THE TREND

IS UP

Books by ANTHONY WEST

HERITAGE

ANOTHER KIND

THE VINTAGE

THE TREND
IS UP

by ANTHONY WEST

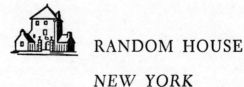

RANDOM HOUSE

NEW YORK

For Lily

THE TREND
IS UP

Chapter One

~~~~~~~~~~~~~~~~

ONE day in the summer of the year in which he turned
nineteen, Gavin Hatfield had one of those moments of clair-
voyance which can, for good or ill, change a man's entire life.
At the time, he was standing on Bailey's Beach at Newport
talking to a girl called Diana Osmington who could, by straining a point, be called a cousin of his, and with whom he had
been on familiar terms for as long as he could remember. She
was a pleasant girl of undistinguished appearance whose abun-
dant good health made her seem prettier than she really was.
She looked her best when she was animated or excited, and
when she was talking to Gavin she was still excited, or as she
put it, thrilled to bits, by something her legal guardian had
told her on the previous day. "So I'll inherit the whole nine
and a half million dollars the minute I get to be twenty-one,"
she said in a voice filled with an innocent delight. "Isn't it too
utterly fantastic?" Until that instant, Gavin had thought of
her as a girl whose only important dissimilarities from himself
resided in her femininity. He now realized with a shock that
there was another difference between them. She was rich in a
way in which he was not. There was no question of his being
poor, but his family was wealthy in a genteel un-pushing Bostonian sort of way belonging to a bygone order of things in
which values were established, and in which it was prudent to
conserve capital. Gavin's future was provided for by a trust
which gave him absolute security, and which would give his

3

children absolute security. But he would have for inheritance one-seventeenth part of his grandfather's wealth, just as his own children would inherit one-fifth of his father's wealth divided by their number, whatever that would turn out to be. Gavin listened to Diana's words and poured a little sand from the palm of one hand onto his toes. As he did so he knew for the first time that he belonged to a race which was killing itself with prudence. He knew that there was something very good about the family house in Wychbury, as there was about his father's house in Louisburg Square in Boston. The summer cottage at Newport which was his father's special delight had the same quality. It was still the white clapboard structure his grandfather had built in 'seventy-eight, and its Spartan, Republican simplicity mocked the later efforts to impress with marble and stone which lined Bellevue Avenue. But it was all very well saying that this was Henry James' Newport, or Henry James' New England, and that it was amusing or "fine" to be loyal to it. Gavin suddenly wondered if his family weren't in bitter truth loyal to something else, something which could be called failure or, with a little less brutality, inadequacy. Gavin poured more sand onto his foot and looked up to see a yawl floating on the milky, gray-blue water offshore breaking out a huge red spinnaker. The sail hung flat for a moment and then filled out into a full bosomy curve. "There goes Matty Fielding with that outlandish red rag of his," he said, and realized too late that it was a Hatfield remark. He liked the colored sail as a matter of fact, and didn't share the correct view that all sails worn on a gentleman's yacht should be white. His mind wandered away to recollections of family gatherings at the Wychbury house at Christmas and Thanksgiving, when the whole clan gathered to exchange family jokes, and to write the names of all the newly born cousins into the back of the Hatfield family Bible. Sooner or later someone attending one of these occasions would say that nothing was the same since the war, and that it was hard to see how this sort of thing—a gesture at this point indicated the whole mechanism of the Hatfield tribe's intense group life—could be kept up. He was sick of it

4

all, the good taste of it, the restraint, the politeness, and the abstention from the roaring, vulgar, vital American adventure which was leaving them behind.

"Come on," he said to Diana, "let's go in swimming. Let's swim out further than we've ever been before, let's go way out until we wonder if we're going to be able to make it back."

She wouldn't go, and he made what turned out to be a six-mile swim alone. He had decided on this as the way to fix his mind on the resolution he had just formed. When he got back onto the sand, with his legs and arms like rubber, so exhausted that he could barely summon the strength to stand up to walk up out of the water, it had become his aim in life. He told his father what it was, in his second year at Harvard, when they were about to have a serious talk on the subject of the careers open to him. At least, it was his father's intention to hold such a discussion and to steer the boy wisely into one of the gentlemanly professions.

"I wonder if you've ever given really serious consideration to the question of your future?" he said, stroking his cheekbone with his long elegant fingers, looking about him at the room full of good, but not ostentatiously good, antiques, and the brown portraits of the men who had been on good terms with Emerson and Lowell and the Lodges.

"I'm going into business," Gavin said. "I've made up my mind. I'm going to be a speculator, and I'm going to have my first million before I'm thirty."

"I should have sent you to Yale," his father remarked, after a brief silence.

"Why? What do you mean?"

"Oh, nothing in particular, it's just that it's a Yale man's ambition, that's all." He sighed. "I could have hoped you would have had more elevated aims; you have your share of the world's goods, after all. But it's your life, not mine when all's said and done, and I shan't say any more on the matter."

And with that he dropped the subject, following his son's subsequent career with a detached ironical interest which

5

stopped short of any inquiry into sordid details. When Gavin was twenty-eight his father died, slipping quietly out of life in the beginning of the autumn after a summer of what had been an increase in tranquility rather than an illness. That was three years after Gavin had bought his partnership in the First National Bank of Maramee, a town on the gulf coast of Florida which nobody in Boston had ever heard of. At an urgent call from his sister, the wife of a Harvard geologist, Gavin flew North from this remote frontier post and was able to speak to the old man before he lost consciousness for the last time.

"How's my banker son?" he asked faintly, and with an exhausted smile, as Gavin came to his bedside.

"Oh, I'm just fine, father, I get plenty of tennis and I feel pretty fit." He felt idiotic making small talk with a dying man, and almost forgotten feelings of tenderness overwhelmed him. As a child he had ridden on the shoulders of this frail white-faced creature. His father saw the affection wakening in his face and fended it off.

"I didn't know that bankers played tennis. I'm sure my banker doesn't."

"Ah, but he's a Bostonian, father. We do things differently in our part of the world."

"When are you coming back from that place, wherever it is, with the extraordinary name—"

"Maramee."

"Marryme! I can't imagine what you can be doing there."

"I'm making that million I told you about, father."

"You've got two years to go. Are you going to manage it?" Gavin nodded, unwilling to risk a smile. He felt like crying. "Really—tell me."

"I've only seventy-eight thousand dollars to get."

"Then I'm sure you'll swing it."

There was a brief silence in the room in which a girl outside the house could be heard calling for some animal called Midge. The day nurse came to the door on tiptoe and signed for him to leave. He got to his feet and stood for a moment holding the back of the chair on which he had been sitting, reluctant to go.

"Well, father, I must be getting along."

"Come and see me tomorrow."

"I will."

His father suddenly looked at him with clear eyes.

"It was good of you to come up here to see me. I've never been able to face the journey down to your place." He stared at his son, fighting for strength to go on. "Why you chose to clear out—turn your back on us all, I'll never understand." The nurse was now pulling at Gavin's sleeve. "Come home soon," he said in an exhausted croak, "come home before it's too late."

Gavin never heard him speak again, and when he thought of his father later he preferred to think of his next to last words rather than his last ones. He had for a period a recurrent dream, which came to him with an hallucinatory force almost as vividly actual as real experience, that his father was visiting him in Maramee. They walked together through the business district and the waterfront neighborhood, Gavin in his white linen suit and his father as always in his stiff collar, white shirt, dark town suit, and beautifully polished and very old handmade English shoes on his feet. As they walked, he was explaining with facts and figures just why he had chosen Maramee, and why he had been right to choose Maramee, as his place of business. The choice had not been lightly made, in fact by the time he was twenty-five Gavin had already seen more of America than many people see in their lifetimes. While he was still at Harvard he had started looking over the new areas which were opening up as investment and development possibilities, after the lull caused by the depression. The East had little attraction for him, even though he realized that it was picking up again after its check. The ground floor there was not wide open to newcomers, and there weren't many chances for young men like himself to find the openings to the channels which led from that traditional point of entry to the top. Gavin learned to look for his openings where industry

7

and trade were immature, and where new men needed new money so badly that they would pay off, not in discreet percentages of future earnings, but in shares in the total value of their enterprises. Gavin spent most of his time in country gashed open with new roads, in the sprawling ugliness of towns that were springing into life or being hideously reawakened, and in the peculiar hideousness of new factories, mines and opencast workings, or sprawling new oil fields. His existence had a quality related to his interests. It had no center. He had an apartment in New York but he was rarely there. He moved from one hotel room to another. While he occupied it, its appearance, however it may have been decorated, was always the same. Every flat surface, including that of the unused twin bed alongside whichever one it was in which Gavin slept, was stacked with company reports, data sheets, financial newspapers and magazines, geodetic survey maps and aerial photographs. The evenings he spent with this room waiting for him to come back to were passed in the company of men who called him Gavin, and whom he called Ed, Tom, Charlie, Newt, and so on, who had been his intimate friends for the three or even four days which comprised their entire knowledge of each other. They took him to the Oak Room, the Cedar Room, the Chippewa Room, the Grub Stake Grill, or whatever the place was called in that town that year, and they told him why they must succeed with whatever it was they were trying to get started. Sometimes they were simply criminals looking for a sucker, sometimes they were even more simply men who had gone a little crazy from thinking too much about quick and easy ways of making money. But eighteen times in twenty, they were men who had a scheme which would work and which would make money once they were given the capital which would set them rolling. Gavin bought in at the speculative stage at which faith was necessary and sold out as soon as the extravagant dreams and hopes involved had become realities recognizable to bankers and conventional investors. Ed, Tom, Charlie and Newt were never grateful to him for seeing them through this phase of their enterprises, for he drove a hard bargain and took for his money a share in their ventures, which was neither fair nor reasonable but a crude measure of their desperation. The kind of gambler Gavin had elected to be was their last chance, they would only turn to him and others like him when every other way of raising money had failed. Secure in the knowledge that they would not be talking to him if they had not tried every possible alternative and failed, Gavin would ask for, and often get, a quarter or a third share in an enterprise to which he had come late and contributed nothing. Sometimes Ed or Tom or Charlie would suddenly break down into furious denunciations of the robber who had come out of the East to skin them. They dwelt on his youth, on his Eastern accent, and on his buttoned-up manner, as they lit into him with scarlet, angry faces. He learned to take it, poker-faced, concealing even his amusement at the parodies of his speech and the imputations of homosexuality which sometimes went with them. After the worst of these attacks he could always say, in what he recognized unwillingly to be something like the ironic voice with which his father had often brought him to heel in his childhood: "I'm going to forget all this, and I'd advise you to go home to bed and think it over. Forget what a fancy-pants son of a bitch I am, and try to think where else you'll raise the money."

It was a rough life for a young man who was not by nature a son of a bitch at all, and Gavin found that he was unable to give it the ten years he had intended. He made the mistake, so far as his original plan was concerned, of taking a liking to a man he was doing business with. The man was a wild-catter with a set of expiring oil leases and a dry hole in the ground three thousand nine hundred feet deep to offer as security for an urgently needed fifty thousand dollars. He had an absolute certainty that his well was going to come in within a month, but meanwhile he had nothing with which to keep up the payments on his hired drilling rig, or even to feed and pay his crew. For all that it was absolute, his certainty was no greater than that of any other wild-catter with a hunch that this time

9

it was really it, and Gavin was aware that he was not a business-man any longer when he let him have what he needed to see him through that last month. He sweated blood for twenty-four days until the hole turned at last triumphantly into a well, and was amazed to find just what a friendly impulse had cost him in anxiety. A fifty-percent interest in a producing field was compensation of a kind, but of the wrong kind. Gavin felt when the wild-catter, now a successful oilman and a solid citizen, bought him out that he had done something about as intelligent as putting his fifty thousand onto the daily double at a race track. And because Gavin had behaved irrationally, because he liked the other man's smile, the way his eyes were set in his head, and the way he talked, he expected gratitude. But when the time came to end their relationship, and a certified check for a million dollars was about to be handed to Gavin in the presence of lawyers who were sliding all the completed documents into their briefcases, the oilman spoke his mind.

"I don't mind telling you how much I hate to do this," he said. "I spent the night before I got tied up with you calling everyone I knew between the gulf and Toronto to see if I could raise the money any other way. I hated your guts when I signed up with you. I hate them right now. Ever since the well came in, I've had a team of lawyers working on finding some way round the agreement we made. If there had been any legal way of getting out of paying you this money, I'd have tried it. So far as I'm concerned, the good Lord made a mistake in not making you a Jew, you're one piece of the same material the whole way through, and I hope I never have to deal with you, or anyone like you, ever again."

The lawyers all eyed Gavin covertly while pretending not to have heard what was said. His eyes briefly met those of the Jewish lawyer who was in the oilman's team. A tiny, almost invisible, shrug of the shoulders conveyed sympathy and advice—that this was the sort of thing one had to take and learn to ignore. Gavin disregarded it.

"If it hadn't been for me," he said, "your leases would have run out and the people who owned that drilling rig would have taken it back long before you had brought that well in. Right now you would be telling a hard-luck story in some bar—if you could get anyone to listen. You may have oil and money now, but you had nothing but hot air to offer when I came along. If I hadn't come along that's all you would ever have had. I hope you won't forget it."

"Why you damn parasite, I found the place and I did the work, and you did nothing, and you get a million dollars for it . . ." He choked into incoherence and left after throwing the check onto the table between them. Gavin heard his angry bellowing through the open door of the hotel suite as he went off down the corridor toward the elevator with his lawyers. The older of his two men twinkled at him through rimless spectacles.

"Our friend's quick success doesn't seem to have sweetened his temper any," he said.

"Have you known him long?" Gavin asked.

"My son knows him better than I do—they were in engineering school together—University of Colorado—he was a nice fellow then, quiet, good natured. He'll settle down when he gets used to it; I hope so anyway. He has a nice wife. . . . Well, Mr. Hatfield, I think that just about does our business. I hope you have an enjoyable trip."

"Trip?" Gavin gathered himself. "Oh, yes, I'm sure I will. Well, I thank you gentlemen very much. It's been very pleasant doing business with you and I hope we meet again."

His face was stretched in a smile as they shook hands, and they smiled back with the same charm-school grins that meant precisely nothing. He picked the check up when they had gone and looked at it. A whole million dollars. For a moment he thought that it was the moment of arrival, but then he remembered the bite that would be taken out of it by taxes, and the fees of the lawyers who had just left him. There was still a way to go. But the oilman's words, bitter and unreasonable as they were, still rang inside his head. "I hope I never have to deal with you, or anyone like you, ever again." Their sound had

11

a powerful effect upon him. It changed the nature of his ambition. He still wanted the whole, round million before he was thirty, but he also wanted a good name, and gratitude and friendship. He was not hard-hearted enough to do without these things.

At that point he thought of Maramee, a place he had visited in order to look over the prospects of a sulphur bed nearby. It had struck him as soon as he reached it that it was not a dead town but an unawakened one. Its business, when he first saw it, was cigar-making, and it was largely a Spanish town. Almost all its slow-paced life was built around the cigar factories which had been brought in, lock, stock, and barrel, from Cuba at the turn of the century to beat a steep rise in the tariff on imported made-up cigars. The factories were un-American in almost every respect, most of all in their interior arrangements. Inside the thick-walled buildings there was an unfactory-like coolness and the atmosphere of an educational or religious institution. The girls who rolled the cigars by hand, with an almost incredible deftness, worked in silence at their benches while a reader, seated at a raised lectern in their midst, read aloud to them in Spanish. When Gavin was being shown over one of these places he paused to ask some questions of one of the girls who worked almost under the reader's lectern. He pretended an interest in what she had to do to prevent the outer leaf splitting, but he was really interested in the line of her cheekbone, the proud arch of her neck, and a certain fullness of mouth and nostril which seemed to promise well. While he looked down at her bosom and thought what a great lay she would be, if he could get her, he suddenly found his ears full of the words coming from the reader's mouth. They were not, as he had assumed they would be, part of a romance or a novelette suited to the idle minds of uneducated girls, but part of an argument in favor of syndicalism, written by some Spanish follower of Bakunin. Gavin asked the plant's manager, who was standing at his elbow, inwardly amused as usual by the tendency of male visitors to ask their technical questions of this particular girl, if he knew what the reader was giving the girls. He got an offhand reply. "I wouldn't know—it's nothing to do with me—the girls chip in and pay the readers—I guess they get what they want." The answer shocked Gavin, and brought home to him just how old-fashioned the Maramee cigar business was, with its handcraft basis, and its old-fashioned approach to selling and distributing. He could see that the girls were working to the limits of their skills—that the quick, beautiful movements of their practiced hands could not be speeded up or improved upon by any number of time and motion studies. In a few years, these women, or another crop of them a little further from their Cuban origins, a little closer to America, would be caught up by the new appetites and cravings, for radios, for iceboxes, washing machines, and all the other things which were becoming necessities. They would want more money. And if their demands were met, the handmade domestic cigar would be priced right out of the reach of the sort of man who smoked it. As it was, the business had no future, and yet Gavin was sure that the foundation of a future was there. In the quietness he said to the manager, "These girls will have to learn to use machines," and the older man smiled as he said that he'd retire before that happened. "You can't make a good cigar with a machine. No, sir, it can't be done." "I'm not talking about good cigars," Gavin said. "I'm talking about a cheap cigar that would sell." The man shook his head. "I can't see why anyone would want to make a cigar if they didn't want to make it a good one." "You're way behind the times," said Gavin. He walked round the town and saw many other things that didn't make sense. The docks and wharves had run down steadily since their heyday of activity between 1917 and 1919, and the railroad yards looked as if they hadn't been touched in twenty years. And yet the place was a natural shipping center for the growing fruit business and the new meat and cattle trade, which was springing up now that the zebu-Hereford crossbred steers were proving that they could stand up to the ticks in the palmetto. Gavin lunched with a Mr. Steinhardt of the Maramee Mechanics Loan and Savings Bank and found him unenthusiastic about the prospects for his sulphur project in particular, and for business in the neighborhood of Maramee in general.

"Of course, we had our fling during the European War, but we learned our lesson in the 'twenties when we had to pay for it. Frankly, Mr. Hatfield, though you may be right when you say that this town needs new capital and the interest of younger men like yourself—new blood was your phrase as I recall—I take leave to doubt it. There wasn't much reason for Maramee in the first place, there's even less reason for it to expand now. I wouldn't myself advise anyone to put any money into the district now, or in the foreseeable future."

"But doesn't everything point to the most dramatic possible change?"

"That's what people used to say to me at the time of the land boom, Coral Gables—that affair—I suppose you're too young to remember it at all. I thought their optimism was unfounded then, and I was right."

"But that was just an incident."

"I suppose it was, but there have been others. Tell me, have you noticed the Alhambra Court Hotel?"

"I should just think so." Gavin smiled, remembering its six large domes, and its countless fretted Moorish arches. "It's hard to miss."

"And it looks comical now, but it was the latest style when it was built—just before the Spanish-American War. The fellow who built it, a railroad man—you wouldn't know his name if I told you—he was sure Maramee was the coming place—a year-round paradise for young and old alike is what he called it. But it isn't just a matter of history that made me think of it, though it is a warning, if you want one, of the number of men who've gone broke backing Maramee, win, place, or show. The point is that a group of our citizens have been trying to turn that place into a small two-year university for some years now. We've had everything planned for some considerable period—since the last attempt to run it as a hotel failed. But in spite of a great many liberal promises of help from one quar-

14

ter and another, nobody has so far come across. The plain fact is this town is on its uppers and I'd be dishonest if I told you anything else. I may tell you in absolute confidence that I have had some very sharp discussions in the past with the Federal Bank Examiners over the real position of some of the local people, older men, whose accounts I have been carrying with my own funds when prudence might seem to dictate another course. I dislike humbling young men, and I hate disgracing old ones even more. I've had plenty of opportunities for both in recent years. You can take it from me, young man, that the tide is going out so far as Maramee is concerned."

"It's coming in fresh and strong in so many places."

Mr. Steinhardt took his glasses off and polished them. He pursed his lips before he spoke.

"You speak with the fire and ardor of a young man. I dare say that in years to come Maramee may feel the benefit of a general rise in prosperity, but its glory will be reflected. The big money, the easy money, which is, if you'll excuse me for saying so, what you are so single-mindedly in pursuit of, is to be got elsewhere."

After they had parted on the steps of the mission-style bank building, and Gavin had walked a few paces down the street, something made him glance back over his shoulder. The banker was standing looking after him with a quizzical expression on his face. Gavin took in his stiff collar, his pinch-waisted suit, and his narrow trousers as he raised his hand in salute, and thought that he looked less like a living person than like a photograph of some intimate of Teddy Roosevelt or President Taft. He spoke of this feeling a couple of days later when he went out fishing on the gulf with a local real-estate man named Harry Bodiner.

"I'll tell you what, Gavin, old man Steinhardt just doesn't believe in change. He'll talk you out of anything, if you go to see him about it. He gives me the feeling there's a wider gap between his generation and ours than there's ever been between grandfathers and grandsons before. He grew up before the war, before abroad was quite real, before cars counted for anything, before any of the things we accept without thinking appeared on the scene. He doesn't really believe in our times; he thinks the newspapers are full of things they've got up—'stunts' he calls them. He's pretty sure that in back of all the racket there's a real America, carrying on quietly just as it did when McKinley was President. He thinks that someday everybody will stop pretending and he'll be proved right."

"So I can just forget anything Steinhardt says?"

"Hell no, not if you want to locate here in Maramee. Don't make any mistake about that—he's the man who runs the bank. We all have to get along with Steinhardt. He's been a daddy to us all at one time or another."

Gavin didn't go into the sulphur project at that time, but he remembered Bodiner's phrase and the sleepy place between the brilliant green water of the gulf and the dark molasses-like flow of the wide river, which seemed to be on the very edge of waking up. For better or worse, it had attracted him, and when he was at the bottom of the slump into which the oil-man's words had thrown him he was seized by his recollection of it. His money could do some good there. He would go to Maramee and turn that dead-and-alive bank of Steinhardt's into something which would really give the town some service. From now on he would make his money in a way which would make money for other people, people who would have the sense to realize what he was doing, and who would thank him for it. When he got back, Mr. Steinhardt seemed almost to have been expecting him, and smiled his thin-lipped smile in welcome.

"I had a feeling you would be back," he said. "There was something in your eye when you looked me over as I said good-bye to you on the steps of the bank. I could see you thinking that I was probably what was wrong with Maramee." He sighed. "Well, you may be right, at that; at least there's a hell of a lot going on nowadays that I don't begin to understand. If you've come to talk me into letting you have a partnership in the bank, I can tell you right away that, subject to certain safeguards, I'll agree. I'm beginning to feel the need of help in dealing with the incomprehensible."

It all worked out very well, and Gavin's training as a speculator stood him in good stead when, about a year after his arrival, Maramee began to break wide open. He smelled death in the books of R. H. Champin, Finest Seeds and Feeds in Any Town, but detected whatever it was about the rival and somewhat dingier firm of Leitz and Hendrix, Feeds and Fertilizers, which was to take it upwards and onwards through a series of reorganizations until it was the unrecognizable monster Gulf Chemical. Roy Allendorf came to Gavin, hat in hand, for a loan to cover a refit of his firm's two small freighters, and was shaken when Gavin suggested a big R.F.C. loan and two brand new ships. Because he was persuasive, the Allendorf house flag, a red A in a white diamond on a black ground, which had till then fluttered somewhat uncertainly in the winds of the gulf, of the Caribbean, and of the Atlantic coast, became known to deep-water pools all over the world. The two new ships became nine, and then fifteen, and their black slab-sided hulls, lettered enormously with the names of the Allendorf brothers Roy and Alfred, their wives Susie and May, their children Gunther, Ulric, Wilma, Heinrich, Manfred, Dorothea, Stephan, Gottfried, Elizabeth, and their sons' wives Lois and Juanita, were familiar sights wherever there were cargoes to be had and wherever money was to be made. Eddie Riemann's little hobby laboratory at the back of his house, where he had puttered for years with cans and freezers and hand-crushed juices and pulps, underwent the same kind of transformation. It became the research block attached to the plant where Mother Goose's Juices were made and bottled in the seven flavors known to every child old enough to spend money in the whole area between New Orleans, St. Louis, and Baltimore. As things looked up, the town began to spread. Traffic and parking became a problem, and the police increased their squad cars from two to ten. Gavin persuaded Mr. Steinhardt to retire altogether and to leave everything in the hands of his junior partner. He brought in New York money

17

and reincorporated the Maramee Mechanics Loan and Savings as the First National of Maramee, and marked the change by tearing down the old Spanish-mission-style building to make way for the first of the city's towers, a fifteen-story construction which caused Mr. Steinhardt to sell his home in Maramee Heights and to move to Sarasota to get out of sight of it. The raising of the bank tower started a building boom in which the Heintzinger Building was pushed up to eighteen stories, and the Beverly Hotel to twelve. And in the middle of all the stir and excitement of making his success, Gavin found the Grove.

He knew the house was sooner or later going to belong to him the minute he first saw it, coming on it by chance one Sunday afternoon when he was exploring the countryside. It was a hot day in early summer and there was nobody about when he drove through the drowsy stillness, up to the front of the huge, empty place. He got out of his convertible, smelling the sweetness of its vastly overgrown gardens, of the surrounding orchards of oranges and lemons, and of the clear blue lake beyond them. "I simply don't believe it," he murmured to himself, as he faced the turrets, the carved and fretted bargeboards and porches, and the wild aesthetic extravagance of the building's design. It was at once marvelous and absurd. He walked up the steps and peered in through a huge plate-glass panel in one of the two leaves of the enormous front door, seeing beyond the shadowy magnificence of the wide hallway the cranky sweep of a Walter Scott Gothic staircase. The glass was cool to his forehead, and he could hear echoing from its surface the remote barking of dogs some way off in the afternoon's heavy silence. "My children are going to run up and down that stair," he said to himself. "I'm going to bring this place alive, too."

At that moment, there appeared on the glass in front of him the reflection of a Negro in faded blue workclothes who had stepped out from among the trees, and who was standing watching him, nervously clutching a hoe. He spoke, as Gavin turned to face him.

18

"If you want to see over the house you have to go down to the Lascombs' place to talk to Mister Manuel."

"Do they let people look over it?"

"Yes, sir. I understand they is considering selling it, or that's what I did hear. But you better talk to them for I don't truly know."

"How far away are these Lascombs?"

"It ain't far, you can hear the dogs barking down there. It's a quarter of a mile, no more."

"Well thanks, I'll go down there. What's your name?"

"Charlie, sir."

"I expect we'll be seeing a lot of each other, Charlie."

He felt in his pocket and drew out a quarter which he threw across to the black man, who held it until Gavin had gone out of sight. He then spat on it and threw it upwards and away so that it flew off over the tops of a row of orange trees and fell to earth somewhere out of his or anyone else's knowledge, edge upwards, half-buried in the warm, sandy earth.

The dogs had stopped barking by the time Gavin reached the Lascombs' place, and silence enveloped it just as it had enveloped the other, almost identical house, up the road. A swarthy man appeared in the front doorway as Gavin was getting out of his car, and as he came down the steps to meet him Gavin found himself wondering if he was colored or not.

"Have I the pleasure of speaking to Mr. Lascomb?"

"Yes, I am Manuel Lascomb. Can I be of service?"

A dinge! thought Gavin with a quickening interest, as he explained who he was and why he was there, he must be a colored man with that soft voice.

"So I thought I'd come right on down," he said.

"I'd be happy to show you the house," Mr. Lascomb said, "and the very considerable property which goes with it. There's the orange grove, a commercial proposition, incidentally, and there are the cleared fields by the waterside. Altogether it amounts to some four hundred and eighty acres of the best land in the state. If you've serious intentions I'd be very glad to take you round."

19

"Oh, yes, I've serious intentions." Gavin laughed. "Perhaps I should tell you that I run the First National Bank in Maramee."

"That's where I've heard your name, then. My mother, Donna Anna, did business there in old Mr. Steinhardt's day."

"Your family has Spanish connections?"

"Rather remotely, my mother was from Cuba." Manuel Lascomb smiled. "But my father was a Northerner like yourself."

"Oh, yes?" Gavin politely concealed his incredulity.

"He came here more or less by accident, because his first wife's sister was lonely," he paused. "I'll tell you the story as we drive up to the other house. It explains why these two monstrosities are standing all by themselves out here in the back of the beyond."

"Don't you like them?"

"In a way I do. But as architecture they appall me."

"I think they're quite wonderful."

"They're certainly unusual, in this part of the world at least. But I gather they're of a type which is fairly common round Troy in New York State. Perhaps you know that neighborhood?"

"I do. But I've never seen anything up there quite as fantastic as this."

"I suppose not. You see, the Mr. Culver who built them wasn't really an architect. He was a contractor and he built these houses after he'd retired, from his memories of what he'd built up North. I understand that during his building days he kept a notebook into which he put rough drawings of any architectural details that caught his fancy. When he came to build for himself, he worked in as many of them as he could; if that's true, it would account for the very odd way the houses turned out. He came down here, in 'seventy-eight I think it was, and built first the one house—its real name is the Grove, though in my family it's always referred to as 'the other house' —and then the other a couple of years later. He had a young wife and she was bored and lonely here—we've just crossed the boundary between the two properties—so he brought her sister and her sister's husband—he was my father—down here for company and built them a house. It all ended rather badly. Over there behind that clump of live oaks, that's where there were some stables at one time. They were burned down out of spite by some local figure whom Mr. Culver had annoyed in some way, and fifteen of his horses were burned alive in the fire. Mr. Culver had a stroke while he was watching the blaze and died soon afterwards. His wife and her sister went back North just as soon as he was buried, taking their children with them, and only my father remained here. He married my mother late in life, after spending many years here as a recluse."

Gavin stopped the car outside the Grove and sat looking up at its shuttered windows. Lascomb sat beside him, watching his face.

"Perhaps now you've had a second look at it, you don't want to bother to go inside?"

"I was wondering if I wouldn't make you an offer right this minute. I don't have to see the inside of it. I know I want it."

"Are you serious?"

"Of course I am."

"It seems to me that you don't really begin to realize what you're saying. I don't believe you know what buying a house means." A heavy, sullen expression passed over Lascomb's face. "When you take it on you take on so much more, neighbors, a way of life, duties and obligations—I find it hard to describe. You even take on some part of the history of the house. Local people have always hated them both, my house and this one. Two Sundays after Culver moved in the Baptist preacher down at the chapel took Daniel 4 Verse 1 for his text 'I Nebuchadnezzar was at rest in mine house, and flourishing in my palace.' The crackers have delighted in every misfortune that has fallen on the Lascombs and the Culvers ever since. We came from outside. We were too fortunate, and they hated us for our good fortune. They rejoice to see us humbled. Think twice before you move in here, and, if you must, come in with discretion."

21

They walked round the silent building to a terrace which looked down a broad avenue cut through the orange grove to the shining water of the lake. Manuel Lascomb leaned on a rattan cane and fanned his face with his panama, as Gavin stood admiring the view.

"This is not a neglected property, even though the house has not been lived in for so many years," he said. "My father admired George Culver a great deal, too much I should say, and he wasted more than half his life keeping this relic of his foolish dreams in order."

Gavin paid him as little attention as a small boy with his first bicycle gives to the adult who warns him how dangerous the roads can be; when he looked at him it was less to listen to what he was saying than to confirm his suspicion that Lascomb was a colored man. The soft voice murmured on.

"He used to come up here every day at least once, and sometimes twice—in the morning and in the evening—to see that everything was 'all right' as he put it. He was sure that Culver's children would want to come back someday."

"But they never did."

"No. They had been indoctrinated with a disgust for the place by their mother. I was able to buy it from Mrs. Culver's heirs after the crash—they'd never seen it; they were glad to find they had something left which they could turn into money. They sold it without regrets as quickly as they could."

"You've taken very good care of it yourself." Gavin smiled at him. "You seem to share your father's view that it was worth looking after."

"It is a valuable property. I knew I could turn it into more money than I gave for it, given time. Meanwhile I've been making a commercial success of the grove. Citrus fruits are chancy, but with good management they pay when the gains and losses are spread over the years."

"Can't you see what a strangely beautiful place this is? How magnificent these gardens are? What a wonderful place it is to live in? It's the most perfect thing of its kind I've ever seen."

"Our roles seem to have become reversed, Mr. Hatfield. One

22

would think you were trying to sell the place to me." He put his hat back on his head. "I suppose it has a great deal of charm. Perhaps I've become hardened to it." His eyes were fixed on Gavin's face, but his thoughts were back in the great days of the K.K.K. after the war, when he was growing up and there had been a good deal of local talk about burning out the family of dinges who had got hold of the Lascomb place. Fifteen or twenty colored farmers had been burned out, and there had been several whippings, all within a few miles of the Lascombs. But their wealth had seen them through—there was always to be taken into account the possibility that Donna Anna really had been a woman of Spanish origin from Cuba. He took out his handkerchief and dabbed round the back of his neck.

"Different people see different things in different ways," he said. "This is merely a saleable property to me, and my sights are set on forty-eight thousand dollars. I don't mean to take a penny less, so it's really up to you to decide if it's worth that to you. I don't have to sell, and I can wait for my price."

Gavin looked at him and decided that it was probably true. He did not know that Lascomb was devoting his life to his son's future, investing every penny he made in an ambiguous fortune which would enable the boy to go North to school and to a university to be reborn, not as a Cuban Spaniard, but as a simple Lascomb, christened Herbert Wingfield, whose grandfather had gone to Florida to make money, and who was going back to his ancestral New England now that the fortune was an established matter. The money raised by the sale of the Grove would provide a great many solid blocks in the wall of money he was building between the child and the dark world of the cabins, and of the shuffling figures walking in the soft dust along the edges of the roads. He had no inkling of what Gavin felt for the Grove, he assumed quite simply that he had come down from the North with his head full of storybook stuff about the old South and wanted to play ol' Massa in the biggest house he could find. To have Gavin so eager for it gave him much the same pleasure as he had derived from

23

the eagerness the parents of Angelina Madriaquix had shown
to have their daughter marry a landowner with a big house.
They were Spanish immigrants, from Spain beyond any doubt
or question, and their approval of the marriage had given a
kind of retrospective authentication to his father's story about
Donna Anna. His son really had cousins in Spain whom he
might one day visit. If Angelina kept her mouth shut on whatever suspicions she might have formed in the course of caring
for Donna Anna in her last years, and if he succeeded in getting his price for the other half of the property before the boy
got to be ten, then he might grow to manhood in the North
without ever having to face the knowledge of what he was or
that his blood involved him in any kind of a problem. Gavin's
arrival out of the haze of the hot afternoon represented the
first giant step towards securing the child's freedom from the
past. With intense inner jubilation he heard him say:

"Well, Mr. Lascomb, I think that's a fair price. I think I can
see my way to letting you have it. Shall we go ahead at that
figure and put the lawyers to work at making it a deal?"

The house assumed control of Gavin as soon as he was in
full legal possession. The day after the formal completion of
the sale he drove out and walked through the high-ceilinged
rooms, with his hands full of keys, measuring their space and
feeling the force of Culver's desire to have a family bearing
upon him; life in the Grove would be meaningless if there were
not a woman and children under its roof. It was unthinkable
that, owning it, he should remain single for long. He threw
back the shutters of the big bedroom that looked straight
down the vista to the lake and saw the margin of white sand
at its edge. Children would run down there and swim before
breakfast. They would have a boat which could be kept from
the sun in the shadow of the swamp of cypresses over to the
right. He recognized the loneliness and emptiness of the road
he had been planning. In the ten years in which he had been
getting his first million, he had laid a number of women for
the sport rather than from any affectionate interest in them
as people; he had lost touch with his college friends and made

24

few new ones; and, even though he had a number of drinking and fishing companions chosen from among his business
acquaintances, there was no one in his circle with whom he
could share his pleasure in the Grove. He had contrived to cut
himself off from his own, and from almost every other, generation, and the sense of isolation abruptly overwhelmed him. A
few days after this discovery, he proposed marriage to Nedda
Riemann, a good sport who had been away with him for several weekends and short trips just for the hell of it.

"We get along pretty well, why don't we make it legal,
Nedda?"

"You must be out of your mind, Gavin."

"I'm not, I'm perfectly serious."

"You mean you can't think of what to do with that great
barn you've bought, and you want me to come and play house
in it with you? Oh, no Gavin. There's more to marriage than
that. Fooling around's fooling around, but marriage is something else again. I've got my ideas about that, and this getting
along pretty well doesn't come within a mile of it. Sorry,
old man, but that's how it is."

"I'm sorry too." He stubbed out his cigarette in the ash tray
on the table between them. "Shall we dance?"

The band was playing well that night, and there was a cool
wind from the gulf which swung the long fronds of the pepper
trees surrounding the club lawns. From the dance floor they
could see a few people swimming in the lighted pool below the
terrace. Gavin felt the choked, choking, emotion which afflicts
young people whose real trouble is that they have not had
sufficient experience to know if they are deeply moved or not.

"I guess this fixes things between us," he said.

"I suppose it does. I think so. Yes." She was a good dancer
and often led him without his knowing it. "I think we'd better break up this little thing before you begin to get difficult."

For several days after this incident, he allowed himself to
believe that he was desperately in love and bitterly hurt, and
his sense, that he had been through something, was revived
at the end of a month when Nedda's engagement to Harry

hands stuffed into his pockets. Eddie Riemann came up and slapped him on the back.

"These affairs are the end, aren't they, Gavin? I can't believe any sane person would deliberately ask Margie Wiley to a party they were giving, yet she always gets invited. I must even have asked her to this damned thing myself. It beats me."

"Everything's beyond me these days—I think I'll take a long holiday—knock right off for a couple of months. Come to think of it, I haven't had a real holiday in years."

"You don't look right at the top of your form, old boy," Eddie said. "Maybe it would do you good to get away for a spell. Meanwhile, how about a drink?"

"I could use one."

As they went over to the drink table, Eddie threw an arm over Gavin's shoulders and patted him encouragingly.

"I guess I shouldn't say this," he said, "but it's too bad it isn't you. I'd much rather have you in the family than that guy Crane. He's a jumpy s.o.b. if you ask me."

"I think it's too bad, too. But I suppose Nedda knows what she's doing."

"Well, I hope so, I hope so."

"Say, do you know what? I'm forgetting all about Margie's coffee."

"Have a drink before you bother with it, Margie can wait."

Gavin was weaving a little when he at last got Margie's coffee out to her, a judge of these things would have said that by then he was a little further gone than she was. The cocktail hour had passed and it was getting to be dark. Margie had passed through her noisy phase and was entering another.

Hours later Gavin woke up in the studio, hung with Navaho rugs, at the back of Margie's roadside Arts and Crafts Shoppe. Moonlight was streaming into the room and the deep shadows it cast made the shapes of the huge, useless pots and jars, placed on stands round the walls, look sinister and goblinish. Mexican tinplate ash trays and sconces glittered on rug-covered stools and on the walls. The cold aseptic light was merciless on the lean body, with its slightly shrunken breasts, lying naked beside him. She was in really wonderful condition for a woman of her age; but it was not his age. He raised himself slowly into a position from which he could swing his legs off the bed, moving deliberately with the hope that he could get up, get dressed, and get away without waking her. As the soles of his feet touched the cool tiled floor she woke and grabbed his arm.

"Don't go, don't leave me."

"I've got to go—it's late—it's nearly morning."

"Do me once again before you go."

Her arms were tightly round him, pulling him backwards onto the bed. He lost his balance and rolled back onto her.

"You're so strong," she said. "Jesus God, you're so strong, your muscles are so hard. Give me that thing. Do that thing to me. God how I love that thing. I need it so badly, that lovely thing. You lovely man, oh, yes, you lovely man, lovely, lovely, lovely . . ."

Later, when he was exhausted, she cried, stroking his body.

"I need that so badly, Gavin, I can't get enough of it. Promise you'll come and do me often, darling, promise. I can't live without it. I sometimes think I must be going mad, I need it so much."

He listened to her voice running on, not quite believing that he heard what she was saying, fascinated by the way that her tears ran slowly, one by one, down her face before falling onto his body.

"Perhaps I ought to kill myself," she was saying. "Do you think I ought to kill myself? How can I go on, the way I am?"

He hardly listened to her monologue, although every word of it burned deeply. He was more immediately concerned with the thought that he would probably go on getting himself into messes like this one, and worse, so long as he remained unmarried. She was not a woman to him, just something awful that had happened to him. He shouldn't have allowed it to happen. He fell heavily asleep and did not waken until it was daybreak. This time he managed to get off the bed without disturbing Margie and succeeded in getting clear away. She

29

called him that afternoon and the following morning. When she made her third call, he had already left town. His secretary knew that he was to attend a convention of small-town bankers in Philadelphia and that he was going on from there to attend a family wedding at which a Wychbury Hatfield boy was to marry a Murray girl from Barnton, Connecticut, but she did not tell Margie that; she just said that Mr. Hatfield had left town on a business trip and that she did not know when he would return.

At the wedding Gavin felt rather lost. He discovered that a whole new generation of Hatfields had grown up since he had moved South, and that the Murray clan was an even bigger one than his own. Among the two closely knit groups he felt himself to be an outsider, and when the reception broke up into knots of intimate friends scattered across the green lawns under the big maples, he found himself drifting on the fringe of things. When people had said, "Why, Gavin, I haven't seen you in an age," or some variant of that remark, there wasn't much left to be said. He felt very much out of it all until he noticed a young woman with dark-blue, almost violet eyes, a mass of coppery-red hair, good features and a well-proportioned body, who seemed to be of the party but not in it, as he was.

"I'm Gavin Hatfield," he said, "my guess is that you're a Murray. Tell me if I'm wrong."

"You're quite right. I'm Ilona Murray."

"Do you live in Barnton?"

"Not any more, but I spent most of my childhood here."

"It's an attractive place."

"Oh, if you're dealing with Murrays you have to be more positive than that," she said. "We think it's the only place. Our story is that God made Barnton on the eighth day, and then regretted all his previous mistakes."

Ilona did not share this view of Barnton, which was, for her, a place of long-drawn-out misery and humiliation where she had eaten the bread of charity and hated every mouthful of it. Her father had come into his patrimony in time to treble his fortune on the easy upward slope leading to November, 1929. He had faced the crash with the confidence of a man who had proved himself to have a real flair for a good thing. He was sure that his luck was just going to change, and that everything was going to come out all right up to the point at which he was sold out. By then all his inheritance was gone, and almost all of his wife's, with the exception of a trust fund which brought in three thousand dollars a year. The house on Sixty-fourth Street in New York and the summer place at Easthampton, the chauffeur-driven Packard, and the snappy little Chrysler convertible with the rumble seat, which Stewart used to drive himself, Peggy the cook, and Maureen and Hannah the aproned maids, Fräulein, and many other things and people vanished abruptly from Ilona's life. The family moved to what had been the coachman's cottage beside the stables on Alston Murray's place at Barnton, and there they lived, rent free, while Ilona was growing up. Stewart Murray never did anything again after he had been sold out of the market. He watched the financial pages as closely as if he were still in it, bitterly keeping check on the stocks the bank had taken from him. They had all come back—any fool but a banker would have seen that they would—and in some cases they had done better than reach their old values. Every morning Mr. Murray figured out, on the basis of the previous day's closing prices, down to the cents, how much richer he would be if the bank had not stepped in and ruined him. He cherished this ghostly fortune night and day to the utter neglect of all practical matters. It was Ilona's mother, Carmel, who did the housekeeping, although she had never learned how to balance a check book or indeed any other sort of account. She felt that as they had a fixed income they could pay for anything, if only they were given time, it was just a matter of waiting till the money came in. So they were always a few months behind, and the income was always pledged before it came in. Each month the bill at the top of the list, or the one that was being most rudely and embarrassingly pressed got paid in full, two or three others got part payment, and the rest were passed on to wait their turn.

31

As a girl, Ilona was always lifting the telephone in the hope that a friend had called her, to hear instead the softly threatening complaint of somebody's bookkeeper. And there were often men at the door who had come round to try to get a little something, just to show good intent. Ilona came to know their technique very well.

"You ought to write to explain your position, Mrs. Murray, really you should. It's when we don't hear anything that we don't like it. We get the idea that—well—I'll be frank—that you're trying to put something over on us. Now what say we try to work out a little scheme, you and me, Mrs. Murray, so you let us have a little something regular, on the first or the fifteenth of each month, however you like it, till we get this thing straightened out?"

Mrs. Murray's hands would flutter softly, like doves, from her bosom to her back hair, to her chin, to the mysterious figured bits of paper in front of her. "Why yes, why yes, that seems reasonable—I'd never thought of it that way—it does seem best like that. You young men are all so clever with money nowadays."

She would agree to one little scheme, and then to another. The pressure would build up. Then Mr. Murray would be forced to beg from his elder brother, who made it a practice to let him have half what he asked for. Or Mrs. Murray would go to her parents for help. They were old, they felt the money would soon be hers anyway, so they let their only daughter dribble her inheritance away little by little, out of kindness. The trouble was that, like all genteel beggars, Ilona's father and mother were dishonest and unable to admit to themselves or to other people how far they were in debt. And because they were ashamed of owing money, they were afraid of shocking the people to whom they turned for help so they never asked for quite enough to do them any good. They lived year in and year out with their heads just under water. Had they owned the house they lived in, or its furniture, or the car they used, they would have been in trouble. But as the debt collectors found out when they checked the possibilities, these things were not available to be attached. The house was Alston Murray's, the furniture belonged to Mrs. Murray's parents, the car belonged to Stewart's young brother Geoffrey, who didn't need it—or the few dollars he would have got by selling it—while he was with the State Department in Madrid, in Tokyo, in Prague, and later in Bogotá. Sometimes there were bad scares that one creditor or another was going to attach their bank account, but that catastrophe was always, somehow or other, fended off and the family dodged on month after month in an atmosphere of perpetually renewed crisis.

Ilona found it hard enough to bear when she was younger with a child's sense of shame, but this was only at the beginning. At eighteen she blossomed startlingly and became an undeniable beauty. Her naturally graceful movements had nothing coltish about them, and her body seemed to have been made for love. Until this flowering took place, she had been just a poor relation, little Ilona, an unlucky old friend's daughter, who could be patronized and invited to parties and on weekends to receive kindnesses. In the middle of that summer she turned into what was, from her world's point of view, one of the worst menaces a young man could possibly encounter, a dazzlingly attractive girl without a cent. Parents of young sons in the circle to which the Murrays belonged became acutely aware of Ilona, and watchful. They saw that their boys did not spend too much time with her, and they "forgot" to ask her to picnics and dances. "Oh, lord, I'd forgotten all about her, well, we'll just ask her some other time." When these measures failed, hints were dropped. Ilona was a perfectly nice girl, but not a girl to get involved with, or to think about seriously. If the boys argued the point, and stood out for their God-given right to pursue whatever girl they fancied, they were told, more or less brutally, why Stewart Murray was no good and his seed was accursed. The boys would drop her suddenly in a clumsy and shame-faced way, or worse, begin to treat her with a sort of condescending kindness. James Stanton, who was writing to her two or three times a week all through his last two terms at Groton, spent the summer before he went on to Harvard living with a French family in Burgundy, learning the language and forgetting Ilona. And Morton Harris, who was even more seriously in love with her, broke a family tradition which had been built up in four generations, and went to Cambridge in England instead of going to Yale like every other male Harris.

And then at the age at which she would have gone to college if only things had been different, she started work in New York. While all her friends were tasting the excitements and freedoms of university life, she was learning business method and office routine. A cousin of her mother's lent her an unused servant's bedroom in her big Park Avenue apartment. It had its own bathroom and its own entrance. It was, up to a point, just like having her own place, and it had the advantage of being free. But it was not her own, and the help came in and the garbage went out through the dark green service lobby, with its scratched walls, onto which her door opened. And when she was inside she was faced by the sort of blank stout furniture which employers choose for servants who live in, things of which no one could complain and which would stand up to hard use. Ilona never felt at home in the place and never wanted anyone she knew to see it. At weekends she would ride out to Barnton on the train, hoping that some of the friends who had liked her when she was one of the boarding-school crowd would be around and inclined to take her out. But generally, from the time when her father greeted her with his favorite, "Ah, here's Tilly the Toiler home for a few free meals!" she spent her weekend with her parents, doing a little mending, or making herself new clothes on her mother's sewing machine. She was being dropped by her own generation. When she was asked anywhere it was because some older relative among the clan of the Murrays—or of her mother's race, the Pakenhams—was making up a party for the younger members of the tribe, or because it was a matter of a wedding or a funeral to which every last cousin had to be asked by the iron-clad rules of the tribal game.

What depressed her most of all was the increasingly clear vision which she began to have of her horizon, and of what lay between it and her present situation. She did well in the secretarial post she had been given—through Pakenham influence—in the City and Central Bank, and she had earned herself praise. "Why, Miss Murray, I believe I can trust you to write a whole letter in the English language." And even better than that: "Well, Miss Murray, it's a relief to find a girl of your age with what I call common sense." These declarations, meant sincerely, and the product of a genuine appreciation, meant that she had a good start on the ladder which would take her slowly up to the position of confidential secretary to one of the bank's great men, and to compliments of another kind. "Why, Miss Murray, I believe you know the business of this bank even better than I do myself." And "My goodness, Miss Murray, it's easier to imagine this place without money than it is to think of it without you." Between the bottom of the ladder and the top there would be twenty years or so of nickel pinching, of subway rides, drugstore breakfasts and lunches, and office politics. It was not a prospect in which she saw many possibilities of pleasure, or even of interest, and her dislike of the routines and mechanisms of banking made her doubt if she would, in the outcome, have the endurance and the patience to make a success of the climb. She saw herself sticking somewhere near the middle of the ascent, becoming disheartened and dowdy, and turning into one of that large army of graying, thickening women, who spent their days waiting for five o'clock to release them from the desks at which they automatically performed their meaningless tasks. The way out was to get married. But the marriages open to her seemed even more appalling than the career which she saw in front of her. She could angle for some junior executive in the bank, or she could accept the brother or a friend of one of the girls she met through her work. She went out on dates with young men who were, by the standards of her new station in life, perfectly all right, and had glimpses in these contacts of lives happily lived inside confines so narrow that she felt that to accept them indicated something not too far from mental deformity. Her snobbery, which had consisted in the days when she was a child of nothing positive, but only of a negative total disregard of nine-tenths of humanity, and which had been instinctive and unconscious, now became acute, conscious, and unrelenting. She could not, she would not sink to the level of the dull crowds of ordinary people living ordinary lives. She was a Murray, her mother was a Pakenham, she had a birthright which she would not resign. She would one day get back to her true social level if she only held out, she was sure of it.

She had almost given up, when a Pakenham cousin who had taken a fancy to her as a child left her a legacy of five thousand dollars. She was at once grateful and irritated, for although it was a handsome gift if one thought of it as money to spend, it was an almost meaningless capital sum. At best it would produce three hundred dollars a year. Her father tried to persuade her to let him have it, telling her with bright eyes and a glassy smile that he would double it for her within a year, and make her comfortably rich within ten years. She turned him down coldly, and was even colder to her mother, who begged her for a loan that would get her out of all her crowding difficulties.

"If I could just get straight I could pay you off at the rate of a thousand dollars a year. You could have it all back at the end of a few years."

"Oh, mother," said Ilona, "how can you try to get away with that? You know you'll be in just as big a muddle as ever in six months—all that would be different would be that my money would be gone, too."

"You've turned into a hard woman, Ilona," her mother said. "I don't know what's changed you."

"Let's not discuss that."

"You were such a dear good baby, you never seemed to cry. And then you were such a happy, open, little girl . . ."

"Please, mother."

"We did everything we could to make you happy."

Ilona got up and left the room. In the hallway she hesitated, undecided between going upstairs to her own attic bedroom, and putting on a raincoat and going out for a walk in the steadily falling spring rain. The alternative to a soaking was waiting until her mother clambered up the stair to cry, whine, and plead for reconciliation. It was unbearable to think of it, so Ilona strode out hatless into the downpour. It was raining harder than she thought and she did not get very far, no further than the summerhouse by Alston Murray's pond. She sat on a bench inside it, watching the raindrops strike the gray water between the lily pads, and listening to the rush of the stream pouring out of the pond and over the dam. The trees were in full leaf, but their leaves were still brilliant with the flaming green of spring. Across the pond, beyond a couple of paddocks laid up for hay and starred with a thousand yellow, pink, and white flowers, she could see part of Alston Murray's big center-chimney house with its gracefully graded clapboard and its black shutters. She had learned to ride on the well-bred ponies which had once been kept, for the children, on those expensive pastures. She spent the long hot summer afternoons of her adolescence swimming to and from the raft out in the pond, baking herself brown on its rope-matting deck or on the huge flat stones along the top of the dam. She was the last of the gang's girls to remain unmarried, the only one still living in Barnton for even part of the time. She had dropped right out. It struck her that the legacy of five thousand dollars had given her a last chance of making her way back in. If she reappeared on the scene behaving as if, to use a favorite phrase of that set to whom money in the last analysis meant everything, "money doesn't really mean anything after all," they might forget that she had become an outsider for long enough for her to get married to some insider who would never let her be driven out again. She would live in a center-chimney house, and there would be an orchard where Shetland ponies would munch windfalls. They would have the ponies so that the children could learn to ride. There would be a terrace where they could eat by candlelight from the end of May through into mid-October. In winter they would sit by a large open fire-

37

place heaped up with large logs. The only furniture in the house would be very good, very plain, early American, and on the walls there would be a few of her husband's family portraits from the period up to the 'forties and a few very good modern pictures, nothing in between. They would stand out against the white walls of the rooms like jewels. She would have an English or a Swiss nannie for the children, and they would grow up with lovely, grave, somewhat continental manners.

The rain stopped. She left the summerhouse and walked home, planning her campaign, she would spend a thousand dollars on clothes and shoes right away, and she should have a roadster so that she would be able to get around without bothering people and being a nuisance.

A few days later, a young married man who was standing on a Saunderstown lawn packing a freshly dried out Genoa jib into a sail bag, with his wife's help, looked up from his work and saw a red-haired girl in a dark-green linen dress getting out of a white car which had just driven into the driveway and stopped.

"Wow!" he said. "Who is this dish?"

"I don't think it's anyone we . . ." his wife was saying when the woman took off her sunglasses and stuffed them into her straw handbag.

"Hallo," she called out. "Are you at home to a casual dropper-in?"

"Why, Ilona," said the wife. "You're looking gorgeous! Dick, it's Ilona Murray—you remember her."

"Why, yes, of course I do. This is just wonderful, Ilona. Where have you been hiding away? We haven't seen you in ages."

"Oh, I've been around, I'm on my way to spend a few days with Ned and Mary Stevens in Newport. I had to come right by Saunderstown anyway so I thought I'd look you up. Kick me out if it's inconvenient. I just dropped in to say hallo, really."

"Oh, we're not doing anything special. Why don't you come and have a swim and have lunch with us before you go on?

We'd love it. Jackie Pierce and Tod are coming over around noon, and I know they'd love to see you. Do stay."

The campaign was off to a flying start, and in its first few weeks she felt that she was sweeping everything ahead of her. But at the end of six months, her heart was dropping towards her boots. The old crowd had welcomed her back, and they were really glad to have her around. But almost all the men were married, and most of the women, with their second and third children beginning to walk, were happily involved in a way of life which was friendly, warm, and easy as an old shoe, but over Ilona's head. She just wasn't in the young married set, and its members had had seven years of experience which was to her a closed book. Her money was going with amazing speed, and she was beginning to soften her attitude towards discontented husbands. She found herself arguing Jesuitically that if a marriage was going so badly that the man in it was already looking outside it for something he lacked, she could hardly be accused of breaking it up. But, though she tried to tell herself that what she was doing when she encouraged Sydney Clavering to find in her the warmth of sympathy and understanding which he didn't get from his wife was perfectly all right, she couldn't in the end go through with the final practical stages of shattering the framework of two other people's lives. She felt that she was sinking pretty low even to think about it—and then, when she was telling herself that it was unthinkable in order to get herself ready to do it, she met Gavin Hatfield, rich, unattached, and interested. The night on which he proposed and was accepted Ilona looked into her bank book, and after subtracting the amount of the most recently written checks arrived at a balance of three hundred and eighty-nine dollars and seventy-one cents. When she had finished adding and subtracting she gave a sigh of relief. She had made it after all. And she was not really putting anything over on Gavin either. He was a nice guy, a perfectly wonderful man, really, and if she didn't love him, she did respect him and value him as a person. She would never let him even suspect that she did not love him, or let him have any inkling of the way things

39

really were. And, it was more than most of the girls in her set could say, she was giving him her virginity. She undertook to be loyal and true, no matter what, and really, all things considered, she was giving Gavin a good deal. But when she was undressed and in bed, she felt so ashamed of what she was doing that she almost cried. And when her fit of childishness was past, she lay rigid for a while imagining that she was in for a sleepless night. In fact, she slept very well, and when she came down to breakfast the next morning she looked as radiant as a girl should who has to tell her father and mother that she is to be married. Her mother was unaffectedly delighted, but she was distressed to hear that her little girl was to live in Florida.

"It seems so far away, like another country, almost," she said.

Her father, however, who was never going to forgive her for not letting him have that legacy to gamble with, took another line.

"This fellow, he's not a Jew is he? Hatfield—Hatfield. It's a suspicious name. I went down to Miami once from Palm Beach with young Tom Custis—Amy's brother—the one who was mad about foreign cars. The place was swarming with Jews then."

"Oh, father. It wouldn't matter if he was. But he isn't. Gavin lives in Maramee, over on the west coast, hundreds of miles from Miami."

"I'm sorry I asked, but you don't expect me to relish the idea of your being married to a Jew do you?"

"Gavin was born in Wychbury, Mass., in the house his great-great-great whatever-it-is built in 1784. He's as much a New Englander of the old stock as he could be."

"Well, I'm glad to hear it. At least I know one thing about the man my daughter's going to marry." He looked down into his coffee cup with what he intended to be a wounded expression, but which was in reality both sly and smug. Ilona looked at him and thought how mean his face had become since his disappointment. She could remember him with the open face of a good-natured man. She felt a surge of affection for what he had been.

"I'm sorry, father, I should have told you all about him, I suppose. He's tall—he's about six feet two—his eyes are gray-blue, his hair is fair. He looks as if he took care of himself—he's hard and thin, and he's a little older than I am, three years to be exact—"

"Ah then," her father broke in, "he will have been married and divorced a couple of times in the modern fashion. You'd better make sure he really has been divorced properly from his previous women—those Nevada and Mexican things aren't good enough if there's any really important question of property involved. You must see that—"

"Father!" She flushed. "He's never been married."

"Never married? Hmn, that's odd, very odd. I wonder why not. Do you know him at all well?"

"I intend marrying him. I know him quite well enough, thank you."

"Ah, but I wonder if you do. Wychbury is a place which has gone a great way downhill since its best days. Mr. Hatfield's people could be swamp Yankees for all we know. Many of these old families have become unspeakably degenerate in the last hundred years."

"Gavin's relatives keep up the house in Wychbury for sentimental reasons, more as a family meeting place than anything else. His parents really lived in Boston where his father's house was—and they had a summer house at Newport."

" 'Had'? I hope you are not speaking of departed glories?"

"No, I'm not. Gavin's sister has the house on Louisburg Square—her husband teaches at Harvard, and his mother still has the cottage at Newport."

"The cottage at Newport!" Her father raised his eyebrows in a mockery of delighted surprise. "Well, well, then I suppose I need worry about your future no further." He dropped his arched eyebrows and gave her a watery smile. "You are cleverer than I am after all, I'm forced to admit."

"I—clever?"

41

"Yes." He laughed unpleasantly. "Putting your keep, clothing and amusements at the barest minimum I should say they cost three thousand a year. Supposing you rub along with this fellow Hatfield for ten years you'll be thirty thousand to the good at the end of it. Now I couldn't have turned a stake of five thousand into a thirty-thousand-dollar asset in a year, I'll admit that. So I have to concede, you're much, ever so much cleverer than I am."

"That's disgusting." She got unsteadily to her feet.

"You should be the best judge of that, my dear."

"I won't speak to you again until you've apologized."

"I see that I've touched upon an open wound!"

Ilona looked desperately at her mother for some support or assistance, but found that lady staring vaguely away from them and their discussion, out through the screen of pot plants on the window ledge. The robin which had come to tap on the glass three mornings in a row, would it come again? Why did it come? To catch midges perhaps? Or had it come as some sort of mystic messenger to warn her of the important family event which was about to take place? Life was full of hidden marvels which science could not explain. She heard a voice saying, "Mother!" with an accent of urgent appeal.

"I'm sure we both wish you every happiness, Ilona darling," she said.

"Quite so. Perhaps we had better remain on speaking terms until after you are married. It will look better, I think." Stewart started to chuckle but broke into an old-fashioned guffaw. The startlingly loud, "Haw, haw, haw," which burst from him as he flung his head back drove Ilona from the room and angered her so that she slammed the door onto the sound of it, with the idea of cutting it off. She stood in the narrow hall beside the steep staircase, resting her hand on the baluster rail, uncertain if she would be better off in her room or outside the confining house. She heard the conversation going on in the dining room.

"You were hard on her, Stewart dear."

"Hard! When I think of all I've put up with from her!"

42

"She's not been happy in that bank. It's not her fault that she's impatient with us."

"It's a simple matter of manners, I should say. Perhaps she's right to despise me—I am after all a failure—but need she show me that she thinks so all the time?"

"Perhaps marriage will sweeten her temperament."

"That's another thing. I wonder where on earth we're to find the sort of money it takes to marry a girl these days."

Oh God, Ilona thought—that's it, that's why he's been so horrible about my becoming engaged. Thank heaven Gavin has money. In a few months more, I shall be out of all this and all right. I shall never think mean thoughts about money again.

That evening her father walked up the shadowed path between the double row of maples to the big house at the top of the hill to borrow money from his brother Alston. He outlined the situation and asked his brother for four thousand dollars to enable him to do things properly. As he talked, Alston slowly filled a large English briar pipe with tobacco and lit it. He did not start or give any sign of surprise when he heard the amount Stewart was asking for, he simply looked at him steadily and began to think of some alternative course to that of giving his brother the amount of money he had named. He knew that, if he did let him have it, less than half of it would go on the wedding festivities, the rest would be converted to Stewart's own purposes and frittered away. When his brother had finished speaking, he smiled with a mouth full of beautifully cared-for teeth.

"I've a better idea than that," he said. "Up here on the hill we've got the business of marrying off our daughters worked out to a fine art. We know just about all you have to know about it, after three efforts in that line. The old coach house is too small for the big affair Ilona's entitled to, anyway. So I suggest we do the whole thing up here. You leave it all to us. Let me have the lists of who're to come and my secretary will handle all that end of it. You won't have a thing to worry about."

"We couldn't possibly . . ."

"Oh, now, Stewart—think it over if you like, but I'm sure you can see it would be fun for us and much the best thing to do."

"Well, I suppose Agnes would be pretty much at a loss with a big wedding on her hands."

"It would be a kindness to her to let us do it all. Why not? Say you will. We're all so fond of Ilona, it'll be the greatest of pleasures. Don't deny it to us."

And so Ilona, all in white, came to stand in a receiving line under a green and white striped marquee on the lawn in front of the big house. There was a good band from New York and dancing on the smooth floor of the made-over barn. The champagne was good and there was enough of it to float a small dinghy. Everybody had a marvelous time, both on the Hatfield and Murray sides, and it was generally agreed that the bride and groom might have been made for each other.

Chapter Two

LIKE most women who dive into marriage without any clear idea of what they are doing, Ilona took refuge from the problems of adjusting herself to her new condition by breeding. It was a joke between her and Gavin that their son Thomas had been conceived in the Plaza on the night of their wedding day, so prompt had been his appearance. They both looked back on that night with somewhat different feelings. Gavin had been surprised to find that his wife was a virgin, and the discovery had given their first night of lovemaking a grave and sacramental quality in his eyes; afterwards he felt an increased tenderness for her and a responsibility for her that he hadn't foreseen. She had been surprised too, but in another way. She had been brought up in an era of knowledge, in which ignorance was the thing to be ashamed of, not anything else. She had always pretended to know about the mechanics of sex because the smart leaders of the bands of girls and boys among whom she had grown up affected to know all about them: it would have been a confession that she was an outsider to admit that she knew nothing in this matter. And so, it was always assumed that she knew what men and women did together when they made love, nobody ever told her. She concocted her own rough idea. But it was all guesswork and conjecture, and when she at last found herself in bed with Gavin, all she had to go on was will power. She kept repeating to herself "I mustn't be scared. I mustn't give myself away—I mustn't let anything he does disgust me." She was terribly surprised by Gavin's weight pressing down upon her, and even more surprised to find herself possessed by him. She looked through her eyelashes into his face and found him with his eyes shut looking just like some little boy dreaming of some delicious thing to eat. She was not prepared for the pleasure she would find in touching the smooth skin of his muscular body, nor for the electrical excitement which would pass through her when he kissed her breasts. The pumping effort between her thighs turned without warning into an exquisite rhythm to which her whole body answered and presently a moment arrived which she hoped would last forever. Her whole body treasonably dissolved into softness, while she exerted all her will to hold onto it. There was nothing in the world but Gavin, and then an eternity, no world, no Gavin, nothing but the overflowing of that rhythmic pulsing in a flood of pure delight.

Ilona slept well and woke early. A white gauze curtain billowed softly in a cool breeze. Sitting up in bed she could see the wide expanse of Central Park heavily mid-summer green, and beyond it, across the roof tops of the upper west side, a strip of the Hudson bright blue under the crags on the New Jersey shore. Gavin lay beside her, still naked, with the sheet flung back from the upper part of his body. She studied him intently, the golden fuzz of tiny hairs on his strong arms, his powerful muscles between his naval and his sternum, his ears, and the structure of his face. This was the man who had, the night before, given her such intense pleasure. He was a complete stranger to her. She was deeply shocked to find that this was so, and still more shaken by what she learned about herself from it when she found a hunger for that new sensation of being first possessed and then transported rising within her. It did not matter that he was a stranger. She stroked his shoulder until he woke. His eyes were blank when they opened, and for a terrifying instant she saw that he did not know where he was, who she was, or anything. And then his eyes cleared and he smiled.

"Ilona," he said and put an enormous strong male hand on her hipbone. She felt her flesh beginning to melt in anticipation and she bit her lip. She had to go on biting it for fear of what she would say while he spent what seemed to be an endless waste of time nuzzling at her breasts and shoulders, kissing the line of her chin, her ears, her eyelids. And then there at last he was, and this time it was better than before. Afterwards she lay face downwards with her head buried in her pillows in utter astonishment, until after a while Gavin kissed her shoulders, stroked her buttocks and thighs and left her. Then she sat up and, ignoring the sounds from the bathroom, stared at herself in the full-length mirror on the closet door. There she was, Ilona, the same as ever. But utterly, utterly different. She had done this wonderful thing, the most marvelously personal thing you could do, with a man she hardly knew and certainly didn't love. How could that be right? She did not find the answer during the month of their honeymoon on Andros. They ate, made love, swam, played tennis, ate, and made love again, day after glorious day. Then shortly before the end of their stay, Thomas gave the first hint of his arrival. One morning Gavin woke at dawn and shook her gently awake with more lovemaking on his mind.

"No, please, Gavin," she said, "please not."

"Oh, come on, darling, see what a gorgeous new day we've got."

"No," she said. "Let's just swim this morning."

He was a little sulky as they went out onto the long sweep of silvery white sand, and they said nothing to each other as they walked out to stand waist deep in the jade-green, dazzling pure water. Gavin half turned and looked back at the row of cottages and the palms behind them.

"It's going to be awfully hard to leave," he said.

She looked round, fiddling with the white strap of her bathing cap.

"I don't know."

"What's the matter with you this morning, old sourpuss?" He took a step towards her and put an arm round her shoulders. "I haven't done anything to upset you, have I?"

"No." She nestled in against his body and he felt reassured. "Then what is it?"

"Nothing. I don't know that I should tell you so soon—not until I've seen a doctor, anyway."

47

"You're going to have a baby!"

"There you go! I don't know really. All I know is I'm late with that thing—over a week. I shouldn't have told you until I was sure—no, I don't mean that, I'm sure, in my bones somehow—but I oughtn't to have told you until it was made official by a doctor."

"Oh, no, it's wonderful news." He seized her by the shoulders and kissed her on the mouth. "It's the best news." He let her go and plunged into the sea, swimming out for a long way with his fast untidy crawl. She swam after him with her slow, comfortable, breast stroke. When he was nearly two hundred yards ahead of her he rolled over onto his back and swam back stroke. "Yai, yai, yai, yippee," he yelled, and turned several somersaults, kicking his legs up high out of the water. It struck her strangely that he should leave her behind to make this demonstration. Was he really delighted at the idea of a new life stirring in her, or was he triumphant over the confirmation it gave his virility? As she swam towards him she formed a determination not to let him touch her, or rather to do *that* to her while she was carrying the child. The defenseless creature might be swept away and lost in the appalling melting and liquifying of her body in which she so often lost herself. To give way to her base appetite for it would be simply a criminal betrayal of her new responsibility. He swam close to her in the water and kissed her salty cheek.

"Darling, I love you so. I love you so," he said, and she smiled back at him with the mysterious, veiled expression which women sometimes assume when they do not wish to speak.

When the child came it was a boy, and in his delight with it Gavin bought a piece of property he had been wanting for some time. It was alongside the state route number 189, which originated just outside the Maramee city limits and went south, dead straight, until, after an involvement with the outer suburbs of Tampa, it passed on to Sarasota; and its frontage stretched from a point just beyond the Marracombee County Arch to a burned-out gas station a mile beyond the house jointly owned by Edwin and Marsen Bunce. It looked like any other stretch of country on either side of the road in question which was bordered with wide stretches of open grazing land interlarded with drifts of woodland. Black birds with uptilted wing tips circled over it searching for carrion, a thing which they often found along the margins of the road in the shape of dogs hit by passing cars. As hardly anyone other than the Bunces lived beside the road until Halesville, halfway to Tampa, it was something of a mystery where these dogs came from, but this was not a problem which engaged the minds of many people who traveled the road. They gave their minds to two questions, how rapidly they could get down the straight-away without knocking themselves and their cars to pieces on what was, when all was said for it, a poor surface; and who on earth had built the Marracombee Arch. This was a paper-thin version of a Roman triumphal arch with Welcome to Marra-combee County written on its face, and Come Back to the Big County with the Big Future written on the other. Standing up in the middle of the miles of burnt-off palmetto scrub, it looked odd—welcoming the traveler to nothing, in a country which was all future and very little present. Gavin was drawn out there by a desire to meet Marsen Bunce on his own grounds and to have a look at him as a person. He knew him through the bank as an eccentric figure who held a portfolio of excessively conservative investments, and who carried an unnecessarily large cash balance.

Gavin felt about this account much the same feelings as a farmer who sees a rich field in the middle of his acreage lying fallow year after year. He had an urge to put that money to work somehow or other, not as much for the sake of making profit out of it as for seeing it put properly to use. Marsen was a client after Mr. Steinhardt's heart, but he was a source of active distress to a banker of Gavin's temperament. At first he promised himself that he would have a word with Mr. Bunce when he came into the bank. But he never did. Dividend checks appeared endorsed in a sprawling scrawl for deposit Marsen F. Bunce, and a check for seventy-five dollars was

49

drawn every other week to the Halesville Quality Market. Months passed and Gavin found out nothing more about his depositor of a personal nature. He went down to Sarasota one day to have lunch with old Mr. Steinhardt, who was failing and glad of a friendly visit now and again, and in talking of old times in Maramee, the name Bunce came up. Mr. Steinhardt remembered it very well.

"There were two of them," he said, "Marsen and Edwin. You could hardly tell them apart. They both had the same shrewd, dried-up look, thin hands, thin lips, lean faces. I don't suppose they'd ever done anything on impulse in their lives. They looked like book salesmen, or storekeepers on holiday when I first saw them. They were both wearing blue serge suits straight off the peg, and their wrists and necks seemed to come out of the center of their starched cuffs and collars. They came into the office to see me with a beat-up, black Gladstone bag between them and I thought they wanted advice about where to look for jobs. They sat down in my office and allowed it was a mighty nice day and we beat about the bushes until I said, 'What can I do for you young fellows?' And then Marsen said, 'We'd like to open an account if this bank is sound.' I gave them a patronizing run-down on my situation, and the sort of insurances on depositors' accounts I carried and then Marsen snapped the bag open and began reaching into it. Every time he dived down Edwin's eyes followed his hands all the way down and back. By the time he was through he'd piled one hundred and sixty-eight thousand dollars onto my desk. Oh, those two surprised me, all right. They'll surprise you. You ought to go out and see them some time." Steinhardt chuckled.

"I'll tell you one thing. Edwin can't read or write. He's the younger of the two, and I believe Marsen has mothered him since he was a boy; they were orphaned when they were only kids. Marsen was very upset when Edwin kicked over the traces and married a few years ago, and I think there's quite a situation developing out there—they all live together in the one house out on Route 189. Yes, you really ought to get out there, if only to tell me what you make of them."

"Why did they come here?"

"For the same reason locusts move into new territory," Mr. Steinhardt said. "They started up in Alabama logging with their father. After he died they worked central Mississippi, and then northern Louisiana. Then they came on down here, in 1915. They bought themselves fourteen thousand acres of virgin timber land and a piece of waterfront property for a timber yard. All through the war and for a year after, they were shipping the stuff out as fast as they could cut it. They must have cleared something like three hundred percent on their investment by the time things quieted down."

"They were pretty lucky."

"They've done well out of having people underestimate them. Don't you make that mistake."

With this warning in his ears, Gavin went out to see the Bunces. He found them sitting in a row on rockers on the porch of their house, Marsen reading, Edwin and Lorene, hands folded across their stomachs, apparently content just to watch what went on in front of their noses. As Gavin came up the steps, Marsen folded his magazine back so that he would not lose his place and spoke.

"It's friendly of you to call, young feller, but if you're selling anything forget it. We have a rule against that sort of thing in this family and there's a law against it in the county."

"I'm not a salesman, Mr. Bunce. I'm the man who looks after your money, I run the bank in Maramee. I thought I'd come out and have a look at my invisible client."

"I heard Steinhardt was giving up. You'd be Mr. Hatfield."

"That's right. And I'm very glad to meet you at last."

Gavin noticed that when he said he was from the bank Marsen looked sharply at him and showed, by the movement of his hands, a certain uneasiness. Edwin's eyes brightened and he moved his hands from his little round paunch to the arms of his chair. Lorene Bunce's face remained absolutely expressionless but her right hand stole out and covered her husband's, as if she were reminding him to keep calm and to do or say nothing rash. Marsen made the introductions and they talked of nothing for a while. A huge clump of bamboos near the house made a dry rattling and a large truck traveled across the landscape from right to left.

"Getting to be more of them things each year," Edwin said, nodding at it.

"Horrible noisy things they are, too," Lorene said. "On a still night we can hear them a mile off—more than that—I say with the wind right you can hear them when they speed up after slowing down for the crossing at Halesville. But there, it's all noise and hurry these days."

"Surely not out here."

"Oh, we take our time with things out here," Edwin said and grinned at Marsen.

"I've been after Marsen to have that clump of bamboos there grubbed for four years now. I say it harbors snakes. He says it breaks the winds from the north and the east. I say when the wind blows the everlasting clattering those little leaves make would drive a person crazy—and he says he'll think about getting one of those big tractors in one day. That'll be the day!"

"We don't want to bother Mr. Hatfield with that sort of thing," Marsen said with a certain firmness.

"I wonder you've never thought of moving nearer the sea now you're retired," Gavin said idly. "Did you ever think of a house on one of the keys?"

"Don't think I haven't, Mr. Hatfield," Lorene said.

"I'll show Mr. Hatfield why I for one don't want to move," said Marsen. He got up and went indoors for his Panama hat. Edwin and Lorene got up uncertainly looking at each other.

"He'll be going to show you the boil, I expect," Edwin said. "It's a kind of natural wonder we have in these parts."

Marsen reappeared looking more like an old turtle than ever in his age-yellowed hat.

"No need for all of you to start milling around. It won't take the three of us to show Mr. Hatfield what I'm going to show him. And don't you go spoiling my surprise, Edwin, telling him what it is." He turned to Gavin. "It ain't everyone as

52

comes out here that I show the boil to, and when I do show a person I like to surprise them. If your car isn't good in sand, we'd better take my Model T. She's no beauty but she's hard to beat on a sand track." He turned back to Edwin and Lorene. "You've both seen the place a hundred times, there's no point in dragging out there like an outing. I'll be back presently."

So they went off alone, up 189 for a mile, and then turning across it onto a sand road which headed for a woodlot seeming like any other which stood up like a wall beyond the cleared ground. The old Ford trundled them sweetly along at a steady fifteen miles an hour, kicking up a pall of reddish fog behind them.

"Well, you've got a head on your shoulders, young man," Marsen said. "You certainly found out a lot about us pretty quick."

"I'd no idea of probing into your concerns when I came out here."

"Come on now, Mr. Hatfield. I know better. Still, the plain fact is I don't get on with Edwin the way I used to and it bothers me. I don't feel I can talk business in front of him any more. His attitude has changed. I could say more on this subject but I won't. Not until I know you better. The thing is what did you come out here for?"

"Two things, three really. You've a lot of idle cash in the bank which could be earning you money. It ought to be invested. That's one thing. Another is that the investments you have made are all right but they could be better from the point of earned income and capital appreciation. The third thing is that those wharves of yours down on the waterfront aren't bringing you in a proper return. You oughtn't to be leasing them as cheaply as you are. You ought to sell them and set the capital working for you. There's very little benefit for you in your ownership as things are."

"I was afraid you'd say something like that to me when I saw the young, eager look you've got on you." He was silent for a minute as the car passed through an opening in a wire fence and into the shadows of the wood. "Can you give me any good reason why I should be richer than I am? I don't believe you can. There's the saying in the scriptures, 'It is easier for a camel to go through the eye of a needle, than for a rich man to enter into the kingdom of God.' That text troubles me. You know something else, it troubles me to be as rich as I am. We, Edwin and me that is, we made a mint of money in that European war. We were cutting timber. They wanted it. They had money to burn, or so it seemed, and we took the money and let them have the timber. I never thought any more of it than that. Cutting timber and selling it was what I'd been doing all my life. Then one day I had the fancy to fill in the coupon and order this illustrated history of the war they mentioned in the advertisement. I never was a man for reading newspapers. I'd no idea what had been going on over there, millions of men dead, women and children suffering, and me and Edwin making a great wad out of it. I felt ashamed." He paused. "I still do." He paused again, and drew the car to a standstill under a huge live oak whose fronds of blue-gray Spanish moss hung down within a few inches of the ground. "We walk from here."

There was a cool shade under the trees, and the footfalls of the two men were silent as they moved away from the car across the floor of soft, powdery white sand. A few widely spaced clumps of palmetto spread their stiff fanlike leaves in the gloom. They walked along, side by side, without speaking until they abruptly emerged into the full blaze of sunlight. It took Gavin a few seconds to realize what he was looking at. In the center of an almost complete circle of spotless sand there was a jade-green pool of translucent water. It was alive and in constant agitation like a crystal dome, rising a foot or so above its surface, it rose, now a little higher, and fell. Gavin was puzzled by it as it swung to and fro, always within a short distance of the middle of the basin, and then recognized it as the top of a column of water thrusting up out of the ground at the rate of thousands of gallons a second. An underground river of almost unimaginable purity was breaking out into the light of day. It made a chuckling happy sound as its dome rose and collapsed again and again, and Gavin's heart leapt with joy at the glory and beauty of the sight. Still in silence Marsen led him round half the circle to the point at which the underground river began a new life, flowing away down a sandy channel floored here and there with clumps of vivid green weed to become a tributary stream of the Marracombee river. Marsen looked at it and cleared his throat.

"Some of the crackers from round about will swear blind that this water comes clear down from the Tennessee hills, but you don't have to believe all you're told."

Gavin knelt and tasted the water. It was sweet and good, without any hint of saltness or any suggestion of a mineral flavor.

"Cool in summer, warm in winter, I've never known it vary a degree either way, from sixty-four." Marsen's voice was flat, even, and matter of fact. "It's a sign and a wonder to magnify His name, sure enough," he added without changing his tone in the least. "When the good book fails me I often come out here just to look at it and take comfort." His voice now changed, perplexity and discouragement entered into it. "You'll probably think I'm an old blabbermouth to tell you all of my affairs, but something about you makes me feel I can tell you what it is that bothers me. It's Edwin, more than anything, and that woman of his. I've always looked out for Edwin ever since we were boys. Our mother died a long way back and our father got killed logging. I was seventeen then, and Edwin was fourteen. A wire cable snapped, whipped back and cut father all to bits. We were alone there out in the wood with his body. 'What are we going to do now, Marsen?' Ed said. So I told him. We were going to take the body into town on the wagon, get some woman to wash it, and have father buried proper. 'And what are we going to do then, Marsen?' Ed said, and I told him. 'We're going to come back here and finish logging off this tract we got.' We had this sawmill, we had fifteen hundred acres of uncut timber, we had a gang of niggers, and we had two hundred and fifteen dollars in cash. There wasn't anything else we could do. But Ed couldn't see that, he had to be told. And he got the habit of asking me the ques-

55

tion, what are we going to do now. And I got the habit of telling him. Well, sir, all the time we were building ourselves up I knew what we had to do. Keep working and stick to what the good books says. My generation and yours are different. You know lots of books; I've never really taken stock of any but the one. I can quote you reams of it, all the rest goes in one ear and out the other, but I know the book. 'For the seed shall be prosperous; the vine shall give her fruit, and the ground shall give her increase, and the heavens shall give their dew; and I will cause the remnant of this people to possess all these things. And it shall come to pass, that as ye were a curse among the heathen, O house of Judah, and house of Israel; so will I save you, and ye shall be a blessing: fear not but let your hands be strong. . . . These are the things that ye shall do; Speak ye every man the truth to his neighbor, execute the judgement of truth and peace in your gates: And let none of you imagine evil in your hearts against his neighbor; and love no false oath: for all these things that I hate, saith the Lord.' I can follow that, see what it means, and try to do it. I used to think we did well because I followed it out. And then when I found we'd made ourselves rich out of the war I began to wonder. The way we got rich was one thing. And then Ed. I'll be level with you. Ed is wedded to untruth. I don't mean Lorene. I mean he couldn't tell the truth if he was to try to. He's just a born natural liar. You see a sparrow fly through the room. Ed'll say see that yellow and red bird go through here just now, I never saw one like that before. It's harmless, I guess, wanting to add a bit of interest to things. But it gets to be a habit. Ed can't give you a straight answer on anything no more. He lies to me, he lies to Lorene, he lies to anyone he can get to listen to him. And he's a fornicator, too. He always was after women, girls, anything in skirts he could get to lie down with him, young or old, married or unmarried. Well, after the war he says to me in the usual way 'What are we going to do now, Marsen?' and I said 'Nothing. We aren't going to do anything. We're going to take it easy. Taper off and retire.' He said 'You mean that?' I said I did, and he said 'You mean we've got enough money to do

56

whatever we like?' When I told him, yes, he let out a sigh from deep down inside him and he said 'Well, Marsen, if that's the way we're situated I'll tell you what, I'm going to get me a woman of my very own.' What he did beat everything. He took up with one of them bureaus and presently he was exchanging photographs and sending letters all over the United States to women who were seemingly willing to pledge themselves to any well-heeled feller who asked them, whether they'd set eyes on him or not. Oh, it was a fine exhibition I can tell you, seeing my brother squinting at the photographs, like a cattle dealer, trying to figure out what the woman who sent them was really like. Finally he settled on a bunch of women right here in the state of Florida. I asked him why, with all of the United States to choose from he'd picked on a set of local girls after all and he looked at me as if he pitied me. He said to me 'Marsen, you may know God's own amount about the timber business, but there's one hell of a lot you don't know.' He wouldn't tell me. But later on he had to. He has to tell someone every mortal thing."

They stood back in the shade looking out at the sunlight gleaming on the jumbled surface of the pool. Gavin leaned back against the lichened stem of one of the oaks and lit a cigarette.

"Well, sir, later on he told me, as if he was expecting me to admire him for his cleverness, that he picked those girls because he could drive over and see them; and when he'd been over a couple of times he'd say, How about a picnic at the beach and a swim? That way he could get them into bathing suits, see, and have a good look at them, what they'd got or not got. Finally he picked on this Lorene from down near Fort Myers, because she came out of the cabin she'd changed in wearing one of those one-piece Jantzen affairs with a little skirt on it that wouldn't hide nothing. He came back carrying on about her in a way that disgusted me. I said to him, How can you marry a woman you don't know, you talk as if you were buying a steer or horse. He laughed and he said something a long way too vile for me to repeat. I tell you, Ed is an ungodly man. I'm not worried about his state. If he wants to spend eternity in hell's fire when the way to heaven is set straight before him, that's his foolishness and his fate. But what am I to think of my life? I lived my life for Ed now I look back on it. All that work I did was to make him rich. When I pass on it'll all go to be squandered on fornication and high living by him and his woman. That's why I'm not interested by that money in the bank any more. You turn it into more money and what'll you do? Just feed up a fool in his folly. You're a young man, Mr. Hatfield, you may not understand an old man's feeling. I just look back on my life and I wonder what the hell I've been at, and I wonder if all that money ain't somehow tainted. All my life I've labored and worshiped, and somewhere along the line I sinned. I feel sick at heart when I think about it, and I don't know what I can do to put it right."

They both stared out at the living water leaping in the sunlight. Gavin threw his cigarette down and stamped it out of sight in the sand.

"Have you talked this over with the preacher of your church?" he said. "It sounds more like his problem than mine."

"I did once. His eyes popped right out of his head. He looked just as if he'd seen a boiled pork chop and a slice of apple pie fly in at the window to offer themselves to him. Greed! You could have taken a photoportrait of him and printed it in a magazine with greed for a title. The first piece of God's work he had for me to do was to rebuild the presbytery. Seems it was forty years old and getting real inconvenient."

"You don't want to leave Edwin high and dry, do you?"

"I've no wish to spite him, nor that woman of his."

"Suppose you left him and his wife a lifetime trust fund which would see to all their reasonable needs, would that suit you? Then you could provide that on their deaths the capital would go to serve some institution that you approved of—a hospital, a university—anything you like."

Marsen considered it.

"Sick people always disgusted me, I can't say why, and I know it ain't right that it should be so. But I just don't want to think I worked my life long to fatten up a parcel of invalids and doctors. And education's another thing. Not having had much of it I can't say I know a lot about it, but let a fellow who wants an education work for it, I say, then he'll appreciate what he's getting. I don't believe in spoon-feeding young people. The trouble with Edwin is I spoon fed him."

"You make things very difficult for yourself."

"I guess I do. But how was I to know all that time that I was working for so much more than I would have any use for?"

The two men watched the joyous leaping and surging of the water for a time.

"I'm sure we can put your money to good use if we put our minds to it, Mr. Bunce," Gavin said.

"Don't think of it that way," Marsen had rounded on him, and had hold of his jacket by the lapel. His other hand, with one finger outstretched like a pistol was waving up and down in front of Gavin's nose. "No, sir." Gavin for a moment wondered if he were a little mad. "No, indeed. It's not a matter of putting the money to good use, or better use. It's a matter of putting something right. I've got to find some way of dealing with it that will cleanse my soul. You young people may not take much stock of such language, but I've got a burden to put down before I can die in peace. Can you understand that?"

"I think, perhaps, I can." Gavin felt himself released.

"I'm sorry I flared up on you that way." Marsen moved a little way off and kicked at a twig covered with brown leaves lying on the sand. "I get desperate thinking what I ought to do. Maybe I just ought to let Edwin and that woman have some damn big house out on Steamboat Key, with a dock for a motor cruiser, and a swimming pool, and a mess of barbecue pits and little tables with those dam' fool striped umbrellas over them. Maybe I ought to just let the pair of them go to hell by the route of their own choosing. But somehow when I get out here and think about it I can't bear to think that's what I worked for all my life. I don't believe that's what the

59

book means when it says the seed shall be prosperous. There's something about this place tells me different."

He stopped. Something about the set of his jaw and his mouth told Gavin that his mood of loquacity and openness had come to an end. Marsen turned to him again and gave him a level-eyed inspection, looking deeply into his face to see if there was anything there in the way of pity or contempt. Gavin seemed to pass muster, and the older man's face cleared.

"I'm sorry, boy, I'd no call to bother you with all this."

"I'll try to help if I can."

They turned away from the spring, walking back towards the car, and the drive out of the cool shadowed wood across the hot open land to face the quick-eyed curiosity of Edwin and the dead-pan suspicions of his wife. The pair of them, with their road-company performance of indifference, hardened Gavin's determination to help Marsen. They took to lunching together once a week in one of the cool, tiled-walled Spanish restaurants in downtown Maramee, eating soup, paella, and dessert for seventy-five cents on separate checks, talking over coffee afterwards and becoming friends. Gavin persuaded Marsen to let him reorganize his estate even though it grieved him to be made richer with no solution to his problem in sight. At the end of a year and a half, Gavin showed him that he was worth a million and a half dollars, and that there would be an income of ninety thousand a year to deal with from then on. Marsen looked at the figures in silence for a while.

"I remember I took Edwin and Lorene over to the east coast one time and we had lunch there in Miami," he said. "The waiter brought me this bill for nine dollars and thirty-eight cents and I told him that's the most I ever spent on a meal in my life. He seemed to be amused. What are you doing to me, Gavin, boy?"

"I'm setting you up for the biggest jolt you've ever had in your life." Gavin was half-joking, and half-scared by what he was going to do. When they had finished their coffee and paid the bill they went out into the harsh glare of the sunshine and drove over to Morgantown across the river from Maramee City.

At the far end of its sprawl of run-down streets, potholed and neglected, Gavin pulled up in front of an archway of red-painted tinplate crowned by a cross set slightly askew. White letters against the red proclaimed that this was the Ethel Coring Munson Home for Orphaned and Abandoned Children. "Suffer the little children to come unto me." Inside the gates a few listless teen-age girls tended a mob of forty or so ragged urchins with shaved heads, who all fell silent and stared as the two men came into their playground. Marsen looked at the tumbled-down sheds which served as dormitories and class rooms, and at the patched clothes on the children, without any change of expression.

"Reverend Stevens, that man here again," called one of the girls, and an elderly Negro, white-haired and with his eyes blue with untreated cataract came to the doorway of a decayed frame house at the far end of the yard. A younger man appeared in the dark room behind him, peering uncertainly over his shoulder.

"It's that fellow from the bank across the river, Reverend Stevens," he muttered, "brought another fellow to look us over."

"Goodday to you, Mr. Hatfield, goodday," said the preacher smiling blindly towards them, "and goodday to your friend."

"Good afternoon, Mr. Stevens," Marsen said crisply. He turned to Gavin. "Do I understand you correctly?"

"You do." Gavin smiled. "I think you do."

"I provide so much for new buildings, and so much for their upkeep, and so much more for the food and clothing of fifty or sixty or even a hundred nigger bastards? Is that it?"

"That's it."

"And it'll be renamed the Marsen Bunce home for black bastards, I daresay."

"No. That's not legally possible. It's got its name forever. It's the Ethel Coring Munson Home till the end of time, or so Scott Hansen tells me. Your name will appear on the trust deeds, but very few people will know anything about it."

Marsen looked wonderingly at the children who had lost

61

interest in the strangers and who had begun to pick up their games where they had left off.

"Well, I'll be eternally goddamned," he said softly. "Do you mean this, Gavin?"

"Yes, sir, I do. Mrs. Munson left them the ground and ten thousand dollars in 1874. The money hasn't been wisely managed and the whole place has an income of three hundred a year. The rest is done by cadging. The Reverend Stevens spends his time begging, a few dollars here and a few dollars there. It's all done on a hand-to-mouth basis." Gavin paused, looking at the old man who was being led towards them. There was something a little cringing and uncertain on the blind face, and the younger Negro who was leading him looked suspicious and apprehensive. "You could change those faces with your money," he said softly and rapidly. "If you let them have it, then they won't have to think of anything but getting on with the job. God knows they might even look happy for a time, and some of the kids might turn out all right, too."

"All right, Gavin, all right. If you say so."

Marsen spoke up when they were driving back into Maramee across the new swing bridge the army engineers had put in.

"You have hell's own amount of gall, getting me into a thing like that, Gavin," he said. "Do you know I never shook hands with a coon before in the whole of my natural life? To think I should end up playing Santa Claus to a pack of piccaninnies." He threw back his head and laughed, slapping his thigh.

"I never heard you laugh before."

"I haven't felt like laughing in a long time." He split wide-open again. "Oh Gavin, boy, you do me good."

With his income cut down to six thousand a year Marsen became rosy and cheerful, so much so that he seemed to have dropped ten years from his age. Edwin and Lorene watched the change with deep suspicion but without understanding. They knew Gavin had somehow got hold of Marsen, but they could not make out what was going on. Edwin supposed that the banker had got Marsen interested in some get-rich-quick scheme or other, and that his brother had become obsessed with the new kind of business venture. He felt that he was being left out of things and decided that he would show his elder that he was to be reckoned with when it came to money spinning. He found himself his own sweet scheme. There was this man in Halesville who had a site by the railroad track where this man who was planning to go into business with bottled drinks was willing to locate if they could guarantee him a pure water supply. Pumping it out of the Marracombee, the old thick and dirty, wouldn't do. It had to be pure well water. Well, there was this spring, the boil, out there across Route 189 doing no good to anyone. So the man down in Halesville agreed: He'd pay a third of whatever he got for the lot by the tracks, plus whatever it cost to cap the boil and lay a pipe line down to Halesville, with a guaranteed minimum of forty thousand dollars. Edwin explained the whole thing over a special lunch he had had Lorene cook up of Marsen's favorite food; a leg of lamb like a young angel's thigh, new potatoes, green peas, and a pecan pie that was a joy to put in your mouth. Marsen ate every last bite that was put before him in silence and then spooned a great deal of sugar into the cup of fresh coffee Lorene put down by his empty plate.

"That pie was real good, Lorene," he said. "Real good."

"But what do you think about what I've been saying," Edwin said. He had been letting Marsen have the scheme between mouthfuls all through the meal.

"I think you've got a lot to learn, for one thing." Marsen drank his coffee and wiped his lips with his napkin. "I'm going to remember that pie for a long time, Lorene. It was delicious." He smiled at her. She wished she had put arsenic in his coffee. "Well, Edwin, with that source of water out there on it that three thousand eight hundred acres of ground on the far side of the road is worth a hundred dollars an acre at present land values, perhaps a little bit more. Without water it's just palmetto scrub worth twenty to twenty-five an acre, like any other bit of logged-off sand and gravel hereabouts. Do you follow me?"

63

Edwin cheered up. This was like the old days when Marsen took time to explain things to him. He nodded.

"I can see that, Marsen."

"Well, that's nice. Now you're considering a proposition that will bring in forty thousand dollars cash in return for reducing the sale value of the property from three hundred and eighty thousand to seventy-six thousand. If you add seventy-six to forty you get one hundred and sixteen. One hundred and sixteen from three hundred and eighty is two hundred and sixty-four. That's what you would have me lose on this deal of yours, two hundred and sixty-four thousand dollars."

Lorene had gone round the table a way to Marsen to get to a spot where she could look at the three hundred and eighty thousand dollars across the road. She ran her hand along the hem of her apron as she gazed out of the window. Marsen took a quick look at her, and then turned to Edwin, whose eyes were glazed with the difficulty of mastering the calculations put before him. He felt fond of him for the moment.

"I never did have a head for figures, Marsen," he said weakly. "But that forty thousand was a guaranteed minimum, he said."

"Guaranteed nothing! He only gave you that figure to see how far he could take you. You'd best get down there and tell him the deal's off, your skinflint brother wouldn't agree to it. You tell him that, and first thing you know he'll raise that guaranteed minimum to a hundred thousand or so. But tell him no, the deal's off." Marsen sighed. "I'd just like to sit around this afternoon and think over the beauty of that pie of yours, Lorene, but I've got to get into Maramee to see a feller about some business I've got. Too bad." He went out into the hall and took his Panama off the peg, sighed deeply, and went out through the screen door. He paused near the clump of bamboos behind which his going-to-town car was parked and heard the beginning of a diatribe from Lorene.

"You damned fool, putting a half-baked scheme like that up to an old sharpie like Marsen. If you'd gone over it with me I could of told you."

He sighed again, put his hat square on his head and marched off towards his car. It was a terrible thing in a home when the wife could call the husband a fool, and worse when she was right. When he got to Maramee he found Gavin in his tenth-floor office looking out over the spreading town to the green expanse of the gulf beyond it. An Allendorf ship was coming in through the dredged channel and a white-hulled French boat which had been loading at the Gulf Chemical wharf was waiting in the pool with one anchor down, ready to leave as soon as the channel was clear. Gavin beamed when he saw Marsen.

"Well, this is a nice surprise! I was going to come out your way this evening to give you a cigar."

"A cigar! You know I've had to give those things up."

"Oh, but I have to give you one, all the same. It's what fathers are supposed to do isn't it?"

"Mrs. Hatfield's had her baby?"

"Yes, she had a boy this morning. They're both just fine."

"Well, that's great news, boy, great news. I don't suppose you'll want to be bothered with business today, though."

"Oh, yes, I'm doing a little business between my spells of jubilation. What can I do for you?"

"It's about my land, that piece with the boil on it. I thought of all things I could trust Edwin to be sensible about land, but I find I can't. He came up today with a hare-brained god-damned scheme for capping that spring and piping the water off down to Halesville where some fellow wants to bottle pop. I was sick to my stomach when I heard him tell it. They'd put some concrete box on top of it, and have the whole flow running through precast pipe across that flat ground—hell—and he'd even lose money doing it. I can't trust that boy with any-thing. I've got to sell that ground to keep it out of his hands, and put the money in trust like the rest. Get busy on it right away, will you, Gavin, and fix up something fast. I've got no time to lose with this heart of mine beginning to act up."

Gavin looked at him, remembering the intense beauty of the welling spring.

65

"If you really want to sell it I might buy it myself. What's your price?"

"My price." An interior struggle took place within Marsen. Gavin was his friend, and yet land was land and money, money. "Four hundred and twenty thousand," he said. "There's three thousand eight hundred acres in the piece, and some odd. I don't know. Land's going up around here all the time. You can't lose."

"No, I don't suppose I can." Gavin suddenly thought of his son, pink, barely shaped, lying beside his exhausted mother. Perhaps there was something providential in the coincidence of the boy's arrival and the offer of the land, it was as if it was intended that they should have something to do with each other. "All right," said Gavin. "I'll buy it. I'll get the lawyers working on it today. What do you want done with the money? I think those little coons have about all the money they can use for the present. Any ideas?"

Marsen looked down at the hat he was holding in his lap with a curious expression before he spoke.

"Well, Gavin, I wouldn't say but what having this trouble of my own hasn't changed my view on sickness the least bit. Anyway I feel differently about hospitals from the way I did. And I've been thinking about the Reverend Stevens' eyes that got so bad without being attended to, and the way he died like a dog for lack of proper care last spring. Well, hell man, they could do with a little bit of a hospital over there in Morgantown. See how far you can stretch the money in that line, Gavin."

"I'll do that," said Gavin, thinking inwardly, Hurray, hurray, this makes it a perfect day.

As soon as the bank's doors were closed he went off to pay a second visit to Ilona. She was asleep when he arrived, and he sat beside her for half an hour waiting for her to wake. Sunlight filtered into the room through a slatted blind and she looked very lovely in the soft light. There were a great many flowers in the room and the stirrings in the bright outer world seemed very remote. He dozed and his head nodded. When he felt himself falling and snapped out of it he found that Ilona was awake and watching him. He went and knelt by her bed, kissing the palm of her hand and its fingers, one by one.

"It was sweet of you to come again." She was still a little dopey. "Did you have a good day?"

"Yes. Wonderful." He thought of the spring which was going to be his, and one day his son's. He wanted to tell her about it. "Marsen Bunce came to see me, he . . ."

"That dreadful old man."

"Oh, Ilona, he's not dreadful. Shush now."

"He is too dreadful. He disgusts me, with his scrawny neck, and that mean, mean mouth. I can't see how you can bear him."

"You're wrong about him, but we won't talk about that now." He squeezed her hand. He could tell her some other time.

"He's a dreadful, horrible, ignorant old thing," she said and fell asleep again. A starched nurse came and beckoned him out of the room; his news would wait until some other time. That came over three months later when Gavin took Ilona and Thomas in his basket cot out to see what was now safely his property. They swam and ate a picnic, slept a little and swam again, testing their strength against the surging water which always flung them back no matter how hard they tried to reach the crystal dome in the center of the pool. They came out of the water hand in hand, and went dripping to look down at Thomas, sleeping in his basket under a muslin cover stretched over a frame. He was beginning to look like Gavin after a spell of resembling Ilona.

"Did you ever see anything so beautiful?"

"Never." She kissed his wet shoulder.

"Nor such a beautiful place?" She shook her head. "I bought it for him."

"Clever Gavin to find such a wonderful place for our Thomas," she said.

"I didn't find it," he said, "Marsen Bunce showed it to me a long time ago, the first time we met."

"Oh, him!"

"What have you got against Marsen?"

"I don't know. I just can't bear him."

"I wish you weren't such a snob, sometimes."

"I'm sorry, darling. I just don't like him. Please don't try to make me like him."

Gavin looked round at the circle of trees, with a profound sinking of heart. There was a gap between them which he could not bridge with words. There was only one time when they were truly together. He took her by the shoulders.

"Please, Gavin, not here, anyone might come!"

But in spite of her protests, and some physical opposition, he possessed her under the trees on the rug which had been spread for their meal. The physical magic worked as powerfully as it had ever done and she was swept away out of herself into that terrifying world in which she knew nothing of what was fitting and proper, or right and wrong. When it was over she leapt up and ran, with some thought of cleaning herself, into the pool. He came lazily after her, deeply content.

"You look like a wood nymph," he said. "You look so lovely in that green water."

"I don't feel lovely. And I don't feel like a nymph." She swam a few strokes away from him and then turned her head. "You may not know it, Gavin, but that was rape."

"Rape." He was astounded. "Good God, Ilona, what are you saying?"

"You did something to me against my will and without my consent. You could do it because you're stronger than I am. That's rape." She looked at him. "Please don't ever do that again."

He looked into the face of the stranger he had married with a gathering sense of horror and the first true awareness that some important thing had gone terribly wrong at the heart of his life.

"Forgive me," he said.

"Let's not talk about it any more." She smiled. "We'd best forget the whole thing." She swam back to the shore with

68

smooth powerful strokes, and he watched her walk up the bank and dry herself from the far side of the pool. He had heard the sobs of joy and delight coming from deep within her being a few minutes before. How had they been the preliminary to this—this cold awfulness? It made no sense to him. He suddenly remembered Nedda Riemann. He had brought her out to the pool several times in the old days and had enjoyed her under the trees. And she had, to all appearances enjoyed him. "Oh, Gavin, oh God, Gavin," she had once said to him, "isn't this the best thing in the whole world." He had known just how to give it to her, too, and then she had suddenly gone off with Crane. He left the water and found Ilona feeding Thomas at the breast. She smiled at him.

"This greedy little beast is always ready for a feed," she said. "He's growing so fast I can't believe it."

Gavin tickled the baby with his little finger. Without taking his lips from Ilona's nipple Thomas rolled his eyes at his father and grabbed the finger tightly.

"He's the dearest little thing, isn't he?" said Ilona. "Aren't you, precious?"

Gavin took his finger back, and stood up. He wondered if he had dreamed the scene in the water.

"Let's go back to the Grove, Ilona," he said, "let's go home."

Six weeks later Ilona came into Maramee to see her doctor and to have lunch with her husband at the Merchant Adventuress Club in the Beverly Hotel. She came into his office unannounced after saying good morning to his secretary, and she was so full of her own news that she scarcely noticed her husband's preoccupied expression. He got to his feet absent-mindedly.

"Oh, hello, dear, there you are." He looked at his watch. "I'd no idea it was so late. The morning seems to have slipped away." He wiped his chinbone with his fingertips in a questioning gesture that was beginning to become habitual with him. "Well, if you're all through with your morning I guess we might as well go on over to the club and eat."

69

"Gavin. You're being terrible. Aren't you even going to ask me?"

"Ask you? Oh, great heavens! How could I forget. How did it come out?"

"Well, Dr. Miller's quite certain, just as certain as I am. We're going to have another child."

He kissed her on the forehead, and held her in his arms for a moment. Although he was pressing her body to his she felt that he was still thoughtful, and concentrated on something other than herself. She broke out of his arms and stood with her hands on his shoulders looking into his face.

"There's something the matter?"

"Oh, it's nothing . . ."

"But it is."

He contemplated her concern, which was perfectly genuine, with a renewed feeling that he was at sea. After the scene at the spring their relations had been resumed as if it had never taken place, and had indeed become if anything better than ever. But Gavin now achieved her release and his own at the price of the disagreeable knowledge that this perfection of physical experience meant nothing in terms of understanding. They had a carnal knowledge of each other which was absolute, and which was not knowledge. Now she was asking him to tell her something which would only turn her away from him, and to expose a feeling which would be bound to make her impatient.

"Shall we wish for it to be a girl this time," he said.

"No, Gavin, you're not to put me off."

"Well, darling, I was just having some grim thought on a subject which doesn't really go very well with your news."

"I expect you'll feel less badly about it when you've told me."

"A friend of mine came to see me," he said. "He wants his affairs put in order because he's got an inoperable cancer and he's going to be dead inside six months."

"How cruel of them to tell him!" Her eyes glowed with sympathy. "They shouldn't have, surely."

"I don't know," Gavin said. "I think if I were Marsen Bunce's doctor I would have told him. He's the kind of old-fashioned man who likes to be told important things about himself."

"Poor old man." She kissed him on the cheek. "I wish I understood why he means so much to you. I'm sorry I can't like him. I hope he doesn't have too horrid a time."

"I hope not." He suddenly felt fonder of Ilona than ever. "Let's go on over to the club. I could do with a drink."

Out at the Bunces' house another conversation was going on. The midday meal was drawing to a close, and ice cream and cake were on the table.

"A funny thing I've noticed," Edwin said, "lately."

"Such as what?" Marsen asked.

"It used to be you going over to the spring all the time, and now you don't go any more. But that fellow Hatfield, he does."

"Does he indeed?" Marsen said, smiling into his plate.

"You're not to go upsetting each other," Lorene said.

"I merely stated a fact I'd observed," Edwin said.

"It don't surprise me in the least," Marsen said. "There's an explanation for everything, when you get down to it."

"There is?" said Edwin.

"Now you two stop chipping at each other," Lorene said.

"Well, Edwin, when it was my place I used to go out there. Now it's his place, Hatfield's, it does seem natural he should be going, or don't it strike you that way?"

Edwin stopped a spoonful of ice cream halfway to his mouth.

"You sold that ground? But you said it was worth three hundred and eighty thousand dollars if we held onto it."

"That's right, Edwin, and I sold it for four hundred and twenty thousand."

Lorene flashed a warning look at Edwin who stared first at her and then at his brother with an expression of amazement. Lorene smiled at Marsen.

"That's a real nice sum of money."

"It is." Marsen sipped from his glass of water, and then fished a phial of pills out of his vest pocket. Lorene watched him swallow two of them with interest.

"You take a lot of them things these days."

"For discomfort, after meals, it says on its label," Marsen said.

"You've been losing weight lately," she said, with something near tenderness.

"I'll be losing a lot more, some day," Marsen said.

"What are you going to do with all that money?" Edwin said, poking at his ice cream with his spoon.

"I'll think of something," Marsen said. "I'll let you know when I do." His mouth shut like a trap. "You'll know soon enough," he muttered from one corner of it, and his forehead broke out into beads of sweat. He half rose from his chair, and then sank back into it.

"Why, Marsen," Lorene said, "you're sick, you're a sick man. Let me help you over to the couch in the parlor. You have a nice lie-down while I telephone Dr. Willis and have him come and look you over."

"I'll have a nice lie-down when and where I feel inclined. And I've a better doctor in Maramee than poor old Willis will ever be who's told me all I want to know about my condition. I value your concern, Lorene, but there isn't anything you can do for me so just take it easy."

"Lorene's right though, you should take care," Edwin said.

"You let your brother alone," Lorene said. She went into the kitchen, signing from behind Marsen's back that her husband should follow her. Before she left the room she took one last look at the grayish-white tinge which had begun to replace the healthy color on Marsen's cheeks. When the kitchen door was safely shut on them both she went up to Edwin and whispered into his ear.

"He's real sick. He hasn't got far to go. Don't you go tormenting him in his last days."

"You mean he's dying?"

72

She nodded, and a look of alertness dawned on Edwin's face.

"Do you suppose he's made a will? I've heard of people having a mess of real trouble in cases where there's been no will."

"You'd best not trouble him with any of that. We'll make out all right when the time comes."

"Poor ol' Marsen," Edwin shook his head. "Poor old Marsen."

Lorene looked at him, nodding, thinking that Edwin was no chicken either, and that with any luck she'd be shot of them both and free to do what she liked within ten years. Four hundred and twenty thousand dollars was a tremendous amount of money, and she was reasonably sure that it was only a part of Marsen's property, and a small part. Involuntarily she licked her lips with the tip of her tongue. Edwin caught the action and sniggered. He dug her in the ribs with his elbow.

"A penny for your thoughts, Lorene," he said, and she slapped at him as he dodged away.

"Oh, you, I've got the washing up to do." But she couldn't help but laugh.

Marsen found the heavy weight of their sympathy much too hard to bear after a couple of weeks and moved himself all of a sudden to the care of the Sisters of Mercy on Maramee Heights. Lorene and Edwin were profoundly disconcerted to find that he had put himself in the hands of a pack of Romans and visited him in a spirit of stiff disapproval as if he had committed some such eccentricity as taking up quarters in a bawdy house.

"Do you think you're doing the right thing coming here, Marsen?" Edwin asked.

"Yes," said Lorene, "shouldn't you stick with your own kind in your trouble?"

"I never could trust them Romans, and I've always been sorry when I did," Edwin said.

"And think, Marsen," Lorene said, "suppose when you get weak they start working on you, the way they do."

"I never was a hellfire man in matters of religion," Edwin said, "but I sure enough wouldn't feel happy thinking of my chances on the last day if I'd let them people get a hold of me."

Marsen assumed a look of great piety and raised his hand in a gesture which he had seen a preacher use with a powerful effect somewhere back in his youth.

" 'In my Father's house there are many mansions,' that's what the Redeemer said His own self, and I'm not one to raise my voice against holy writ." He deliberately weakened his voice. "And I have it on my mind that when the time comes for me to say 'Lord, now lettest thou thy servant depart in peace,' He won't be particular who I've been boarding with the last few weeks. I'm pretty tired right now, Edwin, I think I'll take a bit of a snooze. It was real good of you two to come in. Come in again early next week."

"This ain't but Wednesday, Marsen, we'll come in tomorrow," Edwin said severely.

"You better not come tomorrow: they've got some saint's day tomorrow. You'll find them singing in the chapel, ringing little bells and such, and there'll be a stench of incense. You won't like any of it. Like I said, you better not come tomorrow."

"You're just teasing, Marsen," Lorene said.

"Maybe I am. But I came in here to die in peace if you want to know, and teasing's about the one way I've got left to protect myself."

"Well, we'll look in Monday," said Lorene stiffly. "We wouldn't wish to force ourselves on you."

They got up and left the wandering sheep. Nuns passed them and smiled at them as they found their way out along the high-ceilinged passages in the rambling old European-style building. They did not smile back, and as they reached the street Edwin observed that it broke his heart to leave his own blood brother in such a place. He simply did not like Romans.

"I've never had any truck with them before," he said, "and

I don't know that I want them meddling between me and my own brother now."

There was no saint's day coming up, and when Gavin called in on the following afternoon he found Marsen seated in a comfortable cane chair on a vine-covered terrace, looking out over the town and watching the movement of the yachts and the ships on the river. He was one of a row of old men spaced along the terrace tranquilly yielding up what remained of their lives. A young sister sat knitting within call in an arbor covered with a mass of plumbago in vivid blue flower. They played chess for a while until Marsen suddenly broke the game up on the grounds that it was muddling him to have to concentrate.

"I've something on my mind, Gavin, concerning you."

"Well, fire away."

"You go out to the boil, the spring, far too much."

"I'm surprised that you should say that."

"It's your going out alone I'm talking about. It's too soon in your life for what you'll get to realize out there. A young man can't afford ideas that an old one can handle naturally. I can tell you that life doesn't mean anything, and that it won't ever make sense because there's no sense in it, and you'll be able to shrug it off. You'll be able to say, poor old Marsen, he's going to die and he's sort of given up. But if you come to know that, you'll be badly off. I know you think you showed me something when you got me giving money to those little bastards and the sick niggers over in Morgantown. So you did in a way, but it wasn't what you thought. I believe you thought you could get me to find my life wasn't wasted by showing me some way I could do good."

"I—"

"Don't you go on interrupting me, young feller. I'm privileged by age and infirmity to lecture you just as much as I please." Marsen gulped. "You showed me something different though. I had it all worked out what it was this morning but it's all gone soft in my mind since then."

"Don't worry about it. Just let's sit for a bit."

75

"Yes, I've got it now. What giving that money to those niggers taught me was simply this. There wasn't one damned scrap of point in my life from start to finish, and it don't matter a bit. Nothing matters except whether you feel good or bad about it."

"Oh, Marsen." A tremendous surge of dismay swept through Gavin. "There's got to be something more to it than that." He looked at his old friend's emaciated face, the tendons now prominent at the back of his neck and on the backs of his hands. The poor old man's mind was letting go of life just as his waxy white flesh was melting every day. He was beginning to think the thoughts of an empty skull. "I know there's something more to it all than that," he said. "I know it."

"Oh, yes, boy, you know it. You've got a long way to go before you'll know anything different. Now take me, sitting here waiting like a baby in its pram with that young woman over there watching like a nursemaid so's the minute I let out a holler she'll come and see what ails me, there was a time when I just knew in my bones I was on mighty important business. I always loved forests. I never liked anything so much as the silence and the dignity of big trees, and it always gave me a kind of wrench to see the first one topple. But then I believed in the principle of growth or some such damned thing. I felt those trees were somehow better as board feet of timber; men were doing something with them, making things, making houses and workshops and I don't know what. So I turned them forests into thousands of acres of stump land, with a pile of sawdust here and there, and opened the way for a lot of land-hungry red-necked white trash to get cheap farms. And I kept on saying to myself it's all for something. It's got to be, and then, by jim, you showed up to give me a sense of purpose, to put meaning into my poor old lost life by taking all my money, that I was so all-fired afraid Edwin was going to squander, to give it to a bunch of coons. I despise niggers, always have done. I think of them as a bit less than human and a lot more trouble than animals. I liked you, I even respected you. You surprised me when you came up with that wet-hen do-gooder's idea. I went along with it just to find out how far you were going with it. And then, by golly, you went the whole way, the whole way down the line. I saw it when it was done, what it was all about. I'd been sick—ill—for ten years worrying what ungodly things Edwin was going to do with that money—and there it was doing good. I might as well have put it down through the hole in the old back-house seat. I used to lie awake nights wondering if you knew that you'd shown me that what I did with that money mattered even less to me than what's going to happen to my poor old carcass when I'm through with it. Then Edwin came up with his idea of turning that spring into a sort of glorified water works for a soda-pop plant. I knew you knew better than that so I got you to buy it. But I still didn't know what you knew about the other thing. So I cooked up that hospital scheme. I can see your face now, just as it looked when I told you. Glory, glory, Hallelujah, you thought, the ol' sinner's seen the light."

"Morgantown needed that little hospital, Marsen," Gavin said unhappily.

"Oh, sure." The old man leaned back. "I'll tell you what, Gavin. You make me another heap of money and I'll set up a mission to the lions in Africa and the tigers in India, and we'll teach them all to be vegetarians. And then the world will be a whole lot better." He paused and thought. "I'm an old man, Gavin, and I've got the thoughts that make it easy for me to go. I never figured that out till just the other day. 'Lord, now lettest thou thy servant depart in peace.' It don't mean a thing but 'put me in a frame of mind where I shan't want to hang on,' that's all. I know now I didn't make good use or bad of my life, I didn't improve anything, or waste anything. I was just Marsen Bunce, and it didn't mean a thing."

"But," Gavin said desperately, "if that's really so why do you give a damn what Edwin does with the spring?"

"I did. I can't say I do any more. I was cooling off in my room the other day. I had my hands cupped under the faucet to gather up some to throw over my face, and when my hands

77

were full and that plain city water was running back down my wrists I just suddenly stopped worrying about that, too."

A bell rang, a weak tinny note, and the sister put away her knitting and rose to her feet. She came over and told Gavin that visiting hours were at an end. As he left she walked beside him, saying what a pleasant-natured old gentleman Marsen seemed to be. They paused beside the door opening from the terrace onto the stairwell down which Gavin would go on his way out. Someone out of sight on the landing below whistled a cheerful tune, perhaps relieved to have the gloomy business of visiting a sick relative over and done with.

"Mr. Hatfield," the sister said, "if you know other friends of Mr. Bunce who would like to see him, tell them not to put their visits off for too long, the old gentleman is failing fast now."

"Does he have much pain?"

"We try to make it as easy for him as we can."

"He's drugged a great deal of the time, I suppose."

"He would have a bad time at night without drugs."

"Well, I'm sure you take very good care of him."

"We do what we can."

Gavin went on his way much cheered up. Marsen was no longer truly himself, poor old man, he thought. His opinions were not to be taken at their face value, his mind was affected by the drugs which were dulling his awareness of the rebellion of his body, and the notions that it produced could be attributed to a lesser being than the redoubtable old Marsen Gavin had first known.

As the child his wife was carrying approached its term Gavin wondered if Ilona would allow him to call it Marsen, a name she detested almost as much as she disliked the man who bore it, because she suspected that it was an illiterate garbling of Marsden. The point, however, remained an academic one because the child was a girl, who was named plain Mary Hatfield after a minimum of discussion and dispute. The child was a pretty baby and Gavin found himself moved by her whenever he saw her. But he did not feel the depth of emotion he had felt at the birth of his son Thomas. Mary had kept him from Ilona for eight months before she was born, and afterwards she stood between them. Ilona's labor was long, and she came home from the nursing home weak and tired. And then Mary remained at her breast for a long time, and seemed to remain attached to her as Thomas had not. Months went by and Ilona slept alone with the child's cot beside her in the spare room across the upper landing from the room where Gavin slept in the big double bed. He began to feel neglected and rejected, and he slept badly. When he reached the office in the morning he found it hard to settle to business, and took to spending longer and longer over the morning papers, following the war news from Europe. What was wrong with the world seemed to make what was wrong with his life seem a very small matter. And out there, in Europe, there was a tangible evil which could be destroyed and broken unlike the nagging, evasive, and untouchable trouble in his own being which could never be fixed and brought to combat. At the height of his self-questioning Marsen Bunce died, long after his due time. The doctor tried to explain his survival. "Most people are afraid of dying, or of death, and they fight, and exhaust themselves. Your friend seemed absolutely indifferent—utterly relaxed—he just remained alive, I really can't tell you how." The doctor did not quite like what had happened, because it was in conflict both with his medical knowledge and his religious faith. He did not enjoy having patients who emerged from the mass to impress themselves upon him as memorable personalities. He looked almost ashamed of himself when he met Gavin's eye at the funeral: "I'm damned if I know what I came for," he said. "I know my being here wouldn't have meant anything to the old boy, and what I know of his brother I don't much care for. But here I am." Edwin was relieved to see the doctor, who was white, just as he was relieved to see Gavin. Lorene was beyond relief. Every place she looked she saw more Negroes in their Sunday clothes. At first she thought it was just coincidence, but as she drew closer to the mortuary chapel in the Vale of Hebron Incorporated Burial Ground she was forced to recognize that all the serious dark faces in the crowd were bent on hers with sympathy and respect because she was closely akin to the man whose funeral they, too, were attending. Edwin did not appreciate the situation as quickly as Lorene, and his anxiety took another form.

"Great God, Mr. Hatfield," he said, darting up behind Gavin and plucking at his sleeve, "ain't the Vale of Hebron restricted?"

"I believe it is, in fact I'm sure it is."

"Well . . ." Edwin looked anxiously back along the path leading to the cemetery gates between a row of meager young palms. There were only two or three whites in the reverent black column which was moving up towards the chapel. In the middle of it there were eighty-five boys and girls between the ages of five and fourteen in scarlet blazers marching in fours behind a group of senior boys carrying a large open book of white lilies with a scarlet ribbon as a bookmarker. Picked out in cornflowers on the white pages were the words, Bunce Our Benefactor. The staff of the Ethel Coring Munson Home followed the children, each of them carrying a wreath of brilliantly colored paper flowers. Edwin's jaw dropped at the sight, but Lorene's mouth hardened into a thin line.

"Someone's playing a game with us, I believe," she said. "Mr. Hatfield, where are all these niggers coming from?"

As she spoke the sinister sound of a band striking up was heard just outside the cemetery gates, and blasts of a recognizable tune presently reached the chapel steps: "When the Saints Come Marching In." The band came in sight, headed by its uniformed drum major and a special honor group carrying a massive tribute in the form of a floral clock set at the hour at which Marsen passed on. A white dove representing the dead man's soul taking off on its heavenward flight hovered on a wire over the clock face.

"This mockery has gone far enough," snapped Lorene, "call the state troopers, Edwin, have these people turned out of here."

"What can we do, Mr. Hatfield?" cried Edwin. "Can we call the state troopers like Lorene says?"

Gavin looked down across the black mass of orphans and abandoned children and recognized the band leader who beamed and gave his gilded staff an extra twirl when he saw Gavin turning towards him. He was Immortal Maggs, formerly Bugsy Maggs, the owner of the noisiest and most disreputable club in Morgantown's bar and whore-house section, perpetually in trouble with the police and with even tougher rivals over drug distribution and profits from prostitution. A few months before he had been cut to ribbons in a razor fight, and would surely have died if he had not been hustled across the street into the Marsen Bunce Hospital and Dispensary. He emerged from it with an enhanced reputation as an unkillable man, and his new name, and here he was under a huge feather-topped shako expressing his gratitude to the man who had saved him. As anyone who knew Morgantown at all was well aware, if there was one thing Immortal Maggs liked better than leading a band it was the excitement of a riot or a street fight, and it forcibly struck Gavin that if the troopers did show up to clear the Vale of Hebron, Marsen's funeral stood a good chance of acquiring the status of an historical event.

"I wouldn't call the police," he said, "I'd just carry on as if nothing out of the ordinary was happening."

But there was a hitch up ahead at the chapel doors. The undertaker's men, who had had the coffin halfway out of the hearse and almost onto the rubber-tired trolley on which it would have reposed during the service, were now pushing it back into the hearse on the instructions of a scarlet-faced newcomer to the scene who had appeared with coattails flying, half running, from somewhere behind the chapel a few instants before. When the coffin was safely back in the Cadillac, and the pallbearers were clustered in a cowed and demoralized group round its doors, the newcomer came bounding across the gravel towards the chief mourners. He was incoherent with rage.

81

"That band, never in all my life have I been so— There's never been anything like this in the Vale of Hebron, I—" He wiped his forehead with a handkerchief and fixed his attention on Lorene. "You get him out of here, I say. That's my last word to you as sure as my name's Howard Grainger, get that, that, outrageous *thing* out of here before I send for the police."

"This man is insane," cried Lorene.

"You know perfectly well that this is a restricted burial ground," shouted the manager of the Vale. "You've no one but yourself to blame if you find this scene unpleasant. Trying to sneak a colored man in here. Take him away where he belongs. Take him away from here!"

"Edwin!" Lorene's eyes blazed with fury. "He's trying to say Marsen was colored!"

"If he wasn't, what are all these niggers doing here? I tell you I shall need documentary proof . . ."

Edwin struck him squarely on the mouth. The manager leapt for his throat, spitting out some blood and a tooth, and tried to throttle him.

"A decently run place! That's all I try for, and you do this to me!"

Lorene leapt upon him scratching, and Gavin grabbed her round the waist to pull her off. The doctor tried to part Edwin and Grainger. The children in their red blazers screamed with pleasure or dismay according to their temperaments, and then scattered like quail as Maggs, terrible in his baby-blue, scarlet, and gold uniform, crowned with his huge tuft of white and scarlet feathers, flew through them flourishing his razor followed by three or four of his more dashing bandsmen. Gavin, as the man obviously attacking the chief woman mourner, took the first cut, from beside his left eyebrow down to his jaw. He felt an exquisite pain as the steel grated over his jawbone, and a cry escaped him. He fell to his knees covering his head with his arms, and took another slash which cut the sleeve of his jacket from shoulder to elbow, but only went skin deep. The doctor took the rest of what was going. Gavin

82

saw him go down just as he heard the sirens on the cars of the state troopers coming up the hill. Someone at the cemetery office down by the gates must have called for them just about the time the band appeared, Gavin thought woozily as he fainted. He was dimly aware that Lorene, with her hat tilted sideways, was screaming as she stared at him, and he had a fantastic vision of the crowd of mourners and Immortal Maggs' bandsmen sprinting off in all directions among the bright new grave markers and the leggy young palm trees. Even the undertakers' men, infected by the general panic, were running with the crowd. When he came to, feeling deathly sick, the hearse with the coffin in it was standing all alone by itself in front of the chapel. State troopers walked among the abandoned tributes scattered where they had been dropped along the driveway. Lorene and Edwin were denouncing the manager of the cemetery to one group of policemen, and Mr. Grainger was denouncing them to another. Gavin's wounds were being attended to by two interns from the city hospital. They prevented him from rising, and he noticed that he had been put onto a stretcher.

"You'll have to come on down to the hospital to have this gash stitched up," one intern said. "You've had a close call with your jaw muscles."

The doctor, greenish-white, with a dressing on his neck, and his shirt front covered with blood, sat on the back step of the ambulance watching Gavin with interest. They could hear Lorene.

". . . the vilest slander. If he can't be locked up for it, you can tell him he won't get away with it, we'll sue him for defamation and take his every last cent. . . ."

"I have a feeling Marsen would have enjoyed all of this," the doctor said, and Gavin, feeling the full pain of his wound for the first time, fainted again. As things slid upwards and sideways away from him, and one of the interns said, "Oh, oh, there he goes again," Gavin saw something, like a river or a lake seen from a great distance across a thirsty landscape. In what was, so to speak, the foreground, was Lorene's voice running tirelessly and interminably on, and his awareness that her natural talent for grievance would inevitably find its focus on him before too long; but beyond that, at a great distance, was the knowledge that he was going to be in conflict with Marsen, fighting with him for his own soul, for what might be the rest of his life. He could see that the battle was to be fought, and he felt that if he could hold on he would find out where it was to take place and what his weapons would be. But his feet and hands were wet and slippery with his own blood and though he tried he couldn't hold on, the fuller vision eluded him.

His sense that he had been cheated of a mystical experience was strong on him when he recovered his senses, but he immediately recognized that the change in his life of which he had been forewarned as he lost consciousness had taken place. He was already deep in the battle's ebb and flow. State troopers were all around him, and they had Immortal Maggs. Gavin looked into Maggs' face with a certain curiosity, thinking of him as the enemy who had struck him down and hurt him so terribly, with the why of it uppermost in his thoughts. And then he saw Maggs, first the wild, hate-filled, trapped face of the man who had just been violently taken, and beaten by the troopers in the taking, then behind it the puzzled, scared, and exhilarated face of one of the children in the scarlet blazers. His face was discolored by fear, and shiny with sweat, so was his chest. Gavin could see his muscles laboring as he fought for breath. His absurd uniform had been ripped open as he tried to get away, and the cheapness of the pink and blue cloth was glaringly obvious now that the gilt epaulets were askew and some buttonholes torn. Maggs' white underpants showed round his trousers-top. A trooper held him by an arm, his handcuffed wrists were behind his back. A few paces away another trooper held his shako, stroking its feathered plumes with an enormous sun-browned hand. Maggs' pitifulness accentuated an appalling reinforced reality which belonged to the troopers. His pretend uniform was mocked by the superb quality of the cloth in their shirts and their breeches, the overpowering strength of their leather belts and pistol holsters, their thick-soled boots, the hideous weight and solidity of their effective weapons. A Captain Manson who was well known to Gavin knelt by him, his warlike harness creaking a little as he knelt. Manson was a man who had eaten well and followed the regulations all his life. He had never had any doubt of where his duty lay or of how it should be done. His face carried an appropriate expression of solicitude as he looked at Gavin and uttered a few brief phrases of conventional sympathy, but in an instant Gavin saw that he didn't give a damn about him, he just wanted to see if Gavin was in shape to make a statement. It appeared that he was.

"Is this the nigger who cut you, Mr. Hatfield?" The trooper holding Maggs shook him, as if shaking him would somehow bring him into sharper focus and help in his identification. Maggs looked at Gavin without shame, and without fear, but in a remote and exquisite passion of enmity. Gavin heard his unspoken words. Boy, I sure cut you good, you'll remember me every which time you look in a mirror from now on. The lines for their battle were clearly drawn, and Maggs, although temporarily the tactical victor, was already defeated, Gavin's counterattack would send him to the stone piles and the ditches of the work-camp jails for a third or a half of what remained of his natural life. But that is not my battle, and I don't want any part of it, he thought. He saw Marsen's grinning ghost, the real enemy, moving in on his open flank. Well, he would put him to flight. He was suddenly resolute.

"I doubt if he can speak," one of the interns said. "He'll hurt himself if he does."

"Can you speak, Mr. Hatfield?" the Captain said. "If you can't, nod if this is the man."

"No," Gavin said. The intern was right, and speaking hurt him a lot. "No. He was just here to lead the band, I don't think he had anything to do with it."

The Captain stared. Maggs' look of wild fury changed to one of blank incomprehension behind which the enmity remained. What is this damned ofay up to? was his thought.

85

"Are you sure of what you're saying, Mr. Hatfield?" the Captain said. "I think the man did cut you. I'd swear, from the way he acted when we took him that he'd done it."

"Damn it to hell we know he cut you, mister," said the trooper holding Maggs. He sounded disgusted with Gavin.

"No, he had nothing to do with it." Gavin felt blood flowing inside his mouth. He was suddenly afraid that he might choke or drown in his own blood. "I won't charge him," he said faintly. "You can turn him loose for all I care." Behind the troopers he saw the greenish-white face of the manager of the cemetery, frantic with anxiety and with anger. The Vale of Hebron's timetable had been thrown into disorder, three funerals due to follow Marsen's in orderly sequence were piled up outside the cemetery gates already.

"Couldn't you question Mr. Hatfield after he is at the hospital?" the manager said irately washing his hands with invisible soap and water. Gavin recognized the enemy. The whole thing was his fault—Maggs was his victim. "Mr. Hatfield has had a terrible shock, he hardly knows what he's saying." Gavin rolled his head sideways to take a better look at him, and, looking at him, made a vow that he would ruin him if he possibly could. The man met Gavin's eyes for a second and read them correctly, recognizing him at the same instant as the head of the bank to which he was substantially indebted. His face fell and he began to stammer in his misery.

"Oh, Mr. Hatfield, please I—I had no idea—nothing was farther from my thoughts—I merely—" Something like a sob escaped him. "Why does everything seem to happen to me?"

The ginger-haired captain of the state troopers looked at him and looked at Gavin. He understood the manager, who was greedy and cowardly. He did not understand Mr. Hatfield at all. It was odd, a white man getting cut by a nigger in a cemetery. He wondered for a few seconds if Marsen had been one of the white men who ran the numbers racket in Maramee and the northern part of the state behind a screen of colored stooges. But everything he knew of the Bunces made the idea ridiculous. He dismissed it and gave the manager a swift knuckle punch on the upper arm to bring him to his senses. He reeled away, rubbing his arm and looking as if he might burst into tears.

"Thanks," Gavin muttered.

"You want me to turn Maggs loose, Mr. Hatfield?" the Captain asked, probing the situation further. "Is that what you want?"

"Yes, please do that."

The Captain nodded to the trooper holding Maggs, who sulkily unlocked the handcuffs. While he did so the tall Negro looked first at the Captain then at Gavin with baffled amazement. He wondered what Gavin had on the Captain, and more importantly what the wounded man hoped to get from him. The phrase, I got important friends across the river, took shape in his mind. All I got to do when the police make trouble is pass the word over there. Pleasure warmed his face a little. He took a step away from the trooper, swinging his free arms, looking about him. The third trooper silently held out his shako to him and he accepted it with a not undignified gesture. He put it on his head and, now the tallest man in the group, smiled condescendingly about him as, adjusting his jacket as best he could, he set out for the cemetery gates. In his imagination the biggest and best band in the world marched right behind him playing "Here the Conquering Hero Comes." Death couldn't touch him and the law couldn't touch him. He had cut a white man, and he had got clear away with it. The ofay he'd cut was scared of him. I got big men, important men, across the river eating out of my hand. They're afraid of me, and the police are afraid of them. Captain Tiger Manson himself couldn't hold me when they said to turn me free.

The troopers watched him go off at the head of his invisible procession. They would kill him the next time he was fool enough to get into trouble in their jurisdiction. He would resist arrest according to the report, but it would simply be the carrying out of a sentence. Captain Manson gave his proud back a glance and then turned to take a look at Gavin's face.

An expression of deep satisfaction was on what was visible of it. Gavin was thinking that he had found the answer to Marsen. Of course life in itself was meaningless, you gave it meaning by doing what you thought was right, fighting injustice and wrong, and creating order and right out of the chaos of mere happenstance. Maggs, the innocent victim who had been chosen by society, or its representatives, to serve as scapegoat on this occasion had been set free. In the weeks to come Gavin would make it his business to execute natural justice on the son of a bitch who had stirred up the whole mess. It was clear to him, too, what his money was for. It was to give him power to do justice. He pitied poor Marsen who had had so much, and who had never known what he could do with it. Manson looked at him in silence and spat swiftly on the ground. The son of a bitch means to do good, he thought. Well if Maggs got the idea that he could get away with anything, he was likely to start carrying a gun instead of a razor, and if so, somebody on the side of the law might get shot before he was cut down to size.

"I hope you know what you're at, Mr. Hatfield," he said. He took his cap off and put it back on again. "Yes, sir, I hope you know what you just did." He nodded to the interns. "Take him off and patch him up, boys, take very good care of our Mr. Hatfield."

They slid him into the ambulance and rolled him away past the waiting hearses and the groups of curious and irritated mourners outside the police cordon at the gates. Behind him Edwin and Lorene were the sole witnesses as Marsen was put away on the run to clear the way for the next burial. While the service was read at break-neck speed some of the cemetery gardeners collected the trampled and broken floral tributes and hustled them away; others raked the graveled drive until the last blood stains were gone. Within an hour all traces of the incident had vanished and the peaceful routine of the Vale of Hebron had been restored.

But Gavin's life had been scored even more deeply by Maggs' razor than his flesh, which healed swiftly and easily. The inner

88

wound, at first undetected, suppurated and generated powerful poisons. It was amusing, in the beginning, for Gavin to explain the vivid white scar running down the side of his face by saying that he had got mixed up in a razor fight with a gentleman of color, but then he found that the scar and the manner of its acquisition filled Ilona with a profound horror. He discovered that she could not bear to touch it, or to come into contact with it. Her disgust made her a stiff and unwilling bedfellow, always averting her face from his, and holding herself back. They both began to sleep badly, and often one waking would find that the other had slipped quietly away into the bed in the dressing room to read until sleep came. One morning, after a lost night, Gavin spoke up at the breakfast table. They sat on the terrace under a vine, looking down at the dazzle of morning sunlight on the lake. The ripening oranges showed on the dark trees of the grove as if flocks of goldfinches had alighted there.

"What in heaven's name is the matter?"

"Oh, Gavin, it's such a perfect morning—do we have to discuss it?"

"What is it?" He drank his coffee irritably. "I seem to disgust you."

"I had a rough time with Mary," she sighed. "Can't you understand that? I just need a little time to get over it."

He tried to meet her eye, but she was resolute in her evasion.

"It's got something to do with this scar," he persisted. "Hasn't it?"

"It's certainly not very pretty." It had slipped from her. "But it would be ridiculous to say that had anything to do with it."

"I try to tell you everything I think and feel," he said. "Because I love you. But you always hold back . . ."

"That isn't fair. You know it isn't . . . it's blackmail. You want me to be false to my nature and true to yours. I can't discuss things—certain things. If it's a defect it's my defect and I can't help it. What would be the use if I did say yes, your scar disgusts me—it stands for something I can't and won't ever understand. What good would it do if I said sex frightens me and disgusts me with myself because I like it so much? You take it so easily. I can't. Just as I can't deal with vulgar and awful people like your friend Marsen. Can't you see I'm not like you in all sorts of way? Do I have to put it all in words and tell you every time you outrage my feelings? Aren't some things better left unsaid?"

"No." He buried his head in his hands. "No. If they are, I'm all wrong about life, about everything."

"It might occur to you sometimes that you could be."

"All wrong, about everything?" He lifted his head and stared at her. "An awful lot of things, but not everything. I hope not everything."

This conversation, which blighted that day, turned out to be like the catch in a piece of woven material which proves to be the start of its unraveling. A few days later Immortal Maggs, snappily dressed in a white suit, sauntered up to Gavin's car as he was having it filled up with gas at the garage behind the bank building where he usually left the machine during business hours. Gavin noted the sharp hat, the waisted suit and the pointed two-tone shoes, and noticed too, as he was intended to, that when Maggs adjusted the handkerchief in his jacket's breast pocket the handle of a folded razor was briefly visible.

"Hallo there, Mr. Hatfield, I'm glad to see you're quite recovered from your little misadventure."

"Well, I'm glad to see that the police didn't make things too rough for you, Immortal. You could have been in trouble that day."

"That's what I've been meaning to have a little chat with you about, Mr. Hatfield." Maggs' hand strayed lightly to his breast pocket again. "That police fellow Tiger Manson has been pushing me around an awful lot lately. He—"

"You mean Captain Manson, don't you?" said Gavin.

"Some people do call him that," Maggs said. "But I call him Tiger."

"You'd better not, Immortal. I don't think it would do for him to hear you were calling him by his nickname."

"Oh, I ain't afraid of him." Maggs swept the razor from his pocket and lightly trimmed a fingernail. "Ain't many people scares me. I just wants you to tell this Mr. Manson—"

"Captain Manson . . ."

"Like I was saying, Mr. Manson, that he ain't got no call to push me around. People are liable to get hurt if they push Maggs around." The razor blade swung lightly across Immortal's palm as if it were being stropped. "You tell your friend in the police that." Maggs smiled. "We don't want no trouble between us, do we?"

"Are you by any chance threatening me, Immortal?"

"Me? I wouldn't do no such thing." Maggs stepped back from the car grinning. "You draw your own conclusions as to the meaning of my words." The razor had disappeared. He lifted his hand, waved it at Gavin and sauntered away even more jauntily than he had come. Gavin suddenly became aware that all the colored garage men, poker-faced, had been watching the whole incident. Fury possessed him, and on his way home he called in at the barracks to see Captain Manson. He was received without pleasure or displeasure in an office which had nothing personal in it whatever. Manson's hat, hanging on the wall, could have been any policeman's hat, he always wore it and handled it as if he might one day be called to account for any difference in its condition which might have arisen since it was issued to him. He sat behind his desk solidly and impenetrably, just as he thought behind his smile.

"That man Maggs came to me and threatened me today," Gavin said. "He said you were pushing him around."

"You want me to stop?"

"Good God," Gavin stared. "Why do you think I would?"

"I don't think anything. I just wanted to know."

"You sound as if I'd annoyed you."

"You have. You come to me to tell me Maggs threatened you. You asked him to threaten you. You set yourself up for trouble. Man, you must have been looking right into his eyes

91

when he cut you. You said he didn't cut you. What did you expect would happen?"

"I don't know. I thought—hell I don't know."

"Well, I can tell you what he did. He went around saying he'd got such good protection across the river he could cut a white man and get away with it. He said he could do any damn thing he wanted. He moved in on a lot of rackets he'd been trying to get into for years, and ran a few people like himself out of town. I think, I'm not sure of it, that he murdered two of them, or had them murdered. He marked up a couple of whores to impress the others. He's caused me some trouble."

"I'm sorry."

"Well that's nice. Maybe that'll make him melt into the ground like a sugar lump. You know what he means when he says I've been pushing him around?"

"No." Gavin felt sheepish.

"I've told him he's through in Morgantown. I've told him to get out of the state, get over into Alabama or Louisiana, to peddle his papers where he won't have any illusions about being God Almighty's brother Charlie. He won't go. Because he's got this protection across the river. That means you."

"What's the answer?"

"You really want to know? If you want to know I'll tell you —though it's not the kind of thing you solid citizens care to think about when you don't have to." Gavin nodded. "Well, there ain't but one thing to do when a nigger gets to the point of thinking he's God's friend. I'll have to kill him, or one of my men will the first chance we get to do it. Till then he'll be cutting people, and threatening people, and raising Cain all through this part of the state. God knows what he won't do."

"Can't you bring him up on a proper charge and send him to the pen to cool off."

"Mr. Hatfield, that's what we had a chance of doing when he opened you up. We couldn't raise a witness to speak against him in a case involving an assault on a colored person now if we was to offer cash on the line for testimony. Immortal can get away with murder any time he feels like it so far as Morgantown is concerned. All he has to do is keep out of sight of white witnesses and he can run forever. Unless we go beyond what the law says we can do there isn't a thing under God's heaven we can do to stop him. I had a chance when he cut you. But you had something else in mind. So here we are." He drummed on his desk with his fingers. "He bought himself a gun ten days ago. Sooner or later he'll start flourishing it around and firing it. Then we'll go and get him." He got to his feet and went over to stand by a map on the wall. "I can tell you just how it will be—it'll begin in some lousy joint or other like the Club Select. He'll get into a row there and draw that damned gun on somebody—there'll be shots and some poor slob will be killed or wounded. Then Maggs'll try to get away and we'll corner him in a block between here and the river —they all head that way. We'll have a cordon round the block and floodlights. He'll have nothing but that miserable pistol he thinks he can blow the world apart with. He'll wound a couple of troopers—maybe he'll even kill one. And then we'll smother the place he's holed up in with tear gas until he runs out into the open and we cut him down." He tapped the map with his finger tips. "Maggs was born and raised in this block here between Meridian and Old Dock. If I know him the way I think I do he thinks he knows all the alleys, passages, nooks and corners in there so well he can dodge a lot of thick-brained white cops forever once he's inside. We'll kill him within fifty yards of that old livery stable in the center of the block. He thinks it's a kind of castle because it was big and solid and full of mystery to him when he was a kid. When he finds it ain't but a trap, he'll try to run for it. He'll lie in the street where he falls with a bit of cloth over his face until the dead wagon comes to get him, and you know what? From the second he stops twitching, every black son of a bitch in Morgantown will forget he's a bully and a killer and half of them'll stand round in the crowd on the street hating me and my boys for shooting down a poor colored man who couldn't mean no harm. That's the way it's going to be now because

93

there ain't no other way for it to be. And don't think I relish any part of it."

"You should have told me what sort of mistake I was making on the day of the funeral," Gavin said. "I wish you had."

Manson turned his back on the map and sat himself down in his swivel chair. He picked up a pencil and poised it between his two index fingers. His blue eyes strayed over Gavin's face with curiosity and without malice.

"I could have told you," he said. "But you wouldn't have listened. Some things you have to learn, they don't tell. And there's people you don't tell things to, not if you're a captain in the state police. You're one of the big men in Maramee. I've seen you with the Governor, and on platforms with the Senators and the political high muck-a-mucks. I'm a policeman. I don't tell you things. You tell me, and I do 'em. That's my job."

Gavin left the barracks in a chastened mood and spent a night smoking, reading, and occasionally trying to sleep, in the dressing room. When he dozed off after the first light of dawn had begun to break, he slept for three hours until a nightmare brought him back. His father, in the uniform of a state trooper, flagged him down for speeding on the road to the state capital. When Gavin went over to the police car to show his license he found his father lying back in the driver's seat, dying. Captain Manson was leaning over from the back seat sponging his face with a cloth dipped in cologne. "You see what you've done to the poor old man, don't you? He's real worried. He wants you to go home before it's too late."

The dream brought home to Gavin the extent to which he had discovered a new world through Marsen, and how lost in it he was. He had another hammer blow a few days later when Neil Parker, an assistant vice-president in whose hands he had put the matter of the Vale of Hebron, came and put the folder on his desk. He was a year or two out of the business school at Tulane and no fool. He looked at Gavin with admiration.

"I thought you were crazy, forcing that fellow Grainger into liquidation and taking over. But now that all the outstanding

94

claims are settled it looks a pretty good little business. As I see it the only thing wrong with it was Grainger and his lack of capital. Now things are squared away we look like clearing a steady profit of about two hundred percent on our money. The beauty of the operation is that the Vale of Hebron is on almost the only bit of ground within half an hour of Maramee where you can dig a hole six foot deep without hitting water. The Romans have the only other spot, and the old City Cemetery's going to be filled right up two years from now. We're sitting pretty, and all we have to do is keep a watch on maintenance costs and count the cash as it comes to hand."

Gavin took the folder uneasily and checked the figures as Neil explained them, item by item. As the young man's pointing pencil flicked across the columns, Gavin recognized that he had, in breaking Grainger, brought off one of the best deals in real estate in his career. He leaned back in his chair.

"I see the outline of the thing," he said. "You've done a good job—a very good job in fact, from the time you organized that credit squeeze on Grainger right through to the end. I congratulate you." He hesitated for a moment. "You don't happen to know what became of Grainger, do you?"

"I do, as a matter of fact. After we closed him out he went up North into Alabama and took a Ford agency in Mobile, or rather just outside it. His brother-in-law has a laundry there and took out a personal loan to set him up. We can't hit him up there without wiping out the brother-in-law, too. I didn't think you would want to go that far—particularly when you'd seen how well the affair had turned out for us. So I held back. But I can get the bank up there to call in their money any time you say."

"Forget it." Gavin stirred irritably in his chair.

"I'm glad you feel that way about it, sir." Neil smiled. "It gave me an odd feeling marshaling all our forces and resources against that poor little weed. He always seemed on the brink of tears, and I'm told his wife keeps after him with a sort of whining that drives him frantic. He wasn't much of a man, and

95

we gave him a hard time. Still he was in the way, and he had to be forced out I suppose."

"Well, it would take a lot of explaining," Gavin said, "just why I went out of my way to give him a rough passage."

"Getting cut up at that funeral was reason enough to me," Neil said. "I gather that the whole thing was started off by some sort of hysterical outburst on Grainger's part. I'd have gone after him myself if I'd been in your place."

Neil smiled at Gavin, and Gavin smiled back at him. I just took my revenge on the poor slob, he thought, looking at the young man, and hit him because he'd hit me. Can I have done something as mean and ugly as that? And in cold blood, too?

He drove out to the spring before he went home that night, and sat watching it until the light began to go out of the sky. He smoked a pipe and wondered at himself, and at his situation, and enjoyed the cool breath which came across into the shadows under the trees from the basin of lime water. He heard a cough beside him, turned his head and saw Edwin Bunce standing a little way off. Edwin had aged since his brother's death, and had lost weight. Lorene's disappointment with the size of their inheritance weighed heavily upon him. Her action in grubbing up the clump of bamboos had struck him as revengeful and barbarous, and it had come between them.

"Mind if I join you?"

"Not a bit. Want some tobacco for that pipe of yours?"

"I've already filled up. I'll try that sweet-smelling brand of yours some other time." Edwin lit up. "I've been . . . trying . . . to catch you . . . for quite a while." He spoke between draws, and the rising and falling flame lit up his face. Gavin saw more there than he had expected; less simple greed, more character and patience.

"Marsen liked to come out here to be off by himself," he said. "I never liked to intrude upon him when he had one of his solitary moods on him. I was part afraid it might be the same with you."

"Oh, that's all right. What's on your mind, Edwin?"

"I don't know. I just wanted to tell you I didn't hold anything against you, about the way Marsen saw fit to give his money away to all and sundry barring his own kin." He paused. "It's Lorene as minds."

"I'm afraid it must have been a disappointment."

"I won't say it wasn't a shock. And then I thought, that's what you get for wanting a dead man's shoes. If I'd never thought on whether Marsen was rich or poor maybe he would have left me the whole of it. But there. You know what did disappoint me?"

"I don't think I do, Edwin."

"Well Mr. Hatfield, I'll tell you. Right after father died as I remember I said to my brother Marsen, what are we going to do now. And he told me. He kept on telling me. And I kept on asking him. After a while I got to thinking it ain't right, always following his lead and I set out to show him I could think out an idea for making money or whatever just as good as he could. But I never could. Right up to the end I couldn't outsmart him or get the respect from him I hankered after. I had a sort of dream one day I'd say to him, 'Marsen, what are we going to do now,' and he'd come right back and say, 'I ain't sure, Edwin, what do you think we ought to do?' But it never got to be that way."

"I know he was fond of you," Gavin lied with kindly intent.

"That's as may be. Once upon a time, I daresay it was true. But he never forgave me for marrying up with Lorene, and for having affairs with women before that. Something in Marsen always revolted at the touch of a woman. He never could bring himself to get further than shaking hands with one of them. He died a virgin if the truth be told. I cain't prove it of course, but I'd swear my Bible oath on it. That's what made him take against me in the end. I couldn't say if he despised me, or if he was sort of mad at himself. Lorene says he was just mean, but I tell her there ain't nothing so simple as that."

Edwin sat on the sand and drew thoughtfully on his pipe for a minute.

97

"I'd like to have died when I saw all them coons and jigaboos shewing up for his burial. I didn't know then they was beholden to him for all the money he'd given them. I thought they was springing up out of the ground. I just couldn't make a thing of it. I could of cried. I expect I would have if Lorene hadn't been there. I was feeling pretty badly about Marsen being gone just then, and then by God he was getting a burial that was laughable, the sort people would break up talking about for years afterward. And I knew Marsen wasn't a man to laugh at, virgin or no." Edwin broke off to give his pipe his attention before he went on. "Whatever Marsen may of thought of me, he was my whole world, even taking Lorene into account. Many's the time I thought of clearing out and leaving him. But I couldn't do it. It didn't seem right to leave him alone, no matter how cranky and peculiar he got. To my way of thinking it was seeing father cut in half, or near enough cut in half, right in front of him that did it. 'Look out there, Marsen,' father yelled, and he leapt across and knocked Marsen over just as the cable gave way. The frayed end of it just about cleaned father's guts right out. He gave a scritch like nothing I ever want to hear again and then he never let out another sound till he was gone. We was kneeling each side of him holding his hands and he'd roll his eyes over to me for a minute and then at Marsen, then he give a sort of shudder, and that was the end of him. When he was gone Marsen knelt there just like he wasn't gone, holding his hand. He was stunned by it happening so quick, I suppose. Anyway he didn't move till I said 'Marsen, you got to get washed up, you're all covered with blood.' That brought him to and he went off and got out of his clothes and took a shower under an oil-drum affair I'd rigged up. While he was going over there all the niggers we had working for us who'd been clustering round sort of shrank back from him looking scared. I can see their way of looking at it, it ain't every day you see a kid spattered from head to toe with his father's own blood and entrails, but all the same it had a powerful effect on Marsen, as if they thought he was accursed or unclean, like it says in the book. He was never easy

98

with niggers after that, and never easy with himself. Though I didn't see it at the time, father's death altered things, up till then I'd been the hex in the family. Our mother died whilst I was being born, and I carried the burden of having taken father's wife and made Marsen motherless. Father giving his life for Marsen that way evened things up in a terrible sort of fashion. Anyway, after that he had to stay out in front of me and be the big I am, and I had to be the stupid, helpless, brother. It was all I could do to stand it at times, but then, there it was. I couldn't outsmart him, and now I look back on it I have the feeling his world would have fallen apart if I had ever succeeded in getting out from under. He needed me the way I was to make him feel all right with himself." He paused again. "Lorene can't see it. I've tried to tell her, but she don't seem able to understand. And another thing she don't understand. I loved Marsen, and I think I still do. She says how can you say you love him and cherish his memory when he despised you and let you know you disgusted him, and I tell her that don't matter a bit. There was some part of Marsen I knew about that Marsen never let show to me, and so far as I know never let on about to anyone else, and that was what I loved. He was a real good feller in back of it all, no matter what he did and said."

Gavin was silent. The sky was a clear green in which a few stars showed themselves. The pool was darkness itself in its circle of white sand. Edwin got to his feet, dusting sand from the seat of his pants.

"It's getting to be my supper time," he said. "Lorene don't like to be kept waiting when she's got a meal prepared." He sighed gently. "I miss Marsen all the time. I don't feel but half-alive now he's gone. His being underground makes me see how much of the last years I had with him I wasted thinking about his money and how he didn't treat me right. I should of just taken ol' Marsen as he was without worrying about his not being some other way. But there it is, we live and learn, and we mostly learn too late."

You damned corn-ball cracker-barrel philosopher, Gavin

99

thought with a quick flush of resentment, you dare to talk to me like that, "we live and learn, and we mostly learn too late." He tried to think of some of the specialists in rhymed home-spun philosophy who had graced the newspapers with their work when he was young. Edwin must have been one of their readers. When Marsen's brother had left him and he was alone again, facing the black water of the pool, the bleak realization that the remark he had found so objectionable was nothing more or less than the plain truth about human experience, overwhelmed him. He had patronized Marsen and Edwin. He had made a complete mess of things since the day he had taken over Marsen's affairs. He understood very little about life, and practically nothing about people. He had lived the first third of his allotted span like a blind man or a fool.

Gavin felt that he had touched bottom at the pool, and that having felt it under his feet he would be able to thrust against it to start himself on his way back up towards the light. But there was still a depth beneath for him to plumb. When he got home he ate with Ilona outdoors in the softly scented night air. A moon a little beyond the full hung in the sky beyond the lake, silvering the surface, and lighting the sky so that all the trees and vines around them were velvety with deep shadows. Ilona's face was shadowed too. He kept looking at her as he talked but saw only darkness where her eyes were. He tried to tell her of the whole landslide of events which had threatened all his beliefs and drew nothing from her but a motionless tension. He knew she was following his every word, but her expression was as well concealed by the shadow as if she had been masked.

"The only thing I have left now is my love for you," he said.

"No!" It escaped her like a cry. "I can't bear it, Gavin. All this—it's just to get me to sleep with you again isn't it? Be honest."

He got to his feet, thunderstruck, and his chair clattered as it fell backwards. Ilona got to her feet too, with the thought in her mind that he might take out his anger at having his real intentions unmasked by beating her. She steeled herself for the first blow, and as she did so discovered something new, and frightening, about herself. She wanted the blow to fall. But there was a stillness in which she listened to his strained breathing, and which ended at last when he spoke.

"I've been telling you that I love you, Ilona," he said.

"Thank you. I think, by now, that I know what that means, or what saying it is the prelude to . . ."

"I wish you did know what it means." Gavin's voice was level. "I don't think you do." He hesitated a moment, appealing to her silently with his whole concentrated being, then turned on his heel and went indoors. Her body, all her instincts, clamored for her to go after him, to fling her arms round him, and to make the reconciliation that would lead to a night of lovemaking. Every part of her body was ready for the act. But her mind was cold and in command. She would not let that disgusting side of herself take charge, and humiliate her. Gavin disappeared into the house and she buried her face in her hands. "God give me strength not to go crawling to his room tonight," she said. "Give me back my self-respect."

Gavin picked up the Maramee evening paper from the table in the hall as he made his way up to bed. He unfolded it and read the lead story. "War threat looms in East and West, says President. Calls on U.S. to prepare." Idly Gavin took in the details of the program for the expansion of the armed forces which Roosevelt had proposed. It struck him that they were going to need an awful lot of men to come anywhere near the goals which had been set, and as soon as he saw it he knew what he was going to do. My life is impossible, he thought, perhaps the answer to it all is to try to live another one for a while. I'll do that, if there is a war I'll be doing what I'll have to do anyway—if it blows over I'll have had a couple of years to think things out—and then we'll see. He felt solid ground under his feet. The Nazis were a rotten crowd by all accounts and they had to be stopped sooner or later. Stopping them was a man's job which involved no tricky questions: it was the right thing to do, and no doubt about it.

Chapter Three

WHEN Gavin met Helen Brassey in London, he had flown eighteen missions and he was introduced to her as a Major. The introduction was informal. "Helen darling, this is Jack's Major Thing, do give him a drink or something." Pretty bouncy little Mrs. Cranshaw had then gone off to the kitchen of her mews flat with Colonel Jack Littlefield to unpack the parcel of what she called "goodies" he had brought her from the PX, with a bottle of whiskey from his liquor allowance and a bottle of black-market gin. Littlefield's invitation had been informal, too. As Gavin's commanding officer, he had thought that Gavin was showing signs of strain which an affable woman could easily remove. "Come along and meet Betty Cranshaw," he had said. "Her flat's always full of randy little women looking for great big healthy American boys; and even though you are a beat-out old man, you'll have as good a chance as anyone."

"I'm Helen Brassey," Helen said, smiling, giving him her hand.

"I'm Gavin Hatfield."

"I'm sorry?"

"Hatfield—you know—like that Elizabethan house—north of London."

"Oh, where the Sissles live."

"Sissles?"

"Oh dear! C-e-c-i-l-s—Lord Salisbury and all those people."

"Oh Sessels—I remember now." He looked at her, liking the way she carried herself and hoping that she was going to turn out to be one of the randy little women. "I'll promise to be good and say Sissle for Cecil from now on if you promise to go and get me that drink right away."

"It'll have to be whiskey or gin and lime, I don't think Betty's supplies will run to anything else." While she spoke she thought she detected something in his face which disturbed her. And when she brought him the good stiff Scotch he had asked for, she wasn't especially surprised to see him spill it almost immediately on his trousers. He mopped it up with his handkerchief, and as he did so she could see that he was frightened by his clumsiness, and scared that anyone else should have noticed it. The room began to fill with Littlefield's noisy cronies and their pretty British girl friends, some in A.T.S. and WRAF uniforms. The flyers gave Gavin friendly greetings as they came in, calling across the room, "Hi, Pop," "Hullo, there, Pop," and "Good evening, Paw," and the room began to fill with chatter, party noise, and cigarette smoke. Helen stayed with Gavin watching him, and listening to his loud, cheery talk with Littlefield and the boys, full of almost meaningless running jokes which were fired off to produce easy automatic laughter. She suddenly pulled his sleeve and beckoned to him to put his head down near hers.

"I've got a splitting headache, Major Hatfield, would you terribly much mind seeing me home?"

"Oh, no." Gavin took a quick look at his watch: eight ten. The plan had been to meet at Betty's and then to go on somewhere to eat and dance. This would separate him from the group and bitch up the evening nicely. "Not at all," he said. "I'll see you home with pleasure. Let me help you up." He gave her a hand and hoisted her up off the cushion where she had been sitting at his feet. As she rose up towards him he was surprised at the ease with which she moved, and at the pleasant expression behind which she concealed her migraine. He wanted to ask her if she was sure she really had a headache, and he rather sulkily followed her out into the street. It was late twilight and darkness was beginning to settle down onto the blacked-out city. Gavin looked across the way at a gap knocked in a row of houses by a German bomb. He was always

103

disturbed at this hour in London by the silence of the streets after the rush-hour traffic had taken the office workers and the people from the ministries away. An occasional cab passed them, and an infrequent bus rumbled down a nearby main street. Otherwise the only noises were those of hushed conversations, and of footsteps, strange sounds to be dominant in a great city.

"I have a jeep parked in the square over there, if we've far to go," Gavin said.

"Thanks. I'd rather walk, if you don't mind."

Well, there goes my last chance of dumping her off inside of a quarter of an hour and joining up with the crowd, Gavin thought, I might as well face it, the evening's a washout. The one consolation was that the crowd would assume that he had taken the bloody woman off to lay her, an illusion which he would do all he could to foster.

"A nice walk would be just swell," he said.

"Wow," she said.

"Eh?" he was startled.

"I was just admiring your subtle use of irony. We—English people, I mean—are always supposed to be too dumb to detect it when Americans use it, aren't we?"

"I'm sorry," he said. He decided on honesty. "I didn't mean to be rude. It's just that I was looking forward to a night on the town to raise a little hell with the boys and, well, when I've seen you back to your place it's going to be pretty difficult to find where in hell they'll have gone to. I'll have a damned dull half an hour or so on the phone calling a lot of clubs and bars to find out where they are. And to be frank, I don't like your phone boxes. I don't know if the British have always used them to pee in, or if that's something they've just been doing since the blackout came in, but they sure as hell seem to like the idea for some reason. And frankly, Helen (you don't mind my calling you Helen, do you?), I wouldn't plan an evening round a phone booth if I was meaning it to be a pleasant evening— Watch it, soldier!"

A fully equipped British infantryman bumped into them.

"Sorry, mate. Am I heading right for Waterloo Station?"

"I'm afraid I can't help you on that."

"Ow, not another bloody Yank! Ain't there any of the aboriginals left to tell me the way out of their bloody town?"

"I can help you." Helen Brassey gave him crisp and easy directions.

"Thanks, miss," said the soldier coldly, and vanished, his steel-capped army boots clicking on the pavement as he went off.

"They pee in phone boxes, and they all hate us deep down," Gavin said.

"Oh, dear, Major Hatfield. Won't you come out of your sulk, please? It's a lovely fresh June evening and you're walking with me. Couldn't you find some tiny crumb of comfort in it somehow, if you were to try very hard?"

"Comfort? I don't think so, a night like this smells of fear to me. All these damned people tiptoeing about in the darkness waiting for the early warning, and when the warning comes they'll be even quieter passively waiting for the bombers and the bloody racket the barrage makes, and then, when all the shit has fallen out of the sky and the streets are full of rubble and broken glass, they'll come quietly out of their holes to carry on and wait for the next packet. You know, unless I've had quite a bit to drink I can't stand to be in London at night. I like it, or I like a lot of things about it, but I can't stand it." His voice died away. "Do you know what I mean?"

"Poor Major Hatfield," she said. She slipped her hand under his arm. "It is horrid being afraid, isn't it?" She said it softly, and he wasn't sure that he'd heard her correctly. A cool wind played gently on his face, and reminded him of her excuse for leaving the party.

"How's the headache, now we're out in the fresh air?"

"What's your name? I can't go on calling you Major Hatfield."

"Gavin."

"Gavin? Well, Gavin, if you must know, I never had a headache."

They walked along in silence for several paces.

"You must think me an awful clod, Helen."

"Let's not talk about that, just now." She put a little pressure on his arm. "We go right here, and cross the street. We're almost there."

They walked under the imposing stuccoed arch which formed the entrance to Curraghan Mews. It towered over them, magnified by the darkness. They walked down a slope of smooth cobblestones, and along past a row of old coach houses and stables once converted into garages, and since then converted again into small cottage-like houses. Helen Brassey's front door was a small green one with a brass knocker. It had a tub of hydrangeas placed on each side of it. A steep and narrow stair led directly up from the front doorstep to a low-roofed apartment with a bedroom, a sitting room, a tiny bathroom and an even smaller kitchen. Gavin felt too large for all of it. He caught sight of himself in the bedroom mirror through the living-room door, and thought how strangely his uniform at once enlarged him, made him seem more massive, and dehumanized him. He took off his cap and folded his raincoat into the smallest possible bundle, looking about him for somewhere to put it. As he did so he encountered the pleasant smile of a British officer looking out of a photograph frame on the far side of the room. He recalled, unhappily, Jack Littlefield's phrase about randy little women, and a spasm of distaste made him shiver. He wondered where Colonel or Major Brassey was. He particularly didn't want him to be a prisoner of war, or overseas. Still nooky was nooky, he told himself, and who cared what the woman was like if the lay was good. Helen Brassey was beside him. She had taken off her coat and was now offering to take his things. She sensed the change in his manner, and looking about for something to account for it she saw the photograph.

"My husband's dead," she said. "He was a Lancer. He was killed in Libya, in the first fighting there. I ought to put that photograph away, it's so long ago, and he looks so alive in the picture." She smiled. "His sister sent us the salmon we're going to eat, as a matter of fact. She's a nice woman. I ought to get dinner. There's a little whiskey in that cupboard over there if you want it, and I can even give you some ice."

She went out and left Gavin standing in the little countrified room. Everything in it was so small. He lowered himself into an armchair, which took him even though it looked hardly big enough to do so. He stretched out his legs and put his head back on the cushion. The Lancer smiled at him—a friendly, decent chap.

"How was it, you poor bugger?" Gavin muttered. "How did you get it?"

Helen rattled briskly in the kitchen, and outside there came the agonized wail of the sirens sounding the first warning of the evening. Gavin's flesh crawled. The flat seemed to grow a great deal smaller. He noticed that there was a beam running across the roof which would fall across his legs if the roof fell in. He drew up his knees. He put his hand to his forehead and covered his eyes. A few minutes later the barrage began and a minute after that the first German plane droned into earshot. Mrs. Brassey carried the cold boiled salmon and a salad of thinly sliced cucumber into the room and put them down on the table. She went out and came back with a sauceboat full of mayonnaise.

"It isn't often I have an egg and olive oil these days," she said, "but as I happen to have them I thought we'd have the real right thing that salmon deserves." She saw that Gavin was fast asleep, lying with his head thrown back and his mouth wide open. She took in the expression of pain and grief on his face and almost cried out. "Oh," she said faintly. "Oh, you poor beast." There was the sound of a bomb explosion a long way off, then another and another as the rest of the stick came down, falling through the darkness into the naked black mass of the town. Gavin stirred in his sleep. More bombs fell closer and shook the building on its foundations. The photograph of Captain Brassey fell on its face with a small flat sound which came with a strange clarity through the hubbub and the noise. Helen crossed the room and sat herself on the arm of Gavin's

107

chair. She took his hand and held it. A faint whistle, like a hole in the other noises, began to drown out all the rest of the world as it rose in pitch. Her body stiffened and Gavin woke. They looked at each other across an immense desolate plain of terror. The noise ceased to have the quality of audibility, although it shut out all other sounds. The immense roar of the explosion came as a relief. Everything shook, some soot fell from the chimney. A few flakes of plaster fell from the ceiling. The lights went dim and then recovered. From close at hand there was a noise of glass falling like a cascade from dozens of windows as the backwash from the shock wave sucked their panes out into the street. What seemed to be silence followed and lasted for several seconds until the sound of the guns, the drone of enemy planes, and the thumping of bursting bombs seemed to come back as if some sound engineer were turning up their volume. Gavin opened and shut his mouth several times. But the brave remark he wished to make was not to be found, or rather something in Mrs. Brassey's face made it impossible for him to use any of the stock sayings that had in the past served to destroy the tension bred by such incidents.

"It's horrid being afraid, isn't it," she said. "Poor Gavin, are you afraid all the time now?"

"Jesus Christ!" He threw her hand away. "Jesus Christ, Helen, how can you ask me that? You don't seem to know what you're saying!"

"Oh, yes I do," she said. "Don't you come heroic over me. I know a whole lot about you. You're seven or eight years too old for the job you're doing—much older than all those boys you fly with. You're beginning not to believe in yourself any more. You're afraid you're going to crack up. And you don't believe in the bomber you have to fly, or in the way it's being used. You're afraid it's only a matter of time before you get killed, even if you don't break down. And you daren't say a word to anyone about any of it, you poor lamb, and that's doing you in faster than anything else."

"Jesus," muttered Gavin, climbing out of his chair. "Jesus. You've got some nerve. I don't know what you think you're doing to me, but I want no part of it!" He tried to pass her but she blocked him and grabbed his arms. He tried to shake her off. "Now that will be all of that."

"Admit!" she cried. "Admit! You bloody fool! Say it before it poisons you. Say it before you go rotten inside." She let go of his arm and began to beat on his chest with her clenched fists. "Admit! Say it after me. Get it out in words, for the love of God. Say 'Helen, Helen, I'm afraid, afraid all the time.'"

He took her by the shoulders to shake her into silence, and once more heard the rising pitch of a bomb whistling down not too far away. He found that he was holding her tightly to him, and that her pleasant smelling hair was against his cheek. He bent his face into her protecting shoulder and held on while the room shuddered again.

"You know," he said, "you know, all right. It's been since—oh—it was my tenth mission or the eleventh. I didn't think I would ever forget which. We went into St. Nazaire at the wrong height. Everything went wrong. And nothing's gone right for me since. I have nightmares, just the way I did when I first started flying, about landings and take-offs. I didn't think they'd ever come back. At one stage I thought I couldn't go wrong with routines like that. Now I know better. There's one dream about an intruder—an enemy fighter who picks you up and follows you until you're coming into land at base. Then he lets you have it just as you drop in over the end of the runway. I'm drifting in with the flaps down and the wheels down, slow and easy, and suddenly we're shot all to hell by this stream of cannon shell from in back of us. The plane starts to come apart and the controls go soft. We hit the runway and burst into flames as we hit. That's one dream. I don't know for sure how it ends, I always wake up when I see the flames breaking out round the engine nacelles. When I'm awake I'm in a cold sweat because I screamed in my dream and I don't know if anyone heard me in the barracks—and I can't go around asking. The other thing—another thing—is taking off for a deep-penetration raid with a huge load of gas and all the bombs we can carry. We get along the runway and she won't come unstuck. The runway goes on for miles, it seems like forever. We've got flying speed but she's glued on. I've done something wrong. There's something I could do. But I can't think what it is. I try everything I know but I haven't a clue to this one thing. I begin to sweat and my hands start slipping on the comtrols. Now I'm trying to throttle back, but I can't remember how to do that either. She keeps slamming on down that everlasting runway. And about now I recognize the field. It's some damned place in Gloucester where we were for a month, and just beyond the end of the runway I'm on there's a group of stone farm buildings with a barn like a bloody church. Now I've got her six inches or a foot off the ground but that's all I can get her up. And now the runway's gone and we're skimming over the tops of the markers and there's the gable of that bloody barn filling up the whole sky in front of us." He broke off, stroking her hair. "The next one's silly, but Christ, knowing it's silly doesn't make any difference. I'm over Germany in this one. We're in formation. The air's full of planes stacked up around my flight. There's a little cloud, but not much. During the briefing for some special reason we've been given a warning. When we're over Germany we're not to look down towards the ground on any account. There's no flak and there aren't any German fighters anywhere in the sky. I look over to Jack Littlefield in his plane and he gives me a thumbs-up sign. I'm damned if I see what harm just taking a peek down at the ground will do, so I risk it. I can see a big river coming round under a dark forest, and a town on the far side of the river. It's about twenty thousand feet down, but all the same I can see a gun emplacement on the edge of the town and I can even see a particular gun. The men round it are all looking right at me and grinning in a nasty kind of way and, as I notice that, the gun fires. I see the muzzle flash and then the shell starts up, straight up towards me. It floats, but floats fast, I can't describe it exactly. And when I've looked at it for a second I know it's going to hit my ship. I do every damned thing I can think of, jinking, twisting, turning, every damned thing. But that shell keeps sliding up at me." He stroked the back of her head again.

"It's hard to explain to anyone because flying's supposed to be romantic and dashing. It's hard to explain—but we go into action sitting down. Up above the enemy. Well, hell, we're sitting over them—on top of them. If they looked up—if they could see through the bottom of the ship that is—well, we'd be there with our feet towards them. Oh, Christ, don't you see, we go into action arse first, that shell's going to hit me in the arse or in the balls, that's what I know all the time the bloody thing is coming up to me, that's what I know all the time I'm over enemy country, and that's what the Huns are grinning at when they fire their bloody piece."

He let Helen go and turned his back on her. He felt through his pockets until he found a packet of cigarettes. Then he faced her again and offered her one. She shook her head.

"I suppose you don't think much of me after this."

"I'd think more of you if you weren't holding something back." She listened to the silence outside. "I think they've gone for tonight. You don't have to tell me. But it would be much better if you did."

"Tell you?"

"The thing which really does scare you—which isn't a thing you dream about. I mean the real thing, the worst thing of all. It's still there behind your eyes. I can see it."

He fiddled with his cigarette and with the matches. He leaned back against the mantelpiece, supporting himself on his elbows. They heard the eerie moaning of the all clear. The raid was over.

"You want an awful lot," he grumbled. "Don't you?"

"Oh yes. I hate secrets—and bottled up things which turn nice people nasty. You're turning nasty."

"Am I?" He started to light the cigarette, looking at her over the flame.

"Yes. Talking tough, being one of the boys, putting back drinks you don't want—all that phoney stuff." She saw that his hands were shaking so badly that he couldn't bring the lighted match to the tip of his cigarette. The match went out and he flung it into the fireplace. The cigarette was scorched underneath. He looked at it and scrabbled it into a little ball before throwing it after the match. They heard fire engines going to a nearby fire.

"You press me pretty hard—too hard."

"Perhaps I was wrong about you at the party, perhaps you aren't worth it after all. I don't know. I fancied you at Betty's —you seemed so out of place among all those young toughs. You seemed nice—and I thought I could help."

"You meant to do good," Gavin said sourly.

"No, you silly ass. I just wanted to get that sick look out of your eyes and the blur that's between us out of the way." She stroked her thigh with the flat of her hand, and bit her lip. "Oh, you're hopeless. What's the use of my going to bed with you when you're so stiff with misery you can't tell what's going on?" She yawned, overtaken by weariness. "Oh Lord, I've got to get some sleep. I'm off to bed. You can sleep on the sofa if you want—or if you want to get back to the officers' club you can let yourself out. Give the door a bang or the lock won't work. You'll find pillows and blankets in the cupboard over there."

"Thanks." He felt that his position, leaning against the fireplace, was an oafish one and straightened. She put the uneaten dinner away, and was busy between her bedroom and the bathroom for a few minutes. He stood woodenly, watching her comings and goings. She didn't say good night to him; she simply made a last disappearance through the door, and a minute or two later her light went out. Gavin felt miserably that he had failed himself and had failed her too. He turned off all the lights but a small reading lamp and settled himself into the easy chair beside it. His hands had stopped shaking and he could light a cigarette easily. The smoke streamed up from it in a long straight line of brilliant blue. The clock ticked on top of the bookshelf near him. Twelve ten. He would take it easy for ten minutes and then he would walk back to the club. The jeep would be all right parked in the square till morning. He closed his eyes for a second and—he looked at the clock again. Two thirty-two. For a moment he thought he was misreading the dial, and then he realized that he had been asleep. The cigarette was gone, and there was no trace of it anywhere. There was a light blanket over his knees. He thought he would go in and thank Helen for looking after him, and for the evening, although it had turned out so strangely. He switched off the light and went to her door. He opened it quietly and saw that she had parted the blackout curtains to let in some air. A faint light from the stars and the last of a waning moon showed him where the furniture was. He could barely distinguish the woman on the bed.

"Are you awake, Helen?" he whispered, and got no answer. He took a step forward to the foot of the bed. "Helen?" he said. He heard her breathing change, and knew that she had been lying awake waiting for him. "Helen," he whispered again. "I'm sorry I didn't trust you. You see, I went to Betty's place to find what Jack promised me I'd find there, an easy lay. And it's sort of upsetting when an easy lay starts turning your insides out. I wish I'd had the courage to tell you what I'm afraid of, but I wasn't ready to do that. If you could see my face I don't believe I could tell you now. The thing is that when the chips are down I'm a coward and I don't want anyone to know it. I found out the second time we went to Hamburg." He licked his lips. "We were crossing the North Sea, going out. It was six in the morning and the most beautiful morning you've ever seen. We were in a big formation, more than a hundred and fifty of us, just sailing along in one big thumping mass to knock hell out of the navy yards there. And I knew I didn't want to go. What I wanted to do was to give number three engine a rich mixture. That would make it throw a lot of smoke out of the exhaust and cough a bit. The crew would see it and feel it. And pretty soon someone would speak about it to me over the intercom. They'd say, Gavin, take a look at that inboard engine on the portside. I don't like the way it's acting up. And I'd fiddle around for a bit and then I'd say too bad, men—that engine ain't right, we'll have to turn back. Just about then I'd fix it so that the engine let out more smoke than ever. I'd feather the prop and break formation. We'd swing round in a big arc and go home. I wouldn't get away with it. They'd know just as soon as they looked the ship over at base. But it wouldn't matter. I'd never have to go again, Helen, they'd treat me as if I was sick. I'd be poor old Pop who couldn't take it, and I'd be sent off to liaison or intelligence with all the rhubarb on my chest. But I'd know and everybody would know and God knows how it would work out. That's what I'm afraid of, Helen, because I've figured it all out, and I can do it any time, and I wouldn't have figured it out if I wasn't going to do it. I've seen planes leave formation like that, and the guys have disappeared by the time we get back to base. It makes my stomach knot up when I see them go, it's like the feeling I had about sex talk when I was thirteen or fourteen, and the feeling I had before I was going to masturbate. I didn't want to dirty myself by talking that way or doing that thing, but I knew that I couldn't stop myself. So there you are, Helen, that's what I couldn't tell you. I'm a pretty rotten sort of man when you get down to it, and there's nothing you can do about it."

"Gavin, you poor love," she whispered. "You aren't different from anyone else. It's just not wanting to die. Nobody wants to die. We'd all get out of it if we could."

He went round and knelt by the bed, taking her hand.

"And what then?" he said, "Helen, what's going to stop me doing that God-awful thing?"

"Nothing. Just you. And having me. You'll be wanting to get back to me to show me you didn't do it." She ruffed his hair with her free hand. "Now come to bed like a dear man and we'll forget the beastly war and everything to do with it. Oh, Gavin, you slept for so long. And I was scared to death you were going to go. I thought I'd gone too far with tormenting you. I'd have cried and cried if I'd heard that wretched door bang. Gavin, you can stop pretending to be brave, and soldierly and all that, and start thinking of your beastly operations as horrid things that take you away from me."

Later, when Gavin had come to be known at the newspaper shop on the corner, and at the dairy next door to it, as the

114

Yank from Number 10 or Mrs. Brassey's Yank, he wondered if it could really have been as easy as that. And strangely enough it had been. She had changed his life by presenting him with an immediate future. He no longer thought of the real demand that was being made upon him—to complete his tour of thirty missions and then to volunteer for another—nor did he think of himself as being engaged in a one-sided conflict with the law of averages. Before he knew it his next mission had ceased to be death itself bearing down on him; it had become an obstacle to be cleared before he could return to the little house with the green door in the mews. All he had to do was to survive being burned alive, maimed, or taken prisoner, just once and then he could be back with her at Number 10, for a few hours, or a whole night, or even for a couple of days. After a honeymoon of intense sexual activity, they settled down into an easy routine of intimacy in which he discovered her life and became a contributor to it. He began to do chores as well as to have things done for him, and would sometimes try to get into the city early so that he could have the place warmed and ready for her when she got back from her job with the censorship. Walking across the flat desolation of the base, with its vast lunar perspectives along the tarmac runways, crossing from the ugly Nissen huts where they had eaten breakfast to the even uglier huts where the briefings were held, with a chill dawn's east wind coming in across the North Sea, Gavin could think of Helen sleeping like a child in her wide bed under the patchwork cover in her cottage-like place and believe that life was possible and pleasant. Across the mews, facing Number 10, there was the gaunt array of the burned-out shells of the houses in Carraghan Terrace, hit by incendiaries two years before. Their neglected gardens were filled with a wild profusion of self-sown sycamores, unpruned shrubs, sprawling fig trees, willow herb and hollyhocks. Gavin, waking, even with Helen beside him, at the routine hour for the beginning of an operational day, found that these overgrown gardens were haunted by hundreds of small birds who filled the air each morning at first light, no matter how bad the night had been, with a chorus of breath-taking purity and innocence.

The birds singing among the grasses as Gavin and his crew climbed out of the jeeps which had taken them out to the dispersal point where the B-17, called *Plain Jane*, had been armed and fueled, seemed to sing the same songs, and to tell him that life was to be lived in one piece, and that there was no taking one part of it and rejecting another. Gavin found that he had a new grip on himself, perhaps better than he had ever had before. His flying hands came back, and Littlefield stopped sweating every time *Plain Jane* started down the airfield to take off or came in across the elm-tufted landscape to land after an exercise or an operation. For him it was quite simple—Gavin had found a nice piece of tail, not a piece he, personally, would have chosen for himself, and he was over the hump. He would not go bad for a long time, perhaps not ever. Before Gavin knew it he had finished one tour and was halfway through another. It was almost complete when he ran into trouble.

On the way to Jena, plane after plane had been knocked out of the huge formation of over three hundred machines. Some burst into huge smears of oily black smoke, others, torn and damaged, suddenly seemed to become heavy and sank down through the formation to shed a little swarm of parachutes, as, with a wing crumpling or part of the tail gone, the wounded ship stopped flying and began to fall. Two or three times Gavin had to move in on the leaders to fill up holes which had been knocked in the formation, and several times he felt *Plain Jane* shuddering as her waist and tail guns fired at enemy fighters. Once he saw a Messerschmitt, pock-marked with bullet holes, gliding a hundred feet below him on a parallel course. Looking into the cockpit Gavin saw the dead pilot lolling back green-faced with his hands off the controls, frozen in the act of trying to fling off the Plexiglass canopy. At the moment in which Gavin realized that the man was dead, every gunner in the flight woke from a momentary paralysis and opened fire. The fighter came apart in the storm of heavy machine-gun bullets and exploded in a vast flower of orange flame which flung *Plain Jane* upwards and out of her place in the defensive box for half a minute. When she was settled back into her slot Gavin looked across at Littlefield guiltily. Jinking away from close bursts was not allowed and Gavin hoped that he was not going to be accused of having done so at the interrogation. Littlefield read his mind and grinned at him across the intervening street of their German upper air, wagging his finger at him inside his Plexiglass carapace in mock reproof. There were forty minutes to go to Jena. Out in front of them an enemy plane, pressing a frontal attack too hard, struck an American bomber head on between the outboard and the inboard engines. They spun with a waltzing motion for a few seconds, apparently welded together, and then broke apart, tumbling downwards, dissolving into hundreds of large and small fragments of metal. Five of the bomber's crew bailed out and floated off into the vast hostile landscape below, swinging under their gleaming white parachutes as if they were holiday-makers playing some amusing game. Gavin looked at the hands of his watch and found that they seemed to have been glued to the dial. "Oh boy," said a voice on the intercom, "are we taking a beating today. That makes seventeen." The formation tightened and began to lose height as it went in for the bombing run. Bursting anti-aircraft shells filled the air below them, and then all around them. Three more planes went down; two went in flames, leaving long streaks of dirty black smoke behind them, the other folded its wings at the roots, like a bird, and plummeted eastwards so fast that Gavin lost sight of it almost at once. Sixteen parachutes drifted towards the ground. Gavin wiped his face. Someone seemed to try to pull *Plain Jane* off course by grabbing the right wing. Gavin looked across and saw through the thinning smoke of shell burst that part of the engine cowling and some of the skin of the wing were gone. There was no sign of fire for the moment but a mixture of oil and cooling fluid was being blown off the trailing edge of the wing. They were hit once again just before they got their bombs away, and came out of the bombing run with two propellers feathered. Gavin's mouth was dry. The formation was inexorably leaving them behind and the two dead propellers were a sign saying Come and get me to any German fighters they might run into. Gavin looked southwards towards Switzerland and saw a vast expanse of empty sky between him and safety in that direction. Some instinct told him that the air in that direction was full of hostile fighters. "And besides," he said to himself, "I don't know anybody down there." On the route back to base he could see thickening masses of cloud building up in the direction of the Atlantic and the southwest. There was a chance, even though the ship would be bucking a headwind, of dodging from cloud mass to cloud mass, and making it. Gavin had had luck with the fighters, but *Plain Jane* was more badly damaged than he had at first supposed, and their luck had its price.

All the way across Germany they lost altitude steadily and sickeningly, and when they passed through the flak belt on the Dutch coast it was at an agonizingly slow speed and at moderate height. The bomber was jarred as it was hit again and again, and by the time they slid out past the dunes and the line of surf at the edge of the gray cold sea, Gavin knew that the ship was a wreck and that every man on board was wounded. Gavin did not at first know that he himself was wounded. At one point he had felt a sharp blow on his seat, and imagined that a loose strap had slapped his thigh. Then, a minute or two later, when something solid hit the plane aft near the rear gunner's position, he had suddenly realized that he was sitting in a pool of warm stickiness. He thought with a pang of shame that he had betrayed himself with the classic manifestation of extreme fear, but he soon found that he was sitting in his own blood. He had a moment of panic in which he became terribly afraid that he would lose consciousness before he could get the seven wounded men behind him home. But he fought it and refused to give way. He would get the ship across the sea. The clouds were full of rain now, and hung low over the sea. For minutes at a time the plane slammed through heavy showers which drenched him and blinded him altogether.

When the rain stopped there was nothing to see but the whirling rags of vapor. Time passed slowly and he could not figure out if the *Plain Jane* was getting anywhere or not. The navigator mumbled in delirium at his position, bent over blood-smeared maps. The co-pilot was slumped forward green-faced in his seat, breathing like a man who had had an overdose of sleeping pills. Nobody answered to calls on the intercom, either because they were too badly hurt or because the system was out. The ship slowly broke out through the bottom of the cloud mass to face the sullen gray sea, flecked with white caps, a few hundred feet beneath.

She seemed to want to settle into it. Gavin tried to gain altitude, but she wouldn't give it to him. He talked to her as an old friend, begging her to give him just another thousand feet, but she remained leaden in the air. Gavin began to feel cold and wondered why he should be sweating. The hands of his watch crawled on their dial and the gauges showing him how much gas he had left gave him worse news than he expected each time he looked at them. The gray sea under its mantle of gray cloud seemed endless and there was no sign of land ahead. He wondered if he could be off course enough to be flying out down the Channel parallel to the English coast. If that were the case he would run out of gas and fall into the sea somewhere off Dungeness. He read the compass and was relieved for a moment until he realized that he would be just as badly off if he was on the right compass bearing but too far south. Pain was now throbbing in his thigh. He thought he would head the ship a little more to the north and began to ease her round ten degrees. The starboard motor coughed, spat, and died. Oh God no, thought Gavin, I'm so cold and that sea is so cold, I don't want to ditch, I don't want to drown my boys. Blood ran across the floor under his feet. He leveled off on the new course. He hardly had enough strength left to do it, and he knew that if he did get to England he would in all probability not now have the strength to make a proper landing, and that he certainly would not have time enough left to look for a regular airfield to land upon. He saw a line of slowly breaking surf beneath him and a long, unfamiliar stretch of beach. Behind it there were salt marshes and twisting tidal creeks lined with reed beds. A man in a small boat turned a white face up at the plane. He had a dog sitting beside him. "Oh, Jesus Christ, help me now," Gavin said, "I can't have more than a hundred and fifty feet." He saw a sea wall ahead with a row of trees behind it, rounded and shaven by the salt winds from the east. Further on there was a patchwork of meadows, each ringed by a hedge in which a few trees had been left to grow. *Plain Jane* failed slowly towards them. The fields grew larger, but now they were divided by long lines of towering elms with hideously massive trunks. A woman in a white apron ran to gather up a child as the plane swept over a red brick farmhouse and a black tarred wooden barn. Gavin looked away to his right and saw a square battlemented church tower of gray flint and stone rising out of the clustering roofs of a village. The clock face on it showed the time as clearly as he could wish it, three twenty. He checked it against his watch, and found it a minute or two fast. Ahead there was another row of elms at the far side of a field with a herd of dairy cows in it, knee deep in lush grass. Gavin fingered the controls and nerved himself for a last effort. Even if *Plain Jane* cleared that row of trees she would not clear another. As she headed inevitably for the top branches of the solid-looking elms, he cut the last engine in the hope of reducing the chance of fire. He would just have to put her down with the wheels up and slide into whatever was waiting for him beyond the trees. He shut his eyes and counted five. When he opened them again he saw in front of him sixty acres of almost ripe wheat. I believe, so help me, it's going to be all right, he thought, easing her nose up and settling her in. If she just doesn't catch fire, if she doesn't catch fire, some of us may get out of this alive. He thought he might black out after the wrenching, scraping and sliding of the landing was over, but he found himself sitting back in the unlikely quietness, looking out over the waving wheat, wondering in a detached way what would happen next. He heard the alarm call of an excited pheasant. He heard a cock crowing and he thought he heard a horse whinny. Then he heard shouting a long way off, and a confused medley of human voices. Help was on its way. His fingers seemed to have become very large, sticky and thick, but he managed to get his notebook from his pocket. Slowly and carefully he took out a ballpoint pen and wrote a message: *Please call Kensington 5272 at 6 p.m. this evening and tell Mrs. Brassey that Major Hatfield has been slightly wounded on operations but is safe and well. He will call her in the morning.*

While he was writing, the cold slime in which he had been sitting began to grow still colder, half of his being wanted to slide off into it to be at peace, the other half resisted. He had a feeling that he should hold on a little longer, until the last of the crew were out of the *Plain Jane*. He had no reason for it, he just felt he would be happier if he held on till then. The church clock struck once to mark the half-hour, and the wind ruffled the wheat between him and what looked like a small woodlot. The first amateur help reached the plane, a voluble and excited group of red-faced and blue-eyed farm workers. They wanted to be kind and they were filled with good intentions but they couldn't get into the interior of the machine. It had seemed so fragile over Germany and over the sea, but now that it was lying dead in an English field it had hardened its surfaces and become impenetrable. Gavin watched their faces as they wrenched at the shattered Plexiglass and the metal caging around him and was half afraid that they would succeed. They would hurt him terribly if they moved him. They would mean well and they would try to be gentle. They would lift him out and lay him down on the ground among the trampled wheat. His wound would start bleeding again and he would die. He looked at the anxious earnest faces outside and understood that their good will was as great a danger as any which he had yet had to face. He smiled at them and with enormous effort shook his head from side to side. "Better not," he muttered, "better not." But they couldn't quite hear him, just as he couldn't quite understand their excited conversation, until out of their burred country murmurings he heard a voice pitched a little higher than the rest saying, "Ah, thank goodness, here come th' ambulances." R.A.F. uniforms replaced the open-necked shirts and the dark trousers of the farm workers, and *Plain Jane* began to open up like an oyster in the hands of an expert barman. A doctor came in through the escape hatch in the roof behind Gavin's position, and before many more minutes three plasma bottles were hanging over the wounded men. Life was being poured back into their bodies. Gavin saw that the doctor, after having looked him over, was getting ready to give him an injection of what he guessed would be morphine. Outside a tripod was being erected which would lift off the plane's nose, and presently swing him out on a stretcher. His life with *Plain Jane* was almost over.

"Doctor," he said.

"You'll be all right, Major, everything's in hand."

"How many of my men are hurt?"

"Oh, they have a scratch or two among them. We'll do our best with them."

"I want to know, doctor."

"All right. One's dead, the rear gunner. One man in the waist will die. You and five others will live, unless we have some perfectly rotten luck between here and the hospital. You're all pretty badly hurt, and groggy with loss of blood. Does that ease your mind?"

"Thanks. There's one more thing. Call my base at Padgham Market. Ask the duty officer to tell Colonel Littlefield where this ship is and what the state of the crew is. And another." He handed the piece of paper with the message for Helen on it, to the doctor. It was odd that an R.A.F. man should look so like Marsen Bunce, he thought. "You'll do those things for me, if you can, won't you?" he said.

"Of course," the doctor said. "I'll be glad to. And I won't forget the lady. Now what you want is a good sleep." He pressed the hypodermic needle into Gavin's arm.

"I never even felt you cut my sleeve," he said. It was funny how like Marsen he was. He even could be Marsen. "You're too old to be in the R.A.F.," he said. And then he added, "I'm doing better this time, aren't I? Better than I did in the cemetery."

"You aren't going to any cemetery," the doctor said sharply. "None of that!"

"Let now Thy servant depart in peace," Gavin murmured.

"I shall do no such thing," said the doctor. "You're going to be all right."

It seemed to Gavin that the crew of the *Plain Jane* were standing around under the wings as the ambulance took him off through the wheat. Evans, Enright, Harris, Janowicz, Taubmann, Thurston, Wiess. They waved good-bye and smiled. "I don't know which of you is the dead one," he muttered, and Thurston shouted back, "It don't matter, old boy, it don't matter a good goddamn, it'll be all the same in a thousand years." Then it came to him: It would have been Weiss who was in the tail turret, and the dying man in the waist would have been either Enright or Taubmann. He tried to see from their faces which of them it was, but their features kept melting into each other. Then he felt miserable because he remembered that nobody could be standing under *Plain Jane*'s wing. She was on her belly in the dirt, where he had put her.

"Well, damn it," he said. "I did the best I could."

There was something wrong with the remark even when he made it in the presence of armed death. Later, lying in bed in the big U.S.A.A.F. hospital near Padgham Market, he began to be visited by doubts. They arrived soon after his first request for writing paper had been met. He had been intending to send a cheerful, newsy letter to Helen assuring her that he was all right and that they would soon be together. But when the blank sheet of paper was in front of him, and the cap was off his pen, the words Darling Helen did not appear on the paper. Major Hatfield, it appeared, had received a mortal wound on the long flight home from Jena, and if he was not dead already, he very soon would be. Gavin Hatfield the Maramee banker and civic leader had come back. He was,

123

among other things, a married man. It would be absurd to pretend that Major Hatfield had forgotten that he was married, but his ideas of marriage had contracted while he was in the air force much in the manner in which men's stomachs contract when they starve for long periods in drifting ships' boats, on desert atolls, or in concentration camps. His thoughts on his relationship with Ilona had refined down until he had reached the stage at which it was possible for him to think that all his duties and obligations had been fulfilled when he had written Ilona his weekly letter, a thing which he had never failed to do. It had pained him to find, after he had been wounded, that he had not been bothering to read Ilona's letters properly for over a year. A bundle of them had been brought to him, and looking them over he had discovered that they were much better, and much more full of interest, than he had imagined. On their first arrival, as mail from home, he had always ripped them open eagerly, and then found them flatly disappointing; wordy, forced, and unbearably trivial. He had always, at the beginning, hoped for the passionate declaration of love and longing which he had wanted from Ilona. But what he got was the news of happenings at the Grove, news of Thomas and Mary, news of the quarrels, feuds, making-ups and breaking-aways in their set in Maramee. Against the realities of war these things had possessed but very little power over his mind, it was all news from far away, next door to nowhere. Now that he was out of the war this small beer had become, once again, the warp and weft of his future. The war itself had lost its domination over him. Jack Littlefield came in to congratulate him on the fine job he had done in bringing *Plain Jane* home in what was, technically, an unflyable state. Littlefield bored him, and he bored Littlefield. He was off the fighting strength of the wing, and had ceased to be of any real concern to its commander. The Colonel smiled, patted Gavin and left him. Contact between them had been broken. Thurston, ever-cheerful Thurston, the Florida man who had been the crew member whom he got along with best, came in to see him, grinning with pride in his own quick-healing flesh. "They didn't but mark me up a little, Gavin boy," he said. Talking to him out of uniform for the first time, Gavin found it too easy to remember that he was the head of the biggest bank in his part of the state, and Thurston was a man who lived with his wife's family between failures at store keeping, running gas stations, salesmanship, and poultry farming. That they had both lived in Florida seemed less of a bond than it had been. And then re-reading Ilona's letters it came to him with ugly simplicity that he had been two-timing her all the time she had been writing him these simple, good-hearted letters. And he had been less than honorable with Helen, too. It was quite true that she had never asked him if he were married, but then he had never told her either. They had just made a tight little formation organized to exclude the whole of the external world, it had been a good thing. But, he thought, he had been a heel to let things go so far. The time had come, or had damn nearly come, for a little honesty. He spent an hour looking out of the window and then wrote evasive and uneasy letters to both women. The problem grew a little larger in his mind, and when the two envelopes were addressed and ready to go out he contemplated them for a while, stroking the line of his jawbone with his finger tips as he did so in a gesture which was the banker's, but which had never been in Major Hatfield's repertory of movements.

While his splintered thighbone was being put to rights, he had ample opportunity to work out a program. He would have to face Helen Brassey to tell her that he wasn't free, and to tell her all the other things about himself which had never come up. On the question of whether he would be able to marry her or not he wouldn't be able to give her a definite word until he'd been home to discuss things with Ilona. Reasonable explanations, and long explanatory speeches formed and re-formed in his mind. The only thing was that he could never begin to see them as anything he could conceivably say to Helen if she were in front of him, or that she would listen to if he brought himself to spout them at her. He even found it harder and harder to write to her, his words looked so false and insincere on the page when he tried to conjure up the old spirit of their interchanges. He felt miserable about the way he was treating her, and escaped from his misery by writing longer and longer letters to Ilona full of the joking small talk with which married people who are in difficulties fill in the long silences in which incomprehension and failure lie in wait. Helen called his bluff in her child's handwriting.

Dearest, your last letters have been so awful I've had to pretend they weren't from you. Don't write any more trying to be nice. I expect they will give you a week's leave before you go home—or won't they—if it isn't the usual thing, ask for a week or ten days to settle your urgent domestic affairs before you go. I have leave due to me and we could go somewhere together if you could tell me dates. But please, darling, no more solemn letters full of gassy nothings. Still I forgive you even for them. Lots of love, Helen.

And so he found himself walking slowly, and making much play with a rubber-tipped cane as he walked, beside Helen through the streets and lanes of a small village on the Welsh coast. They had rooms in a gray stone farmhouse at the head of a small grassy valley running at an easy slope down to the sea. The clean beach beyond a small stretch of sand dunes lay between rocky headlands which sheltered it from the searching winds of spring. Crystal streams ran down from the moors behind the farm, chuckling in their pebble beds between lush banks of peppermint and balsam. On the way to the post office, where they called at noon to pick up the London papers, there were several small stone bridges with wide parapets to lean upon, while they looked down at the swiftly flowing water. On sunny mornings it was pleasant to sit on the lawn in the aggressively fertile garden in front of the house, and in the evenings they had a whitewashed sitting room with an open fireplace in it all to themselves. The slow battle round Caen was breaking up, and the invading army was beginning its end run round the flank at the neck of the Cherbourg peninsula into

France. There was exhilaration and hope for the end of it all in the air. The wind came freshly off the sea, and the waves broke on the beach with an intense sparkle. But Gavin was profoundly bored, he was counting the hours, now that he could walk and get about, until he got home. Their first day in Wales dragged, even though he was delighted with the place. And Helen was different. She was exhausted, and had clearly come to the farm as much to get sleep and to get away from the flying bombs as to be with Gavin. She had nothing to give him, and for the first time he had the impression that she had lost her physical confidence in herself. On the way she had told him that for eight summers, from the time she was six till the time she was fourteen her family had taken the front part of the farmhouse for August and two weeks in September each summer holiday, and that she was taking him to a precious part of her life. But she seemed almost to be disappointed with it when she got there, or at least disappointed to be in it with him. She spoke up on their second morning.

"It's all right, Gavin," she said. "Really it is." She had stopped in her tracks halfway down the grassy track to the beach.

"What?" He was startled.

"You don't have to try so hard. You don't have to pretend anything tragic is happening. It's just that you're through with me. I've known that ever since I knew that they wouldn't make you fly again. You've got your real future back, and I'm very glad. I've got mine back too—well, that's not quite true—but I can see it now anyway. We don't need each other any more. Everything's just come to a natural end. So we don't have to pretend fate's being cruel or anything."

He considered it. "I've treated you very badly."

"Oh, dear Gavin, please not to have awful ideas about us. It isn't even sad, what's happening. You're just going home safe after all you've been through and it's marvelous—don't you see?"

"Do you mean you're bored with me, and you don't want

127

to sleep with me any more?" It had not occurred to him that she could just have become tired of the affair.

"You must be mad, darling," she said. "I adore it with you, you know that. It's just that you've had the sort of walk out soldiers do have with women in countries they fight in, and it's almost over. It can't go on because you'll be in America and I'll be here in England."

"Can anything be that simple?"

"Of course it can." She took his arm and moved him off towards the beach. "You don't have to feel a bit guilty. You've been a dear, and I've loved having you. When Martin was killed I felt so glum and sad and utterly pointless I thought I'd die. And then along came poor lost and frightened you, and I knew you'd be all right if you had somewhere to go and someone nice to go to. And now you are all right, and I don't feel pointless any more, and we can go on to whatever it's going to be."

"You British can be so—I don't know—bang on about things sometimes," he said. "You scare me."

"Do I?" She squeezed his arm. "People who pretend scare me. Please don't slip back into pretending. Not ever, Gavin, not to yourself or anyone."

"I'll try. I promise." He took her hand and they walked on towards the shore. He felt happy, but in some inner recess of his being still scared, as if he were with a spendthrift who had inspired him to embark on some wild spending spree. He wondered if he had quite enough of the necessary coinage. It would take an awful lot of courage never to pretend about anything. He looked sideways at her good, strong profile and saw that she was not a pretty woman, but that she was brave and true. It surprised him that he liked what he saw better than prettiness, and with a sudden sense of intense pleasure he knew that he had five and a half days of certain happiness before him. He was going to enjoy every minute of what remained, not because there was a term set to it but simply because Helen was Helen. They reached the turn in the path which was the first point from which they could see, through a gap in the dunes, the curving line of the beach, the rocks, and wheeling gulls over the breaking waves. She turned to him a face illuminated with delight and found him, without doubts or regrets, in her own world of pure joy at last.

Chapter Four

THE trouble with discoveries of the kind which Gavin Hatfield had made in England is that for any two people their magic essences are rarely even remotely the same. While her husband had been finding his paradise, Ilona had been finding another of quite a different nature. At first Gavin's decision to enlist before America had been drawn into the war had seemed willful and cruel; it was as if he had cunningly found a way to desert her and abandon his children without incurring any of the odium attached to such a proceeding. It was almost intolerable to her in the early months of her solitude when little lacy women in Maramee's society bustled up to her at parties and receptions to say that they thought Mr. Hatfield's splendid gesture was one of the finest things they'd heard of in their whole lives, and that he had set an example to all the young men in the State. Ilona was tempted to snap rude answers to these well-meant congratulatory speeches, but she checked her impulse because she knew that in the instant in which she exposed her real feelings it would be all over town that her marriage was breaking up and that Gavin had walked out. She preferred congratulations to condolences; since the wound of Gavin's departure was to her pride, sympathy could only be salt rubbed into it. But her feeling grew all the stronger for being kept secret, and before long she had slipped wholly into the role of the wronged woman. Whenever she petted and nursed the thriving and rapidly growing children she told herself that there was a specially strong bond between them because "Daddy went away and left us, all to ourselves, didn't he, my poor pet?" An expression of patient sweetness came into her face and took away the hint of hardness which some people had detected beneath her superficial prettiness in the early days of her marriage. "You can see she's really missing Gavin," her friends said, commenting upon the change. In a sense she was, but not in the obvious sense. With Gavin out of the house, the storms of desire which occasionally flamed through her body went unsatisfied and left behind them, in place of the self-disgust which had followed their satisfaction, a feeling that she had advanced a step in the conquest of something vile within herself. Choked back without release her bouts of lust became less frequent and much easier to control. Serenity added itself to the patient sweetness in her expression. By that time America was deeply into the war. Gavin had long been gone across the seas, and many other husbands, fathers, and sons had left Maramee. Women whose marriages were not in the least like Ilona's came to her to confide in her and to cry a little on her more experienced shoulder, the usual pretext being that they had come at last to understand the sacrifices Ilona had made by letting Gavin go to war so long before he had to. At the word sacrifice Ilona would smile a secret smile and cast down her eyes, in the manner of one who knew a lot but did not wish to talk about it. To her proclaimed virtues there was added another; Ilona never complains. As a matter of fact she was truly happy for the first time in her life. She had all the money she wanted, she had a beautiful house and two lovely children, she was widely respected, and she was a powerful figure in the world of Maramee's committees and wartime activities. And her day was her own, the whole way round the clock, from the time she got up until the time she went back to bed she decided, without reference to anybody else, what she would or would not do. It was all quite perfect.

And then, suddenly, before the war was properly over even, Gavin was back. She was able to extract some comfort from her imagination when the first news of his wounding reached her. They would not be sending him home unless he was much more badly wounded than anyone was admitting. He must, really, be quite helpless. Unable to do anything for himself. She quickly planned his existence. His old study—or perhaps the little dining room—would become his bedroom and the downstairs toilet could be converted into a bathroom for his use. On fine days he could be wheeled out onto the terrace, and when it was too hot, he could lie on the north porch in the cool shadow under the huge old wisteria vine. In winter he could catch the sun in the shelter of the south porch. She inspected the way the rooms and porches were laid out and worked out routes a wheel chair could take which would avoid steps and changes in level. The only unavoidable steps led down onto the terrace, but a board ramp could be put over them with very little trouble. He would be pale and helpless, and as a serviceman he would realize that she could not interrupt her war work just for the sake of one sick individual. She would have breakfast with him—no, he would need rest—all the rest he could get—it would be a mistake to wake him just to fit into her routine. She would take her breakfast alone as she had become used to do, and she would call him from her office during the morning. She would sit with him in the evenings, when she was free. She would have to dine out several times a week as she had been doing—so much valuable preparatory work for the committees which took up her days was done on what seemed to be frivolous social occasions that she sometimes felt the dinners were even more valuable than the regular committee meetings, when it came to really getting things done. But he would understand all that. At least they would always have half an hour before she went to dress, even when she was going out. She had a clear mental picture of him lying stretched out, white and still, wearing dark glasses, motionless, in his special wheeled bed—poor devil—it would almost have been better if he had been killed, there was so little of the old powerful, eager Gavin left. But that was a horrid thing even to think.

Gavin's letters, in which he said he first learned to walk on crutches, and then with a stick, came as a rude shock. It struck her as quite fantastic that men who were really still useful in all sort of ways were being let go when the war seemed as far from being won as ever. She began to make quite stirring speeches to her committees and at lunches to support various drives. There must be no relaxation just because there was a hopeful glow in the sky. In fact the hardest efforts and the greatest sacrifices still lay ahead. They had all done well, and they could congratulate themselves on what they had done, but now was the time when even those who had given most and done most must give just a little bit more. Gavin, she felt sure, would find idleness intolerable when he got back. He would, surely, not want to hang about Maramee after having been in the thick of the fight. He would want to go to Washington, where they must be crying out for men with just his combination of business and combat experience. Gavin's rehabilitation became a matter of concern to her, she could not bear to think of his talents going to waste for any length of time, and she inquired of the Murrays and Pakenhams in Washington just where Gavin would be most likely to fit in. Being in the hospital, and being babied by nurses, might have softened him and weakened his powers of decision. It might help him to get a grip on himself again if there was a clearly marked path for him to follow. She had three good openings in Washington for him to choose among by the time they sent him home: it was the least a good wife could do for a husband returning from the wars.

Ilona would have liked to go up to New York to meet Gavin, but there was too much to do and she was simply not able to get away. Even on the day of his arrival in Maramee she had to leave a committee in session to go down to the station to meet him, and that evening she was going to have to go—as a member of the organizing committee she was forced to put in an appearance—to a ball to raise funds for comforts for seamen in the merchant marine. It was a shame to have to do such a thing on their first night, but the date of the ball had been fixed a long way ahead and his return was something of a surprise. She waited a few minutes for the train to come in and rehearsed an account of this bad news. If he didn't, she thought, like the sound of the ball he needn't even go—he probably wouldn't want to. She clung to her mental image of

133

him as a man with a consuming need for rest and sleep. The engine wheezed past her and the long line of dark brown coaches came to a standstill. She didn't see him for a long time in the crowd of descending passengers because she was looking for a white-faced wounded man hobbling along on a cane. Gavin was suddenly close to her, smiling. His hard lean face had the glow of happiness on it and his shoulders seemed to have broadened. The uniform, which had seemed to be in the nature of a fancy dress when he had visited her on home leaves during his training, now seemed to become him and to belong on him. He limped very slightly and he moved with a physical assurance which frightened her. She looked at his hands and then up again at his face. As she did so her blood turned to water; he had become more desirable than ever. The three years of independence behind her in an instant acquired the character of a desert of deprivation in which she had starved for lack of him. She flushed with eager sensuality and he smiled broadly as he took her in his arms.

Her body and her instinctive being retained full control until three o'clock the next morning when her mind snapped awake. Gavin lad dead asleep beside her, all muscle, health, and content, in the bright moonlight. He lay on his chest with his head turned sideways towards her and with a look of innocence on his face. In his soldiering his physique had acquired a new quality of real strength; he was in immensely better condition than he had been when he took exercise to keep in shape in peacetime. Sitting up in bed she despised herself utterly for having given way so completely to the mere animal magic that he exuded in this state. Her eyes traveled down from his wide shoulders past his narrow waist and small buttocks to his thighs. She shivered as she saw the bright white line of the new smooth flesh which had grown to mend the long gash torn through his meat and sinew by the shell fragment. It was horrible to her that a few hours before she had been able to kiss this loathsome disfigurement in an ecstasy of what she now saw as self-abasement. She looked at it and tried to imagine what that tearing and rending must have felt like. Without her knowing it, her hand stole out and touched the satin smooth skin of the scar. Gavin woke and smiled into her eyes. She was once again entirely his. He rolled over and she went down into his arms, her mouth thirsting for his. Her mind tried to fight against what was happening but Gavin's gentle strength and the absolute certainty of his caresses liquefied her will. In an instant she no longer wanted anything but what Gavin wanted, and she hoped he would want it forever.

Ilona remained upon this seesaw between passionate intoxication and intellectual repugnance while the season of hope after the invasion died away into bitter winter, and while the sour victory in Europe showed itself as the ugly beginning of a new conflict which made even the war in the East seem a small affair. Ilona inclined to this pessimistic view of what was happening because her public position had degenerated rapidly after Gavin's return. She had made herself, or she had been made, ridiculous by calling for greater efforts and sterner sacrifices just before taking a week off, canceling all her engagements, to welcome her husband home. It made things no better that Gavin had insisted, and that she had not wanted it that way. The damage was done and the image of the Ilona of the sufferings and sacrifices had gone forever when the seven days were over. As one of the more vulgar women who had forced her way into the upper levels of the local Red Cross organization put it, "I wouldn't mind a week looking at the ceiling myself, pretty damn soon." Presently, when Gavin was back at the bank, resuming control and taking up the public responsibilities he had put aside when he went into the air force, the sense that Ilona was privileged and fortunate became widespread among the women who still had husbands or sons away from home. "We aren't all as lucky as you are, my dear," was snapped at her one day when she was calling for an intensification of discipline among the Gray Ladies, and the cancellation of the credentials of some of the more irregular and uncertain of them. "Madam Chairman, this isn't a personal matter at all," she answered angrily, "and I very much

135

resent the suggestion Mrs. Aldington has just made." "I'm sure Mrs. Aldington will apologize, won't you, dear?" said the chairman, smiling a waxy smile. "Why yes," said Mrs. Aldington. "I'll apologize when I've had my say. We're talking about silly Polly Cummins. Everybody knows she's been falling down on the job for the past two months. I know both her sons have been missing since that thing in the Ardennes, and on top of that her husband, who's dressed up as a Colonel to do some administrative job or other up North, has left her for some little floozy of a WAC and isn't sending her enough money to get by on. She's in money trouble, she's mad with worry and anxiety about the boys, and she's been drinking too much lately. A good brisk slap in the face from us is just what she needs right now, I'm sure. I quite agree with Mrs. Hatfield that Polly's attendance record has been just terrible in the last few weeks, but situated as she is I don't think she comes within a mile of knowing how to handle that poor woman. If that's being personal, I'm very sorry to hear it, and I withdraw it as a personal remark." "I don't think Mrs. Aldington realizes that this is a matter of detail in the routine operation of a large organization, not a matter of sentiment at all," Ilona said crisply, getting ready to drive Mrs. Aldington into the ground with some good sound common sense. But as she said the words, she saw the expression, bored, indifferent, and long suffering, on the faces of the seven other women in the room. She realized for the first time that she had become unpopular. Well, that was the fate of responsible practical people who got things done; the only thing to do was to keep your chin up and to keep on slogging away. She drove Mrs. Aldington into the ground, right was on her side after all, and derived a certain satisfaction from getting a majority of the committee to vote with her against their own inclinations.

She had her reward later in the day as she waited, reading the evening paper, for Gavin, in the lobby of the Beverly Hotel. Her table was behind the dwarf wall crested with potted plants which divided the Play Hour Bar from the wide avenue of beige carpeting leading from the main entrance and the

136

reception desk to the restaurant and the ballroom where the late afternoon dances for servicemen were held. People came and went, and if anyone looked across the low hedge all they saw was a woman's lap and legs and the outside pages of the Maramee *Evening News*. Two of the women on the committee, now transformed into chaperones for the dance, passed along in the flow of men and women walking towards the ballroom, leaving a scrap of talk to rankle behind them. "I never could endure that horrid cold northern woman, and I declare I detest her for the way she behaved this afternoon." "Oh, I liked her well enough at first, but then you know how she is . . ." They were out of earshot before Ilona could learn how she was. She put her paper down and sipped her Baccardi. She was staring straight ahead of her and Gavin bent down and kissed her before she noticed that he was there.

"Hallo, love," he said, "have you been rowing with your lady battle-axes again?"

"Oh, Gavin you surprised me." She looked up, startled. "How did you know? Has anyone said anything to you about it? Behind my back?"

"Hell no." He laughed at her without concern. "You were just looking so fierce and stern, as if you'd been in one hell of a fight with someone."

"Don't joke about it, Gavin, please; I really want to know."

"Cross my heart," he said slowly, looking at her and seeing for the first time some of the shortcomings of the way of life he had learned from Helen. It was perfectly all right creating your own zone of happiness and welcoming those you loved or were fond of to join you in it, unless they were utterly determined to cultivate some sour private acres of discontent and misery of their own. He put a hand kindly on her shoulder. The way the war was dragging on was making everyone tired and nervy, these last extra months of futile endurance on the part of the Japanese were being very hard on those who hadn't, like himself, been formally acquitted at the assize of arms.

"You've been doing too much for too long," he said. His

137

sentence crossed her thought which had been concerned with his recognition that she had been quarreling with someone. She had wondered how he could at once know her so well in small things and so little in large. Now she detected a note of patronage in his voice.

"You think I might just as well have devoted myself to hop-scotch as to all these committees, don't you?" She challenged him with it, and watched him decide to respond to the challenge with a twinge of dismay. He lowered himself into the chair beside her and looked round for the waiter.

"That's a big question," he said, flapping his hand at the man behind the bar. "I'll tell you. It opens up another, about whether married people ought to be honest with each other. I'm damned if I know the answer to that one. But if you really want to know what I think your committees are worth when it comes to winning the war or not winning it . . ." He broke off. "There—you're angry already, because you don't like what I think. If you haven't thought it once or twice yourself how do you know what I think so instantly?"

"Oh, I know you, and *men*," Ilona snapped. "But we did want to do something, and we've been doing our best."

"Well, there's your answer. And why let it worry you?"

"Do you really suppose it would make me happy to be told that I'd been doing something quite pointless ever since you went away?"

The waiter brought Gavin his usual very good plain whiskey and water, and set it down in front of him. He looked at the drink in the glass for a few seconds as if he were a fortune teller looking into a crystal ball. In it he saw the last days of pure happiness which he had enjoyed with Helen, like a distant view of a far country. Beside that image he saw another, of the sticks of bombs, like some obscene kind of bird droppings, falling from the planes in front of his in a big formation towards places and people he had never seen. He wondered if she knew anything about the horrors of napalm, or if the censorship was still keeping secret the news of the sort of weapons the side of good was using in its fight against evil.

138

He was almost certain that some of the bombs he had dropped had burned some human beings alive, though he would, in the nature of things, never be absolutely certain.

"All I know about the war is that I'll be very glad when it's over," he said.

"You were in such a hurry to get into it," she snapped.

"I know," he answered her gently. "The issues were so clear then, but the closer I got to the whole bloody mess the more confused I got, and now when I look at the news from Europe I'm damned if I know what we were doing over there. As for the East, all I know is the Japs kicked us and we felt we had to kick them right back. I'm damned if I see ten-bucks worth of sense in any of it."

"You don't mean you would stand by and let half the Jews in Europe be murdered if it was all to do over again?"

"Ah, there you have me," Gavin stroked his chin in the old way. "But do you remember how disgusted you were when Captain Manson shot that Negro Maggs—the man who cut me? You said it was a disgrace to us all."

"I still do. That man Manson went after him as if he wasn't a human being. They didn't even pretend to try to arrest him —there was no trial or anything—they just went after him and shot him down as if he'd been tried and sentenced to death already. It was horrible."

"Well, nobody brought any of the Germans I killed to trial either. I don't know if they had any hand in that Jewish business or not. They certainly hadn't had a *prima facie* case established against them. They just had it, sudden death, dished out to them."

"You didn't deliberately kill civilians! That's a ridiculous argument."

"Honey, we just offloaded our bombs at fifteen to twenty thousand feet, we didn't know too much about where they hit. There was generally a factory somewhere around, and some of our bombs usually hit it. But they clobbered an awful lot of the local scenery as well."

"But that—those were accidents of war. It wasn't a bit like

139

Manson going after Maggs. He stood close enough to him to see his face, and just shot him. Manson had something—a Thomson gun—I don't know—and he nearly cut Maggs in half. It was a ghastly story. I got together a group of women and we went to see the Governor about it—that awful man."

"What did he say?" Gavin couldn't help smiling wolfishly.

"Oh, he was unbearable. He showed us a big photograph of the state trooper Maggs shot before they got him, and another of his wife and children—just as if it was a matter of sentiment, and not a matter of principle at all. When we tried to get some sense out of him he started clowning. He passed us out deputy sheriff's badges and swore us in. He said he'd call us his special posse and that next time there was a jigaboo on the rampage anywhere in the state he'd call on us to go and reason with him. He just wouldn't discuss the questions of human rights and common decency which were involved. He was so awful it still makes me mad to think about it."

"Poor Ilona! You should have known just how far you'd get with him." A thought crossed his mind. "You didn't go to Manson and say what you thought, did you?"

Ilona flushed scarlet.

"You did? Why you nervy old thing. What did he say?" Gavin downed his drink with relish.

"I can't possibly tell you." Ilona's blush was replaced by a look of cold fury. "It was one of the most disagreeable experiences in my life. God, how I hate these Southerners."

"Go on—what did he say?"

"He lounged back in his swivel chair in the most insolent manner you can imagine, holding a pencil or something between his fingertips, and he didn't say anything until I'd finished. And then—oh, it's too beastly—he gave himself away for the horrible Nazi he really is underneath. I didn't realize until then how many people there are in America who could be the worst kind of facist . . ."

"But what did he say?" Gavin said.

"I don't think I can repeat it—well, if you must know—he said you'd been away at the war too long and, and, well that

140

I needed something doing to me. He said—I can just see his face—that he thought I was forgetting what a woman was naturally for. And then he just got up and went out, and left me sitting in his office . . ."

Gavin stared at her for an instant and then, before he knew it, had laughed.

"He said you wanted a good . . ."

"That's what he said." Ilona was on her feet, frozen-faced. "Is it so funny?"

"Yes." Gavin got to his feet, suddenly sobered. "Yes, Ilona. In a coarse, horrible way it is. Funny; just that and nothing more."

"It was the ugliest, most horrible thing that's ever happened to me." She was really angry. "I've never been so humiliated in my life."

"It wasn't, Ilona." There was no trace of amusement on his face. "It was nothing. You annoyed a man beyond endurance and he said something rude to relieve his feelings, that's all. You asked for it. And what you got yourself was a place in a vulgar joke."

"So I was in the wrong?"

"Nobody was in the wrong. You were quite in the right according to your lights, but he lives in another world—beyond your knowledge. You had no business taking your ideas to him; you were telling him how he ought to do his job without having the faintest idea what his job is."

"It's a perfectly simple matter of fundamental principle, anyone halfway decent understands, or ought to."

"Nothing is perfectly simple. And Manson's job is no exception."

"I can see this is something there's no point in our discussing." Ilona saw that people around them were staring and trying to overhear their all too evidently heated conversation. "We simply won't say anything more about it."

They were nearing a breaking point, but there was still a little further to go. It came on the great day when the Japanese surrendered at last, and the war was finally at an end.

141

That morning the air round the First National tower filled with the noise of bells, the whistle of factory sirens, and the booming voices of the freighters lying in the port in their drab wartime paint jobs. The pigeons from the square in front of City Hall and pigeons from a dozen lofts in Spanishtown circled in panic, clattering their wings, and a cloud of gulls milled over the river and out on the mud flats where Morgantown melted into the Gulf for an indeterminate no man's land of reed beds, rat-infested refuse tips, rickety sheds, and boat landings. Gavin had been waiting for it and stood watching at his window. He wanted to feel what he was expected to feel, but he found it difficult to feel even relief. He knew, now, looking out over Maramee, the lesson he had learned in the English wheatfield, and which all men learn when they stand close to the dark angel and live. It was no cheerful message, simply the words of a stay of execution: thou art preserved for another end, and in another place, go thy ways until in the fullness of time I claim thee. He listened to the blaring of car horns and the hubhub of voices in the street below. White-uniformed sailors were starting a snake dance round the monument to the Civil War dead at the crossing of Broad and 17th. They came from the shore-training establishment, out beyond Maramee Heights, for radio and radar operators who, never having been to sea, would now never have to lose their innocence of its dangers. They had, Gavin conceded, something to rejoice about, knowing as little as they knew. Downstairs the bank was emptying. He had given instructions that it should close for the day the minute the rumored surrender of the Japanese was officially confirmed. His employees had all been excited and delighted and he had envied their frame of mind. Miss Lumley, his secretary, had for the moment looked young and pretty again as she exclaimed over the wonderful thing it would be for all the divided families and separated husbands and wives who would now be reunited. He saw some black puffs in the air above Morgantown, rockets. They were letting off fireworks there, of all places. He had heard some fantastic stories of what G.I. insurances had meant to a number of families over there, and of what pay in the war plants round Maramee had done for that section generally. From where he stood behind his big plate-glass window he could see nine new factories and workshops, and there were several others out of sight behind him on the eastern and northern sides of the town. Maramee had done well out of the war, beyond question. And so had he. Gavin left the window and went back to his desk. Miss Lumley had clearly thought that it was bad taste on his part for him to spend the first day of peace looking over his personal portfolio but for some reason he had felt impelled to call on her to bring it to him. And there, spread out in front of him, was the schedule of his investments. While he was being a hero in England and over Europe his man Neil Parker, who looked surprisingly fit for someone with a 4-F rating, had been working all the time to do what was, in his phrase, in Gavin's best interests. He was amazed by the way in which, now that he had money, it was easy to make money. His tax-free income from the oil business into which Neil had put him was now bringing in a horrifying two hundred and eighty-six thousand a year, and the total value of the stocks standing in his name was just over nine and a half million dollars. The sum, as Gavin read it at the foot of the long column of figures, rang a bell in his mind. He saw a sea melting towards the horizon into heat haze, and against it the sudden flowering of a bright red sail. Diana somebody or other, Anstruther? Carrington? No, Osmington, it was, sat beside him on the sand and told him she was to have nine and a half million dollars when she was twenty-one. It gave him a curious sense of loss to realize that it had been towards just this moment of equalization that his life till then had been directed. He had wanted to be on an equality with that girl, on whom he had not set his eyes for God alone knew how many years. He snapped the folder shut and walked about his office. Could that really have been it? He remembered that he had, just about the time Diana had told him about her inheritance, formed that resolution of his to make a million before he was thirty. He wanted very much to be able to think that he had formed the ambition before she had told him how rich she was going to be, but he couldn't. It had been after that. He fought to recall his memories of Diana's physical appearance, but he couldn't. All he remembered of her was that, by mentioning some figures, she had made him feel in some way deficient, and inferior as a man in relation to her as a woman. Now that he had that sum, thanks to Neil's efforts rather than his own, it was borne in on him how little legal title to it related to what he was or was not. He had imagined a vain thing. It brought him up with a jerk to find himself quoting biblical tags in Marsen's manner, and the break in his thoughts allowed him to notice an event in the outside world. The fireworks, or something else, had started a fire over in Morgantown among the shanties at the beginning of the swamps. A star of orange flame glowed among the crazy rooftops and a thickening tower of dirty-looking smoke stood up in the sky. It occurred to Gavin that the reed beds, garbage dumps, and the fish docks over there, were very close to the center of downtown Maramee. With all the new machinery that had been developed during the war for making beaches into landing points, and swamps into airfields it would be a cinch to turn that derelict morass into solid ground. And if Morgantown were cleared up Maramee could grow out in that direction as good sense seemed to indicate that it should. He would get a campaign going for the incorporation of Morgantown into the city so that what went on there could be properly controlled. Then they would get the federal people to put in a second bridge, and then . . . It would be fun and worthwhile, and now that peace had broken out it would be possible. He began to feel the lift of the day. It was worth being alive after all, and a damned good thing to have it over and done with. He began telephoning all over town. "Come on out to the Grove, we're having a party. Hell, that doesn't matter. Bring your party on over to our party, they'll like each other." Easy and friendly, the public Gavin swept his peace celebration together. He got hold of four lambs to broil whole over the barbecue pits, he got a marching band out of Morgantown, and he got all the ice, soft drinks, hard liquor, and everything else needed to keep a hundred and sixty-seven men, women and children of various ages happy for half a day, out to the Grove within a couple of hours. Seeing him at work, briskly getting it all going, everyone who thought about the matter at all concluded that he was filled with delight at the war's end and happy as children are happy when things go well and look like they'll be going better. Ilona watched him with mixed feelings, not far from those of a child who sees a well-designed and well-built sandcastle made into a mud pudding by a random wave. She was mistress of the Grove, and ran it well. Giving parties was after all her department, and she gave pretty good parties— of the candles-in-glass-chimneys and lanterns-in-the-trees variety. But here was Gavin, with his satanic energy, deluging her neatly ordered world with this jamboree, and filling it with more guests than she would dream of undertaking without the help of a caterer on his simple whim. She strayed around her own domain feeling lost and a little indignant. The barbecue pits, where the lambs had been roasted two by two over great mounds of charcoal, bothered her particularly. Where and how had Gavin found the three Syrians who had handled the whole business? They had just appeared out of nowhere with two wives and seven children and become part of the party because Gavin had wished it. And all the cases and cases of bottles, the Coke machine, and the ice cream for all the children? She drifted round stupefied, thinking of all the days of telephoning and negotiating it all would have meant for her, and, as she drifted, smiling friends, acquaintances, and strangers whom she had never in her recollection seen before, came up and congratulated her on the wonderful party she was giving. Gavin was circulating too, constantly moving about seeing that his guests had what they wanted, his face shiny and his suit limp. He seemed inexhaustible and, to Ilona, terrifying. A party was the last thing, as it happened, that she was in the mood for. She had news for him that she had no intention of giving him in these circum-

145

stances. She saw the whole thing as an epitome of the essential difference which lay between them. He was coarse, earthy, vigorous and instinctive, she was delicate and sensitively organized. He could create this sort of thing and she—well, her concerns were with another department of life altogether. Neil Parker came over to her where she was standing, drawn off a little apart, under a dark lovely tree with long pointed leaves whose name she had never learned.

"This is a terrific party, Mrs. Hatfield."

"Everyone seems to be having a very good time."

"They surely are. You know what all this makes me think?"

"No, I can't imagine."

"Well, I tell you, Mrs. Hatfield." He looked narrowly at her with his eyes, still smiling at her with his mouth. She was, he thought, a goddamn Eastern snob, just as a lot of Maramee women were saying. "Well, I tell you, in my opinion Gavin has just a natural flair for this kind of thing—getting a lot of people together and making himself the living center of the occasion. You know what that adds up to—it means he's a natural born politician, and I mean that. Why I believe, truly I do, that Gavin could be governor of this state in five years. And when he gets to be governor he'll be a national figure in no time at all. I'm telling you that with the right kind of backing there'll be no stopping our boy anywhere along the line."

"Oh, Mr. Parker, please. I can't think of anything more utterly awful than having a national figure in the house. It's bad enough trying to keep abreast of Gavin as the big wheel in Maramee, but let's not turn him into a professional windbag in the bargain."

"Before God, Mrs. Hatfield, I do sometimes believe you're the worst enemy Gavin Hatfield has anywhere at all. You don't understand him, and it's my belief you don't even like him. You don't like Maramee, and you don't give a good goddamn for any living person who inhabits it. If you ask me you ought to pack up and git. I mean that. I do. I truly do. Go back up North where you belong."

Ilona's hand striking his cheek made a small sharp sound

146

that was drowned among the noises of the party about them. As she heard it and saw that her blow hadn't even made him turn his head she felt the bitterness that every woman feels when the feminist bluff is called. For all her tennis and swimming it simply wasn't in her power to deal with him as a physical equal. Hitting Neil had been an act of cowardice. She had known even when she was angry enough to do it that centuries of convention had given her an almost absolute security from a return blow. Neil smiled contemptuously.

"I think you've had a little too much to drink, Mr. Parker," Ilona said, pathetically attempting a rally on firmer ground.

"I don't doubt that it would be nice for you to think so, Mrs. Hatfield," Neil said. "And perhaps we'd better have it that way. But if you want to know, I've never let hard liquor pass my lips in all my born days. My father was a drinking man. I've seen him lying in a pool of his own vomit more often than I like to think. That sort of turned me against drinking. I don't ever drink. But occasionally I do get sort of excited and I just can't help coming out with the truth as I see it."

"I see no reason for us to continue this conversation."

"No, ma'am. We're much too well bred to mess with the truth, aren't we? I apologize for talking out of turn."

He bowed with mock courtesy and left her. Almost in tears, she made her way blindly to the house and went upstairs to lie down in her room. Three women were sitting there, waiting for the bathroom to be free and talking about the nursery-school problem in Maramee to pass the time. Was it better to send the children to the Sisters of the Sacred Heart in the Heights, or was it better to send them to Molly Hasbrouck's cute little school out on the point beyond the yacht basin, which meant taking them and fetching them yourself? The Sisters ran two white station wagons to fetch and deliver children, and that was convenient, but they charged for the service. Ilona dislodged the woman sitting in front of her dressing table and bathed her forehead in cologne. She put in her ten cents worth. Thomas and Mary went to Molly's. She thought

147

Molly had such a pretty garden—and, well, the atmosphere was so much nicer without all those nuns about. And Molly had such pleasant, normal young girls working with her. It seemed nicer altogether. "Oh, well, Mrs. Hatfield," one of the women said, "after all, with all your committees you've never had to worry about gas the way we ordinary folks have. You'd just naturally see the whole thing in a different light." The talk turned to hopes that the gas controls would go soon now that the war was over, and various rumors were discussed. Ilona locked the door behind the last of them and lay down on the bed, biting on a handkerchief to keep herself from crying, and listening to the sounds of the party rising, falling, and at last dying away. It was not until after seven that she felt it would be safe to come down again.

She found only the shank of the gathering left. The mysterious Syrians, the bandsmen, and most of the guests had gone. The Coke machine and the two bars had vanished. The field hands of the Grove were already at work picking up the litter on the ground between the house and the lake, spurred on by the promise of almost unlimited beer for their own celbration when the job was finished. A station wagon full of beer cases was already parked round at the back by the kitchen for distribution when the last carton and piece of wrapping paper was safely gathered up. Harry and Nedda Crane, Eddie Riemann, Neil and Jean Parker, Jock and Leila Whitman, and Sue Hollis were sitting rather languidly on the terrace waiting for something to happen. Gavin sat on the parapet of the terrace, reddened, exhausted, but still jazzed up and excited by all that had happened. Ilona was astonished to see that Neil had stayed on after their scene, she imagined that he would have gone. He gave her a curious look, partly of warning, partly of connivance, as if they had committed adultery together. She instantly turned away from him and found herself involved in a meeting of eyes with Nedda Crane. It was in its way even more disconcerting to her. Nedda silently offered her sympathy and pity.

"It's our disappearing hostess!" said Leila Whitman. "Good to have you back!"

"Just a little headache. It's gone now," Ilona said. She felt she had to do something quickly to restore her position in the set. She was within a hair's breadth, obviously, of getting a permanent rating as a drag on Gavin. "I think anything here is going to be an anticlimax, and I don't want to get all dressed up. Why don't we just go over to the spring and swim and roast wienies?"

It was considered to be a wonderful idea. But there was a little delay before they got off, and while Bailey, the houseman, took the franks from the deep freeze and put up the picnic baskets there was time for three rounds of drinks. And then when the baskets were unpacked it was found that they had a great deal of hard liquor in them and no beer. There was more drinking in the dying evening light before anyone went into the pool. Everything was set for trouble by the time Nedda discovered that she hadn't brought a suit. She called out her bad news from the shadows where the women were undressing, a little apart from the men, and added, "The hell with it, why don't we go in skinnies, the way we always used to here?"

"Oh, I say, not starkers, you can't mean starkers," Eddie cried in his pretend English voice, trying to make a joke out of the thing because he had come to know a good deal about Harry Crane's compulsive jealousy and possessiveness, and because he knew that Harry had in the years of his tense association with his sister come to know what her premarital relationship with Gavin had been. "It would be madness to go romping in the buff, old girl."

"I've never swum here naked in my life," Jean Parker said. "You must have been having private orgies, Nedda."

"Well, the hell with suits for tonight, anyway," Nedda said. "Here I come, boys, if the female form is news to any of you, now's your big chance."

She stepped out of the shadows in which she had been just a pale shape and appeared, lean, athletic, and barely marked

149

by the passage of the years of her childless marriage. Gavin looked at her and thought she was as gorgeous as ever, it was too bad they weren't sleeping together still. Neil thought, Jewesses, they're sort of exaggerated in their sensuality, the way they have such waists and hips, such sweetly rounded tummies. Eddie thought, my dear lovely, gorgeous sister, why did you have to chuck yourself away on such a hopeless man as Crane who was bound to make you miserable? Why with all our gifts for being happy have we always done so badly for ourselves? All this was in the frozen moment before Harry, just as mad as Eddie had known he would be, started out after Nedda swinging his belt and shouting at her. "Get out of sight, you drunken whore!"

She ran along the white sand, and the other women screamed. Harry slipped and sprawled. Gavin dived on top of him.

"You get off me, lover boy. You let me alone. You mind your business!"

"Nobody's going to hit a woman while I'm around."

"All right, war hero!" Harry slammed Gavin in the ribs, and took a short-armed jab under his jaw. They rolled over each other into the spring.

"Nedda's nothing to you, nothing, you bastard," Harry said. "Just because you . . ." Gavin grabbed his head and shoved it under water.

"He'll drown him," shrieked Jean.

Eddie and Neil parted them as they flailed at each other in the water. Ilona stood frozen and apart. Sue Hollis pursued Nedda with a robe of terry cloth, laughing hysterically, and Jean ran after the pair of them.

The whole thing burned out as quickly as it had flared up, and within a minute or two of the worst of it everybody was round the fire drying off. Eddie flung a few branches of turpentine pine from deeper in the wood onto the flames and a ruddy glow lit up the spring, the circle of oaks, and even, it seemed, a great vault of the night. Gavin and Harry were bathed in gold and amity, and stood in their shorts with their arms over each other's shoulders and Eddie was burying their hatchet in a mound of words. "Hell, Harry, we were all just kids—it was just growing up—what we did do and what we didn't do—it's all water over the dam—we weren't keeping score and none of it counts." Harry looked into the fire. He couldn't meet Nedda's eyes. He had behaved badly. She had been loyally and devotedly his ever since their marriage, but whenever he got drunk she became in his imagination a lascivious bitch-in-heat open to every passing stranger. Had he tried her patience and her forbearance once too often? He didn't dare to look up into her eyes to find out. Everyone else talked rapidly, eagerly, to cover up the great raw wound which was exposed. As if to prove the harmlessness of that water which had poured away so long ago, the talk turned to the old times which Eddie, Harry, Nedda and Gavin, had shared. Neil and Jean, deeply involved in the local life, delighted in the anecdotes of the extravagant pasts of those they knew as their rather slow and stuffy seniors; they pressed for more. They began swapping anecdotes of Margie Wiley and her desperate search, and of the fantastic evasive maneuvers that her prey had been compelled to take in the last years before her removal to an asylum. The stories were lewd and the laughter was loud. Harry was good at Margie stories. In fact a foul mouth was one of the symptoms of his insecurity and Nedda always knew just what the state of his morale was from the sort of story he was prepared to tell. As he told the story of how Margie had made a platoon of paratroopers break and run during a training exercise in the autumn of 'forty-two, she recognized that his morale had come somewhere near the bottom. What a fool she had been to bring the crisis on. It would have been so easy just to dart across the sand and into the water. God damn my big mouth, she thought. The story reached its climax, so bizarre and so unexpected that everyone was forced to laugh—almost to retch with laughter. Nedda looked across at Gavin and their eyes met. Ah, yes. If they had each known then what they knew about marriage and themselves now, things would have been very different. She broke the dangerous contact and her eyes strayed over to Ilona's face to see if she could gather how their relationship was. She was shocked by what she saw, horror, dismay, intense loathing. She involuntarily gave a little cry, it could not be as bad as that! The sound caught everyone's attention. All round the circle the faces turned first to her and then to Ilona, the stranger, the woman Gavin had brought down from the East, who had never belonged or wished to belong. They all saw the disgust on her face and a silence fell. When she heard their voices die, and saw them all looking at her, to some degree pitying her or scorning her, a black wave swept up from her womb to her brain and she crumpled in a faint. When she came to, with her head in Gavin's lap, and with everyone about her, solicitous and anxious, she was only able to say: "It's nothing, nothing at all, I'm really all right. It's the most natural thing in the world. It's just this baby I've started."

It was in this way that she broke the news of the quickening of his third child to her husband.

"Honey," he said. "Ilona darling, that's wonderful . . ."

Scalding tears burst from her, rushing out with her words.

"Please, please, everyone. I just can't take any more. The party, everything—it's all been too much. Please, everybody. Just to go away—I can't take any more."

And then the whole thing had broken up, not just the party, but everything. The others had driven away, leaving her alone with Gavin.

"Are you sure?" he said in the silence which had gathered about them after the last departure.

"I don't want to talk about it, please. And don't touch me."

He got up and stood back with the firelit trees and the caverns of shadow under them behind him. She sat looking up at his bulky, strongly animal figure.

"You've made love to that Crane woman—here—under these trees, haven't you?" He looked amazed and his silence was assent enough to her. She went on. "I know it. And you've brought other women here—to neck and swim. To make them if you could."

"You're out of your mind. What does that matter now?"

"Oh nothing, nothing—to think that half these women who pretend to be my friends are just your old mistresses."

"How can what happened before we were married, before I even knew you, matter a hoot. It didn't mean much of anything even then—it was just play—young people fooling around."

"And what about the whores, the foreign women, you had over in the E.T.O. The women who taught you to make love with the light on, in broad daylight, any time. You never did that until after you'd been away."

"You're not yourself, Ilona," Gavin said, evading it. "I've got to get you home."

"Don't dodge, Gavin. Don't flinch away. Tell me the truth. You've had any woman you could get, all through your life, haven't you? When you were writing me love letters before we were married, since we've been married, all the time, any little bitch who'd open her legs to you has been good enough for you. Isn't that the truth?"

"No," he said savagely. "If I could think you were drunk I could bear this. But I know you're not." He took her by the shoulders and shook her gently. "What's been getting into you anyway?"

She looked at him owlishly and then went off into a screech of hysterical laughter.

"Why you—that's what—" she said. "That's why I'm having this baby!" She laughed wildly again. "That's good enough for Harry Crane isn't it? You can tell your Nedda next time you lay her that I make dirty jokes too—just like her husband."

He slapped her and she lapsed into sudden silence. He stamped out the dying fire and threw sand on the embers. He led her to the car without speaking, and no further word was said on the drive back to the Grove. While they sat stiffly side by side but utterly apart on the way home, Gavin kept serious thoughts at bay by telling himself that women had odd spells when they were pregnant. This pregnancy must clearly have come as a surprise to her since they had never even discussed

153

the possibility of a third child, and she had seemed very happy to have what she called their pigeon pair of boy and girl. He had, secretly, been reading a book on feminine psychology not long before which had told him that the early stages of breeding were always difficult periods of adjustment if the mother was not consciously desiring a child. He would have to make allowances. Taking a quick look sideways at her as an oncoming car filled their machine with light, he saw that her cheeks were wet with silently shed tears. He felt the familiar pang of tenderness which something about her always moved in him. It was easy to sympathize with her for spoiling the picnic, indeed for resenting the whole hellish day which he had blindly inflicted upon her. She was, as she had always been for him, the other stranger, left out of things at the big wedding. If she was difficult it was not altogether her fault, and there were some feelings you couldn't help giving way to, after all. When she recovered her balance he might tease her about it a little, but he would never hold it against her.

So no issue was made of anything, then, or later.

Because Ilona was so clearly upset she slept alone that night and she slept alone for eight months after that because she had a preference for sleeping alone when she was carrying a child. The girl was born at the end of a long labor, and when born proved to have a delicate stomach. She could not feed except at Ilona's breast. So Ilona slept alone while she recovered her strength, and then slept alone to maintain it against the drain of the child's growing demands. Then when the child was weaned at last, she went into a collapse with physical and nervous exhaustion as its cause. She clung greedily to her solitude. It was only after a full year had gone by that Gavin faced the fact of the new situation in his marriage, when it occurred to him to say that everything had been just wonderful since morning and that it would round out a perfect day to go on over to the spring for a supper picnic. As he spoke the words in which he made this suggestion he put his hand on his wife's where it was resting on the arm of her chair. He did this with conscious affection, and he had been thinking of bending down to kiss her cheek when he had finished speaking. But her hand slid from under his.

"We might go to the beach," she said. "I'd far rather not go to that place."

"Do you mean to say . . ." he began with incredulity in his voice.

"Let's not discuss it, please."

He knew simultaneously that the sleeping arrangements which he had supposed to be temporary were permanent, and that the foolish wrangle and scuffle at the edge of the pool was something he should have talked out with Ilona long since. He drew up a rattan stool beside her chair and sat on it.

"Are you truly jealous of Nedda Crane?" he asked. "Because if so be you are you . . ."

"I said I didn't want to talk about it," Ilona said.

Gavin looked at her for several seconds before he muttered, "Sweet Jesus Christ," and swallowed down the whole of the highball in his hand as he had until then never gulped down a drink. A silence subsisted between them for several minutes until at last he walked across the brick terrace to the trolley with the drinks on it. When he got there he poured himself another drink of straight whiskey, and put it back as if it were water. He stood looking down the broad grassed-over walk at the lake and the landscape beyond, and did not seem to hear when Ilona gathered up her things and went indoors.

"I heard you come to bed last night," she said in the morning.

"I'm sorry."

"It was quite an exhibition."

Bailey brought Gavin his plate of eggs and some fresh hot coffee, and went out again through the swing door. While he was in the room Gavin affected a deep interest in Pegler's column in the Maramee *Herald*. Ilona spoke up again as soon as the door stopped swinging.

"It doesn't really matter to me, though I was personally disgusted," she said. "But the children aren't babies any more, Thomas and Mary—they notice a lot. I don't think it would

155

be good for them to have a drunk in the house. And I'll tell you this Gavin Hatfield, the minute I think there is one around I'll take the children North—out of your reach. I mean that."

Gavin looked across the table at her. He felt liverish after his night of drinking. He was ashamed of himself for having let go, and well aware that drink was no answer to his problem of finding out how he would live with the brute fact that he was not loved by the woman he could not help loving.

"The odd thing is," he said, "that you don't have to threaten me with that much. Even after this last year I'd still be pretty damned miserable if you just went off by yourself."

"Oh, come now," she said stirring her coffee, looking coldly at him. "I'm not a complete fool."

"You're as big a fool as anyone I know," he said quietly.

"You mean I'd be smart to believe a word you say?"

"Listen, Ilona, I've never said the words 'I love you' to you without meaning them," he said. "I'll say them again now . . ."

"Really Gavin." She got to her feet and quickly left the room.

"I wish to God I knew why," he said to the emptiness she left. "I wish to God I knew why I do, but I still do."

Thomas and Mary came into the room dressed for school.

"Haven't you finished your breakfast yet?" Mary said.

"What's your big rush?" He put his arm round her waist.

"We'll be late for school if we don't go soon," Thomas said. "You promised you'd take us this morning."

"Well, I'll keep my promise." Gavin wiped his lips with his napkin. "I may die of starvation, but I'll get you to school."

Gavin enjoyed taking them to their schools on his way to the bank, and looking at them this morning he felt that he still had a lot to be thankful for. He noticed that Thomas was unusually silent as he drove in through the fringes of Maramee and he hoped he hadn't upset the boy by being noisy or saying something he didn't understand while he was drunk.

"You can get things to eat downtown, can't you, daddy," he said, "any time you like?"

"Yes, at drugstores and, oh, all sorts of places."

"Oh, good."

There was another silence which lasted until Thomas spoke again, after getting a nudge from Mary.

"A man couldn't really die of starvation, just because he missed his breakfast, could he?" he asked.

"Oh, no," Gavin laughed. "Were you worrying about me? No, Thomas, it would take a long time for a man to die of hunger, much longer than you'd think."

They all laughed and drove on to Maramee and their new day with a sudden lightness of heart.

Chapter Five

SEVERAL times in the next few years Thomas Hatfield was told that he was a very lucky little boy, and later on that he was a very lucky young man. Anyone who had seen him driving into Maramee with his father and his sister Mary that morning would have agreed that the description was apt. It would have seemed to apply again some several years later when it was a question of water skiing one day early in the summer holidays. Mary came bursting into the north porch where Ilona was having a late breakfast and reading the New York Sunday *Times* which got to Maramee in time for the Tuesday morning delivery. "Mommy, please, we want to go water skiing," she said.

"There's nothing wrong with the outboard, is there?" Ilona said. "Thomas knows how to start it."

"But, mommy, you don't understand. We don't want to go on the silly ole lake, we want to go out on the gulf."

"Oh, must you? Well, all right. I don't see any reasons why you shouldn't." Ilona smiled. "On condition you don't bother me. Go and tell Miss Leigh I say you can have the boat for the day, and tell her you're to be back by seven."

Mary gave her a quick kiss, and ran squealing from the room. "Thomas, Miss Leigh, mommy says yes!"

Miss Leigh had been prepared for the excursion by Thomas, and was ready to go straight to the phone to call Alfred, the yacht captain, down at the Maramee Marina, as soon as she got the word. She was a combination of governess for the children and social secretary for Ilona. She was called Tiny Leigh because she was six feet two. She had mousy brown hair which she dyed an unextravagant blond color, she had good features, and a splendid figure. Thomas was in love with her, so was Alfred, and Gavin had been through a phase of wanting to sleep with her. Ilona had been doubtful about hiring her in the first place because she had no special recommendations and seemed much too attractive. She had left Michigan State in her second year, because "frankly I was bored, Mrs. Hatfield," and she had modeled in New York for two years without success because she was simply too big. She had been married for six months and then divorced. When Ilona heard that at the interview she was already almost determined not to hire her, and was just asking questions for form's sake. And just for form's sake she made some remark about her marriage having been a sad experience for her. "Oh, no, Mrs. Hatfield. It was pretty simple really. I'd never been keen on sex, and when we got down to it I turned out to be frigid. I guess when I was made they just left some part out. Anyway it was too depressing for poor Jimmy so we just cut our losses and called the whole thing off." Ilona wondered if she were telling the truth for about thirty seconds and then decided she would be just about ideal. Her statements about herself turned out to be true. "I adore kids. I just love playing around with them and looking after them," and, "I'm really good at that secretarial stuff—you know, getting airline tickets, and balancing household accounts, knowing where you ought to be at any given time and getting you there. I'm just a natural Miss Fixit." When Gavin bore down on her she said, simply, "All right, but you won't like it." She gave herself to him on his insistence, and proved to be a true prophet. He didn't like it, but somehow or other there was nothing rancid or humiliating in the encounter and he went right on liking her. So did the children. She did not love them, or pretend to love them, but she was always lively, always amusing, and never angry, though she could be firm as a rock in enforcing discipline when she had to. Ilona called her perfect, and so she was, in her own rather special way. For being what she was, she was paid eight thousand dollars a year, a little less than the starting salary of a fully fledged college professor.

159

Miss Leigh now picked up the telephone and called Alfred down in the yacht basin on the far side of downtown Maramee.

"The kids want to go water skiing," she said. "Tell Michiko we'll take lunch on the boat, me and the three of them. He should get black raspberry ice cream for dessert, and some of those pureed vegetables for Bogey."

"Couldn't you leave Bogey behind this once? She's a brat."

"Now, Alfred, Alice is just young, that's all that's the matter with her." Miss Leigh did not think Alfred appreciated the Hatfields as employers and was inclined to treat him as if he were Thomas' age. "And Alfred, check over the water skis and the skin-diving equipment before we come down. We'll be at the dock in forty minutes and we'd like to leave right away when we get there."

"O.K., Admiral. We'll have everything squared away."

When the station wagon pulled up on the dock and the children tumbled out to run helter-skelter across the dock and onto the *Plain Jane,* Alfred was on the flying bridge in crisp whites, the two big marine engines were ticking over, and the two Negro deckhands were at the bow and stern lines ready to cast off. The Nisei cook, Michiko, was beaming out of the galley window, and as Miss Leigh came aboard he put his hands to his mouth and produced a perfect imitation of a bosun's whistle. When he had piped her aboard he slammed the galley window shut and disappeared, the sailors cast off the lines, and the seventy-foot boat moved smoothly out into the channel. Alfred took her out past the point by way of the deep-water channel, and then turned north towards sheltered waters inside the reefs, where the skiing and the diving was good. The boat pulled along at sixteen knots, leaving a dead straight wake behind it on the jade-green water. The skyline of Maramee, sordid enough from close at hand, began to take on the look of a clean and magical collection of towers. Miss Leigh came up onto the bridge to enjoy the breeze. Alfred looked fondly at a lock of her hair dancing in the wind and put his arm round her waist. She shook it off.

"Now, Alfred. You know better than that."

"Like hell I do. The best thing in the world will be when you say yes to me."

"We've been over all this."

"Well, I can't say it too often." He pointed at the two Negroes in their white sailor suits sitting on the forepeak staring ahead of them. "What's the difference between us and them? What sort of life is this anyway, just being a sort of lackey to old Gotrocks? Why won't you let me take you away from it to some halfway decent life where we won't be just dangling round on the end of a phone for some rich feller to make up his mind what he feels like doing to fill up his silly day with."

"I should think you'd be pleased to have this lovely boat to look after."

"But Tiny, it ain't a boat, it's a frogging toy. Real boats are different."

"Oh, I know, dirty rusty old things. I should think you'd be glad of a clean job."

"You know I'd like to quit the sea altogether. I saw quite enough of it in the war. And you know what else? I'd like to get me some stump land in one of the Northwest states. Spend a year or two dynamiting stumps, and at the end of it you've got a real good ranch. Now there's something for a man to do. Why don't you come along with me and give it a try. You're a real woman. You aren't meant to be wasting your best years fooling around as a sort of glorified nursemaid."

"I'm doing what I was cut out to do, Alfred, and I've no intention of changing." She put a hand on his arm. "And if you'd try not to be so discontented you'd be a much happier man."

"If I wasn't discontented doing what I am doing I'd have to admit I was no damn good. I'm nothing better than a chauffeur, and I've always said that's the lowest a man can sink to. Now why don't you and me marry, get our own spread, make our own lives and raise some kids to be proud of us, instead of sticking on with this half-arsed . . ."

"Little pitchers," said Miss Leigh as Thomas, momentarily bored with Michiko's efforts to amuse the two little girls, came up onto the bridge.

"Hallo there, Commodore," said Alfred, "have you come along to take your trick at the wheel?"

"She's on the automatic pilot, isn't she?" Thomas said.

"Well, yes, as a matter of fact, she is."

"Then it would be sort of silly for me to take the wheel, wouldn't it?"

"You're getting to be a big feller. I can't fool you with kid stuff any more, can I?" Alfred said. Thomas looked steadily at him.

"I think it's pretty stinky, making people do assy things just because they're little," he said.

"Well, now, let's leave Alfred to think that one over while we go and see what Michiko and the girls are doing."

When they were out of sight behind the deckhouse, Alfred spat morosely into the sea. The kid was right. It was pretty stinky to assume he was a dope, just because his father had more money than was good for him. And it was pretty stinky to go on taking money off an employer he despised. If he did despise him. He looked out towards the western horizon at a tanker passing southward down the gulf in the full glory of a new paint job; a pretty sight to see. He looked back to the east and saw the long white line of the sandy beach they were looking for. He took *Plain Jane* off the automatic pilot and began to stand into the shallow water at half speed. The two Negroes stood up and got ready to let go the anchor. When it was down, and the ship was swinging to it, you could see every link in the chain the whole way to the white sand bottom twenty feet below. It wasn't worth wasting any time fishing. Alfred went below and lay on his bunk reading a text book on profitable sheep farming. Michiko prepared lunch, and Miss Leigh lay in a deck chair sleeping lightly with *Time* open on her lap. The two sailors whirled the white dinghy round and round and round on the green sea, sometimes with Mary and sometimes with Thomas behind them straddled on the red skis. Bogey bounced up and down with pleasure in the little boat urging the sailors to turn more sharply and to go faster so as to topple the skiers off their balance sooner. Mary and Thomas both preferred long straight runs and slow swings on which they could practice tricks so there was soon a row, and Bogey was put back on the yacht screaming and kicking. Once she was on board her tantrum was soon over. Miss Leigh was familiar with the development of this situation as the inevitable first phase of a day on the water and was ready for it. Bogey was soon settled down under the awning over the afterdeck with a pile of new comics, Batman, The Lone Ranger, and the rest. When she grew bored with that she went into the galley to watch Michiko making birds, flowers and strange fish out of radishes to complete the decoration of the table. After lunch, eaten in the blue-painted saloon with the reflected light from the rippled sea outside making dancing patterns on the ceiling, the children were bedded down for their rest hour, one to a cabin. Alfred generally made his main effort to make Miss Leigh in this part of the day, but today she had him outsmarted and was busily playing Go with Michiko before he could get anything started. Alfred watched the, to him, incomprehensible, game for some time, trying to keep himself in the players' minds by asking questions that would not allow them to forget him. But the answers, fully explanatory and crystal clear, from Michiko had the effect of making him seem foolish and he soon gave up. He went over to the rail and smoked, looking down at the shadow of the boat's hull on the sand below. It always struck him as amazing that these transparent southern seas should be as buoyant as the opaque waters of the North. They seemed like different substances altogether. When he had exhausted the possibilities in that line of speculation, and had worn out his interest in identifying the few small fish which had gathered in the shadow, he turned himself round and gave himself up to a lecherous survey of Miss Leigh's person. He reached the conclusion that she was physically perfect, but that she had been ruined by her two years at Michigan State. It was a terrible thing, educating women. Education was something they didn't need. What did a woman with breasts and thighs like that want with education? As a babe she would have been terrific, as an educated woman, a college girl, she was—Miss Leigh. Well, one day he would see if he couldn't reform her. It irritated him seeing her sitting so close to Michiko, hanging on his words, interested by the cook in a way he was never able to interest her. He went briskly up to the table and spoke. "Better finish up that game soon if we're going over to the reefs to give the kids their skin-diving."

"Oh, you can take off any time, Alfred," Miss Leigh said, "I told the children they could get up when they heard the boat getting under way." She turned back to the Japanese. "What did you say was wrong with that last move of mine?" she asked.

"It just wasn't the right move, Miss Leigh," Michiko said. "You're remembering your own plans, but you aren't remembering that I have other plans. See what happens now!" He made a move which made no apparent difference to the situation.

"Oh, my goodness," squealed Miss Leigh, to whom it apparently made a lot of difference. Baffled and discontented, Alfred went forward to the bridge and began the routine for getting the boat moving. At about half past two they were over the reefs where the big bath sponges used to come from and Michiko went over the side with Thomas and Mary to teach them the art of undersea hunting. Bogey was not old enough to go with them, so this time, too, was lost for Alfred. He sourly stayed on the bridge and watched the surfacings and divings of the hunters through his glasses. When they had been gone an hour by the clock he hoisted a recall flag. The colored sailor who was supposed to be on the lookout for it didn't see it for another twenty minutes, by which time Michiko and both children were well under with the aqualungs. It was another ten minutes before they surfaced, and fifteen more before they were all, with the load of expensive equipment, masks, cylinders, undersea guns, and the catch of three big red snappers, back on the boat. Alfred started to give the sailor a piece of his mind as the launch was being hoisted on board on the stern davits, but as he began to get going Miss Leigh came up to him smiling sweetly to tell him that she didn't want any of that sort of thing in front of the children.

"All right, all right, but mind you say how things werc when I get hell from Mr. Hatfield for bringing the kids back late."

"Oh, Alfred, relax, you know we aren't that tight on time."

He took the *Plain Jane* back to the yacht basin in a fury. The smoke trails left on the horizon by real ships going to real places, and the sight of the ships lying at the wharves in the port of Maramee increased his temper. All his ambitions had come to this, a lifetime of fooling around as a rich man's servant, with all his free energy concentrated on making another member of the staff. He decided to punish himself.

"Mister Thomas," he called, "come up here on the bridge."

"Did you want me for anything special?" Thomas appeared in fresh shorts and a blue and white singlet, fair-haired and flawless-skinned, the perfect example of a soft, know-nothing, rich kid.

"I'm taking her off the automatic pilot now. I thought you might like to have the wheel as we go in. I'll tell you what to do. It'll be a kind of lesson, really."

Thomas took the wheel gravely and trustingly. Alfred told him what leading marks to look for at each turn in the channel, what engine speed to ring down for, and what signals to give on the hooter as they passed through the traffic in the roadstead and the river.

"I'm going to let you take her right in to the dock, Mister Thomas."

"Do you think that'll be all right?"

"You do as I say and it'll be all right." In an obscure way Alfred felt much better for teaching the rudiments of his job to a twelve-year-old boy. "We'll get you a master's certificate before you know where you are." They slid between the yachts

165

riding to buoys off the marina and then slipped in through its narrow entrance. The blank wall of piling under the glass-fronted club house loomed up straight ahead, terrifyingly close. Thomas bit his upper lip and tasted blood.

"Count five, slowly, and then put the port engine full astern and the starboard full ahead, while you put the helm hard over to starboard. Two, three, four, five," said Alfred. "And now full astern on both while you count fifteen. Three, four, five, six," he went on, ". . . fifteen. Now cut both and in she floats. There, I couldn't have done better myself."

The boat gently came into the wharf and touched with the faintest perceptible shudder. The Negroes leapt ashore with the nylon mooring ropes and the outing was over; Alfred switched off the ignition keys and the boat died. Thomas remained rooted to the ribbed rubber mat in front of the wheel, holding its spokes as if he couldn't really believe that the boat was in and safely alongside.

"That was just fine," said Alfred. "You did all right."

Miss Leigh came round the deckhouse to fetch Thomas, and to tell him to be sure not to leave anything in the boat he would want back at the Grove.

"I had the wheel the whole way from the outer mark, beyond the point," he said proudly. "I brought her in all by myself."

"He did," said Alfred, grinning.

"Of course, Alfred told me what to do, really," Thomas said.

"Well, you are a lucky little boy," said Miss Leigh. "First you catch us a great big red snapper, and now this!"

There was real enthusiasm on her face so far as Thomas could see, and in the glory of the moment he did feel that he was indeed as lucky as he could possibly be. He wanted to get back to the Grove quickly so as to tell his mother what a wonderful day it had been. He let go of the spokes of the wheel at last and ran towards the deck. When he was almost down at the far end of the deck where the gate in the rail was, he remembered something and ran back to the bridge.

"I was forgetting to thank you, Alfred," he said. "It was just great, every minute of it. Thanks a million." He ran off again.

"You nearly had the pee scared out of you, you poor little sod," said Alfred. He stayed on the bridge until the station wagon rolled out of sight, then he went back to *Profitable Sheep Farming* in his cabin. If he saved at his present rate for five more years he would be able to go ashore and get so far inland that he would never see the sea or even a bloody sea gull again. He turned to his favorite page in the book which showed a nice toppy lot of young lambs fattening on an open mountain meadow under the watchful eye of a mounted shepherd with a rifle in a saddle holster. There were mountains and pine woods in the background. Looking at the photograph Alfred could almost smell the cold, fresh, upland air. That would be the life. He rang the bell at the head of his bunk and waited for Michiko to appear. When the Japanese opened the door Alfred was lying back on his bunk with his arms folded behind his head making a kind of cradle.

"Michiko," he said, "I want you to bring me about a quart of vanilla ice cream with a real big dollop of butterscotch sauce over it. Let's see how quick you can get that up here."

"You'll be getting dinner in about three-quarters of an hour."

"O.K. O.K. What am I going to get?"

Miss Leigh was kind enough to give us one of the red snappers. I was going to boil it."

"The hell with fish. I'll take lamb chops. You can eat fish if you want. And send one of the boys ashore for a pie if you haven't time to make one for dessert. Tell him to go to that pastry shop on Basin Street. They have good pies."

"If that's what you want."

"That's what I want, Michiko." Alfred beamed happily. "See to it. And I'll still have that ice cream."

It was not at all bad, when you got down to it, being a yacht's captain for a man like Hatfield who had the money to do things properly.

At that moment, Miss Leigh with, as she put it, her fingers crossed, was driving up the avenue of live oaks dripping with gray streamers of Spanish moss which led up to the Grove from the old river road. She saw that Thomas, sitting beside her, was tense with his excited desire to tell his mother how he had handled the big boat, not just the outboard, right up the deep water channel and into the dock. Pity stirred in her. Looking straight ahead through the windshield and avoiding any sort of sideways glance at the boy, she tried to prepare the ground.

"I hope this isn't going to be one of those days when mommy has one of her headaches." She was aware that Thomas was scrutinizing her face carefully, but she was determined not to look at him.

"Do you think it will be?" he said quietly. "It's been a nice day."

"It could have been a headachy day inland."

"Oh."

"We'll just have to go in very quietly at first to find out. Then if your mother does have a headache we can tiptoe away without disturbing her."

"My mother has an awful lot of headaches, doesn't she?" he said. "More than most people."

"Oh no, dear, not really. She's just not very well sometimes."

They passed between two tall gate piers smothered in trumpet vines and entered the gardens of the Grove. The tires made an expensive crunching as they left the tarred surface and came onto the washed gravel of pale gray stones. Huge clumps of bamboo towered over them with shivering leaves. Culver had taken the design of the garden from a handbook on the subject which he had found reliable in New York State. In Florida it had let him down, or rather he had run into trouble by making certain substitutions. In the design he had pirated from the book, clumps of pampas grass had been called for at certain points, notably in a series of positions following the curve of the driveway as it led up to the house. Culver had substituted bamboos, thinking of feathery canes which would be seven or eight feet high, and which could be cut back to the neat rounds shown in the woodcut illustrations. Instead the ground had flung up thick muscular looking bamboo poles thirty to forty feet high which made a solid palisade along the track, giving the Grove the character of a place hidden deep in a mysterious jungle at the end of a shadow-dappled tunnel When the house came in sight, hidden till the last moment by a sharp bend in the drive, it was not less surprising than its approach. It was half a castle from some romantic Brontë land built round a tower which would only have been designed for the confinement of a gently mad prince, and half a dream of Persian luxury conceived by some merchant adventurer who had grown lecherous for shade in a lifetime of journeying across sun-scorched deserts. Wherever it was remotely possible to extend it by adding another veranda it had been done, and it was easy to imagine some dark and almond-eyed owner in the past ordering his builders to roof in yet more space and more shadow whenever he found himself within sight of a shaft of sunlight. Up the pillars, and over the roofs, of all these porches, crawled every kind of flowering or strangely fruiting vine and creeper. Thomas already knew a dozen ways to get in and out of the house by these green ladders and across the roofs without going near any door, and he had several times led Mary along these secret routes to go down through the darkness to swim in the lake in emulation of the night excursions of Tom Sawyer in search of treasure. Ilona knew nothing of these outings but Gavin did, Miss Leigh had asked him what she should do about them and he had told her to watch them but not to say anything. "Kids have the right to a little of that sort of thing after all, it'll be time to step in when they get to slipping out too often or to the wrong places. A moonlight swim now and again never hurt any child that age." The incident confirmed Miss Leigh's view that Gavin was a wonderful father and the Grove a wonderful place for a child to grow up. The familiar sprawling outline of the house came into view as the station wagon came out into the sunlight. In front of it Gavin could be seen setting himself into the seat of his pale-blue Cadillac convertible, its engine was running and as the station wagon pulled into the turning circle by the front steps the Cadillac began to glide forward.

"Blow the horn! Stop him!" cried Thomas. "He mustn't go now!"

"Daddy, daddy!" screamed Mary out of the window as Miss Leigh blew the horn.

"Well, you just caught me," said Gavin, pulling the Cadillac up alongside the other car. "What luck did you have?"

"Mary and I both got snappers, and I . . ."

"Those are really big fish. You're getting to be hot stuff," said Gavin looking at the trophies Mary was holding up. "What have you done with Bogey. You didn't chop her up and use her as bait, did you?"

"Oh, the sun and the sea air got her, Mr. Hatfield," Miss Leigh said. "She's asleep on the back seat."

"Can't you stay with us for a little while?" Thomas said, noticing that the engine of the Cadillac was still running.

"I'd like nothing better, old son," Gavin said, "but the Governor asked me to come along and see him before we go to dinner, so we could have a very important private talk before the other guests get there. So I have to be in his suite in the Beverly Hotel thirty minutes from now. I'm sorry, but that's how it is. Good night, son. Good night, Mary. Give Bogey a good-night kiss for me when she wakes up. See you tomorrow, Tiny. Now I've got to fly."

The car slid away from them into the shadowy tunnel of bamboos, and Miss Leigh drove up to the foot of the steps. Thomas looked up at the huge double doors with their bands of dark-blue and claret-red stained glass surrounding the big central plate-glass panels. From where he sat the hall looked to be full of darkness.

"I hate the Grove, I hate it," he said.

"You're overtired. You were under water too long. Michiko shouldn't have let you make that last dive. And then there was all that excitement on the trip back." Miss Leigh wanted him to believe her.

"That's got nothing to do with it," Thomas said. "The Grove's a horrid place. I wish we could leave it."

"Now you're being silly. Stop it and help me get the things out of the car." Miss Leigh paused. "And remember what I said about going in quietly. Something tells me Mommy does have one of her headaches."

They all went in on tiptoe, Miss Leigh carrying Bogey who snuffled into her shoulder sucking her thumb, still three parts asleep. They found Ilona lying back in a rattan chaise longue on the north porch, a glassed-in one which was almost entirely smothered by a furry stemmed vine with large heart-shaped leaves, and which was consequently filled with another-worldly greenish light. There was a tall jar of lemonade on a low hourglass-shaped cane table beside Ilona's chair. When she opened her eyes she seemed to have some momentary difficulty in focusing them.

"Oh, you've come back, my darlings," she said. "Did you have a good day?"

"We had a nasty day," Bogey said waking up. "Mary and Thomas were horrid to me about water skiing, and then Thomas was silly in the car coming home."

"Oh, you two big ones, you have to make allowances for my poor Bogey," Ilona said, yawning enormously. "How did it go, whatever you were doing?"

"Oh, all right," Thomas said.

"We each got red snappers, big ones," Mary said.

"Why that's wonderful," Ilona said, pouring herself a glass of lemonade. "Give them to Bailey, he'll be terribly pleased." She drank down the glass, and poured herself another. "I don't know why," she muttered, "I just have this terrible thirst."

"I'm afraid you've got one of your headaches again, Mrs. Hatfield," Miss Leigh said, noting something a little confused in Ilona's movements and a tendency for the liquid to slop awkwardly about in the glass as she held it. "I don't expect

171

you want to be bothered with us. We'll be getting along. Come on, kids, let's go."

"Yes." Ilona raised her eyebrows and let them fall, and then passed her hand dramatically across her forehead. "I've been on the rack all day—the afternoon was terribly oppressive. I'll say good night now, children, I don't think I'll be able to come upstairs later."

Mary and Bogey went over and kissed their mother good night, but Thomas said the word from where he stood and then left the room. Miss Leigh and the girls followed him up the huge staircase after they had taken the fish through to Bailey in the pantry.

"Bailey was delighted with your fish," Miss Leigh said when she found Thomas sitting on the end of his bed firing ping-pong balls out of a plastic machine gun at a teddy bear sitting at ease in an armchair. "He's going to give you some of the big one for your supper." She sat down beside him and put an arm round him, disregarding the shower of white balls which were rolling about the floor after having bounced off the bear's chest. "You really are a lucky kid, you know. Just think of all the things you've got. And all the things you do that other boys would like to get a chance to do—like going skin-diving out on the reefs whenever you want to—you won't go getting the idea you have it tough, will you? Just because your mother isn't well, I mean. You know, when people are ill they can't help themselves. They can't do what you'd like them to do, or what they'd like to do."

"Oh, I know," Thomas said. "It was just a letdown, that's all." He got up and gathered the white balls, loading them back into the gun. He walked away from the bear and thoughtfully shot at it again until the magazine was exhausted. He held the weapon in the aiming position for a couple of seconds, and then grounded the butt. "One thing you do I don't like, Miss Leigh, I hope you won't mind my saying this, you keep calling me lucky. I wish you wouldn't do that. It makes me nervous."

She got off the bed with a quickness which startled him, and knelt at his feet, tightly holding him to her.

"I'm sorry, Thomas. I'm truly sorry. Please forgive me."

"Oh sure," he said. He smelled her hair and stroked it. "I'm sorry if I upset you. I didn't mean to, honest I didn't."

She got to her feet running a hand through the gold stubble of his crew cut. "You may or may not be lucky, Thomas, but you're all right." She left the room briskly, telling him to take a shower to get the salt off his skin before he came down to supper. He said he would, but he stood where she left him for a good minute after she was gone, nervously cocking and firing the empty gun. He then went slowly up to the bear and eyed it for some time at close range as if weighing its tact and discretion. "I'll tell you what," he said at last, adopting a confidential manner. "I'll tell you what goes on here, B'ar Hatfield, my mother gets stinko, plastered, or however you like to say drunk, every time she's left alone." The bear said nothing although Thomas gave it a chance to reply, and stood attentively by it as if it might answer him. At the end of the silence the boy cried with indignation, "Well, you're a fine friend! A lot of help in a situation like this." He whacked the bear in the belly with the gun butt, and it burst, leaking bright yellow sawdust over the chair cushions. Thomas looked at his victim in horror and then flew to the door yelling for Miss Leigh.

"It's B'ar Hatfield! He's burst again."

Mary came running in her dressing gown with Bogey behind her in pyjamas.

"Gosh he's really sick this time!" Mary said. "We'd better get him into surgery right away."

"Have you got the sawdust for a transfusion?" Bogey said.

"He's lost one hell of a lot this time." She was scooping up sawdust from the cushion. "He looks emptied right out."

"It's funny how you can never pick up as much as comes out of him," Mary said. "You have still got that can of sawdust the carpenter gave you, haven't you, Thomas?"

"Yes, I have." Thomas was hopping from foot to foot. "Why doesn't Miss Leigh come?"

173

Miss Leigh came on the run as they all simultaneously cried "Miss Leigh, Miss Leigh."

"What's the matter, for heaven's sake."

"It's B'ar Hatfield. He's burst again. You've got to do something."

"Oh, my goodness. You kids are the limit." She was out of breath and indignant. "It's really too bad. I just refuse to mend that ridiculous bear again."

"You've got to, you've got to," the three children screamed together. "Please, Miss Leigh, it's a special bear—it's the B'ar, the only B'ar Hatfield."

"Oh, well. I'll mend it again. Just this once. But I won't do it unless you promise me you won't throw it about any more, or hit it, or whatever it is you do to it. The stuff's getting quite rotten. I'll have to patch it as it is. Give me that spare sawdust, Thomas, and I'll do my best."

They all crowded round her as she did the mending job. They had handkerchiefs over their faces as surgical masks, and Mary gave the bear anesthesia with a folded Kleenex soaked in cologne. It all seemed like a joke, but Miss Leigh realized that Thomas was in a desperate state of anxiety until the last stitch was in the new patch. All through the operation he kept muttering apologies to the bear, as if it were a real friend he had hurt in a hunting accident. She felt suddenly uneasy about what was going on. With deliberate casualness she hefted the bear by the leg and threw it over to Thomas.

"There you are. And that's for the last time. I must say I'm surprised at you, Thomas. You're too old for this sort of thing."

"I guess so." Thomas looked at the old toy. "Poor ol' B'ar," he said and looked at Mary. "You aren't too old for him, are you? Because if you are I'll hand him right on to Bogey, God help him. But it is my wish, purpose and design that you should become from this day forwards the guardian, custodian, and friend of B'ar Hatfield, formerly my trusted companion and adviser, to cherish and preserve him to the best of your ability, so help you God."

174

"So help me God," Mary said solemnly.

"I want him," Bogey said.

"You'll get him later," Thomas said. "Don't worry. You'll have him in good time when Mary's through with him."

When Miss Leigh went downstairs after the children had eaten their supper and gone to bed she was thinking how incalculable children were with their combination of inexperience and intuitive knowledge. She was wondering too if she ought to take Mrs. Hatfield in hand. She went across the hall and through the darkened drawing room into the north porch. Ilona was still lying in the cane chair. The jug of lemonade was almost empty and Ilona had half a glass in her hand. There was only a single, rather dim, reading light on in the porch, but Ilona had put on dark glasses. Miss Leigh sat down on the arm of the chair and put a cool hand on Ilona's forehead.

"How's that headache, Mrs. Hatfield," she said, "getting better?"

"Oh, it's a bad one, Tiny, one of my worst."

"Couldn't I get you something more effective than lemonade for it?"

"Honest to God, Tiny, when I have one of these headaches I think lemonade is the best drink there is for me. I'd sooner have it than anything I can think of. And I've come to think that our lemons here at the Grove are the finest and sweetest you can get anywhere on earth. Shall I ring and have Bailey fix you some, dear?"

"No, thank you, Mrs. Hatfield," Miss Leigh got up briskly. "I don't think I want any before my supper. I hope you're going to eat something tonight. You ought to eat, really you ought."

"With this headache I don't think I could."

"Oh, Mrs. Hatfield, would you take those dark glasses off and look at me, just for a minute?"

"The glare in here hurts my eyes."

"Why do you do it, Mrs. Hatfield? Why don't you stop

it? I wish you would. You know you must have had an awful lot of whiskey before you got onto lemonade."

"Maybe I did have a little shot round about four or five, just to steady my nerves."

"Please don't talk like that. You know you started drinking right after we left the house, and you were drinking all afternoon."

"Why that's ridiculous, Tiny, you know I don't like whiskey. When I take a little drop just to steady my nerves it's all I can do to swallow it down. I have to gulp it—like medicine —that's what I use it as really—and it makes me screw my face up. I really don't like it one bit. You're all wrong about my drinking too much. I can hardly bear the little I do take against my own inclination."

"I think Thomas is beginning to notice, Mrs. Hatfield."

"Notice what, Tiny? I hope you haven't been putting ideas into his head." She put her glass down and wagged an index finger at Miss Leigh. "That would be a wicked thing to do, oh, an abominable thing."

"Of course I haven't."

"I don't see where an innocent child would pick up such an idea." Mrs. Hatfield took off her glasses and stared penetratingly at Miss Leigh. "Maybe there's more to this than meets the eye." She faced the clear blue eyes which had never known passion, love, envy, fear, or hatred, for a few seconds and then faltered. "Yes, that's a silly idea, I'm being ridiculous."

Bailey, a tall, dignified colored man with a distant manner, came in and announced dinner. The meal was set out on the other side of the house in the little breakfast room at the end of the terrace, the masterpiece of Mickey Thurston, the Maramee decorator. It was modeled on a room in a Provençal farmhouse and had brightly checked pink gingham curtains which contrasted with the coarse white linen with which the chairs were upholstered. Mickey had provided appropriate table settings for the room and had taught Bailey how to set them up precisely and without variation. Bailey showed his contempt for what he called a fat-assed fairy of an ofay by carrying out the instructions given him to the letter. Everything was now neatly in place. The homespun napkins were on the thick ironstone soup plates from Normandy, the sets of eighteenth-century German cutlery with the procelain-handled knives were beside the plates, the heavy provincial silver pepper casters and salt pots from London were just where Mickey had insisted they should be beyond the green glasses from Majorca, and the candles burned serenely in the engraved glass chimneys bought in the Rue Royale in New Orleans but of unknown origin. Mrs. Hatfield ate two spoonfuls of the soup and crumbled a slice of bread, she ate a bite of fish, and a slice of tomato from her salad, she did not touch the guava jelly and cream cheese which was served as dessert.

"You better make a real big pot of coffee," Bailey said to Julia the cook when he took the fish back into the kitchen. "The Madam is really liquored up tonight."

Julia clucked. "Pore thing. That woman really do have something on her mind."

Bailey grunted. He knew what the sleeping arrangements in the house were as well as did the people who actually slept in their separate beds. "Ain't nothing but she-devils in this house," he said, and Julia flapped a dishrag at him. When they had finished their dessert the two women moved out through the French windows onto the terrace and sat down in the basket chairs grouped around a glass-topped table. There was no sign of a moon and the clear sky was crusted with brilliant stars. Ilona sipped her coffee and looked upwards.

"Do you ever think about God, Tiny, and what in hell it's all about?"

"No, Mrs. Hatfield. I'm pretty well content to accept things just the way they are."

"Well, I've been thinking about God a lot lately, Tiny, and you know what, this Protestant God I've been going along with all these years isn't good enough. Father Prieto's been showing me he's full of holes. I don't believe he stands up for me, any more."

177

"Are you thinking of becoming a Roman, Mrs. Hatfield?" Miss Leigh asked curiously.

"To tell you the truth I am." Ilona drained her coffee cup. "There's more comfort in what Father Prieto says than in anything I ever heard before. With that church you know where you are."

"Does Gavin know you're thinking of this, Mrs. Hatfield?"

"Him? Oh, no. He's too busy chasing other women to pay attention to me or anything I do. Why should he care what I think."

"I should think he would care a great deal."

"He will in good time. You can bet your bottom dollar on that."

"Oh, no! You aren't thinking of becoming a Roman just to make divorce difficult—"

"Difficult! I'm going to make it impossible, Tiny. I don't trust my own will power."

"That's horrible, Mrs. Hatfield, just horrible. You must be out of your mind!"

"Oh, my dear innocent Tiny, you've got a lot to learn. An awful lot." She yawned enormously. "I'm tired, terribly tired. I'm going to bed if you don't mind." She got up unsteadily and walked round the table. "Good night," she said and on an impulse kissed Miss Leigh on the top of the head. "I'm really fond of you, Tiny," she said, "you dear simple-minded thing. I feel about you just as if you were my own child. Good night and sweet dreams." She vanished into the depths of the house.

Miss Leigh watched her silhouette approach a softly lighted doorway and then saw her acquire color, texture, and volume as she stepped across the threshold into the light; Ilona turned and waved, as if warned by telepathy that she was being watched. Her smile seemed easy, natural and free from malice, she moved gracefully and she was attractive and pretty. Miss Leigh waved back and then walked down to the lake in the darkness. She sat on the boat dock with her long legs dangling over the edge towards the water. Peering downwards she could see the reflections of the stars in the water. The night about her was full of mysterious hushed noises. She felt that there was something absolutely terrible about life and wondered what it was. Ilona, she thought, was playing a really dirty trick on Gavin, and she would like to make it up to him in some way. She decided she would go to Dr. Kaleciewicz at the Buena Vista clinic again and have him give her the hormone injections he had once spoken of as an extreme last resort. She felt Gavin deserved a woman who would appreciate him and who would respond normally. She did appreciate him and if she could fix up the normal response perhaps she would be able to give him some of the happiness he deserved but which he was being denied. She turned back towards the Grove and saw it blackly outlined against the glare from the hundreds of neon lights and arc lamps of Maramee which filled the western sky.

The hormones proved to be a sensational success, and Miss Leigh was married a year later to a veterinarian from her home town in Michigan who had fallen in love with her in high school and who had never abandoned hope. She was what he had always wanted, and he was blissfully happy when he got her. His content quickly made her forget how little she had been able to do for Gavin by giving herself to him. She knew she had given him pleasure, and she had enjoyed herself increasingly each night they had spent together. And yet their acts had changed nothing so far as the trouble in the Grove was concerned. When she had been Gavin's mistress for a month she felt more helpless and irrelevant than she had ever done in the whole of her life. Ilona, whose conversion had taken place without other notable effects than the introduction of a crucifix, a prie dieu, a few crosses of palm, two or three religious books, and a picture of the Madonna into her bedroom, had instantly divined their relationship and had tormented Miss Leigh with ambiguous remarks which had left no room for doubt as to the extent of her knowledge and the state of her feelings. Miss Leigh's departure had had about it a quality of panic-stricken flight. She was overwhelmed with

179

distress when the time came to go and wept copiously all her last morning, new freshets of tears being set off constantly by familiar things which would not come her way again, such as seeing Mary brush her hair, or catching sight of B'ar Hatfield's much-patched person on Mary's dressing table, or getting an awkward hug and kiss from Thomas. After Gavin had driven her off down the drive on her way to the airport the children came in from the steps where they had been waving her their farewells.

"What do you suppose made her so weepy?" Mary said to Thomas. "Isn't she going home to marry some man she's in love with?"

"I don't know." Thomas kicked the edge of a rug. "I used to have her figured out so I could pretty well tell what she'd do or say, in a situation, but then I sort of got lost with her, I mean I couldn't tell any more."

"Tell what?"

"Oh, you know. What would make her mad, what you could get away with, how she *was*." He emphasized it. Lying in his room on hot still nights he had been able to hear the whisperings of lovers across a creeper-covered roof, the agitations of lovemaking, and the gaspings of release. He brushed his face as if a spider's web had fallen upon it. Straining to overhear, he had never actually heard a single word, nor had he ever known for sure that the whisperers had been Tiny and his father, nor what that strange shuddering drawn-out sigh had meant. The whole subject was one which he felt doubtful about, he felt with equal strength a desire to know much more about it and to know a great deal less.

In the car Miss Leigh wept uncontrollably and Gavin pulled in to the side of the road halfway to the airport to try to comfort her. He cradled her in one arm and dried off her tears with a handkerchief as if she were a child .

"Look, if you don't want to go North you don't have to," he said. "But I thought you'd decided you really wanted to marry this man of yours."

"I have. I do," she sobbed, and bit the hand she had put up

to her mouth. When she took it away he saw the tooth prints in her flawless flesh. "I feel such a fool," she said. "Forgive me."

"What's it all about?" he said. "If you spit it out you'll feel better."

"I wish that was true," she said. "But you won't even understand what I'm saying if I do tell you." She fingered his lapel. "You're being so nice, and I'm being so awful. I'm ashamed. I really am. I'll tell you. I wanted to give you something, I don't know what, something important that would make you happy the way you deserve to be happy and, oh, what's the use . . ." Two large tears ran down her cheeks and he mopped them up with his expensive square of linen. "I couldn't do a damn thing for you, Gavin, could I?"

"You were very sweet to me. You made me just as happy as I deserved to be." He took her hand and held it. She looked down at his hands and then swiftly up into his face, so that she caught him unprepared and with a naked face on which his knowledge of life was exposed. He jerked up his wrist and looked at his watch.

"We'll have to get on if you're really meaning to catch that plane."

"Oh, Gavin," she said. "I knew so much a year ago. I knew how to live. The way I know how to ride a bicycle. And now I don't know anything at all."

"Will you promise me something?" he said. "When you get up there promise me you'll think what you're doing. Don't just marry that man up there because you can't think of anything better to do. Make sure it's a real thing, because if it isn't . . ."

"Oh, it's a real thing, all right. He's hell bent on having the biggest and best animal hospital in the central part of the state. That's an ambition I can understand. I can help him with that. I'm sure of it. That's about all I am sure of now. I cling to it. It's got to work out. And I'm going to make it work out." She patted his knee with a that's-that gesture and sat up straight. "I want to get on that plane, Gavin. Don't think I haven't thought of a lot of other things, because I have. But they wouldn't any of them do."

When Gavin saw her last walking across the apron to the plane which was to take her to New Orleans on the first leg of her journey home, stiffly, proudly, and determinedly not looking back, his feeling was primarily one of intense relief. Recognizing it for what it was did not give him any pleasure at all. He stood at the wire barrier watching the rituals of airline departure through to their end and felt that he was seeing an ambulance taking away the victim of some piece of abnormally careless driving on his part. Of course, she had been driving carelessly too, but she had the excuses of youth and inexperience. She had been an idiot, but he should have known better than to take advantage of her idiocy. But it was worse than that. The plane was carrying away a thing more precious than Miss Leigh's delicious flesh and confused warm spirit. It was taking away for good and all Gavin's belief in his own youth. The days in which he believed that a new woman could change everything in his life were over. Once it had seemed to him that there was a whole new future on the far side of every bed which had a woman in it: it might be that she would be the one to set him marching off into another country leaving the ashes of his abandoned boats black and gray on the beach behind him. He had taken Miss Leigh because she was going, an available body. It had nearly got him into trouble because laying the help always did get you into trouble. There was no more to it than that. He had become just another of those older men who took what they could get when they could get it because their passions were dying away and leaving them with mere irritating appetites. It would be nice to think that he was maturing and not just wearing out, but he could not dodge the truth. He had used Miss Leigh as he might have used a cake of soap, he had never come within a mile of opening his heart to her or of penetrating hers. He had never wanted to know her or to be known by her. And his reaction to her distress at leaving him and failing him had been simply to want her out of the way at the greatest possible speed.

The plane came unstuck and lifted into the sky. He watched it diminish and idly watched a two-engined light plane drop in on the field. He heard a noise, an enormous fingernail being drawn across an endless sheet of silk and saw one of the huge obsolete giants of the Strategic Air Command coming in to land at the William Arling Field out across the vast expanse of flat sour land lying to the northeast of the civil airport. Eight million dollars worth of junk drifted in towards the end of the longest paved runway in the country, a road to nowhere floated, regardless of expense, on a bog. The huge silvered machine, with its swept-back wings and its dangling engine pods, touched down and skittered across the landscape for two miles, while another of the big bombers circled in its approach pattern and a third wheeled still further out. It amazed Gavin to think of what the B-29 boys, on the strength of their Pacific headlines, had been able to put over on the Congress and the public since the war. His eye traveled round the mournful plane of salt marsh with its thin groves of stunted turpentine pines growing on the gravel ridges. Unconsciously, as he counted the bombers dispersed all over their field, he smelt the brackish wind blowing off the six-mile-wide, ankle-deep, salt-water lagoon lying beyond the runways and between them and the sea itself. He counted thirty-two planes at eight million dollars each. Somewhere among them all, he knew there was a fighter squadron though he couldn't for the moment pick out its machines, and in any case didn't know their cost. His eye drew in towards the civil airport's brand new control-tower and departures wing, all white concrete and glass brick. MacKaffey and Harmann, the contractors, were lengthening the north-south runway out beyond the little dip which invariably harbored a small mirage at this time of day, seeming to hold a lake of shimmering blue water. A cluster of airliners stood round the buildings, and behind them was the park holding over eighty privately owned and company-owned planes varying in size from DC-3's to little playtime single seaters. Among them all Eddie Riemann's old but beautifully kept up Mustang looked like an enormous shark in its gray and black trim. Eddie flew it more often than he would admit to, but it still amounted to less than two hours a week the year round, even when his flights up to Colorado for skiing weekends were included. It was by any standards an incredibly expensive toy. He wondered idly who owned it nominally, and by what device the taxpayer was made to carry the cost. His *Plain Jane* was the property of something called Tidelands Sulphur. He often wondered if the frequency with which his picture appeared in the paper along with that of the Governor, the state senators, and important visitors from Washington had anything to do with the taxman's readiness to accept the yacht as a necessary part of the company's operations. "We're all getting away with murder," he said to himself, "or at any rate hell's own amount of squalid pilfering." He felt for the car keys in his pocket as he turned away from the fence, and wryly remembered that the blue convertible belonged to the bank and was allocated to his use as the bank's senior officer. "Well, it's all part of the system," he said, "and who am I to want to turn the world upside down."

He drove back into town along the specially built four-lane airport drive lined with billboards, and turned off onto Granby Boulevard at the interchange on the crest of the fifty-seven-foot ridge of sand and gravel which caused that district to be a sought-after suburb and gave it its name of Maramee Heights. Looking down Granby from the interchange Gavin saw the familiar view. His own tower and the five other towers clustered together with a mysterious inanity in the middle of the sprawl of three-to-five-story wooden and brick houses and stores. Right among them was the bottle, or so it appeared from the end of Granby, though it was in reality down on the waterfront. As always Gavin wondered if he would ever see it taken down. Granby Boulevard seemed to be aligned to it the way the Champs Elysées is aligned to the Arc de Triomphe, and from upper Granby it looked like some ironically conceived civic monument. It was a water tank of unusually large size crowning a sturdy metal tower rising up above the roof of a warehouse. As such it was perfectly unobjectionable, but it supplied water to the distillery of which the warehouse was a part, and in the first hectic months of the end of Prohibition, its owner had given it every detail of the appearance, revenue stamp and all, of a fifth of his product—a whiskey which was neither good nor bad, but cheap, wet, and intoxicating. It had been a cheerful celebrant gesture when it was first put up and only the diehard temperance groups had objected at the time. But the joke had worn thin over the years, and finally the bottle had become the bone of contention between the old-timers who thought Maramee was going to hell in a hat and the new men who were running the boom. City Hall was in the middle so far as the record went, but secretly for the bottle, just as it was against the numbers racket for the record and in it behind the scenes. Gavin had once tried to reason with Chuck Hallet who owned the distillery and had told him the bottle was actually doing his business harm by annoying possible customers.

"Mr. Hatfield," Hallet said. "You're insulting my intelligence. You've never considered purchasing a bottle of my whiskey in all your born days. None of your friends has ever considered doing so. And I'll tell you for why. It's not a gentleman's whiskey. I'd puke if I drank it myself. That's a drink for a pig—a man in a bar who wants a drink to hit him in the throat as it goes down. That bottle's a joke. It gets on postal cards that go all over the country. The name's a joke. Old Wool Hat. I hold anyone who drinks such stuff in contempt, and I know damned well that the minute I stop insulting my customers by taking up with genteel advertising methods such as you would approve of, my bar flies would leave me in droves. That bottle up there's a flag for idiots to rally to, Mr. Hatfield, and I can't afford to take it down. I'm sorry if it's an aggravation to you, but it keeps me wealthy and comfortable, and that's my last word on that subject."

So there it was. And even night brought no relief. In the darkness it hung suspended like a vision in the shadowless glare of groups of floodlights aimed at it from the roof tops of the distillery's other buildings. In its constantly freshened

185

paint it outshone even the gilded dome of City Hall four blocks away. It faced businessmen as they emerged through the heavy bronze doors of the First National Bank building, it stared down at the tourists who had been eating pompano in a paper bag in the famous Viscayana restaurant downtown, it leered at lecherous conventioneers coming out of Las Muchachas, the unspeakably bawdy strip joint in the North End beyond the freight yards, it stood between heaven and the worshipers who came loaded with virtue out onto the marble steps of Santa Eulalia, the Roman Catholic cathedral, and it hung, replete with error over the cloister Garden of Reflection at the back of the Church of Christ Scientist. It reminded Gavin always of one of his most complete defeats. He had tried to eliminate it with a trick clause in a city ordnance regulating potentially dangerous rooftop structures, but the maneuver had been detected, and had been beaten not by Hallet and his cohorts of ward-heeling regulars, but by the group of the new men of Gavin's own party who were interested in billboards and sky signs. The advertising crowd had had the clause removed before it got to the floor at the council meeting. The sun twinkled on it as Gavin looked down Granby, so that it seemed to wink triumphantly at him as if to remind him that the postcard with the inscription "The Big Bottle, Maramee's most famous sight" was still being mailed home by thousands of visitors, and as many thousands of servicemen stationed in the neighborhood every year, and would go on being a seller for years to come. There was not much comfort in Granby Boulevard itself when Gavin dropped his eyes from the bottle. Upper Granby had been hit by the backwash of the downtown boom in an altogether unexpected way. What had been the spacious gardens of houses built by the better element in the 'twenties had become used-car lots jam-packed with automobiles lined up, side by side and head to tail like steers in the pens of a crowded cattle market. The quiet old families who had moved out would say that upper Granby had gone downhill terribly since they had left, but such people as Cash Down Schulman, the Generous Dutchman, Martinez of

186

Fair and Square Sales, and Crew Cut Cushman the Bargain King could and did argue that they had brought new life to the neighborhood. "Nothing happened here then, Mr. Hatfield, the place was dead you know that. Now we have here in these six blocks the used-car capital of the gulf, you have to admit that's progress." Gavin looked at the strings of fluorescent pennants, the signs that twirled in the wind like prayer wheels, the balloons painted with slogans, and the tawdry canvas banners, and wondered. In the middle of it all he ran into a traffic jam. It had piled up where two huge army-surplus searchlights were being maneuvered into position in the entry of a newly finished steam bakery which was to have its gala opening that night. The searchlights were eased up ramps past signs showing the usual cute freckled and pigtailed child with enormous eyes saying, "Ooh Mommy, Meltene," as she clasped an immense honey-colored loaf to her chest. As the jam began to melt and to pour on down the avenue Gavin saw another sign at the corner of the block. "You'll feel better if you go to Church next Sunday—the makers of Meltene Bread, your new neighbors, have donated this space to the United Faiths Attendance Drive as a community service." Gavin drove on downtown asking himself who, if anyone, the makers of Meltene thought they were fooling, who was supposed to believe in Schulman's generosity, or in Martinez as a character who would put equity before profit? It struck him with renewed force as he approached the young city's center how much of what was supposed to be new, bright, and gay that its traders were offering to its inhabitants was in fact tawdry and fraudulent, and how many of the offers of finer, better, easier, sweeter, things were simply lies. The drive from the airport to his bank building was a forty-minute study period in a course in cynicism and disbelief. At the lights, he watched the milling streams of people on the sidewalks and in the safety lanes, looking at their faces, and asking himself with amazement how, so abused as they were, they could retain any faith or trust in their society or even in human decency itself.

Gavin drove his car into the entry of the garage across the

street from his building and told the colored man who came to take it that he would want it, gassed up, at four-thirty. "Yes, sir, Mr. Hatfield," the man replied respectfully. Gavin knew him by sight but did not know him well enough ever to have discovered that he had been one of the slightly scared group who had seen Maggs threatening him with a razor in the old days when the nine-story concrete-frame garage had been a simple gas station and parking lot. His respect for Gavin had its origin in that incident as the starting point in a supposed sequence of events faintly relating to reality which had acquired the status of history among a wide circle across the river. Maggs had threatened Hatfield to try to warn him not to move in on Morgantown, but Hatfield didn't scare that easy. He had come on into Maggs' territory just the same and he didn't stop even when Maggs actually went after him and cut him so's he was marked up for judgement day. Hatfield took his time and when he was good and ready had got his gunman Manson to kill Maggs on some no-account pretext or other. Then when he'd come back from the war Hatfield had moved right in. Morgantown had lost its independent charter and had been incorporated into Maramee City. Victory Boulevard had been cut right through the center of it, one way, and the old open sewer and garbage dump called the Canal had been filled in to make a road running slap through it in the other direction. Not only that, but the marsh called Carters Spit by the old-timers had been filled in and built up as a fancy residential district for ofays. Hatfield had made plenty out of that development and they said he had made even more out of floating the bond issue which had paid for the toll-free lower bridge. Morgantown had changed in all sorts of ways. It was certainly cleaner, for one thing, and quieter for another, now that it was run from City Hall and policed by the city police. But it was no longer the colored man's town it had been. While it was all right in a way not to be plagued by men like Maggs any more, and not to have the old bullies with their razors hanging round town, it was doubtful if the Sicilians who took their orders from Amato the Butcher who had, under the new regime, taken over the numbers game and the prostitution were that much better to have around. A lot of the old Morgantown crowd had just pulled up stakes and moved away to other places round the gulf where the ofays didn't give a damn what happened in the colored part of the city. But however you looked at it Hatfield had done the job in Morgantown he had set out to do. He was a big man and a powerful man, and his car would be there, right next to the ramp, at four-thirty, with the tank full and the engine running.

When Gavin got into his office he found Manson, now the head of the state police force, waiting for him there. He was never in uniform these days, unless on ceremonial parades, but his body remained stubbornly uniformed under his Palm Beach suit, and his expensive tropical straw hat with its colored band looked like some improbable piece of fancy dress in his large red hand. Age did not seem to have changed him at all, his hair was the same bright light ginger as ever, and his skin had the same rufous all-over glow. His eyes were perhaps a somewhat paler blue. He was looking out at the view over the city and the port when Gavin came and stood beside him.

"Hallo there, Colonel," Manson said.

"Good heavens, man, do you even follow the postings of officers in the reserve?"

"You know me, Gavin, I like to scare people, or fool 'em a little by pretending to know everything." He gestured at the plumes of white steam and darker smoke rising from a hundred places among the myriad rooftops and towers, and at the fourteen merchant ships in from foreign ports. "This place sure has changed since we first got acquainted. It was a dead-and-alive hole in those days, if the truth be told. But I sort of liked it."

"So did I. Remember the Viscayana when it was a real Spanish restaurant, and they'd give you the best meal you could get on the gulf coast, New Orleans included, for a dollar fifty?"

"You sound as if you'd been fool enough to go there lately."

"Oh, Tiger, it was wicked. A party of seven, a few drinks,

a little wine, some of their wretched steam-table food, and a bill for a hundred and sixteen dollars."

"We're talking like old men, about how good things used to be. We ought to watch it. It can take hold," the policeman said.

Gavin put his hand on Manson's arm. "You didn't come here to trade small talk with me. I know you. What's on your mind?"

Manson licked his lips, and he avoided meeting Gavin's eyes. "I maybe shouldn't of come," he said. "Now I'm here I sort of wish I hadn't." He hesitated. "I've always played my game straight. I've never let any personal matter get involved in any police matter. It's been the rule I've lived by, and the rule I've done a good job by—but this thing has come up . . ." He broke off.

"You aren't in any kind of trouble are you, Tiger? If you are you know you can count on me for anything."

"Hell, no." Manson picked up his hat and looked inside it. "You are. Or you could be—well, it isn't you—though the publicity might affect you. There's talk of running you for governor, and this would kill it."

"Say, have I been seen in the wrong place, at the wrong time, with the wrong woman?" Gavin laughed. "You don't have to worry about that—so far as spoiling my political chances goes —I don't want to be governor or anything in that line."

"You're just making things as difficult for me as you can, Gavin. I don't want to make difficulties between a man and his wife, but there's times when it can't be helped. You're a rich man, Gavin. You can afford to hire a chauffeur. You take my advice and hire one just as soon as you can. And when you've got him take them car keys away from your wife and don't ever let her have them back."

"Has she hit someone?"

"Not yet. But three times now she's been stopped by my cars. Weaves all over the road. Scaring hell out of people. She's been lucky. Luckier than she deserves to be. Twice she was in a condition where one of my men had to take the wheel and drive her home. It can't go on, Gavin. Or if it does there'll be one end to it that I don't want to see. You get that chauffeur, Gavin."

"Thanks, Tiger. It's been good of you to cover up for her."

"Good! I feel ashamed to tell God's truth. Why, she could be out now killing some child or other or a man or a woman. But I thought what it could mean to you, and I did it this way. I don't really have the right to give you privileges, Gavin, so do me the favor back of keeping that woman off the road."

"I'll do my best," Gavin put his hand on Manson's shoulder and let it rest there for a moment. "Thanks."

"Well, you do that thing, and I'll say thanks to you, Gavin boy." Manson smiled awkwardly. "I've got to be getting along. I'll be seeing you." He looked briefly into Gavin's eyes to see how he had taken his medicine and then turned and went. Gavin stood looking at the door through which he had disappeared for half a minute. He was calculating the number of people who knew of the existence of the rotten spot at the center of his life and finding it disquietingly large. He had always thought of what lay between him and Ilona as their own secret; it had never really occurred to him that their marriage was a public performance given before a crowded and not in the least exclusive house. He looked at the large plate-glass windows through which he had so often surveyed the wide spread of Maramee with a new thought that he had set himself up in a high place where Maramee could get a perfect view of him. He wondered how much the town understood of what went on, and he recalled how strange and incomprehensible the action of movies seemed when one caught glimpses of them, distorted and without the clues of the sound track, on the screens of drive-in cinemas briefly visible from nearby highways. The shock of Manson's revelation that Ilona was not only his private problem, but also a concern to the state police began to wear off, and his habits resumed their control. Something would have to be done about Ilona, and he wanted it to be the right thing. He sat down on his desk and clicked down the key of the inter-office telephone. "Come in here a minute, Miss Lumley."

Miss Lumley came crisply into the office looking keenly at him through her contact lenses, neat and correct from top to toe. She had made a career of self-abnegation, having abandoned all her hopes for a normal life when in the year in which she graduated from college she had refused to put her crippled and retarded brother into an institution and dedicated the remainder of her life to his care and support. Her brother, Joey Lumley, was sunnily happy and gloriously healthy and secure at thirty-five in the twelve-year-old boy's world she had preserved for him and he seemed likely to live forever in spite of his handicaps. He might outlast her, but even if he did not he had outlived her youth and would certainly see her middle age go by. She already knew what the greater part of her life would be. Her little house, on the edge of the Heights district, was always bright with flowering pot plants and the new toys Joey loved to play with. Under the grape arbor on the south wall of the house three canaries sang, and the budgies they raised hopped about on their perches. At one time Miss Lumley had thought Joey might earn himself pocket money by selling the budgies, and thus develop a sense of responsibility, or of relationship to the outside world. But he had cried so when it came to parting with them that she couldn't let the man from the pet store take them away. Miss Lumley liked reading to Joey in the arbor in the evenings after she had turned on the little fountain down in the garden which played in a basin between the clipped rosemary hedges she was so proud of. The sleepy birds occasionally let out a peep or hopped from perch to perch and Joey would do a jigsaw puzzle on the tray table pulled across his wheeled chair. They would go through Dickens, the *Tanglewood Tales*, *Tom Sawyer* and *A Connecticut Yankee at King Arthur's Court*, *A Girl of the Limberlost*, and all their old favorites time and time again, and got to love the dear old books more and more. They were two of the happiest people in Maramee, and Miss Lumley was devotedly loyal to Gavin who was the best of employers—not only because he was generous with bonuses, but also because he always remembered Joey on his birthday and at Christmas with some toy with hundreds of parts to put together, but without any of the nasty little buzzing motors with wires which frightened and upset him. Miss Lumley always made Joey remember Gavin in his prayers at bedtime, and remembered him in her own, thanking God nightly for having guided her to leave her particulars with the agency just before Gavin applied to it for a secretary. Gavin often thanked God for the same thing, though in a rather different spirit. He was endlessly grateful for the luck which had given him a girl with so little in the way of ambition, character, and personality, that she amounted to a mere serviceable presence, a factor in his life and in office politics almost as neutral and uncomplicating as another office machine. When she came into the room he smiled and greeted her.

"This is something a little out of our usual line, Miss Lumley," he said. "I want you to get me some books. Find out what the best standard works are on the subject of alcoholics and alcoholic addiction. Call up three or four medical men in the field and get their recommendations—buy the books they all agree on. And one other thing. Find out the books I ought to read on adolescents and their problems; I suppose the psychiatrists who specialize in dealing with young people are the ones to ask on that. My young people are beginning to grow up and I see shoal water ahead of me. I'll be in trouble before I know where I am if I don't watch out. See if you can round me up a little library by the end of the week, Miss Lumley."

The point of her pencil broke with a sharp crack as she pressed it into her pad, an exclamation escaped her.

"Oh, no!"

Gavin looked at her curiously, as Balaam might have looked at his ass. She was staring at him with an expression he had never seen on her face before.

"Don't ask doctors what to do, Mr. Hatfield. They're terribly cruel people. They don't understand human beings. They like shutting people up, behind bars, and doing things to them. Don't turn to doctors, not if it's anyone you love, please, Mr. Hatfield. Trust your instincts. They'll tell you what to do." Her voice died away. "Really they will."

Gavin jingled the keys on his key ring without taking them out of his pocket. He looked sourly at the ruins of the once-perfect secretary who had so unexpectedly betrayed him by turning into a human being.

"That's all right, Miss Lumley," he said. "Perfectly all right. Only what my instincts tell me these days doesn't happen to have anything much to do with what goes on. Now be a good girl, and get me those books. We all of us have to go to hell in our own way you know."

Miss Lumley ran blindly from the room, leaving Gavin alone to look out at his city and his world, places whose perspectives became stranger and less familiar the more he studied them and tried to understand them.

Chapter Six

MISS RODMAN followed Miss Leigh and stayed for a few months until she grew foolish or overconfident and began to talk coyly to Ilona about "our little failing," and to propose a joint campaign to wrestle with it. "I know we're of different faiths, dear," she said, "but it can't hurt for us to pray side by side. If we make a clean breast of all the little tarradiddles and deceptions our failing has led us into, and tell God the whole story, I just know he'll help." Ilona happened to be stone cold sober at the time Miss Rodman made her approach, and had been so for three days because a severe intestinal grippe had been making her feel too miserable to touch a drop. Her nerves were on edge for that reason, and also because when she had strayed into Gavin's downstairs study on the previous day looking for a stamp to put on a letter she had discovered that he was boning up on the medical and psychological aspects of drinking. The discovery had irritated her as much as if she had overheard Gavin discussing some utterly private aspect of their life with a stranger. "Why you common, vulgar, little woman," she said, standing up in her outrage and letting Miss Rodman have the full measure of her accumulated feelings, "you don't know anything about God, and you know nothing at all about me. You can take yourself and all that soft soap you've got from Norman Vincent Peale out of my house this minute, just as quick as you can pack up and go." Miss Rodman had not been prepared for martyrdom in the cause of her amorphous faith, and an acute sense of wrong pervaded her when she found herself undergoing it, at least to the extent of losing a good job. What she had wanted was a nice true-confessions session with Ilona in which she would establish herself in the cozy role of a confidant and hear what all her troubles were. She had some troubles to offer in fair exchange. She had been seduced and abandoned during the war by a dreadful man who . . . but Ilona was never to hear that sad story, she heard instead some frightened bleatings, and then some craven appeals for a second chance. But Ilona had her out of the house within two hours of the commission of her fatal error.

Miss Rodman's successor was a strong-minded young woman who had recently graduated from business school and who had no intention of wasting her qualifications. She stayed for a month and then went to Gavin and resigned.

"I'm afraid I have to go, Mr. Hatfield. This isn't a secretarial post." She hesitated. "I like the children and I'm sorry to leave them. But I don't care for the rest of it all." She hesitated again. "I mean it's a nurse's job, really, if it's anyone's."

Her departure marked the end of the pretense that Ilona had a social secretary. After that there were housekeepers and a governess for the children. Miss Wilbraham the housekeeper, who finally stayed and became a fixture, lived out, in a neat cottage built for her halfway down the avenue. She came and went as unobtrusively as possible, avoiding Ilona so far as she could and referring all questions of difficulty to Gavin through Miss Lumley down at the office. Twice a week she came in during the morning before Ilona was out of bed and did the flowers. She had taken courses in flower arrangement and her knowledge of the art was highly developed. She had the gift of making flowers straight from the garden look as if they had been bought from a florist, or as if they were smartly turned out employees who were on duty with orders to look cheerful. Ilona surprised her at work one morning, catching her as she arranged a vase of white phlox, blue and white irises and pink tulips under a large looking glass at one side of the hall.

"My goodness, Miss Wilbraham, are those real flowers?"

"Yes, Mrs. Hatfield, they came in from the garden this morning."

"I could have sworn they were artificial. Are you sure they're real?"

"Quite sure, Mrs. Hatfield." Miss Wilbraham did not get angry, or even annoyed, although she knew very well that Ilona was trying to get under her skin.

"You really have a knack with flowers, dear, the place has looked quite different since you took them over."

"Thank you, Mrs. Hatfield." Miss Wilbraham pretended to be dumb enough to take it as a compliment. She had learned that a reputation for being a little on the slow side had very real tactical advantages in establishing a relationship with an awkward employer. She did not know what was wrong with Ilona and she was taking care not to find out. But while she did not want to get involved she did not want to seem indifferent, so she put in her time on the flower arrangements. The vases were always full of fresh flowers, and there were a great many of them all through the house. Gavin saw them, and saw that trouble was taken with them. He thought they were rather wooden and formal bunches, and that they gave the house a slightly unsettled resemblance to a well-run hotel, but then Miss Wilbraham was not too bright, and she was trying her level best to please. And so far as keeping the house running with a minimum of trouble was concerned she was unbeatable; she made it seem as if the house ran itself. Ilona wondered vaguely if Gavin realized how God-awful the place was becoming under Miss Wilbraham's regime, and waited for him to make some protest. But while he had become more attentive to her he had become apparently oblivious to much else. She took to reading the books on alcoholism which he was reading in order to find clues to his behavior, studying them attentively during the day while he was at the office. It amused her that he should be steeping himself in so much which so clearly had little or nothing to do with her case; her nerves were bad, and she suffered from these terrible spells of acute tension. A little whiskey enabled her to relax and though she got no pleasure from it she preferred to take whiskey rather than to resort to drugs. She could, she supposed, use Miltown or some such tranquilizer, but she didn't like the idea of drugs which could so easily take a hold of you. Whereas whiskey was something

197

she didn't even enjoy, and had to swallow like some nasty medicine. She explained all this to Gavin, not once but several times, and it seemed strange to her that he should go on believing that she was drinking. As he was so morbidly suspicious she became reluctant to let him see her actually taking a drink. She began to hide bottles in her room, in odd parts of the house, and in the gardens, so that from almost anywhere where she could legitimately be with an iced drink in her hands, she could drift a few paces away out of sight, swiftly reinforce it from a bottle, and return within a few seconds. At first Miss Wilbraham was concerned at the rate liquor was disappearing, bottles and all, but before she was forced to adopt some kind of preventive device Ilona had recognized and circumvented this danger. She gave up Maurice, the coiffeur at the beauty shop she had been frequenting for years, and put her hair into the hands of Jackie Prosser at the Beverly Hotel. Mrs. Prosser's shop opened off the main lobby and had a street entrance on Claibourne Avenue. The chauffeur could put her down and pick her up on the avenue without ever having to know that she had been through to the gift shop across the lobby where they sold souvenirs, stuffed toys, perfumes, candy, and the better grades of liquor in gift packages. Ilona suddenly saw the point of the new enormous handbags that had come into fashion and bought two or three of them in colors that went with her various outfits. They looked smart, and they could hold three full-sized bottles of Scotch without a hint of a bulge or of any strain. As Ilona went into Maramee for her beauty treatments and to have her hair washed and set every Monday and Friday, she had all problems of supply neatly licked. She was worried for a time by the gay ribbons, striped or gilded papers, and the decorative cartons which encumbered the bottles, but she soon found the answer to that one. There were numbers of boxes in her closets holding old hats which had gone out of fashion long before they had been worn out. Her stubbornly surviving streak of New England prudence made it hard for her to throw anything away that had any wear left in it, so there the hats remained, each one in its round cardboard case and in its inner nest of soft white tissue paper. It was a simple matter to double up a couple of hats and to use the hat box left empty as a hiding place for the wrappings. It was surprising how much neatly folded paper and tightly rolled ribbon a hat box would hold. When she had this system of supply and disposal fully organized she was able to face Gavin's attempts to reform her with a serenity which baffled him. He took her down into the Caribbean for a cruise on the *Plain Jane*, thinking that he could dry up her source of supply on the boat and force the subject into the open when she started begging for a drink. He never realized that she had brought three bottles on board in her big red leather and woven straw handbag; that there were two more in her shoe case; and that half the bottles in her fitted dressing case, supposedly filled with liquid shampoos, face lotions, colognes, liquid cleansers, were in fact filled with Scotch. She had known what the trip was all about by instinct from the minute Gavin first spoke of it, and she had relished it from the first minute to the last. She had rationed herself resolutely and had detemined to win the contest. She never allowed herself to get really plastered, but by taking nips at regular intervals all through the day from morning to night had kept herself just on the nearside of the brink. Gavin had only realized what she was doing on the second to last day of the cruise. He had been sitting in his basket chair on the poop deck reading Neil Parker's report on the desirability of getting the bank much more deeply into the business of financing extended-credit purchases of consumer goods. It sounded great as Neil put it, with possibilities of immediate profit and long-term growth. In fact the bank would be going into business with Schumann, Martinez, Cushman and others of that kidney, to become more and more involved in the sort of tricky dealing with innocent customers which went on in Upper Granby. It was clearly, from the business point of view, the right thing to do, but there was something about the rates of interest charged on time-payment agreements that stuck in his throat, particularly as they were never properly disclosed to the buyer. He heard a mellow, fruity snore. He looked up and saw Ilona with her mouth open and her head lolling from side to side on the chaise longue on the other side of the deck. The magazine on her lap slid to the deck. Hair blew across her face and in her sleep she smiled a sly, fatuously contented, drunkard's smile. Gavin leaned across and shook her awake.

"Wha'?" she said. "Oh, Gavin. Sure I am. Yes. You needn't look at me like that. No secrets between old married folks like us."

"Where have you been getting it?"

"It? I don't know what you mean."

"You've just admitted to being drunk."

"No such thing. You must have misheard me." She smiled again, but she had now regained control of herself. "It's silly what a person will say when they first wake up, isn't it?"

"Now, Ilona. Let's stop this nonsense." He took her hand. "Let's talk our problem over. I'm not against you. I'm not your enemy. I love you. I want to help you. Not only for your sake, but for the children's sakes too. Won't you try to lick this thing? We can do it together. Please trust me."

A puff of wind rattled the pages of the report he had put down, turning them over one after another. Michiko threw a box of garbage over the side and the cloud of white seabirds hanging over the wake set up a wild mewing and shrilling as they dived at it.

"I just don't know what you're talking about, Gavin dear," Ilona said. "You worry me sometimes the way you fret about things that just aren't so, or which don't really matter. I'm not always nagging you to get you to give up these women you're always having your little affairs with. I know it's just something you can't help, and I know it's something that isn't in the least important, so I let it go, even when the women you play around with are vulgar little tarts you'd be ashamed to bring to the house—or—it's worse in a way—the servants."

"You've got to stop drinking, Ilona."

"That hurt, about the servants, didn't it? You didn't know I knew about your precious Miss Leigh, did you? Poor girl! And poor you, the great Mr. Moneybags, the successful banker, laying his own children's governess down the hall from his wife's bedroom! What a sordid little mess we might have had on our hands if the girl hadn't had the decency to take herself off. But I didn't say anything then. And I won't say anything about it now. But I won't stand for your taking a high old moral line with me about anything I choose to do or not to do. So let's not get into any discussions of this kind, if you please."

Ilona got to her feet and walked away. Gavin watched her out of sight and then settled back into his chair. He watched the horizon for a time, a harsh line on this bright day which looked like the top of a wall. He pulled his pen from his pocket and started writing on a memorandum sheet attached to the report.

"This is a very good piece of work, Neil. I've no hesitations about your proposal. I think we should go right ahead and take up the block of stock on offer. It will give us full control of Farmers and Mechanics Loan. We should elect our own board at the spring meeting and follow the program of expansion outlined here. Merrick's price is fair and I do not think we should try to bargain on it. Close the deal just as soon as you can."

When he had finished writing he sat for a time brooding with the report on his lap. Then he went forward to his deckhouse cabin and took up the radio telephone. He dictated the memorandum to Miss Lumley and told her to get it onto Neil's desk right away.

"Oh, and one other thing, before I forget, find out Father Prieto's address, will you, and see if you can fix an appointment for Thursday morning. I want to have a talk with him on—ah—say a private matter of importance."

"Very well, Mr. Hatfield."

Father Prieto took Gavin through his barely furnished presbytery on the fringe of the Heights next to the uncompleted parish church of St. Anne's and into the garden behind it. A surrounding cinder-block wall slightly above head height crowned with a single strand of barbed wire gave it something of the air of a prison yard, but every part of the enclosure was filled with a lush growth of carefully tended plants. Father Prieto took Gavin down a little cobbled path into an arbor smothered in the wild tangle of a trumpet vine. Close by water gurgled from a transparent plastic hose as it flowed into a set of channels in the black loam leading to the roots of a dozen orange trees.

"You're a keen gardener," Gavin said awkwardly. "You've transformed this sandy soil."

"In my garden I can most easily evade my vows of poverty," the priest said. Gavin was not sure if the remark was intended as a joke or not, and Father Prieto gave him no help. After a brief exchange of sociabilities Gavin tried to get down to business.

"I don't belong to your church," he said, "and I haven't any color of a right to ask for your help. But my wife is a parishoner of yours and I . . . ."

"Ah, yes, I supposed it would be that, Mr. Hatfield." Father Prieto settled back in his chair. "I don't believe I can be of any help to you at all."

"What's that?" Gavin was startled. "Aren't you her spiritual adviser—or some such thing—I was led to suppose that you had some considerable influence . . . ."

"I do not know what you may have been led to suppose. A parish priest has many problems, and one of them is the church member who loves neither God nor the Church. Vanity, self-interest, whatever it is that brings such persons into the fold brings them within its formal limits but never makes them members of the flock. Your wife has mocked me and mocked God ever since she approached me. I was slow to discover what was going on, and reluctant to credit what my intelligence told me when I did find out how cruelly I was deceived in your wife. I would expel her from my church and deny her its sacraments if I could, but I am not free to deal with her as I would. My Bishop has forbidden me to do so on the simple ground that you are a very rich man. The Church might benefit substantially if your wife were to survive you, or if you were to follow her into the church. I have told the Bishop that I think there is little hope of this kind to be derived from fostering among us a woman who is Catholic neither in deed nor in intention, but he is adamant. He is an older man, and no doubt a wiser man, than I am, and he insists that regardless of the possibilities of scandal I shall treat her as if I were the foolish innocent she takes me to be, to be hoodwinked with a little playacting and a little mimicry of devotion. I have no doubt you wish me to talk to her about her habitual overindulgence in drink, possibly on the ground that it distresses you and upsets your children. It distresses me much more than it can possibly pain you, because when Mrs. Hatfield lies to me about it, or keeps silent about it, in the confessional she lies not only to me but also to God. She has the insolence to pretend that she can keep her little secrets from the Almighty. I am content that a woman capable of such wickedness should contrive her own eternal damnation, and I am not at present inclined to lift a hand to save her from herself. It was malice which brought her into our church, and no sinner deserves more condign punishment than the one who flouts the gift of God's love."

"I don't think I understand you at all." Gavin looked at the man's set jaw and lean face. "Don't you care anything about her happiness as a woman?"

"The happiness of which you speak concerns me not at all. The only happiness I know is that joy and delight of the soul which lies open to God and which comes with complete submission to His Will." Father Prieto paused. "I would be dishonest if I volunteered to help you in a cause in which I have no interest and no belief. I can only offer you the smallest of consolations, that God's purposes will in the last day stand revealed. Out of your wife's wickedness some good that we may never see or know may come."

"You horrify me, Father Prieto." Gavin got to his feet.

"I intended to, Mr. Hatfield. If you had come to me, as God's vicar in this place, to confess your sins and your wretchedness, and to beg from your spiritual poverty of the Church's wealth, I might have spoken to you very differently. I might have told you of the endless bounty of God's love for man, which flows like an unfailing spring of joy for those who have purged themselves of greed and pride and who have learned to love him as the creator and destroyer of all things. But you came to me to do a job for you, as you might have gone to a garage for help with your car, or to a plumber for help with your drains. You wanted me to help you to be happy as if I were a psychiatrist or some wretched Freudian quack. You came to talk to me about some recipe or plan for human happiness, and your own in particular. You want comfort in your home, and you wish me to restore it. I have nothing for you but a rod for your back and salt for your wounds."

"Are you quite sure you are a Christian, Father Prieto?"

"As sure as I am that you are not." The priest stood up and put his hand on Gavin's arm. "The Church has candy for those who have preserved their innocence and come to it for God's mercy like children. For them it was said, 'Suffer the little children to come unto me.' But you have long lost your innocence. I have nothing for you but the hard sayings of my master, nor any crumb of comfort for you until the last ray of pride is off your back and you have learned to be truly thankful that it is given you to drain your cup to the dregs."

"Your last word, if I understand you, is that you will do nothing for my wife?"

"No one can help her so long as she turns her face from God."

"You won't even pray for her?"

"I pray without ceasing, it is my life, for the redemption of mankind, for the salvation of us all. I can do no more."

"It's odd." Gavin studied his unsmiling face. "I dislike your ideas very much. I believe in human happiness. But I have no arguments to support my beliefs. I haven't anything to set up against your horrible conceptions. I ought to have my case in better order."

"There are no arguments which can support your case. You

have no case." Father Prieto smiled triumphantly. "The desire for mortal happiness is in itself a sin. It is a desire for something less than perfection when the example of perfection is before you. Abandon such desires for the trivial and inane things you know. Throw yourself upon God's Mercy, and submit to His Will. There is no other way to endure the human portion."

"I'm afraid we must agree to disagree."

"Oh, no. It's never as easy as all that, or as childish. 'He who is not for me is against me' means just what it says, you know." Father Prieto smiled again. "Compromises are only possible when people aren't very serious about their beliefs. I cannot stop you from walking in darkness, but I can't ever agree to the proposition that you have a right to do so. Your choice is not between joining my organization or not joining it, as if Rotary or the Yacht Club were in question, you just choose between being saved and being damned, between eternal joy and eternal wretchedness. You belong now in the enemy camp, the camp of darkness, mortal desires, lusts, and miseries. When you say: I don't believe what you believe, but let's be friends, you ask the impossible. You are intelligent enough to see that, I'm sure."

"I'm afraid we don't speak a common language. You use words I'm familiar with, but I still don't understand you. I'm not sure that I want to."

"Well, as we're wasting each other's time, Mr. Hatfield, perhaps we should say good-bye. I hope one day, when you have drained your cup, and know how poor you are, you will come back in another spirit altogether to share the wealth I possess as a member of this church. I'm sorry I don't have any bottled remedy for your present trouble. I wish I could help in a way, because you seem a decent sort of a man, but I don't keep the sort of nostrum you require—I don't work in that kind of a shop. And now I must ask you to excuse me."

Gavin was surprised when he found himself out on the street to find that he was still in Maramee. It seemed to him that he had visited a foreign country. Cars—bright, two-toned, and

205

swollen—passed and repassed. A girl went by on roller skates followed by a barking Scotch terrier, and by a puff of wind which mottled the dry leaves of the date palms lining the street.

That's a queer fellow, thought Gavin and remembered the moment when he had looked down at the face of the dead German pilot in the cockpit of his stricken Messerschmitt, and had recognized at once the familiar human features and the utter strangeness of the enemy they masked.

Father Prieto was bent over a part-white part-tabby cat which had strolled out from the scented shade under a clump of lavender to be stroked.

"I'm afraid I was a litle hard on that infidel," he said, caressing the smooth spade-shaped head, "wasn't I, Toby? But what else does an infidel deserve except a stick about his ears to bring him to his senses?" The cat purred and looked at him affably with its green eyes, then stood up to butt his hand with its head to demand a further caress. The priest laughed with pleasure, stroked the cat again with a vigorous motion and then went briskly indoors, humming as he went.

Just at that moment Miss Jelke, more Bogey's governess than the children's now that Thomas and Mary were so much of the time at school, was standing hidden behind a window curtain watching Ilona with excitement and guilt. Ilona was out in the garden and she was just about to discover what Miss Jelke had been doing with her spare time while Ilona had been off on the cruise. In the weeks before it, Miss Jelke had been spying on Ilona and she had managed to locate five out of the eleven places where her mistress had hidden bottles. Careful study of those five had taught her something of Ilona's principles on selecting hiding places and during the week in which Ilona had been on the *Plain Jane* she had unearthed four more caches. She had debated with herself what she should do when she had made her discoveries for a long time, and had thought of several projects. One was to add salt to the whiskey in the bottles, another was to replace the whiskey with salted tea, and a third was to replace it with plain water. Finally she de-

206

cided on a policy of simple disappearances. When Ilona got back, nine bottles were gone from their hiding places. Miss Jelke had taken them down into the grove, broken them with a small tack hammer she had acquired for the purpose, and buried them in the sandy soil. She now watched with breathless excitement as Ilona, having drawn back in the tangle of English ivy in the niche behind the dancing faun at the end of the terrace, moved on to the next place. How soon would it be before she found out the extent of her losses? And what would she do when she found out? Ilona drifted in from the garden looking vague, smiling charmingly, dangling a wide-brimmed straw hat from one hand. Miss Jelke met her in the big hall, leading Bogey in a new sailor suit out towards the front door.

"Good afternoon, Mrs. Hatfield, did you have a nice stroll?"

"Oh, lovely, the place is looking divine, it always looks its best at this time of year. You look sweet in that pleated skirt, Bogey, you really do. Pretty as a little peach."

"You're looking very well yourself, Mrs. Hatfield, rested, after your trip. You were very *tense* when you went away," Miss Jelke said, daringly.

"Oh, me. I'm looking like a hag." Ilona looked in a glass on the wall and patted her hair.

"You don't look like a hag at all, Mommy," Bogey said. "You look lovely."

"Well, that's sweet of you," Ilona said. "But my hair's a mess. All that salt air on the boat played hell with it. I'll have to go downtown tomorrow morning to have Jackie Prosser fix it."

"Well, we must go off and fetch Thomas and Mary from school," Miss Jelke said, rejoicing inwardly. Perhaps finding the whiskey gone after drying out for a week on the boat was going to stop Mrs. Hatfield. It was wonderful that she had taken it so calmly, wonderful. She took Bogey off. Ilona went up to her bedroom and found that her two last-resort reserve bottles were still in their hiding places, one in a hat box, and the other in the tank of the toilet in her bathroom. Reassured, she went downstairs again and walked into the kitchen, pushing casually through the green baize doors separating the house from the quarters, and leaving them flapping behind her.

"Oh, hullo, Bailey," she said. "How are things?"

"Oh middling good, ma'am, middling good. Did you have a pleasant trip, down there among the islands? I've always wanted to go down there. They say there's some mighty pretty places down there, or so I have heard."

"Oh, yes, we saw a heap of pretty things." Ilona looked puzzled. "Now I know I came in here for some reason—oh, yes—one or two things—the way the tables are placed on the terrace, and the way the flowers look in the beds out in the front—there isn't anyone new working in the gardens, is there?"

"No, ma'am." Bailey raged inwardly, thinking, that damn fool woman, what cause did she have to go interfering where she didn't have no concern to meddle at all. "No, ma'am. It's just the same men. Old Charlie Mr. Hatfield keeps on though he really don't do nothing on account of being so old, and Eddie and William who do the work. They're just carrying on the same way as always."

"I just wondered if there was someone around who didn't know our little ways." Ilona smiled. "But I'm probably just imagining the whole thing," she said, "forget about it."

Later she made another slow and thoughtful tour of her caches, trying them first in the hope that she had been looking in slightly wrong places, and then searching for clues. But there weren't any clues. In the next few hours she tried detective work, setting verbal leaps that were designed to bring out guilty knowledge on the part of the person she was talking to, but without much success. Bailey and Julia were clearly uneasy about something, but more she decided about her jumpiness than anything which was on their own minds. They were uneasy about her uneasiness. Everyone else seemed to have a clean bill.

Miss Jelke rode out the storm with ease. She was a little woman with a jolly manner and a high complexion whose brightness of manner was so transparently artificial that it seemed that it must be genuine, anyone really trying to act would be bound to do better. What she labored to conceal and what made her smile so agonizingly and unfailingly cheerful, was constant pain at the ugliness of things. Her own father, a one-legged veteran of the First World War, had become a drunk after her mother's death and her late teens had been spent in a losing battle with his addiction. The concentrated effort of those years had given her a fixation on the situation, and by some sort of sinister gravity she was drawn to job after job in which one or other of her employers was overtly or secretly going under. Long practice had given her enormous skill in the finding of hidden bottles and the rapid disposal of their contents. When she was at work a house seemed to be haunted by a poltergeist working off the thirst of an eternity, all the wretched drinker had to do was to turn his back on a bottle and it would seem to empty itself as if by magic, full one minute it would be dry and rinsed out, or simply gone, the next. Miss Jelke even had special clothes which she had tailored to her own design with huge concealed pockets in the skirts into which a bottle could be dropped in a second to wait for a favorable moment for disposal. The battle of wits she had fought with her father had given her the passion for the task, and in the rest of her life she had built up an astonishing equivalent of a tracker's lore. Had she had the power to write a handbook on the ways of the compulsive drinker it would have been a remarkable contribution to the sociology of the upper middle class, but she had no power to transmit her knowledge, and just as brilliant diagnosticians cannot describe their methods she knew without knowing. When she saw Ilona dressed for Maramee in the wide brimmed straw hat with the red silk band, the pale coffee-colored coarse linen sheath, the plain gold heavy bracelet on her sunburned and slightly freckled arm, the sheer, almost invisible stockings, and the honey-brown linen shoes with their brown leather heels, she took no notice of any of these things. Her eyes fell instantly on the huge, square, red leather and white straw bag swinging from her right hand. "That's how she brings it in," she thought, with precisely the thrill with which a hunter recognizes the track along which his quarry will pass nightly to a favored waterhole. Ilona did a number of things in Maramee, shopped for herself and for the house, took lunch with a friend, had her hair done, visited the gift shop and went home. As she crossed the hall Bogey ran out to meet her; she had made a little theater of cardboard and paper, with sets and a curtain, and everything, Mommy must come and see it at once. She spent ten minutes with Bogey and then came back to the hall on her way upstairs to her room. Her bag was surprisingly light when she lifted it, and as she went upstairs her suspicions grew. A puzzled frown came over her face, and as she climbed she flexed her arm a couple of times the better to gauge the bag's reduced weight. The minute she was inside her room she snapped the clasp and ripped the bag's scarlet mouth wide open. Her wallet was there, a small pack of Kleenex, her change purse, a few make-up things, nothing else. She peered into the various divisions of the bag incredulously and then straightened her back. Well, she thought, it's three forty now, the only people who can have been in or near that damned hallway in the last twenty minutes would be Bogey, Bailey, Julia, that damned Wilbraham woman who hates my guts, Miss Jelke, Thomas the chauffeur, and just possibly, Eddie or William— not that either of the gardeners would come indoors in a million years.

Miss Wilbraham, intent on her task of checking over the curtains and the slipcovers on the furniture in the upstairs rooms, passed quickly between one door and another on the landing at the head of the stairs.

"Miss Wilbraham!" Ilona called to her sharply.

"Yes, madam."

Ilona looked at her deliberately empty face and saw an absolute innocence behind the other woman's instinctive hostility. It was obvious that she had nothing to do with it.

"I'm sorry. It was just something that came into my head and went out again—please forgive me."

"That's quite all right, madam."

She thought, and realized that not one of the possible suspects could have dared the thing if they were in their right minds. It was inexplicable, unless . . . She considered the ugly thought that Gavin might have gone so far as to order someone to watch her and to supervise her life. But that was inconceivable. She remembered how hard it had been for him to make her give up her car keys, because that involved her surrendering them to Fred Bailey. She knew that he could, at a stretch, go behind her back to discuss her with a close friend or a professional man. But that he should secretly conspire against her with her own servants was another matter altogether. The word servant touched the deep reservoir of New England snobbery within her, which was not the less real for never being mentioned. She knew that Gavin was one breed of animal, and that servants, menials, people who would clean your shoes, were of another breed. He was too much of a gentleman still, in spite of his superficial Marameeisms, to make secret plans against one of his own kind with one of them. But which of those people, who weren't quite real as people, could it be who had dared to act alone?

Ilona looked into her bag once more to make sure the bottles were gone, and then considered her position. Her battle of wits with Gavin on the yacht had been fun, but that was because she had known what she was getting into. This blow from an unknown hand was like the first slap in one of the old savage forms of blind man's buff, and it promised to be more wearing and more irritating. If she accepted the challenge she would have to be on the alert, night and day, for weeks, perhaps for months. She would have to set traps, and make schemes. Any incidental setbacks in the struggle would be as tiresome, frustrating, and pointless as the present one. She looked through the cool shadows of the hall out to the hot blaze of sunlit green outside. She had one sure instinct. She

211

knew when not to fight, and she knew how to give up a position, no matter how elaborately prepared, just as soon as it became meaningless. After a moment's consideration, she flung her hat down into the chair beside her bag and went into the downstairs library to make a telephone call.

It was a room in which people rarely sat, and even more rarely read books, and which was in reality a large telephone booth. As Ilona waited for an answer she stood looking at the transparently fraudulent Reynolds hanging over the fireplace. Even Gavin had not believed in it when he bought it, and within ten days of its being hung in its place Mary had renamed its subject General J. Worthington Pish-Posh. It was a dull portrait of a tall horse-faced man dressed in a gold braided scarlet coat, a fawn waistcoat with silver buttons, black breeches and riding boots. It might have been painted by any competent journeyman-portraitist of the period. The face on the canvas wore an expression which was in its totality sad, though there was a hint of amusement about the set of the mouth. "Here I am," he seemed to be saying, "in a strange country among strange people who have no idea who I was or what I did, transformed into a species of ornament. There's no end to the odd things that can happen to a person if they should go in for having their likenesses taken off on canvas."

But Ilona disregarded the small voice of the expensive ornament. She heard a distant murmur in the telephone, and was not quite sure that she recognized the speaker.

"Is Mr. Sigaux there, please?"

"Why, yes, this is he. Isn't that Mrs. Hatfield? Ilona?"

"Oh, Silky—I wasn't sure if it were you. I hope I haven't broken in on your work."

"Oh, no! I'm all through for the day. My last little satin-sheathed deb has flown away."

"That's good. I want to talk to you about a project I have. I want to give Gavin a surprise. I want you to do some portraits of us all, me and the children, up here at the Grove. I've something in mind, like those old English conversation pictures of families in front of their houses. It's hard to explain on the phone. I wish you'd come out to lunch tomorrow to talk about it—if you're free, that is."

"Why that sounds just facinating, Ilona. I've always wanted to paint you, with your wonderful coloring, you know that. And I'd love to come over for lunch tomorrow."

"Good, and we can go into all the details then. If you aren't working too madly hard, you might bring your trunks, we could swim down at the lake in the afternoon. We haven't had a real talk in ages."

"No, we haven't—and I can't think of anything I'd like better. I'll be along around half-past twelve or a quarter to one —is that right?"

"Yes, that would be perfect, Silky, just perfect."

Ilona put the telephone down and went in search of Miss Wilbraham, who was checking over the inventory of the Deep-Freeze with Julia before making her monthly requisitions. There was a slight undertone of tension in the air because Julia had, as usual, been sloppy about checking off items on the list as she used them, and it was necessary to count the frosted packages of this and that to find out what was in fact left in the huge, coffin-like, white machine. Miss Wilbraham was always crisp about inefficiency and treated Julia like a naughty little girl on these occasions, even though there was something like thirty years between them. And Julia secretly felt that the sole purpose of this checking and list-making was to see that nothing was stolen.

"I hates this old thing, and all these little packets. You tell me whatever you like, but this stuff ain't so good as fresh food, all froze up hard."

"You're quite right, Julia," Ilona said, coming into the conversation. "Nothing really has its proper flavor when it's been abused this way."

"Oh, Mrs. Hatfield, please. You just mustn't undermine all my work to get Julia to use the freezer properly. Why we'd be going into market every morning if we didn't make intelligent use of it. And I have to fight Julia every inch of the way."

213

"Ain't nothing to beat stuff you picks out yourself fresh every morning down at the markets."

"I think you're right, in fact I know you are, Julia, but that isn't what I came down here to talk about. Mr. Sigaux is coming to lunch tomorrow, Miss Wilbraham. You know how the poor man drinks. See that there's plenty of Scotch in the dining room, and on the trolley out on the terrace when he comes. He won't drink anything else, and he gets upset when he thinks people are trying to keep him off it. So put out an extra bottle or two. We must keep our local genius happy, mustn't we?"

"I'll do that, Mrs. Hatfield," Miss Wilbraham said, adding in her most dead-pan manner, "It really is too bad about Mr. Sigaux, when he's such a talented man."

"Yes, dear," said Ilona, "but then we can't all be perfect, can we?"

Miss Wilbraham wondered if her employer thought she was really getting away with it, and gave her a steady appraising look under cover of her aseptic smile. Ilona met her eyes and faced her out. Amiably and without malice, she made it quite plain that she didn't in the least care what the housekeeper or anyone else thought of her behavior. She smiled serenely and went on her way. She had completed a maneuver corresponding to breaking off a naval action, turning away under cover of a smokescreen. When the smoke cleared, Miss Jelke was going to find that she had vanished as a secret drinker. The whole business of concealment and precaution against discovery was at an end. Ilona was going to drink openly from now on, but as a matter of social duty. Sigaux was a man who notoriously had a problem, and was accepted as one of Maramee's chartered drunks. "Poor Silky," they said, "poor Silky. It's a damned shame, but that's the way it is with these sensitive, artistic people. And you've got to admit it, his portraits are just wonderful. He's not old fashioned, but he does get the best goddamned likeness you ever saw. If he didn't have his weakness he'd be one of the very top painters working anywhere, and I really mean it, in the world today. We're really damned lucky to have him here in Maramee."

Ilona had never spoken of the painter in this way because she had a strong feeling that luck and Sigaux were not things which could be associated, by any manner of means. She knew that Silky had been born in Maramee, that he had tried to escape from it, and that he had failed. She suspected that he had come back to his birthplace because he had no other place to go, or rather because his one surviving relative there, his Aunt Esther, was the only person in the world who could be relied upon to pick him up, dust him off, and look after him. But even Ilona, with her large fund of imaginative sympathy for anyone who found himself stuck in Maramee without really wishing to be there had no inkling of the nature of his homecoming. He had indeed fallen helpless into the hands of his aunt, as Victorian sinners fed on Bible readings dreaded that they might fall into the hands of the living God. Miss Esther did not exactly scourge him, or plague him with boils in Old Testament style, but she slowly simmered him in his own sense of failure. When he arrived back home, the outward and visible sign of his defeat and rejection by the world he had set out to conquer was a six-year-old Buick convertible with a rent in its canvas top which had obviously been there for a long time. The car's fenders had been crumpled, cheaply repaired, and carelessly repainted with colors which did not quite match the original painting, and the shock absorbers on the rear wheels had given way, so that a ride on the back seat was torture, and the machine, running or parked, looked down at the heels like an old worn-out shoe. It drank oil, and left a cobalt-blue haze behind it whenever it was slowing down or running downhill.

"Where did you get landed with this thing?" Aunt Esther said as soon as she had taken a good look at it.

"A man who was going to Paris, Charlie Evans, he had a Guggenheim and went for a year, he let me have it for almost nothing. For what I gave for it, it was a hell of a good buy, Aunt Esther."

"If you gave legal tender, no matter what the amount, for that thing, you were taken, Silky. It looks like the sort of machine a dealer would palm off on some poor nigra who didn't know any better. Someone who mows lawns and clears blocked drains could be buying it on time."

"It isn't that bad."

"It's a disgrace, and you'll have to get rid of it."

"I haven't the money to buy anything better, Aunt, you know that."

"And so will everyone else who sees it. You get rid of it before lunch today."

She bought a car to replace it that afternoon. On paper it was his. The important thing was that Maramee, thereafter, saw Silky driving around, like any other reasonably successful young tradesman or professional man, in a clean, brightly glittering, late-model car which he could call his, whoever the psychological or actual owner might be. Miss Esther was just as firm about setting him up in a studio of her choosing and not of his. She knew very well that Maramee would refuse recognition as an artist to anyone who tried to work in a made-over room in a house, however big the room might be, or however convincingly it were furnished with artistic properties. Whenever she suspected that Silky was painting in his room she would send her deaf old Negro maid Hattie to sweep it with the vacuum cleaner, or to change the linen on the bed, or to do something, no matter what, which would disturb him. She hoped to drive him across the yard and into the barn, where the hay and feed had been kept when the Sigaux family had owned horses. She succeeded in driving him from the house but not in the direction she intended. She found that he was searching all over Spanishtown for empty lofts and old workrooms which could be converted into studios. She soon stopped that.

"For goodness' own sake, Silky, you must be gone clean out of your mind if you suppose men from the Heights and the Point would dream of letting their wives and daughters go down to an artist's studio in Spanishtown. Why there are brothels all through that neighborhood. You couldn't get a decent woman down there alone in a thousand years. And if you did get a woman down there more than once, they'd say you were romancing her."

"What makes you think I want all these women in my studio, Aunt? I'm not a fashionable portrait painter."

"You aren't now. But you're going to be." She looked at him calmly. "There just isn't anything else you can be in Maramee."

"My dear Aunt Esther! I like to think I'm a serious painter."

"Silky dear, if you try to sell the sort of thing you couldn't sell, or even get to show, in New York or in France, or wherever, back here you'll just be telling everybody the real true reason why you came home. If you settle to portrait we can get away with it."

"With what?"

"With pretending you came back just because Maramee's your home and the sweetest place to live in you know of in the whole wide world, and a place where the sort of painting you've a real gift for is truly appreciated into the bargain." Aunt Esther closed her mouth in a thin hard line, and she looked angry as she saw Silky flinch away from her direct glare.

"I don't fully understand what you mean by the sort of painting I've a real gift for, Aunt." He smiled tolerantly. "You can't mean the sort of thing I did before I was even a student."

"I wish you'd be honest with yourself for just once. It would make it that much easier to help. You know very well you aren't a progressive modern painter by either talent or inclination. When you went up North you started painting plain rubbish. Cheap imitations of what you didn't understand or truly like. I cried with vexation the time I went up there to see you in the Village and found you playing with that stuff you had no business to touch. Anyone could see you were faking. We aren't big-city people down here but we're smart in an old-fashioned way. You won't have any luck faking down here."

"I've always done my best," he said lamely and without conviction. His aunt's forbidding expression was softened towards kindness by his evident unhappiness.

"You had a real flair. You always did understand the way

a girl or a woman saw herself, as she had to be, but still just a mite glorified. You'll just have to do women's portraits like the ones you used to do before you went away and got clever. Everybody liked what you used to do."

"I don't know that I could paint that way again."

"You'll do well to try. I haven't got that much money that I don't have to watch to see where every dime goes. My income, though it's better than it was, isn't much for an old woman to live on, and it's precious little for two. I can't carry you forever."

"You want me to go back to doing blond debutantes in sky-blue silk—with a single row of pearls round their fat necks? I'm to do that sort of thing?" He spoke with loathing.

"It was you wanted to be a painter, not me," she said. "It was you begged me to put you through art school. We all tried to tell you. One sadder kind of fool you might have been. You might have wanted to be a concert pianist, and you might have ended up teaching sulky children to play scales."

She watched him get up and go over to the window, to stand there with his back to her pretending to look through the screen of carefully tended pot plants into the street as he fought back tears of misery and panic. She could tell by the set of his shoulders that there was no real fight left in him. There never had been. It was something which had been lacking in the male members of the Sigaux family for a couple of generations.

"It won't be too bad," she said. "Really, Silky dear, it won't. We'll do over the old barn and make it into a proper studio for you. Though the Point district has gone downhill a trifle and the Heights have gone up in the world this is still a nice neighborhood. I wouldn't care to meet everyone on the block socially, I'll admit, not now that the Remington house has been broken up into apartments, but it's a good address all the same. Everyone who counts for anything in Maramee knows me, and they know who you are. I'll be able to chaperone your sitters. Those portraits you did before you went away are still around, and they're still very much liked. Several people have asked me when you would be ready to accept commissions again. And nobody will tell you what to paint between sittings. You'll have plenty of opportunity, if you want it, to go on."

"Go on?" He faced about. "With what?"

"Something I'd much rather you didn't do. Fooling yourself, pretending you have a talent for being creative and original that isn't properly recognized. That the art world has been unfair to you. That you're a martyr—all that."

"You really want to rub my nose in it," he spoke angrily, "that I'm no good."

"I've never said that, Silky. I say you have a real gift for catching a likeness, and that you know how to paint."

"You want me to set up as a tradesman in competition with that damned photographer, Keyes, or whatever his name is, downtown?"

"That's it, Silky. You are a tradesman. It's rough luck that you weren't a genius, but there aren't so many of them and it's rough luck you share with most of the human race."

"You just want to humiliate me."

"That's untrue and you know it, dear. I'm fond of you, fond of you as if you were the child out of my own body and not my brother's child. And just because I'm as fond of you as I am, I don't get much charge out of seeing you moping around without the energy or the self-respect to get back onto your own feet or to wash the taste of failure out of your mouth. I know what you can do, and I'm urging you to get out there and do it."

They confronted each other. The woman sat upright over her sewing frame. Her fluff of white hair, her flawless rosy skin, her tiny wrists and ankles, and her thin body in its old-fashioned snuff-colored dress with white lace at the neck and cuffs, combined to make her look frail and delicate. She looked, against the large, black, Spanish leather chairback, even less than her five feet two inches, and the size-four shoes on her feet seemed to belong on a doll. Silky was in the bohemian uniform of work shirt and blue jeans. He was eighteen inches taller than she, and twice her weight. But she was the stronger. His rage became sulkiness. He brushed a thin lock of hair off his forehead.

"Are you putting up the money to make over the barn," he said, "because I haven't one red cent?"

"Oh, don't you worry about that," she said. "You can start to pay me back when your commissions begin to roll in." She laughed lightly. "It'll be fun making that old barn over. I've always wanted to see it put to good use, and anyway I love doing places up. It'll do me good, and I hope that getting to work will make you a little happier, child."

She threw herself into the project so eagerly, busying herself with the contractors and the architect's plans, that he was for a time beguiled into sentimentality. Poor dear, he thought, I suppose her life is empty and pretty nearly finished, taking a proxy interest in mine must be some help in filling the void.

But before long he came to recognize the shrewdness with which she was manipulating his affairs. It was worth just over ten thousand dollars a year to him that his sitters could park their cars and station wagons over in the shadow of Miss Esther's porch, change out of their day clothes to their ball dresses in her bedroom, and then walk across to the studio along the moss-covered brick path bordered by camelia bushes and rosemary clumps. There was thus no question of their dressing or undressing amid the supposedly intoxicating smells of linseed oil, turpentine, and paint. Silky had not been back in Maramee long before he recognized the enduring strength of the old myth about painters, models, and the nude, which seemed to be an ineradicable part of the erotic imaginings of almost every man in the place. His fellow citizens had it firmly in their heads that any painter left alone for a few minutes with any woman, no matter what her shape, size, or condition, would ask her to sit for her portrait as a preliminary to getting her spread out naked as a jay bird on some sofa or couch on which he would presently try to make her. "You can't get up to your Parisian tricks with Miss Esther around, can you?" they said, nudging him. "I'll bet you had a real ball when you were over there, and all the time you were up in

New York, too. The Village is the place for quail these days from all I hear, full of hot little numeros pretending to be writers and poets and all that stuff. How did you make out?" Sigaux's stock answer, that he had been much too busy painting to get involved in that kind of thing, caused a sharp drop in male interest in his affairs.

But women liked him. He was a real painter who had studied abroad, and that made him exciting. He had lived where women did—oh, all sorts of things, and men respected them for it. And yet being painted by him was pleasantly safe, because a sitting with Sigaux was bound up so closely with a visit to Miss Esther. It began with a little chat with her in the other house—an affair of a few minutes of the best Maramee gossip larded with Miss Esther's delighted compliments on how well the sitter was looking and beautiful her dress was. And then there was the walk through Miss Esther's lovely old garden to the studio where Silky was waiting. While the hour of the sitting rushed by, Silky talked, so well, about the arts, and people, and Europe, and then he was clean and tidy as so many people who just pretended to be artists were not. And when it was all over, you had something, a likeness so good that it was refreshing to see. And the portraits weren't just likenesses. They were more like the truth than photographs. Women often looked at them and recognized, in their own words, the real me. This was a person a little less marked by life than the apparent me, a little healthier, a little more self-assured, and a little happier. It was this liberation of reality from itself which was his real gift.

It was the key, as Aunt Esther had known it would be, to success in Maramee. Everything could be forgiven an enthusiast, and Silky's portraits were enthusiastic about their subjects. He made them all look like the lovely, wonderful people they told each other they were, and which they, at times, believed themselves to be. Within a few years of Silky's return, beaten and disheartened, to his birthplace, Miss Esther had made him one of the pillars of its society.

A series of sittings with Sigaux was an established part of

the social climb, which culminated when the aspirant became a member of the Garland, the organizing committee responsible for the Pedro Nunez Day cotillion. This affair,
named for a Spaniard who had a somewhat shaky historical
connection with Maramee, was the city's equivalent of the
greatest of the New Orleans Mardi Gras balls. It too was presided over by a king, one of the city's richer and more socially
acceptable businessmen, and a queen of the carnival. The
queen was the product of a compromise between idealism,
which insisted that she had to be one of the prettiest debutantes of the year, and practicality which made it necessary
for her to have more money behind her than any other girl of
her year. Every year Silky, who had already painted their parents, painted the queen of the carnival and six of her attendants, chosen from among either the maids or the matrons of
honor, in their gowns. On the Monday before the cotillion,
Miss Esther held a reception in the studio at which the completed portraits were shown formally before they were delivered. Aunt Esther was much more than a mere chaperone on
this occasion, which she called "my nephew's *vernissage*." She
made up the lists of guests with an acute feeling for Maramee's gossip and its social tensions, and with the full collab-
oration of her faction of ladies in the Maramee parlor, an
institution modeled on the *petit salon* of New Orleans. The
studio was used as a piece of neutral ground, exempted as an
enclave of bohemia from the normal social safeguards, where
social aspirants were allowed to present themselves for a final
inspection before their recognition. Here among the canvases,
still scented with turpentine and linseed oil, and the banks of
pot plants and ferns, the members of the membership committee of every society and club which really signified in Maramee life, were introduced to a selection of newcomers to the
neighborhood who had won the sponsorship of Miss Esther
and the razor-tongued ladies of the parlor. Being in Silky's
studio was a sign of imminent arrival, of being in position to
put one's foot on the bottom round of the ladder, and it gave
the probationer an exciting glimpse of the summit. If, a

week later, at the ball, one of the masked gentlemen from the king of the carnival's train should invite a lady to leave the enclosure beside the floor where the guests invited to watch but not to dance were penned, the way to the top was opened and recognition was completed. Next year the lady and her husband would be invited to the ball to dance, in five years they would become eligible for membership on the Garland. Then they would be entitled both to give formal parties in the week leading up to the cotillion and to present a daughter as candidate for the role of queen or one of her attendants.

Somewhere between recognition and the invitation to join the Garland there would be the confirmation of the family's progress in the upward direction when a wife or a daughter made her appearance on one of Silky's canvases. Miss Esther would never allow him to work on a sitter simply because the money for his fee was available. Miss Esther had, in what proved to be the critical instance for his self-respect, barred the door of his studio to a former Miss Beauty Brew who had married Wilbur Norbert, the contractor who had done all the work on the Arling Field extension program out beyond the municipal airport. Silky had become interested in a paradox in her appearance. The superficial prettiness which had won her title as a beauty queen and a husband, had worn off, leaving exposed a face possessed of dignity and real beauty.

"She's genuine, not a fake at all," Silky said. "You must see it, Aunt Esther, the proportions of her head are terrific, almost noble. She's the real thing, an authentic beauty."

"Well," said Miss Esther sharply, "her husband certainly isn't. He's a coarse-grained brute from heaven alone knows where. And it's not as if he had solid money behind him. Everyone knows his last nickel is in that new coastal highway job of his. He's in hock right up to the limit for his machinery. You can see he's not really a big man just by watching the way he goes about his business. There's always a steel hat in the back of his car, and he's down there on the job every day, sweating into his work clothes, just as if he were still somebody's foreman. That's how he started, and that's how he'll

223

end up again the minute he runs out of borrowed money. There's nothing in back of him but mortgages and bank loans, and he looks like a dressed-up lard hog when he puts on a dinner jacket. That wife of his may be the beauty you say she is, but he's just irredeemably vulgar and you can't afford to take his money."

"Oh, Aunt Esther, I am so confoundedly tired of painting girls who are just little balls of puppy fat, and smooth women whose faces come out of pots. I would like to paint a woman who looks like something just for once."

"I'll tell you what she looks like if you don't know. She looks like a woman who will end up with a job in a store when her husband goes bankrupt. You just can't have anything to do with people like that."

"She's lovely, that's all I know." He felt a stir of rebellion moving in him. "Just when and how did we get so all-fired aristocratic?"

"My great-grandfather was a blockade runner during the war between the states," Miss Esther said primly. "He made a great deal of money."

"And afterwards people never forgot the risks he ran for the Confederacy I suppose?"

"You're just being aggravating, Silky. He ran in luxuries and sold them on what I suppose you could call the black market."

She looked calculatingly at Silky, gauging the extent of his revolt.

"He was a straight-grained scoundrel, all one piece the whole way down the board," she said. "But his son was a good man who lived well and played fair, and so was his son after him. That was my father, and your father's father. He was a finicky man, particular about clean linen and good manners. He would never raise his voice, and he'd never use vile language. Your mother's father came of the same sort of stock. He had a very distinguished manner, as well as his good looks, and people just naturally looked up to him. Don't ask me how these things happen. They just do. Your father and your uncles ran through most of the money there was when

they were young and foolish, but we still have the position."
Her face suddenly hardened. "A position of respect which
you'd be a fool to throw away."

"Me?" He laughed, her vehemence amused him. "By painting the wrong people from the social angle?"

"Don't play the innocent with me, Silky." She picked up
a copy of a magazine, looked cursorily at it and set it down
again. "I know what appeals to you about that woman.
Granted she does have a lovely head, and I'll grant you too
that she carries herself well. But they don't call her Jacky for
nothing. She cuts her hair more like a boy than a grown
woman, and half the time she's in those tight pants and boxy
jackets she wears you could take her for a boy. With all that
tennis and golf, and those long legs and arms, and nothing
here and nothing there, she certainly isn't much of a woman. I
know what speaks to you through her, and I'm warning
you."

"Warning me?" He heard her with fascination.

"Yes, you. One squalid scandal and I won't be the respected
member of one of the oldest families in Maramee as I am
now. I'll just be a poor old maid related to a fellow who had
to leave town in a hurry."

"You can't imagine," he said with mock indignation, not
for a minute supposing that she imagined any such thing,
"that I'm proposing to have an affair with Jacky Norbert, can
you? I declare, I don't know what you're talking about. I just
don't understand you."

"Oh, yes you do, Silky," Aunt Esther said, folding her hands
in her lap. "I'm very fond of you. You've been like my own
child ever since my brother and your mother got themselves
killed in that terrible accident. Perhaps the pain of that loss
made me love you more than I should, maybe it's made me
spoil you. I don't know. Perhaps I should have spoken out before. You must think I've been blind all these years. That's my
punishment for not having said my say sooner."

He lit a cigar, a thin cheroot, and filled the following instants of desperate silence with an elaborately pantomimed

225

concern for bringing its end to an even red glow. He tried to bluff, putting on an amused smile which was sickly.

"I really can't think what you can be going to say."

"Oh, fiddle! Just because I'm a single woman, and elderly, do you suppose I know nothing of life? What do you suppose women talk about when men are not with them, pray? And wouldn't you guess that they might listen to each other? Why I've known about your tendency since before your mother died in that smash, since you were no more than a little boy. You had what ails you now printed on you then. You were always stealing clothes out of your mother's closets and mine for some secret dressing up you used to do. Anyone who wasn't blind could tell even then that you would grow up into a man woman's things would mean more to than any woman. You were able to talk to women, and to understand women's concerns from the minute you stopped being a child. You never gave beans for anything boys or men make their lives of—you've never had me fooled for a minute."

She paused, and he sat speechless in front of her.

"I should have said all this long ago, perhaps when you first came back. But you were too distressed then by being a failure up there where you'd set your heart on succeeding, and I couldn't do it. I should have told you there's one line you mustn't ever cross now you've come back home. You can charm the women the way you do, and come and go in every house in Maramee, just so long as you never disgust any woman or make her fear for her children. Don't you ever have a colored man or a boy up there in the studio on any pretext, no matter what, and don't you ever paint or draw a nude man, and don't ever put a hand on the arm or the shoulder of a man younger than yourself, in anyone's sight or out of it, while you want to go on living in this town."

He looked at her with a wild hope that she might not really understand the full implication of what she was saying, and saw, with horror, pity and the fullest understanding on her face. He could see that she had more to say and worse. She really did know him, and what he had done in Europe with men and boys, sailors and soldiers picked up on trains, waiters and elevator operators in second-rate hotels, working men attracted by his money and his gifts, and those richer, and sometimes older, friends who had often given him clothes, food and lodging for weeks and months. He dropped his eyes and waited.

"And if you should feel inclined to go on up to Mobile, or over to Key West to find what you want, and if you get beaten up or marked by some jig or some rough boy you make a mistake with, don't you come back here until the last trace of it is off you. If you put one foot wrong here, they'll all be on to you like a pack of coon dogs."

Silky felt sick and emptied of words for a while, feeling like a small child all of whose secrets had been discovered.

"Did I do wrong to come home?" he said. "Should I go away again? I don't know what I should do, Aunt Esther."

"I don't think you should run away," she said, mildly. "I think you should try to exercise a little common prudence and self-control. You've got to be an age when you should be able to discipline yourself a little. The longer you keep a grip on yourself, the easier you'll find it to handle yourself. In a year or two, perhaps sooner, you should marry some nice girl with a position who doesn't know too much about life, and you should give her some babies as quick as you can."

"You can say that," he cried out in horror, "knowing as much about me as you do?"

"I know all about you." She put it to him sharply. "But I'm telling you what will be good for you, not what I suppose you will like, or want to hear."

"Can't you see how cruel it would be?"

"Oh, life is a cruel business, Silky dear." She smiled, and not very sweetly. "And old maid knows that as well as anyone, just as well as you."

It was the only time Esther Sigaux had talked in this strain to her nephew, and once was enough. In the course of the exchange, she completed the breaking process which began with his failure to get exhibitions in Paris and New York. It had been bad enough to realize that all his very considerable technical skill and craft knowledge amounted to a thin glaze over the meaninglessness of his work, which any professional eye could penetrate in seconds. But realizing that this old spinster whose innocence he had been inclined to patronize knew both the secret of his inner and of his physical life was far worse. It ended all his pretences. While he was following the international homosexual circuit from New York, Fire Island, Ibizia, Paris, Positano, and Rome he had been able to tell himself that he was living the mobile free life of an artist. And when the little legacy from his mother had been exhausted and he had been forced back to Maramee he had been able to pretend that he was at odds with his home town because he did not, as an artist and a superior soul, truly belong there. But now he was forced to face himself as if in a huge glass, and was bound to admit that all that was special about him was that he was, it was not very special, a queer, a fag, a fairy.

His will collapsed. He became his aunt's creature, living as she told him to live, painting the girls and women she told him to paint, filling empty chairs at dinners in the role of an always available extra man. He was even more obedient and docile than he needed to be, because it was in the back of his mind that if he were unobtrusive enough and, in the nursery sense of the words, good enough, Aunt Esther would forget her master plan, and the ghastly prudent marriage she had conceived for him. He was quiet about the house like a small boy who has been promised punishment, and who sees a greater chance of escaping it with every hour put between him and the promise. And then one afternoon, as Pedro Nunez Day, and with it the parties, the dances, the cotillion, and the *vernissage*, bore down on them again, Aunt Esther, dressed to leave the house for one of the Thursday evening meetings of the Parlor, paused at the foot of the wide, polished stair, faltered and put her hand on the newel post, faintly uttering the words, "Oh, my head, my poor head," in a hissing whisper which she supposed to be a scream. A

228

few seconds later she fell to her knees, poleaxed by a stroke which left her dumb, paralyzed and helpless.

Aunt Esther lived on as a prisoner within her own tiny body, conscious to what extent nobody quite knew, but eternally watchful. The two hundred and twenty pound colored nurse who fed her, cleaned her, and moved her eighty pounds of skin and bone when it had to be moved, swore that she knew little or nothing of what went on about her. But Silky felt her eyes on him all the time he was with her. She watched his face for as long as he was in the room, and he felt exuding from her a terror of what he would do now that the whip was out of her hand and she was helpless. He would sit for long hours reading to her from her favorite books, or just holding her hand, in an attempt to reassure her. And then he would hide from her for days at a time because he could not bear to think of the knowledge of him which was locked up behind the restlessly moving eyes in her lifeless face.

"You pay her too much heed, you pay her altogether too much heed," grumbled the nurse. "You is knocking yourself out for no reason. She don't understand nothing no more. You can see from the way her eyes travels about, and the way she frown, that she don't know where she is or what she seeing. You is just upsetting yourself trying to get any sense through to her poor addled brain, she ain't there no more."

But Silky could not free himself of the feeling that Aunt Esther, in all her menacing, sharp-minded entirety, was peeping out at him through the restless eyes, longing to regain her self-command, and hating every second of her imprisonment.

The disturbance to his routine created in the first few weeks of Miss Esther's illness broke up his program of sittings, and when he began to paint again it was apparent that everything was altered. His first subject was, in the polite phrase, an older woman. Her softening body was braced and pushed into shape by all sorts of elastic devices and her flesh, where it was visible, was subtly corrupted with overcare. It had been subjected to too many greasings, creamings, and waxings, patted and smoothed too often, colored and tinted with too great a number of lotions and rouges. It had the terrifyingly artificial quality which used to be the hallmark of the actor's or the actress's professional flesh. Silky was nauseated and flinched from it. He painted round it. He filled in the canvas with all the accessories which he had painted so often, the bouquet of flowers, white faintly flushed with pink, the distant view of the sitter's house among its live oaks, the matched Japanese pearls, the rings, the bracelets. He became fascinated by the strangely inhuman effect of her head, and traced it at last to her well-washed and beautifully cut hair, so beautifully looked after that it seemed less her own than a helmet she had borrowed from her hairdresser.

"You go to Maurice, don't you?" he asked.

"Yes, I do. It's clever of you to know that, Silky."

"Oh, his—signature—is unmistakable."

"I'll tell him you recognized his touch. I'm sure he'll be gratified."

At the end of five sittings he had everything but the woman, who remained a tentative pink smear surrounded by the harshly glittering detail of her existence. He fiddled with his brushes and palette for twenty minutes, staring at the woman's hands, already ropy with intimations of arthritis to come, and encrusted with bright stones and worked gold.

I can't go on, he said to himself. I can't paint those flabby arms, that beastly face. I can't bear to look at them.

And then with a thrust of panic he remembered Miss Esther's doctor's and nursing bills.

"Excuse me," he said aloud to his subject. "If I could ask you to relax for one minute, I've just this moment remembered the most hideously important telephone call I should have made this morning before I did anything else. It went clean out of my head until this instant. I do hope you won't think me too horribly rude if I just run over to the house and get it off my mind and my conscience before I forget again. It must have been looking forward to painting such a lovely lady that drove it out of my head."

In the other house he leaned against the kitchen wall by

the icebox and poured a tumbler of whiskey into himself, sweating as he drank. The huge nurse taking a break for a cup of coffee sat at the metal-topped table in the middle of the room watching him.

"That ain't going to do you one bit of good, Mr. Sigaux, no sir, not at eleven in the morning, it ain't." She shook her head.

"I don't care if it does me any good or any harm. I only hope it works. It's got to work."

And he went back to the studio leaving her to cluck and shake her head. When he faced the canvas again the woman's face, arms, and hands, went smoothly, just a little too smoothly, onto the canvas; poured onto it as if the picture itself had been in his paint tubes, not just pigment. When the sitter had it at home and it was hung in the place prepared for it, she looked at it with her husband standing beside her.

"Well, I don't know," she said.

"It's sort of like you," her husband said, "and sort of not. He's somehow missed my girl."

"But Silky is good," she said, "that picture of Alice Godstone is just beautiful."

"Sure, I know it is. And I wanted Silky to paint you. But he just hasn't delivered the goods this time." The husband sighed. "It's too bad."

Silky came to dinner a month later, and was placed opposite the portrait. It spoke to him as he spooned his cold Spanish soup, saying "failure even at this level," so loudly that he suddenly called up the table to his hostess to tell her that the portrait would have to come down, and right away. It just wasn't finished. He'd repaint it for free. But it would have to come down that instant. So between the soup and the curried shrimp the picture came down with much laughter, and some hidden annoyance, to stand with its back facing out into the room for the rest of the evening. Silky meant to take it away with him when he left that night, but by then he had taken a little more brandy than he knew and he was forgetting things.

231

When he went round in the morning to fetch the picture away it had been rehung.

"Why Silky, we thought you weren't serious. We thought—well—you know how it is at a party . . ."

"That I had been drinking?"

"Now Silky, don't take it that way. It was a party—we were all pretty cheerful—and you've been having an awful time since this horrible thing happened to poor Esther—we all understand."

"Well, honey, I was sober and serious, and I really do have to repaint that terrible picture. So come and sit for me again as soon as you can."

And this time he fought it out, and stayed sober. But this time the woman was on the canvas as she was, or a least as she was visible, with all her futile and pathetic public aspects brassily to the fore.

"Oh dear," she said, when it was back on her dining room wall.

"Do we have to hang the damned thing?" her husband said. "I believe it was actually better the way it was."

"I'm afraid poor Esther's illness has really upset him. She was a sort of mother to him. Let's just put it away and forget it."

"And to think I could have bought Ted a Volkswagen with the money! Well, what can't be helped has to be endured, I suppose."

Silky had two or three other failures like that in the first year of Miss Esther's illness, and more in the year after. He felt the fabric of the life she had made for him disintegrating round him. The house, which had seemed bright and cheerful in an old-maidish way, began to seem dated and shabby, and it smelt of illness. The garden was running down, and dust gathered on the throne in the studio. By the time that the colored nurse took pity on him and smothered Miss Esther with a pillow Silky knew that his reputation was gone. He had heard that it was all over town that he had to drink to finish his pictures, and that if he worked them over when he was sober he would spoil them. There was a wave of pity for him after Miss Esther's funeral and he was asked to paint the queen and her attendants as usual. But he felt the kindness which lay behind the commissions and knew he wasn't trusted. He claimed to be too upset by his aunt's death to undertake them. And so there was no studio party at the beginning of the great week that year, or ever again. Silky spent most of his time reading the English classic novelists in Miss Esther's old-fashioned library, or he would sit drinking coffee and playing gin rummy with the fat nurse who had stayed on to housekeep for him. The only side of his life that remained unchanged was that which began around six in the evening. He was as quick to accept an invitation as ever, and he got his invitations because he talked his role of the successful, worldly, artist brilliantly —right up to the moment when he fell flat on his face. And a watchful hostess could circumvent that. On the rare occasions when he was allowed to slip past the point of no return to become sodden and incompetent his excuse was not far to seek. He was one who had suffered.

"Poor Silky. He was really broken up by his aunt's death. They were all the world to each other from way back, from the time that awful thing happened when he was kid. He was but seven or eight if I remember, and his father and mother were knocked all to pieces when their car stalled on a grade crossing in front of a train. It's too horrible, but her head never was found, and, well these things can't be helped I suppose, some of the other kids found out and it wasn't too long before he knew."

But it was something else, or a combination of things, that had hit Silky. He missed his aunt's firm hand, but it was more a matter of what he had than what he missed. He had just enough money to live on when Miss Esther's will was through probate. He couldn't afford any of the travelings, and the goings to and fro, with which the rich fill their days and hide their idleness, but he could sit around doing nothing without getting into any sort of trouble. Every now and then he would go to the city markets to get an armful of flowers, and for a day

233

or two would pretend to be working. But these still lifes never got themselves finished before the wilted flowers were thrown out. He dragged his first paintings out of the attic where Miss Esther had stored them and put them round the studio. They surprised him by the amount of old-fashioned promise they contained. He had been designed to fill a slot somewhere between Winslow Homer and John Singer Sargent, but he had been delivered just about sixty years too late. He wondered what would have happened if he had had the nerve to go ahead on the line of his real gift. He had been able to paint people as if they were apples, and to make them look as fresh and innocent and good as apples, too. He tried to get back to that, and failed. He was not that boy any more.

Ilona's invitation came to him when he had not set a brush to canvas in months, and at the psychological moment which arrived every six weeks or so in which he was promising himself that he was really going to pick himself up and put himself together again. It looked like a heaven-sent chance for a break in the routine of laziness which had taken hold of him. He decided it was the dinginess and deadness of his studio, the lingering memories of Miss Esther's long dying in the house, which were holding him back. Out at the Grove in the sunlight, and on the edge of the bright glitter of Gavin's wealth he would be able to get to work. But the first invitation developed into a routine of almost daily visits to the Hatfields. And he always arrived at the house too late to do anything in the morning, and just in time for a drink before lunch. After the meal, the light was too strong and harsh for painting. He talked with Ilona over coffee, and presently the children were home from school, and then Gavin, and the day was gone.

"Since when have you been a collector of lame ducks?" Gavin said.

"Oh, poor old Silky, he's harmless and he tells stories well."

"I don't believe he knows half the people he says he knew over there. He wasn't so grand."

"I know. It doesn't matter though. When he's had a drink

or two he believes he knew them and his stories come out all right. I think he really did meet Dali though, once anyway."

"Well, if he's your choice of lap dog, it's all right with me."

He really disliked Silky, but he was grateful to him because the painter did seem to fill some void in Ilona's life with interest. He knew she drank with him, but her drinking seemed less urgent and less desperate than it had been. I suppose it's really true that misery loves company, he thought, and having him at hand must be the answer to some need I just don't know anything about. He had just come back from Maramee at the end of the day and he was standing down at the end of the terrace watching what was going on. Silky had been going through the motions of starting a portrait that day and his easel and paint box were set up near the breakfast-room door. Gavin could see the roughed-in beginnings of a picture on the canvas. But Silky had forgotten all about that. He was bent over one of the glass-topped coffee tables with a sketching pad spread out in front of him, and with Thomas, Mary and Bogey clustered beside him. He was drawing with enormous speed and facility a new installment in the adventures of B'ar Hatfield. Gavin knew them well and liked them almost as much as the children did. There had been B'ar Hatfield at Valley Forge, B'ar Hatfield on the retreat from Moscow, B'ar Hatfield on the crusades, and B'ar Hatfield crossing the Atlantic with the pilgrim fathers. Ilona lay back in her chair with her feet up, smiling. She looked well, Gavin had not seen her look so relaxed and well in months. He looked at the scene with pleasure. So did Miss Jelke. She was standing near an upstairs window talking to Miss Wilbraham.

"Isn't it wonderful the way Mrs. Hatfield has pulled herself together and found new interests these last few months?" she said, looking fondly out of the French windows opening onto the terrace. The children were clamoring now for Silky to come down to the lake to swim with them.

"Oh do, Silky, and then stay to supper," Ilona could be heard saying.

"You must be greener than you look, dear," said Miss Wilbraham.

"What do you mean?" Miss Jelke was indignant.

"I suppose looking after children all the time slows you up in the end, but I should think even you could see that that one's putting it away just as hard as ever. While they're out there yakking every afternoon they kill a bottle of Scotch between them."

"I can't believe it." Miss Jelke's hand went to her throat.

"Believe what you want. But under that beautiful blah manner of hers her ladyship is halfway plastered right this minute."

"I can't believe it."

Miss Jelke stared out of the window at the figure in the wheeled basketwork chaise longue. Ilona's dress was raspberry pink, cheerful against the bright colors of the candy striped cushions. Silky was wearing white trousers and a yellow sports shirt. The sunburned children in their shorts of denim and their white singlets clustered round him. It all looked pretty, cheerful and gay. Miss Jelke saw the light glittering on the bottles, the glasses, and the ice bucket on the trolley within Ilona's reach. Silky and the children moved on down towards the lake. Ilona reached out and poured herself a drink.

"I've been such a blind fool," muttered Miss Jelke, riveted to the spot where she stood, "such a fool."

"It's none of our business," said Miss Wilbraham sharply.

"Oh, it is. It's everybody's business to save a lost soul."

"Don't be a horse's ass. You just work here."

"That's a terrible attitude."

"If it's anybody's business it's hers and her husband's. You've no right to interfere."

"It's a moral duty."

"This is a good job," Miss Wilbraham said with a slightly raised voice, "and if you make any trouble you'll have me against you for one."

"That woman could be killing herself."

"It's no concern of mine, or of yours."

236

"I'm disappointed in your attitude, Clara, I am indeed."

"Don't you dare to patronize me. I do the job I'm hired to do and I do it well. I'd advise you to do the same." Miss Wilbraham shook her head with irritation. "Some people don't know when to let well enough alone."

The door slamming behind her did not distract Miss Jelke from the fascinated watch she was keeping on Ilona. Her employers drink vanished swallow by swallow over a period of some ten minutes. When the glass was empty Miss Jelke stiffened. Would it be filled again? Ilona lit a cigarette, took a few draws at it, and stubbed it out. Then, without any furtive attempt at concealment whatever, she poured herself another. She had it in her hand when Gavin came sauntering round the end of the house into Miss Jelke's sight, and she quietly put it to her lips as he came towards her. The insolence of it made Miss Jelke gasp, and she wondered what Gavin could find to say to her as he sat down to face her with apparent unconcern.

"Hallo dear," he said. He gestured at the backs of the party heading off for the lakeside. Bogey had one of Silky's hands in a tight grip, his other arm was linked with Mary's, Thomas was leaning forward to see round her head so that he could watch Silky's face. "Silky's the center of things as usual. I wish I knew what it was all about."

"What?"

"What makes you want to have him around all the time."

"Haven't we been through all that? It's just that he's a light amusing man who happens to be at a loose end."

"He's an out-and-out failure—and a quitter too. I wish he amused me."

"You laugh at a lot of his stories."

"Yes I do. I'll admit it. God damn it, I must be jealous."

"You know that's ridiculous."

"Yes, I know that physical jealousy would be—it's not that that I have in mind." He dropped his eyes and touched the pad in front of him. "These drawings are funny, and, and sort

of nice-spirited, too. He could do a wonderful children's book
—if he could go through with anything any more."

"He's going to do something for me. I don't know if he'll
be able to, and you probably won't agree to it anyway."

"Well, shoot, and we'll find out."

"That big dark, ugly old dining room with that pseudo-
feudal fireplace. I know it's full of the character of the mad-
man who built the house but I just can't stand it any more. I
thought of asking Silky to decorate it—scrape it right out and
make it light and bright and cheerful. I thought if he got interested he might want to do some murals for it."

"Would they be any good?"

"I don't know. He'd imitate somebody good. He's got good
taste."

"I suppose he does. It would mean having him around even
more, wouldn't it, if he did this job? That's the real point,
isn't it?"

"Yes."

"I wish, well, you know what I wish."

"We've been through that."

"Well, if it'll make you happy, rip out the dining room and
do it over. Just so long as it doesn't come out green I'll go
along with it."

"That's very sweet of you." She lifted her glass and drank to
him.

"Well, that looks good. I think I'll join you and have one
before I go in and change." He poured himself a drink and sat
sipping it. "Why do you suppose Miss Jelke is standing in the
window there staring at us. She's been doing it ever since I got
here."

"She must be waiting for the children to come back from
their swim." Ilona turned and waved to her with a small gesture of her free hand. Miss Jelke returned her salute with a
wooden movement, turned herself about abruptly and vanished.

"She's an odd one," Gavin said.

"All nurses get odd when their children start to grow up.

Bogey's really too old to have a nurse any longer. I dare say poor old Jelke's afraid of being fired."

"She must know we wouldn't just turn her adrift."

"I don't know. She'll have to go soon. Bogey can twist her round her little finger. It isn't good for the child to have some-one around she can get her own way with all the time."

"It's hard to realize how the kids are growing up."

Miss Jelke was in her room bathing her face and hands in cold water. She was not horrified by the nature of the armed truce which Gavin's and Ilona's marriage had become, and which she was far from understanding. She was shaken by the blow she had received when she had discovered that Ilona was drinking quite openly and in broad daylight.

The nurse's detective instinct was so highly developed by her obsession that she had become almost incapable of straight-forward observation and logical deduction. She had lost the power of accepting anything for what it was. She had come to believe that all appearances were screens between her and a reality which always had to be unmasked. All ac-tions were to her blinds to conceal hidden moves in a secret game of deception played by everyone around her. When Ilona's sittings and long conversational afternoons with Sigaux had begun she had experienced her hunter's quickening of the senses. She had felt sure that she was soon going to find out what Ilona's answer to her intervention would be. She scruti-nized every aspect of her employer's new pattern of behavior for some hint or clue as to its nature. No clue was, however, manifest. There was Ilona on the terrace or on the move, open and transparent. She never visited the now bewilderingly empty caches and hiding places, and all her disappearances were explicable. Miss Jelke searched her room, opening and sniffing all its bottles, and found nothing. She was forced, de-lightedly, to the conclusion that Ilona had dried herself out and stopped drinking. Miss Jelke assumed that the shock of her daring raid on the handbag had done the trick. She was for a time in the seventh heaven. And now she realized how ter-ribly, how artfully she had been deceived. The answer had

239

been right under her nose all the time. She felt wounded and betrayed, as if she were a small girl invited to take part in a game of hide and seek at a party who had found, when it came round to her turn to be the seeker, that nobody was hiding. There she was, playing on in good faith, searching in an empty garden, when all the other players had gone indoors, perhaps over to another house, to play some other game altogether.

Miss Jelke went up to her room and lay down on her bed, near tears. She heard the shouts of the children down at the lake. She felt old, lonely, unloved and cruelly betrayed. A sob gathered like a bubble in her intestines and fought its way through her chest and out. It was a surprise to her to find that she was crying. She did not know quite if she would ever be able to stop. She cried, "Daddy, oh, daddy, why?" through her tears and got no answer from Ilona's choice of furniture suitable for hired help. The brown photograph of her father as he had been, young, muscular, and handsome, when he had gone overseas with the A.E.F., smiled sardonically at her, as it always did, from the silver frame on top of the highboy. She turned her eyes from it to the enlargement of the snapshot she had taken of Bogey a year before, innocent and uncorrupt. A deep passion of love for Bogey welled up in her. The little darling must, must, be saved from the entangling vileness of this house and family, no matter what. She beat her pillow with her clenched fists to help her gain command of herself. It was no time to give way to weakness, no time at all. She got up smiling her brightest smile and jollied at herself in her looking glass as she patted away the traces of her breakdown. "We aren't going to give way now, are we, just because we had a little setback? We aren't going to let that dreadful, scheming woman get us down?" Over the years she had developed a habit of talking to herself in mirrors, a habit systematized to the point at which the image she faced had a personality and character of its own. She spoke to her reflection as if it were her timid and foolish younger sister, a girl who had a tendency to give up in the face of difficulties. "Now," she said, smiling at herself archly, "we're going to get a grip on ourselves, aren't we? And we're going to put on our thinking caps in order to decide what we can do that'll be best for poor dear Bogey. Yes, and nobody must know we're getting to the point of great decisions. We'll give the children their supper just as usual and then we'll really think, won't we?"

Miss Jelke already knew quite well what she was going to do. She knew that her reflection shared her knowledge, so while she said all this she was raising her eyebrows, dipping her head, nodding, and making small gestures with her hands to show that what she was saying was so much chaff thrown into the air to distract any listener who might overhear her and make a counter-plan. She gave one last knowing nod at herself and then went to meet the children.

Down at the lake, Sigaux was off in the kayak, paddling Bogey along the edge of the cypress swamp looking for an alligator which she swore was eighteen feet long. Thomas and Mary said it was the old alligator which had always been in the lake and that it was nine feet long at the outside. Their denials made Bogey stamp her feet and cry with rage. Silky had taken her off to quiet her down and to break up the scene. Mary and Thomas sat on the edge of the raft trailing their ankles in the water and talking.

"What makes Bogey so God-awful?"

"She's just a brat. It's a stage."

"I wish she'd grow out of it." Thomas scratched his thigh. "And quickly."

"I wonder why Silky bothers to be so nice to her."

"He's a creep."

"He is not."

"All right, if you insist. But he seems pretty creepy to me. I mean he just isn't quite there when you expect him to be. I can't explain."

"Silky's a very distinguished artist who has taken part in the creative life of some of the most wonderful cities in the world. He is real. You wouldn't understand what's special about him in a million years."

"I'm sorry. I didn't realize you cared."

241

"Oh, Thomas Hatfield, you're hateful, stuck-up, silly and superior, and I detest you." She reached down and flung a handful of water into his face. He ducked its scattered drops and grabbed at her with his eyes shut. He meant to take her by the shoulders, but while his right hand did find the smooth round nob of her shoulder his left hand missed. It slid down her chest over her breast and nipple. "Oh, you!" she cried and gave him a stinging slap across the face. "Don't you ever do that to me again, Thomas Hatfield. Don't you dare."

"What did I do?" He was indignant. They rose still grappling, overbalanced, and fell off the raft into the clear almost tasteless water. They came threshing wildly to the surface in a flurry of spray. Mary broke water first and found Thomas' wet seal-like head coming up handily close to her. She ducked him savagely once and again, then set off for the shore at a fast crawl. He came up spluttering and swam heavily after her.

"You wait! You just wait till I catch up with you," he shouted. Shouting slowed him down still more and he soon saw that she was out of reach. He swam slowly on behind her, feeling angry, sick, and waterlogged. He promised himself that when he got hold of her on shore he would twist her arm and make her apologize. They were so angry with each other that neither of them saw Gavin walking down the broad walk and out onto the landing dock at the water's edge. When Mary scrambled up the ladder and started to run towards the house she ran full tilt into him. After a first oh! of surprise and hurt she saw who it was and hugged him, laying her sopping head on his chest and bursting into hysterical tears. Gavin's first feeling, after the shock of being almost winded had passed off, was one of irritation. "For God's sake," he said angrily as he felt the water from her hair and her wet suit soaking through his shirt. But then he felt her shoulders moving as she clung to him and realized that she was crying. At that moment Thomas hoisted himself dripping up over the end of the ladder. He ran a few steps along the rope matting towards them and then slowed uneasily to a walk.

"Oh, hullo," he said awkwardly.

"Well, hallo, son. What goes on here?" Gavin said.

"I don't know," Thomas said. "It beats me. We were sitting on the raft talking about nothing much, and she suddenly flared up. God alone knows why. The next thing I knew we were in the water and she was shoving my head under. I must have swallowed half the lake. I was going to make her sorry for it."

"Well, that's nothing to cry your heart out for, old lady, is it?" said Gavin stroking his daughter's wet head. He looked over towards the grove of swamp cypress and saw Sigaux paddling Bogey back towards them. "Now here comes your mother's pet painter and your sister. You don't want them to see you're crying, do you? You'd better run on up to the house and get changed." He put a finger under her chin and turned her face up towards his. "Young Thomas is sorry for whatever it was he said or did. You're sorry for being mad at him, and the whole thing's over, isn't it, now."

She nodded, smiling up at him through her tears, wondering dumbly how they could be so far apart, so remote from each other when they were so physically close. She turned an anguished eye on Thomas and saw dawning comprehension in his face.

"I'm sorry," he said awkwardly, laying his hand on her brown shoulder.

"Oh, everything's so awful," she cried and fled, leaving them both standing.

"Boy, am I just soaked," Gavin said, shifting from foot to foot. He looked at the boy beside him, naked but for his shorts, and saw how rapidly his body was changing into that of a well-made man. He felt proud of Thomas' broad shoulders, his good frame, and his strong muscles, as if they were in some way a personal accomplishment. And at the same time he felt sad. The boy had so much to learn before he would catch up with his body. "Women are funny creatures," he said, putting a hand on Thomas' shoulder and turning towards the house. "They're tougher than men, and more sensitive than men at the same time. They grow up faster. In some ways

Mary's already ahead of you even though she is younger. She's at a very awkward age just now—the awkward age. You'll have to make allowances for a year or two so go slow and try not to tread on her corns. See what I mean?"

"Yes, I think so," Thomas said wondering how anyone who had lived so long and seen so much could seem to know so little.

There was a diversion as Silky brought the kayak in onto the sandy beach beside the landing dock and Bogey came running round to be made much of by her father. Thomas winced as he saw Gavin gather her up off the ground in a bear hug, because that was followed by a lot of customary sweet talk, a parody of lover's talk, which was supposed to be a joke between them. Thomas found it ugly, because anyone could see how Bogey was, even though she was only eleven. He knew, as his mother and father did not, that girls of thirteen and fourteen in Bogey's school in Maramee were already going out on dates with the flyers from the William Arling Field and telling the pilots that they were over sixteen. He thought that Gavin had no business to be amused by Bogey's vamp act, by her eyelash flutterings, her wrigglings, and her cooings. It was all in fun, but even so it was practice which Bogey was going to turn to account some day. His father ought to slap her down, throw cold water on her, and make her behave with some dignity and self-restraint. It might be that Bogey couldn't help having hot pants. But at least she needn't advertise them to the whole world.

"You're a little sugar bonbon, a praline; you're so sweet I could eat you right up," Gavin said, grinning into Bogey's face. She affected to scream. "Can't I have a bite, just one little bite, say from here?" He kissed the top of his finger and pressed it onto her arm. "From there?"

"Oh, daddy, just one little, tiny bite." She rolled her eyes wildly at Sigaux as Gavin pretended to take a nip at her brown flesh. "Oh, daddy, was it good? Terribly good?"

"Simply scrumptious, superdelicious," he said, "the best piece of you I ever tasted."

244

He threw her up in the air and she squealed with delight. Thomas scratched with a toe at the rope matting, awkwardly. It had suddenly come to him just how he had offended his sister, and what had led up to the act which had given her offence. He lifted his head and stared at the painter. His sister had crossed the physical frontier between childhood and womanhood. In their tumbling piece of horseplay he had inadvertently roused a sensitivity in her body that she now held as something reserved and sacred, to be shared only on special terms with a lover. And she was in love with Sigaux. The words sounded so sharply and so alarmingly in his brain that it was surprising to him that his father didn't overhear them. He knew by some sure instinct that Silky was no good, generally speaking. He would be poison for Mary, he was sure of it. He looked desperately and wonderingly at Gavin's smiling face: didn't he begin to realize what was going on? Up at the house Bailey rang the old stable bell hanging outside the kitchen door to call the children in to their supper. Gavin set Bogey down and the instant her feet touched the ground Thomas grabbed her hand.

"Hey you," he said, "race you up to the house. Come on." They both bolted off. It was something to get away. Gavin looked fondly after them as they went. The race petered out within a hundred yards or so of the dock to the tune of squeals of protest from Bogey who couldn't keep up even though Thomas was running at half speed. He stopped for her and hoisted her onto his shoulders where she immediately became a lady bareback rider, spreading her arms widely and gracefully. She knew that Thomas would hold her legs tightly enough to make sure she didn't fall off.

"Children are wonderful, Silky," Gavin said, slapping Sigaux on the back. "You just haven't lived until you've seen your own children growing up and getting a hold on life. I often think it's the greatest experience there is. You bachelors don't know what you're missing. Didn't you ever think of getting married, Silky?"

"Oh, I've thought of it. I just never found the right girl, or

245

the right girl never thought I was the right man. You know how these things are." Silky had long ago arrived at this formula, but he never ceased to wonder at the frequency with which men like Gavin were led to harp on this subject with him. Averting his thoughts from Thomas, he went on, "Bogey's a wonderful little thing. You might think she was spoiled if you didn't know her, but she's really the most natural and uncalculating piece of mischief I know. She's a darling."

"I think she's going to be a dazzler in a year or two," Gavin said complacently. "The boys will be round here after her like wasps round a honey pot." He shrugged his shoulders. "You know, that water looks pretty good to me. I think I'll go in for a swim before dinner. Are you coming in, or have you had enough?"

"Oh, I ought to be getting off home, it's late."

"Stick around for dinner. I know Ilona would like that." Gavin turned away towards the little bath house. "Come on, say you will, and I'll call the house and let them know." His tone became jocular. "You might as well say yes. You know you've nothing better to do."

"Well, I don't have any other engagement to tell the honest truth," Silky said. "So I don't see why I shouldn't."

"That's settled then," said Gavin vanishing into the bath house. In a few seconds Silky heard his voice telling Bailey over the phone that Mr. Sigaux would be staying to dinner. "Oh, you did? You set a place for him?" he heard Gavin say. "Well, that's just fine." He hung up and called cheerily through the slatted door of the men's changing room. "They were expecting you, Silky. You're getting to be a fixture round here." Another barbed shaft went home. Sigaux dived off the end of the dock and came up shaking water out of his hair. I'm becoming these people's toady, a hanger-on in a rich man's house. I'm a jester, and they tolerate me. Where do I go from here? He swam out to the raft and climbed onto it a few seconds before Gavin arrived.

"That was good," the banker said, easing himself down beside Silky. "I may be silly, but I still get a kick out of being able to swim the crawl. When I was in college it was a novelty. You could impress the hell out of girls with it, and anyone else for that matter. It used to annoy my father more than almost anything I did. He swam with his head high out of the water most of the time, and when he wanted to put on a show he used to do something he called the trudgen. I looked it up a year or two ago and found it was named for some British army man who invented it. Whenever he did it when we were in the water together I'd start doing the crawl and I'd shoot past him. He couldn't stand it. He'd say, 'Gavin, if there's one thing worse than a lout it's a show-off,' and then he'd give me a lecture on the way professionalism was ruining games by taking all the fun out of them. We used to row about tennis too. 'You can learn all you want to know about tennis by playing it,' he used to say. 'If you need a professional to teach you how it's not a game and there's no point in playing it.'"

"I see what he meant," Silky said.

"So do I, now. I didn't then. You can be an awful ass when you're young. I spent almost all the money I made working in a lumber camp one summer, on tennis lessons I took secretly from Steven McGill's pro. Father refused to speak to Steven for over a year after he found Steven had hired a professional to sit around that indoor court of his waiting to give him a game whenever he wanted it, and teaching the boys, there were three of them I think, how to beat all their friends right off the court." He suddenly broke off. He stared up into the sky, looking at a minute moving speck which might have been an aircraft passing over them somewhere up above forty thousand feet. The pro, who had never quite made the finals at Forest Hills or Wimbledon, though he often killed off seeded players in surprise upsets in the middle stages of tournaments, was dead; Gavin's father was dead; Steven McGill was dead, and two of the McGill boys had been killed in the war. It was all a long time ago. He remembered the first time he had unleashed his secretly acquired game, beating his cousin Alden Adams Hatfield in straight sets without losing a point. His father had called it a disgusting exhibition. And so it had been, a simple humiliation inflicted on Alden, who had been ready for a friendly game. What did it matter if Silky was a failure? And what, if anything, did failure mean?

"You know, you've done a lot for Ilona," he said abruptly.

"That's absurd, Gavin. Why, Ilona's a wonderful woman."

"Oh, I know that, but she has her problems. I was really worried this time last year, she seemed to be losing her grip on herself. Since then she's been seeing a lot of you, and she's been a different woman. I won't say the problem isn't still there, but she seems to have come to terms with it. I suppose knowing there's someone around who has the same problem as you do helps; anyway I don't think she feels as isolated and as alone as she did."

Silky sat up, uneasily. "I don't think I've done anything I can claim any credit for. I've never said anything about, well, problems, to Ilona. I wouldn't feel justified in doing any such thing."

"You know that's not what I mean. I'm not congratulating you on a piece of successful rescue work. It's just by being here, giving her a new interest in life—in a way that, God help me, I've never been able to do—that you've done the trick."

"I wish I could think I had." Silky suddenly wondered, why do I go on pretending? "I wish I could believe I was any damned good to any living creature, but I can't fool myself, Gavin. You're making a mistake."

Gavin wiped his forehead, as if brushing away water that had run down from his hair. He suddenly saw what it was with a devastating clarity, she had come to that, then. To exist she needed to have someone about whom she could effortlessly and easily despise.

"You're too diffident. You don't want to underrate yourself." He flinched from his suspicion that Silky wasn't to be underrated. "What's this project you and Ilona have cooked up to tear out the old dining room up at the house? Do you think it'll work out?"

"That's just what I mean, Gavin. I can talk that project when I'm a little high, and I can see what Ilona wants done so well that in my head it's all finished and complete. But it's all talk, Gavin. I won't ever do it. I don't have what it takes."

"Come on now, Silky, this is bad. Everyone knows you were upset by the way Miss Esther died, so slowly and sadly. But everyone knows you were a good painter. You've forgotten how good you were."

"People are very kind and very tolerant; I know that if anyone does. But it isn't that easy, Gavin. I never did have much of a gift, and what I did have wasn't a creative gift."

"Well, hell, man. You did your best, and you put on a pretty good show." Gavin gave him a friendly hearty pat on the shoulder. "Up to the time you let Miss Esther's death get you down, and you started drinking, anyway."

"That's what I'd like to believe, Gavin, if I could. But it isn't so. I've just been faking all along."

"Who doesn't, Silky, when you get down to it?" He stood up. "It must be getting on towards dinner time. I feel hungry anyway. We ought to be getting on back."

Silky stood up, his face downcast.

"You don't know what it's like, knowing in your bones that you're no damned good, and that you never have been."

"Come on now. We've all had our moments on the bottom. You know these things pass, Silky." Gavin felt that his voice sounded hollow, he couldn't disguise his misery at the thought that this was what Ilona had need of and hungered for. The image of Father Prieto came startlingly before him, the black-frocked figure with his face dark with hatred for Ilona. He loathed her because she wouldn't crawl and kiss the dirt at his feet. They were competitors for the same offal. He wondered if there was behind the appetite some other thing they shared in common. The priest spent his life celibate and in skirts, and Ilona had slept alone now for, he calculated momentarily, getting on for twelve years. Gavin faltered at the conception of a whole life spent in a torment of disgust at the outrage fate had committed in making the human body what it was; of dozens, thousands, and millions of lives warped and tortured by the same grotesque inability to come to terms with the simple facts of what has always been the price of a man's entry into the world. And it did no good to ask them what was worrying them, since every human being who ever has existed has come into the same being for the same reason, that some woman has taken the shaft from some man. It was precisely that which worried them.

"You have it bad, Silky, and I wish I could help," he said. "But we're getting too damned gloomy. We'd better get up to the house quick, before we decide to sink ourselves down to the bottom of the lake or something. Cheer up, and remember you've got friends and they're with you."

Gavin went off the float and raised a splash that set it swinging. As soon as he was back at the surface he went into the powerful urgent crawl which had become the only way he knew how to swim. If he wasn't just bobbing about, or floating, and deliberately holding himself back he was bound to hurtle, threshing, onwards as if he had some important mission to carry out at a given goal. Silky stood watching his flailing arms and the water churning behind him.

"How that man can throw himself into things," he said enviously, and wondered why he had suddenly fallen into such a confessional mood with a man he hardly knew. Ilona had always been much more friendly to him than Gavin, but he had never been able to speak so openly to her. He felt a little ashamed, and rather relieved at having spoken out. It made him feel less of a sponger so far as Gavin was concerned.

When the two men reached the house they found that a party had materialized in their absence. The enormous, swollen shapes of three Cadillacs, two hardtops and a convertible, filled the graveled circle in front of the house, and the terrace seemed crowded with men and women in play clothes. Bailey had just brought a *quiche Lorraine* out from the kitchen and was handing small slices of it to the newcomers on paper napkins. The air was full of delighted exclamations at the deliciousness and the originality of the offering.

Bailey did not tell them that it would not have figured as a fore bite if they hadn't arrived out of the blue. It would have been the main dish in the light meal that Gavin, Ilona and Silky would have eaten together. It was now being fed to the unexpected guests to hold them off while Julia, grumbling furiously, prepared dinner for ten in place of dinner for three. Ilona was impenetrable behind dark glasses and when Gavin looked at her questioningly to find out what was going on she shrugged her shoulders as if denying all responsibility. Gavin touched his right cheek with one finger in a coded signal they had long before agreed on. If the guests were for drinks only she would pull one of her ears by its lobe in answer, if they were staying for dinner she would touch her mouth briefly. She touched her mouth. Gavin turned towards the guests hoping to recognize at least one of them, but drew a blank. His eye fell on the back of a young woman wearing skin-tight white matador pants, a scarlet sash, and a white-wool jersey blouse with short sleeves. Beyond her there were four men and two women. The fair-haired girl he was staring at turned round as if she sensed his eyes on her buttocks.

"This *quiche* is terrific, I just adore *entremeses*, don't you?" she said smiling.

"I'm glad you like it. Who are you?" he said smiling right back, enjoying the front view of her as much as he had enjoyed the other. "If I knew that I could introduce you to this man here, Silky Sigaux. He's a pretty nice fellow and one hell of a good painter."

"Pleased to meet you, Silky," she said. She laid a limp hand in his, faintly greasy from the *quiche,* and six or seven bracelets, one of them heavily loaded with charms, fell down her forearm with a clatter. She turned back to Gavin with a slight frown. "Say, are you my host or something? I mean I really haven't just barged in. I'm Patti Elliot and I'm here with him —that bald man, Stephen Tollick—and we were over there, out on that key thing—you know—"

"Rummer's Key?" said Gavin.

"Yes, sure, that's it. You really know this district, I must

251

say; well, we were there with Michael Klosky and he called up about getting to see this man—it could be you I guess—Gavin Hatfield, and this woman Enona something—"

"Ilona," Gavin said.

"I'm sorry. I have this terrible memory for names. Well, whoever it was, said oh, come on over and have dinner, and he said but, honey—he calls everybody honey or darling all the time, it doesn't mean a thing—but, honey, he said, I have these guests, and she said oh, that's all right, bring them along and here we are."

"Well, that's nice," Gavin said. "I do know Mike, as it happens. At least I know who he is! He wrote me a couple of letters last week. But the others?"

"Gee, I don't know, except first names. That's Charlie, and that's Alfred, and Grace goes with Charlie and Lola with Alfred."

"When you say they"—Gavin bent his head down towards her ear and whispered—"go with each other, do you mean they're married or just friends?"

"Honest, I wouldn't know, all I know is they're associates, the men, that is, in this thing of Mike's, Mr. Klosky's, that my friend, him, the bald one, Steve, is doing the public relations for."

"Are you in public relations too, Patti?" Silky said.

"Actually no." She took the smile she had been giving Gavin off her face and gave Sigaux a prolonged stare. "I was in this beauty contest once if you want to make anything of it."

"I think you misunderstood the man, darling," Gavin said, beaming. "That was a friendly question he asked."

"It was?" She put the smile back on again, and gave Silky a small part of it this time. She turned and pulled Mike Klosky by the sleeve. "Mr. Klosky, I've located this man that you brought us to have dinner with. He's just dying to meet your other friends."

"What say, Patti? Oh!" Klosky's face assumed a look of desperate cheerfulness. Only his eyes showed his panic. "Mr. Hatfield, this is a great pleasure, you don't know. I had no conception, no thought, of this intrusion when I telephoned your lovely wife. I was merely seeking to get up an appointment for a later date. You can imagine my confusion, my delight, when Madame here urged us to come on over. It's not only for myself that I feel an intense pleasure, it's the thought of being privileged to bring Charlie Pollner and Grace Pollner, old and dear friends as well as close business associates, and Alfred de Laume and Lola de Laume, dear friends too, to your lovely home that pleases me most, and I want you to know my very brilliant young helper, Steve Tollick, and Patti."

"Oh, we've met," Gavin said, slipping an arm over her shoulders, "we're old friends, from two minutes back."

"I want you to know, Gavin, Mr. Hatfield, that Patti is a very talented young person. In addition to her youth she has a very real gift, and definitely ranks as a possible future luminary of stage and screen."

"I knew that just as soon as I saw her, Mr. Klosky," Gavin said gallantly, as he gave the girl's shoulder a slight squeeze. Steve Tollick eyed her nervously and guessed correctly that Patti had decided that Gavin was attractive. He knew that once Patti had formed this opinion about a man there was not far to go, if he wanted to go farther.

"Your husband is a great wit, Mrs. Hatfield," he said sourly. "I see he has Miss Elliot completely under his spell already."

"Oh, Gavin has bags of charm, and money too," said Ilona lazily and sipped her drink. "Nobody's safe with Gavin."

"That's a very sophisticated attitude," Steve said, "on a wife's part, if you'll pardon the remark."

"I adore pictures," Grace Pollner was saying to Silky. "I mean a picture you like is an experience, a new dimension. There was a time when I didn't care a damn. I mean it could be wild geese or September Morn or what the hell, I didn't care . . ."

"Excuse me," Silky said. "Just one moment. Oh, Bailey, I don't seem to have a drink. Give me a good strong Scotch, will you? I'm sorry, that was an uncivil interruption, forgive me, please. Do go on."

"Well, I was naïve, from an artistic point of view, to put it mildly. Then Charlie came to me, he was building the Meadow Motor Court off the Pennsylvania Turnpike then, we were thinking of marriage but his ex was still in the saddle at the time, well, he came and said I want art in the new place. I don't want French prints or Audubon reprints, or anything phoney. I want this to be a tip-top job with a hand-done original oil painting in every room. That meant a hundred and twenty pictures, darling, and you can imagine I was knocked right over. I said, Charlie, I don't know a thing about that stuff, and he said, Grace, you always underrate yourself. You've always shown taste and discrimination in every job you've ever done for me, I've done all his motor courts I may say parenthetically, if you see what I mean, and I'm relying on you in this. Well, when a client, particularly if you happen to be crazy about the guy, shows that amount of confidence what can you do but deliver? I must have walked a hundred miles through museums and galleries while I was getting my nerve up to buy those pictures and at the end of it I was glad. I told Charlie. I said Charlie, something new has been added, I like this stuff. I'm not going to let you open another court without pictures in it. All right, he said, just so long as you don't bring them into the house. We were married by then, you understand, and of course he was just joking, Charlie likes a joke. But to strike a serious note, Mr. Pollner and our good friend Mr. Klosky have constructed a considerable number of motor courts since then and I've seen to it that they've had pictures in all of them, real honest-to-god works of art, and, Mr. Sigaux, I'm telling you nothing less than the truth when I say I've had personal pleasure in buying each and every one of them. And I'm happy to say Charlie enjoys buying pictures now as much as I do. We've bought over eight hundred pictures together, and all by living artists except the set of old stuff, antiques, you know what I mean, we bought for the Colonial Court at Valley Forge. But that was a special Williamsburg-type promotion, we laid on the authenticity with a trowel on that one, but still you can see what I mean when I say I've made painting part of my life."

"It sounds quite wonderful, Mrs. Pollner, wonderful," Silky said.

"Like I'd expect, I find my Gracie talking to a real hand-some fellow," Mr. Pollner said, coming up and clapping Silky on the back with one hand while he patted his wife's back-side with the other. His smile dazzled Silky. His dentures were so much whiter, so much more perfect, than any set of teeth that nature ever put in a man's jaw.

"Mr. Sigaux is a very talented painter, dear," Grace said.

"Then it's a real pleasure, a pleasure indeed," said Mr. Poll-ner. "It's always a pleasure for a business fellow like myself to make contact with creative minds in another sphere. I didn't see it at first, I can tell you. I asked Gracie to get me the pictures for one of our motor courts as a decorative gim-mick, to strike a note of luxury and class, if you follow me, like putting down wall-to-wall carpets. In those days I didn't think too highly of the painting fraternity I may say. Not that I'd ever have said an artist was a bum, mind you, but I didn't rate the profession, that's all. It just didn't rate with me. Sure I knew Nelson Rockefeller or Onassis or some fellow like that would give two or three hundred thousand dollars for this or that picture, but I thought what the hell, you know, I mean what's a prestige item a man like that can afford when you get down to it? I just didn't make the connection between that world and mine. Well, Grace opened my eyes. She showed me hidden values. We had this court we were building in Nevada, a semi-residential type to cream off some of the divorce busi-ness they have out there, you know, very austere, very modern, done by this Jap Klosky was crazy about for a while. We had this spacious entry lobby, and the minute she saw it in the model Grace said for this wall I have to have Jackson Pollock. So all right, I said, you get a Pollock, so I might say all right, dear, if you want to serve caviar serve caviar at a dinner where some occasion is being marked. A month or so later Klosky

255

comes to me looking like death, holding a photograph of that picture in his hand. Words fail me, he says. I've trusted you for years, Charlie, and now this, you sit there facing me without shame when you've spent four thousand dollars of the firm's money for a piece of board some nut has poured paint on. Did I have a time calming him down. And then the battlefield was my own home. Grace, I said, you went altogether too far. At one stage she was packing her bags to leave, if you can imagine. Well, with one thing and another we straightened it out. I gave Klosky my personal check for the sum in question which made him happy, and I got Klosky to leave the picture stay in the lobby which kept my Gracie here happy. But Klosky was so mad he wouldn't meet or speak to Gracie for three whole months. I felt badly myself, because, well, Gracie's all the world to me, but I wasn't convinced by that picture. I told her, frankly, I thought she was in error. Look, I said, granted that type picture is right in the given context, I know there's students, young fellows making their way, who would have been glad to paint you such a thing for a tenth of the money. For four hundred dollars you could have got something perfectly O.K. She just looked at me, you know, with hauteur, as if she wanted to freeze my blood."

"Oh, Charlie, you make it sound as if I'd been terrible."

"It was a crisis, Mr. Sigaux, I'm telling you. And then this feature in *Life* magazine came out, 'The Wonderful World of the American Road,' and there in color, a full page no less, was the lobby of our court with our Jackson Pollock, a splendid picture, a beautiful thing taken with photo floods at night. It was a revelation, right away I could see it was a lovely thing. And an ace to play with Klosky. I took the magazine to him and laid it on his desk. I said, Mike, tell me, since when have you been able to buy a full page of *Life* magazine for four thousand dollars? I crowed over him. I couldn't resist the opportunity. I may say Gracie was a better man than I am on that, the words I told you so never passed her lips, not on one single occasion. She was as wonderful in the hour of triumph as always."

"That's a fascinating story, Mr. Pollner," Silky said, "it really is."

"Well, it certainly taught me to respect the artist. I could see it after that. Pollock's picture was a different affair from what the student, the ordinary fellow, would have done. He had the *je ne sais quoi*, I don't know what, call it star-quality if you like, that made his work outstanding. He was a personality, if you follow me."

"The boys are real sweet about it," Grace said. "These clips I have on my ears were the *amende honorable*. One from each of them, real diamonds, and the green stones are emeralds. I could have died with happiness when Mike gave me a great hug and pushed the box into my hands. There was the sweetest note inside. It proved they were real men and darlings too, if proof were needed. 'We were wrong and you were right, and we both love you, Charlie and Mike.' I cried, I honestly did, I just bawled, it touched me here, right where my heart is."

Charlie and Grace, their eyes misted with tears, briefly clasped hands and beamed fondly at each other. Ilona's voice was heard in a small silence she created by clapping her hands, saying that it was time for them all to go in to dinner. Silky hung back out of the general drift towards the dining room until he had finished his drink and poured himself another stiff one. When he came into the dining room he found an empty chair waiting for him on the left of Lola de Laume. She was an ugly but curiously attractive woman with strong shoulders. She seemed to be lost in some kind of dream as she slowly spooned up the creamed crab soup in front of her. She made no reply when Silky spoke to her and gave no sign of having heard what he had said. He was still trying to decide whether she was timid and withdrawn, or just single-minded about food, when she put down her spoon, and turned her head towards him with heavy grace. She had a noble and serene expression which surprised him.

"I was watching you while Grace Pollner was talking to you," she said. "You have bad posture."

257

"Do I?" Silky was taken aback. "I'm sorry."

"You should do remedial exercises. People don't realize how they harm themselves with bad posture. I don't expect you ever think about breathing either." Her voice was a very soft murmur with a hint of huskiness in it.

"I can't say I do think about breathing. It just seems to happen, almost naturally."

"That's the mistake everybody makes. It's the beginning of everything. Heart trouble, I don't know what else. People talk about diet, but food's secondary. You can eat anything, animal fats, fried foods, whatever you like if you'll only breathe right." She looked across the table at her husband. "Alfred has been a new man, career-wise and sex-wise, since he started taking his breathing seriously."

"You made him do that?"

"It was an emergency. I'm a deeply sensuous woman, Mr. Sigaux. I have healthy instincts. There are certain satisfactions a woman has a right to. That is one of the things I've always cleaved to as a fundamental principle. I told Alfred frankly that we were headed for trouble. We've done our breathing exercises together since then, and the picture, the total picture of our marriage, has been simply transformed."

"Well, that's good news. This rack of lamb is delicious, don't you agree, Mrs. de Laume?"

"It's very good. Now the minute I saw you I could see you didn't handle yourself right. I said to myself, that poor man is wearing himself out with the way he stands. I'll bet he thinks he's in serious emotional trouble of some kind, when he's really just tired. Half the people in this world who think they're unhappy are really just physically exhausted. You know that, don't you?"

"It's an interesting idea."

"Oh it's much more than that. It's a profound truth. Once you fully master its implications, your whole life will be altered. You'll be a new man, and a much happier one." She watched Silky as he drained his glass and as he signaled for Bailey to refill it. Gavin watched him too, through a thick barrage of conversation thrown up by Klosky. Oh, oh, he thought, Silky is going to pass out before this night is through, that's for sure.

"You drink too much, Mr. Sigaux," said Mrs. de Laume. "That's another sign of the damage done by bad habits. I believe we have entirely the wrong approach to alcoholism. Bad posture habits lead to rounded shoulders and spinal curvature, and pressure of the spinal vertebrae on the nerves creates the craving for alcohol. Have you ever seen an alcoholic who stood well? Once you've seen it it's obvious, the answer to the whole thing lies in controlled breathing and good posture."

"I'd love to paint you and Alfred doing your exercises together."

"I doubt that would be possible. You see, we do them in the nude for one thing, and for another they tend to pass insensibly into erotic play. You might say they were an integral part of our marriage relationship. At any rate for me, and I think for Alfred too, they have an intimate and sacramental quality which would suffer in the presence of a third party."

"I can imagine." Silky took a long swallow of his drink.

"You really are a compulsive drinker, Mr. Sigaux," she said, "I can see you need help with your problem."

When the last of the visitors' cars had gone away down the drive, Gavin and Ilona searched the ground floor for Silky. They found him stretched out in a cane chaise longue out on the kitchen porch overlooking the back yard, where the family cars and the servants' cars were parked. Silky looked broken and dead in the ashy moonlight, by which his skin looked to be a pale mauve.

"Well, there he is, poor son of a bitch. I wonder what made him pick this spot," said Gavin.

"His hair is wet," said Ilona, touching him with fingers as light as a moth. "I expect he came out to douse his head under the kitchen tap."

"D'you think he'll be all right here? Shouldn't I get a rug or a blanket to throw over him?"

"He'll be all right. It's a warm night. We'd best just leave him alone to sleep it off." Ilona turned away from the sleeping man and walked back into the front part of the house with Gavin close behind her. Lights were on in all the downstairs rooms and they went round turning them off. In the drawing room, in one of the big armchairs, Gavin found a white evening bag, a flat envelope of cloth.

"I wonder who left this," he said.

"Patti Elliot," Ilona said, barely looking. "And you know why as well as I do. Little tramp." She yawned. "You can call her tomorrow and say you've got it, and then she can ask you to drop by with it sometime when that dreadful little man Tollick isn't around. And then you can have your little romp together. Not that I'd care to get into anything Tollick had been into if I were a man."

"I think you misjudge her. She probably just forgot the damned thing."

"Misjudge her, my foot. Gavin, who were all those ghastly people? Do you really have to do business with a man like Klosky?"

"Oh, Klosky's all right." Gavin put the bag onto the mantelpiece. "Not in your line. I can see that. But he's all right."

"Gavin, he simply isn't all right, and you know it. You must know it." She came and stood in front of him. "I don't understand any of this. I don't know what we're doing or why. I can't see why we live like this. I can't see what you're trying to do, or trying to prove. I can't see what Kloskys and Pollners and Tollicks and de Laumes have to do with us, or what we have to do with them. What is it all about?"

"It's very simple. I run a bank. We have money in it. We lend it to people. Pollner and Mike Klosky have built motels together all over the country—the fancy sort that pretend to be country clubs with swimming pools and landscaped gardens, you know the sort of thing. Now they're trying something new. They've gone in with de Laume who owns a sandbar off the coast twenty miles from here, which he flatters with the name of Rummer's Key. They're going to build a supermotel out there. It's going to be a sort of self-contained fishing and swimming resort. It'll be a four or five million dollar job building a causeway out to the key and pumping enough sand up out of the gulf to build anything on. They'll want that money to start, and they're going to want some short-term loans to see them through till they've got a mortgageable asset out there. So they applied to me. It's what I'm for. I would have handled the whole thing through the bank. We would have had two or three lunches together. We might have gone up to the key in the *Plain Jane*, perhaps. I don't know. I've nothing against Klosky or Pollner, or Tollick for that matter. I'd have been friendly enough. But I wouldn't have had them out here. And well you know it. It wasn't my idea asking them to dinner. That was something you dreamed up all on your own. And God alone knows what put that one into your head."

"I must have been out of my mind. It was just hearing that awful wheedling, vulgar, voice on the telephone. I just had an impulse to see the sort of person you're mixing yourself up with. I wish I hadn't. I wish I didn't know. Marsen was bad enough. I didn't think you could go lower than that. And then I find something like Patti in the house."

"Patti's not that bad. She can't be. A woman like Grace Pollner wouldn't have a real bad egg around."

"Grace Pollner? Don't tell me you respect the judgement of a woman like that? Haven't you any standards left?"

"Yes, I do, as a matter of fact. And I'll tell you about Grace Pollner if you want. I'll bet my bottom dollar she's all right. I'll bet she's never done anything mean or shabby in her life. She's not a liar, and she's not a coward. She's as warm-hearted and as kind and as decent as they come. And you ought to know it."

"I know something else. She's vulgar, vulgar, vulgar, from the top of her head to the tips of her toes." She put out her hand and touched his arm. "Gavin, why don't we go back where we belong. To be with the sort of people we are, the sort we know and like?"

"You can think it odd of me if you want to, but I think we

261

belong here. At least I know I do. The place has treated me well, and I mean to stick with it."

"But, Gavin, look at the life we lead. We're out of everything. The children don't know any of their cousins. We never meet anyone. It's all so empty and meaningless."

"Oh, Ilona. I wish you'd occasionally look beyond the tip of your Yankee nose. You must have been brought up thinking the untamed wilderness began on the far side of the Hudson. People live all over America. A lot goes on outside that little beachhead where the British squatted down when they first got here. This place here, Maramee, is our home now. We belong here. The people we live with are our friends. We don't belong back there any more."

"No, Gavin. It isn't true. It doesn't make sense. You can't, you mustn't just brush off everything I'm saying. I'm thinking of what Thomas is going to grow up to be, about what sort of marriages the girls are going to make. You can't, with what's behind them in the way of breeding and tradition, just turn them adrift in this, in this"—she gestured helplessly— "this hideous place."

"Oh, hell," said Gavin, "what's the use. You lived with your eyes shut when you were up there. You must have. Didn't you ever go over the river to Hoboken when you were in New York? Didn't you ever get to look at Albany? At what goes on on the Jersey flats? Didn't you ever see Philadelphia and what surrounds it—Chester, my God! what a place—didn't you ever take a look at what's within five minutes' walk of the Bunker Hill Monument in your own precious Boston, or drive out to Dorchester? I wish you'd think about your own hideously ugly background as it really is just once—I could say a lot about the dismal social failure we all lived with so complacently up there. We forget it so conveniently when we get down here. But that's not the point. Granting that the East has a lot to its credit as well as to its discredit, and granted that what we grew up to love was something real, what argument is that for quitting on this place? What will it ever become if we all bolt the minute we've got our money out of it, and head for some place where they've made and forgotten all their mistakes? Someone has to stick with it if anything is ever to grow up here that's worth a damn."

Ilona looked at him. She had dropped into a chair and had picked up a glass with the flat end of somebody's drink in it. She sipped it and grimaced.

"At least," she said, in an exhausted voice, "you'll send Thomas North to Harvard or some decent university, and the girls to boarding schools, so that they won't be utterly cut off."

"What you don't seem to realize is that I love this place, that my whole life is here. It'll suit me just fine if the children want it that way too. I hope they will. I don't give a snap of my fingers, not a damned thing, for the kind of rearing, the upbringing, the education, that you had and I had, which taught us to despise nine-tenths of the human race and three-quarters of our country. If we sent our children up there they'd be taught to look down on this place and the people who've made it out of almost nothing in less than half a lifetime. They'd come back wanting to get out, to go somewhere where all the dirty work has been done, and where all the nice side of life is laid on, ready-made. I don't want to have them grow up like my hopeless cousins who really think they're doing the universe a favor by living in Wychbury."

"I don't believe that's what you're worried about," Ilona said. "That's not truly it. I think it's a question of values. I believe you're scared that the children might be taught something worthwhile up there, that there's more to life than just money-grubbing. Isn't that what you're really afraid of, in your heart?"

An extraordinary inner convulsion took place within Ilona as she spoke. She heard the sound of her words clearly and sharply as if they were being said by someone else, and simultaneously she seemed to hear another voice saying, you just said that, and you were the girl who married this man for his money. You got into bed with him and let him into you for cash. There had been a whore in the house ahead of Patti

Elliot, no doubt about it, a real, cold whore, not just a friendly tart. She flushed and drained the glass in her hand.

"You've been drinking a lot today, haven't you?" he said gently.

"I have to. I need to." She brushed her hair off her forehead. "I have my reasons. Let's not talk about it. It will only end in a squalid row."

"Now don't get upset, Ilona. There's nothing to get upset about."

"There is." She clutched at the argument in which she had made her hideous false step. "You aren't really meaning to keep the children in schools down here, right to the end?"

"Yes, I plan to do just that. I meant what I said."

"Thomas is going to that place at Sweetwater? I don't even know its name—what is it called? Nobody ever heard of it."

"I have. I'm on the Board of Regents. It's called Gulf University. If you ever condescended to read the local papers you'd know that. Other people have heard about it, too. They say two of the physicists, Brightman and Hsiuh Long Yee, are in line for Nobel awards. It's a good school."

"But who will he meet there? What sort of friends will he make?"

"Well, he isn't going to spend four years with a bunch of snobs learning how to pat himself on the back. He's going to get a good enough education alongside the men he's going to be working with for the rest of his life."

"You mean we really have brought up three children to be pillars of Maramee society?" She stared at him. "Oh, God. Oh, sweet suffering Jesus."

"Now, Ilona. What use is that? You know Thomas is good stuff as well as I do. It doesn't take one brand of schooling or another to make the most of a good boy. He'll be right wherever he goes. And there are plenty of reasons for sending him to Gulf."

"Maramee High and Gulf," she choked. "And the girls, when they're through with the sisters on the Heights, I suppose they'll go to Gulf, too—or we might even let them skip college so that they can go right ahead with getting married and having children as soon as they're out of school. That's what most of the girls they're in class with down here will do."

"You exaggerate. You exaggerate everything. Our crowd doesn't go in for that sort of thing. The crackers may, the Spanishtowners and the colored people may, we don't."

"Betty Allendorf—whatever she's called now—she isn't twenty yet and her second child is walking."

"It may suit some women to breed early. Maybe you would take things less hard if you'd married and had your babies earlier."

"Before I met you?"

"Let's not get angry and forget the issue. I want Thomas to go to Gulf."

"We're all stuck here for life. We're never going back home. Is that it?" She got to her feet. "Is that what this really means?"

"If you must have it in such terms, yes."

She left the room in silence, took another drink as she passed through the dining room, and went on upstairs to bed. She lay down on the covers without taking her clothes off. Her eyes were open and she stared at the ceiling. She remembered Alston Murray's house, and all the things in the image of its perfection she had married to get. She was no better than that girl Patti. She was worse. She took a large swallow of neat whiskey from the glass which she had put down on the night table beside the bed. Patti offered a good straight lay in return for her keep and some fun, and she would contribute to the fun. Me, Ilona, she thought, I offered love, devotion, fidelity and I haven't delivered the goods, I hated selling myself so much I even gypped him on the lay. I haven't let him have me in eleven years. She took more whiskey, dropping the slow tempo of drinking, which had been keeping her just on the right side of the point of loss of control all day since Silky's arrival. She felt a renewed passion of hatred for her father, whose stupidity had done her out of all the things she deserved as a right and forced her into prostitution. She remembered, as she often did when she was passing out, the last perfect year before her father had lost all his money. She was riding an enormous chestnut hunter called Tiny Tim that year and winning everywhere she went. At Easthampton she had won in all her classes: handy hunter, dressage, and heavy-weight jumpers and won the rosettes for open jumpers, and best animal in the show into the bargain. That year there had been nothing but love in the house, for Tiny Tim, for Fräulein, for Mother and Father, and then after that it had all been mean and hateful, mean and hateful. She split a little whiskey over her chin as she finished the drink. While she was wiping it off with her hand the glass slipped from her fingers and rolled across the bed. It fell with a thud onto the thick pile carpet. Her head fell backwards and she passed into the blackness of night, beyond despair and grief.

Gavin's pill of Luminal had worked by then, too. He had stubbed out his last cigarette and was fast asleep with the novel, from which he had read a few lines, spread out open on the table beside his bed.

Out in the yard, Bailey's dog stirred and scratched, turning itself restlessly round and round as it tried to find a comfortable place on the greasy old cushion in its kennel at the foot of the huge avocado tree. The chain tied to its collar rattled, and the moon, sailing behind the great tree, suddenly cast a beam of shadow across the yard and onto the kitchen porch. Silky, lying there motionless, was one minute as visible as an advertisement on a lighted billboard, and then second by second he slowly vanished into velvet obscurity. At the end of another minute he was invisible. The light left his face last of all. His senses had been adjusted to the moon's silver glare, and when the softness of shadow replaced it his eyes fluttered open. He lay motionless through several panic-stricken seconds trying to think where he could be. He discerned porch pillars, the screens and the screen door, the ashy night sky and the blackness under it. He heard a furtive shuffling behind him and froze. Miss Jelke appeared with two suitcases, tiptoeing through the porch and down the steps leading from it into the yard. She was gone for a few minutes and then she reappeared, empty-handed. When she had gone back into the house, Silky sat up in his shadowed corner wondering what he had seen, and if he had truly seen it. He heard Miss Jelke's light footfalls once more and this time he did not believe what he saw. The governess had the sleeping Bogey in her arms. The child looked like someone's romantic dream of a drowned princess, limp and boneless in the cradling arms which held her. Her hair streamed in a breath-taking fall of shining loveliness from her head, and it swayed with Miss Jelke's movements. "We gave her her sleeping pill so she won't wake up," said Miss Jelke's tiny whisper to her confederate self, "but we still have to worry about the others. We mustn't make a sound. We must be very, very careful." Silky watched her ease the screen door on the porch open so that the spring hardly uttered even a creak of rusty complaint. When she had eased it as quietly shut again and was feeling her way, step by step, down towards the ground, the first awareness of the possible meaning of what he had seen began to penetrate into Silky's conscious daytime mind. He stared, incredulous still, to see what she would do next, his awakening reason rejecting what he had seen. No, he told himself, it can't be *that*. He saw her standing for an instant with a triumphant, scared, mad face turned up at the house before she spun round and ran off towards the line of cars standing in the jumble of shadows on the far side of the yard. Bailey's dog ran out to meet her, plunging out of the pool of darkness under the avocado's mass of glinting leaves with a clink and rattle of its long chain. It whined and whickered with pleasure at this second surprise meeting during the night's long boredom of restraint, with friends, dear friends. It groveled with amity. Silky heard Miss Jelke's hissing whisper to the dog: "Now hush, you silly thing, just hush, Flicker, don't you make a sound, not one more sound." She's scared to have him bark, that's what she is, Silky thought dully, and then his wits began to clear. Because there's something wrong in all this, he reasoned sluggishly, that's why the dog mustn't bark, why she whispers and tiptoes. He stepped out of the shadow and moonlight fell on him. He caught sight of the swaying gleam of Bogey's hanging hair as Miss Jelke, having opened the door of her car, passed the child's slack body in onto the front seat. He heard her trying to shut the door furtively without noise, then giving it a hurried slam. Absolute silence followed the sound, and Silky thought he could almost hear the nurse's heart beat while it lasted. He got to his feet and stood swaying, holding his luminous watch dial up to his face as if it held some clue to what was going on. Three twelve, no sort of time at all for anybody to be doing anything; he knew that there was nothing to be done at twelve minutes past three in the morning. He took two strides across the porch to the screen door and stood holding onto the handle, pressing one cheek and the tip of his nose against the crisscross of fine wires. He saw Miss Jelke flit round her car like a ghost, and heard a second door shut with a furtive crunch. The answer to it all crawled slowly into his mind: why that woman, that woman is, she really is stealing that child. "Hey," he muttered, "hey, I know what you're doing. You can't do that." The unanswerable argument flashed into his mind. "You can't. Don't you realize, it's a federal offense!"

The whirr of the starter sounded like a drum roll against the background of soft night sounds and he was shocked wide-awake and alert. Miss Jelke's car moved backwards and Silky leapt down the steps towards it as she reversed it in a wide arc out into the center of the bare yard. Miss Jelke put her foot on the brake when the car was lined up with the dark, cavernous entry to the back drive. She paused to switch on the lights before she changed into a forward gear, and Silky was upon her. As the beams of yellow light stabbed into the shadow under the overarching trees and the car began to move forward, Silky flung its rear door open and dived in, to sprawl panting across the back seat. Paralyzed with fear, Miss Jelke did nothing for an instant, she kept her foot on the accelerator and drove on as if she and Bogey were still alone together. The effort of getting to the car and into it had stirred up all the alcohol in Silky's blood and he lay behind her fighting it; there was something terribly important he had to do in this machine, that was why he had thrown himself into it, but for the moment he couldn't think what it was that was so terribly wrong with the ride and the driver. Like an automaton, Miss Jelke drove out past Miss Wilbraham's cottage, past the Corners, where the nigras lived, along the winding river road, over the bridge, across the grade crossing, and onto the highway. She started north towards the state line, without hope and without even thought. In her head was the vision of a little white house in a dear little town of little houses, where everybody was nice and kind, the old people mild and the children polite. She was going to go there with Bogey, and she was going to bring Bogey up there, where she would never see anything ugly, sordid, or mean, and never hear vile words slobbered out of drunken mouths. Looking down the bare waste of pavement ahead, with its borders of huge billboards, closed gas stations, darkling houses, and the parallel railroad track, Miss Jelke saw the main street of her little place, with its overarching maples, cosily and happily waiting ahead.

They overtook an eighty-seven-car train crawling north behind a huge Diesel and traveled for twenty minutes in a turbulent arcade of its unbelievably brutal noise. When they at last left it behind, the road and the tracks parted company. They passed a huge traffic circle surrounded by a carnival of used-car lots and gas stations. A few human beings, looking bleached by the greenish overhead neon lamps, walked about in the lunar emptiness between a fleet of vast trailer trucks starred all over with colored lights. The road screamed on into the bleakness of an endless waste of pine barrens. Silky's head slowly cleared. They passed a convoy of brightly lighted trucks traveling south. Each one momentarily flooded the inside of Miss Jelke's car with light as it went by, giving Silky a chance to look at the emptiness and innocence of Bogey's drugged face, and now at Miss Jelke's mask of madness and despair. It had frightened him when he had seen it in its moment of triumph in the yard; now that it was wet with tears, it moved him to a pity in which fear was forgotten.

269

"Miss Jelke."

"Don't speak to me, don't touch me, or try to interfere with me in any way."

"It isn't any use, Miss Jelke."

"If you make one move I'll drive off the road, into a tree. Anything. I don't care what. We're doing sixty-five now. I'll go faster if you do anything. We'll all be killed." Her voice was metallic and dull.

"It hasn't been any use since I got into this car. You know that. You're licked, Miss Jelke. Why not face it?" They crossed a river bridge, a brief incident of metal latticework in nine miles of causeway crossing a swamp. A pale gray beginning of dawn began to ache in the eastern sky. "Come on, Miss Jelke, give up. It was a good try but it went bad on you. You're not going anywhere. I won't make trouble for you when we get back. Nobody will. You're sick, you need rest and help. Everybody will see that. Nobody will want to hurt you or punish you. You've nothing to be afraid of."

"If you don't promise to get out of this car within ten minutes, I'm going to drive it off the road into the swamp. It'll turn over for sure, and if we aren't all killed we'll very soon drown in that black gumbo."

"That's silly, Miss Jelke. You know there's no sense in that. You can't want to kill Bogey."

"I'd rather kill her than take her back." Her voice was shrill and frantic.

"Drowning that lovely child in black mud, you can't mean it."

"I do mean it." She caught a sob. "I'm going to do it any minute if you won't promise."

Silky looked at the speedometer needle, which was steady in the middle sixties, and at the road ahead, running straight as a knitting needle through the flat tangle of marsh, cyrpress and vines. Up ahead there were two dots of light, the headlights of an oncoming car.

"I'll drive straight into it if you won't promise, that's what I'll do."

Silky stared at the oncoming lights, pale in the gray twilight of the minutes before sunrise.

"All right, you win," he said. "I'll promise."

"On your honor?" she said. "You promise me on your honor that you'll just get quietly out?"

"Yes, I'll promise that." He felt not far from sickness. He had not struck anyone in earnest, or fought, since his first year in high school. The knowledge that he had to somehow bring himself to launch an attack on this woman within minutes or seconds made him feel hideously queasy.

"You gave me your word of honor," she said, slowing the car down. "Remember."

"Oh, yes," he said. "Yes. I did that. You can . . ." the word should have been trust, but a scruple held it back. "You can count on me," he said. The car was standing still, motionless, and she was sitting stiff as a ramrod staring in front of her.

"Just get out. Get out as quickly as you can, and leave what doesn't concern you."

He opened the door, and for one panic-stricken instant thought that he wouldn't be able to do what he had to do, and that he would be left there standing alone in the gathering strength of the light, beside the road, nowhere. He heard birds calling to each other in the swamp. He took a long deep breath and, closing his ears against the scream he knew was going to come, grabbed Miss Jelke by the hair and pulled her backwards over the seat and out of the car after him. She threshed about in agony as he hauled her off the road and down onto the bank among the beggar-lice and cockleburs, the beer cans, and the wind-blown candybar wrappers. She wriggled helplessly, clawing impotently backwards at the hands locked in the hair at the base of her skull, while he looked wildly up and down the desolate emptiness of the road. Good God, dear Jesus, he thought, will I have to stand here holding her by the hair until someone comes? I hadn't thought of that. I thought she might quit, just give in, collapse, or I don't know what, when she realized she was beaten. She screamed for help, and

271

when no help came began to curse him with all the profanity which her father had poured out on her in his drunken rages, and which her memory had stored away without her knowledge. She knelt as she cursed, like someone praying. A huge truck came roaring up from the Maramee direction, spraying a drifting plume of foul black smoke out of its towering exhaust into the morning air. Silky waved desperately at the cab with one hand and called to the grinning faces he could see inside it for help. One man leaned out and gave him the thumbs-up sign, yelling some pleasantry.

"Take her home, Mac, and give her a real good . . ." He didn't hear the rest of it. She gave her head a wrench of unbelievable violence and broke her hair free of the grip of his other hand. Now they faced each other. He threw away a tuft of her hair with a bloody piece of scalp still attached to it. Her face was inhuman now, and she was cursing him with the full repertory of 1917 A.E.F. abuse as she tried to work round him to get to the car. He saw her intention and moved in answer to every step she took, keeping himself between her and her goal. They shifted backwards and forwards for a long time, as if it was a strange cautiously played child's game of prisoner's base. The sun climbed slowly into the sky. Traffic became heavier as men started going to work, but nobody stopped to figure out what the man was trying to shout to them over the raging jumble of the woman's obscenities.

"It don't pay to meddle in a thing like that, it's between them, whoever they are. She was foul-mouthed, from what I heard."

Silky did not know how much time had passed when he heard a car stopping, and looked up to see a prowl car and two wooden-faced state troopers standing staring down at the dodging dance from the tip of the embankment. It seemed to him that it must be nearly noon, but when he looked at his watch he saw it was twenty-seven minutes past six. Miss Jelke gave a wild scream of laughter and cried, "The army came, the mother fugging son of a bitch had to send for the army." She sat down and gave herself up to laughter, completely.

"Have you two been drinking, or what?" said one of the troopers, letting the words out of his face as if it hurt him.

"I had. There was a party that is. I passed out. When I came to I caught this woman, she's the nurse, taking the child out of the house, kidnapping her. I got in the car with her to try to talk her into stopping, taking her back, I guess I was pretty drunk still. I didn't realize she was mad. I drove with her, trying to figure out what to do. I got her to stop here and I dragged her out of the car. The girl, it's Gavin Hatfield's daughter, is in the car."

"You charge this woman with a kidnapping attempt? You know what sort of charge that is?" The trooper's voice sounded shocked and thick with disbelief. The other trooper walked away, crunching the grit at the edge of the road under his boots. A bird shrilled with a long skirl of joy in the swamp.

"She's mad," Silky said. "I don't charge her with anything but madness."

"There is a little girl in here. Asleep."

"Asleep. That's right, they're all asleep," said Silky through his hot, dry, drunk's thirst. "They're all asleep at the Grove, where the child belongs. They don't know yet. We must try to get that child back there before they wake up and find her gone."

"We'll be the judges of that." The trooper called to the madwoman. "Ma'am. You. Come up here. There ain't nothing to be afraid of. You tell your side of this. Come on and tell. How come this dispute between you and this fellow got started? Come on now, don't be scared." He took a step towards her. "It's all right, we won't let him hurt you."

"You . . ." She scuttled down the bank, backing away from him, shouting as she went a string of the same World War I obscenities, which seemed to be all that was left in her head.

"You claim she's deranged?" said the second trooper.

"That's what I've been saying all along."

"She certainly isn't in any normal frame of mind right now," the trooper said. "We'll get her, and then we'll all get on down to the barracks to straighten this thing out." He considered the

273

madwoman from behind his expressionless face. "You're the one who upset her, or the one she's mad at. You'd best hang back out of it. Or better, if you know that kid, you better stay with her. She could be scared to death if she should wake up now without someone she knows near her."

Silky sat beside Bogey watching the troopers as they slowly closed in on Miss Jelke, in spite of her efforts to get away from them down the endless strip of waste ground between the road and the cypress swamp. At the last she tried to break away into the cover of trees and the swinging vines, but a few steps out from the causeway she was knee-deep in black rotten-ness and she floundered back into their arms. They brought her back, pinioned, past the line of cars and the little knots of people along the road who had got out of them to watch the fun. She was no longer cursing when she came abreast of Silky sitting at the wheel of her own machine. Her hair was matted round her face, and all the brightness, and some of the mad-ness, was gone from it. There was nothing to be seen on her face but anguish, pain, and the despair of defeat.

"I had to," she was saying to the troopers as she went by Silky. "You see, I had to. I couldn't do anything else. I couldn't leave her there in that house. You must see that. I haven't done anything wrong. I just had to take her away from the vileness, and the deceit, and the wickedness of that house."

The first trooper took her on to the prowl car, and the second paused at Silky's window.

"You said you'd been drinking?"

"Yes."

"You sober now, sober enough to drive, would you say?"

"I think I am, yes."

"Well give it a try. Follow us on to the barracks." He eyed Silky thoughtfully. "You have a valid operator's license?"

"Yes."

"I just wanted to be sure." He took a step away towards the prowl car and spoke over his shoulder, looking back. "You can't ever be sure." He moved solidly away with his measured tread. Up the road, car doors were slamming one after another as the spectators climbed into their machines and drove off. The incident was over for them, and its small interest exhausted. Silky envied them, and envied the unconscious Bogey, still curled up asleep in the light summer blanket which Miss Jelke had tucked around her. He knew that he was at the beginning of what would be for him the worst stretch, in which minutes would leak away slowly like blood in an atmosphere of routine suspicion and doubt while identities were established and his statement was checked and rechecked.

He sat for what seemed like hours facing a man in a uniform shirt seated behind a metal desk who had a pad in front of him on which he never wrote anything. To his left, in back of him against the wall, a plain-clothes man sat on a metal filing cabinet, one leg bent and the other dragging, staring at Silky. At the narrow end of the table, at right angles to Silky and the interrogator, sat another uniformed man, with a pink boy's face, taking a transcript of what was said on a machine with a keyboard. Bogey had been taken away by a starched white police matron.

"What we're tryin' to figure out, Mr. Sigaux, is why you didn't raise any outcry or endeavor to obtain assistance in handling this situation when you saw this woman carryin' the child out of the house."

"I've told you that. I'd been drinking. I didn't fully understand what I saw. I didn't fully understand what I was doing."

"But you knew that wrong was being done. You weren't so drunk but you knew that. And you took this effective action. As you have it here in your statement you had one split second or two split seconds to go to work in and you used them to get down off this porch, across the yard, and into that car. And you were able to pick just that second while she was changing out of reverse to get in there with her. It would take a pretty good athlete in full command of himself to bring off what you say you did when you were all liquored up. Can you explain how that would be?"

"No. I just knew I had to be in that car. It was the only thing I knew."

"This woman was cursing you when the troopers came on the scene. She was mad both ways. Would you be able to give us any reason why she should be angry with you?"

"It's pretty obvious."

"There isn't anything obvious in what people do. Suppose two people, a nurse say, and an artist who hadn't done much work in four or maybe five years, thought up a plan to kidnap a rich banker's child, and carried it out up to a point and then the man, the artist, lost his nerve and couldn't go through with it and said to the nurse we have to turn round and go back, this won't work, if we go back now we can get away with it, we can put the child back in her bed and nobody will ever know, that would make her good and sore wouldn't it? And if she was a tense and unstable character, near enough crazy, anyway, the way a woman would have to be to get into such a half-assed scheme for raising dough, the shock of having her partner quit on her in the middle of the thing might be enough to push her over into a mental breakdown. Couldn't it now?"

"That's not it, this wasn't like that," Silky said. "I need more coffee."

"Get him some more coffee, Leroy. But you see how it could be don't you. If you hadn't been there and you just came in at the end of it. You found the two people mad at each other, shouting at each other, beside the road, with a child in the car that wasn't theirn"—he corrected himself, and even blushed momentarily—"theirs but proved to be this rich man's child, you see how it could seem to be, can't you? If you know different it's because you know a heap more about the whole thing than we do. Now suppose you try and fill us in on some of the detail of what happened, so that we can understand it. When you passed through the traffic circle at Congdon for instance, where all them bright lights are, didn't you see anybody at any of those gas stations, or among them parked trucks?"

"I saw some men. I remember their faces looked greenish under the lights."

"You saw several people?"

"Yes, men in overalls, a boy hosing down the concrete in front of some pumps."

"But you didn't wave at them, or try to draw their attention in any way?"

"No."

"Could you give me any idea why not?"

"I was scared. She threatened to drive off the road. I told you that."

"Yes, you said that. It's in your statement. You said she threatened to drive off the road into the swamp. You didn't get into that swamp until you were seventeen miles on from Congdon. She didn't threaten you before you got to the circle, she did that afterwards. Why didn't you do anything there, under all those bright lights?"

"I don't remember."

"But you remember seeing the color of people's faces, seeing a boy washing off a gas-station forecourt. Why did you ride on so far with this woman before you did anything about what you say you knew from the first was a wrong situation?"

"I was . . . oh, I don't know. I just don't know."

"Well, here's your coffee. We'll take a little break now, and when you've rested up a bit we'll have another try at finding out what was going on."

Leroy put the coffee down in front of him and walked away, round the table.

"The Doc is writing out his report, now," he said. "There's no sex angle to it. The kid is *intacta,* so's the woman for that matter. The scalp wound is consistent with what he says about pulling her out of the car backwards. Mr. Hatfield is on his way up here. He says this guy is a good friend of the family. The woman is the child's nurse, a Dorothy Jelke, like the car papers say. The woman is still talking, rambling stuff about how she has to take the child away because the mother ain't fit. Doc says he inclines to think she's screwy, not that that's his word."

"Looks like the sun's coming out from behind the clouds, don't it," the man in the shirt said. He stood up stretching and yawning. "You can pack up the little old soundscriber, Steve, and go get yourself a bite of breakfast. We won't have to be bothering Mr. Sigaux no more." He stretched again. "You know where I'd like to be right this minute? I'd like to be on my father's place headin' off into the countryside with a couple of the dogs to see if I could find me a couple of coveys of quail before noon. That's what I'd like to be doing. But seriously now, Mr. Sigaux, you've been through an ordeal, and my bet is you've got a great big hollow in your middle. I think you'd better come on down to the canteen and get a real good breakfast into you."

"All I need is about a gallon of coffee."

"That's where you drinking men make your mistake. Kill your thirst with coffee, and you'll be settin' up your nerves for more drinking. You eat your three squares, regular, and plenty of sweet desserts, and you won't have half as much trouble staying off it."

They walked down a long corridor to an aseptic canteen where a scatter of troopers coming off duty were at breakfast. The radio played, turned down low, and a few of the men read papers as they ate. A colored woman came over to them from the kitchen doorway.

"You give Mr. Sigaux the best breakfast we got, Hannah," the man in the shirt said.

"Does he have money or is it to be paid?" she said.

"You don't have to worry about that, Hannah." The policeman was embarrassed. "I should have told you," he said, "before we came in here. There's a washroom down the hallway there where you can clean up." He turned back to the bosomy woman. "Mr. Sigaux has been through an ordeal, Hannah. You treat him right."

"He sure has been through something. When he gets hisself cleaned up I'll give him as good a breakfast as he ever ate. But he can't sit hisself down here in that condition." She suddenly smiled. "And you're going to feel a lot better for a wash-up anyway, I know."

In the washroom, sluicing cold water over his head, Silky

278

tried not to think. It was Bogey being given a vaginal and anal examination to see if he had raped her which he was trying not to think about, and the pain on Miss Jelke's face. He soaped himself and washed, stripped to the waist, but these things would not come off. He dried carefully and looked at himself in the glass above the row of basins. He looked as he had always done, as if he had not heard Miss Jelke's scream as his grip in her hair tightened. She had not let out one single terrible jet of hurt noise as he had expected her to, she had gone back somewhere to something buried and had for an instant relived it: "Oh, daddy, you're hurting me, daddy, do anything you want, I'll do anything you want, only don't hurt me, please, please, let me go, daddy, stop, please," and then as she reached an ultimate threshold of shock, pain, and terror, the meaningless scream had come up from inside her at last and swept her words away. He peered at the glass more closely. It would have been nice to have a shave, but he could get along without it. He went back to the canteen and found Bogey sitting beside the nurse at a table near the door.

"Here's your friend, dear," the nurse said, without taking the cigarette she was smoking from her lip. "Say hello or something." She shook Bogey gently. "The kid is still woozy from the pills that woman gave her," she said to Silky.

He went and sat beside Bogey. She nestled up to him, and he put his arm round her.

"She'll drop off if you do that. She ought to eat her breakfast," the nurse said, smiling. "Your name's Sigaux, isn't it? Mine's Cone, Eleanor Cone. I saw a picture of yours once when I was in private nursing. Mrs. Belling was the invalid, you painted her daughter, Flag they called her, though I believe her given name was Annette. A dark girl, pretty if you like that Elizabeth Taylor type, married to an engineer called, as I remember it, Smeaton, or Stanton, no, it was Lavigne Smeaton, I'm pretty sure. Well, I always just loved that picture, you made her look such a happy girl, and the dress was so pretty and so real. I've always envied the creative gift of a person who could do work of that kind, and I envy the life of a person who can give as well as take, if you know what I mean."

"Thank you."

"Well, I've got things to do. I mustn't sit here gassing away. I'll leave the little girl with you till her father comes. The white You-Know-What is just down the hallway opposite the men's room if she should have a need. It's been a privilege to meet you and I'd love to have a proper talk with you some day. Good-bye, dear," she added, taking hold of Bogey's head and turning the child's face up towards hers. "Now be a good girl, and eat up your breakfast, so you'll be bright and cheerful when your daddy gets here. Keep her awake if you can, Mr. Sigaux. Good-bye for now."

Silky and Bogey sat holding hands for a little while when she had gone.

"You ought to eat some of that cereal, Bogey."

"I don't feel like eating, I feel awful." Bogey yawned. "What happened? Why are we here? Why aren't we home? I don't understand anything."

"It's hard to explain. Miss Jelke went mad. She loved you too much I guess, and she wanted you to be her very own. So she tried to steal you last night. She wanted to drive you away up North somewhere where she wasn't known and you weren't known, and where your parents wouldn't ever find you. I found out what she was doing and I managed to stop her."

"Is she really crazy?"

"She's pretty far gone."

"I said I wanted to see her, but they wouldn't let me. She wouldn't have hurt me would she?"

"No. But she wouldn't have known who you were any more. And she might have said wild things and ugly things that would have upset you."

"Did loving me too much make her go mad?"

"No, that was just the form her madness took." Silky looked at the gigantic breakfast Hannah had put before him. When he had fought to make the night comprehensible to the child there would be Gavin to explain it to in other terms, and after

Gavin, Ilona. The prospect made him suddenly desperately hungry.

"You can't ever tell what goes on in someone else's mind, Bogey," he said. "We'll never know what sent Miss Jelke crazy. Something hurt her a long time ago. There's no knowing what. And something last night made her do this awful thing of trying to steal you away from your own people."

"Poor Jelke. B'ar Hatfield knew. He warned me. He's been saying for months that Miss Jelke is as nutty as a fruit cake."

"It's not play, Bogey. The poor woman is terribly unhappy. Madness is just being more unhappy than you can stand."

"B'ar Hatfield didn't make it up. It's not play. I've heard Bailey telling Julia that that Jelke woman was crazy as a loon. He told me. They said she was crazy because she went round smashing bottles. They said someone was too clever for her about the bottles. And they, this other person had her licked. And Julia said she was scared about which way she was going to break out next. She got a mad look in her eye, Julia said, and when B'ar Hatfield told me that I looked and I could see she was crazy, too. Anybody could who knew where to look. I was scared, because of what Bailey said to Julia, that you couldn't ever tell what mad people were going to do next. B'ar Hatfield told me that."

"Now Bogey, you mustn't make up stories that aren't true. I know all about B'ar Hatfield, but he doesn't get mixed up in real things. I know Mary wouldn't like it if you dragged him into this."

"Mary doesn't care any more. She gave him to me. He's mine now. She made me take the oath, and handed him over. I'm his guardian now."

"Bogey, honey, I don't like this. I honestly don't. I like B'ar Hatfield as a game, but you've got to remember it's a game. Keep B'ar out of real things, because you mustn't get real things and made up things mixed up. That's what happened to Miss Jelke, and you wouldn't want that to happen to you, would you now?"

Bogey ate her cereal thoughtfully. She looked covertly at

281

Silky from time to time. He finished his fried eggs and his toast and jam. He lit a cigarette and took a long draw on it, blowing out a thin pencil of smoke. B'ar Hatfield had told her that for some reason her mother liked Silky better than her father. She knew that what the bear said when she held him by one leg up to her ear, as if he was a sort of telephone, was what was unsayable and dangerous. She could see why Silky would like to pretend that what she heard when she lay on her small bed, with the bear's muzzle in her ear, and the thumb of her other hand in her mouth, was unreal. She knew she didn't actually hear B'ar Hatfield speak, but she did know that while she held his leg she understood things which nobody had ever mentioned or explained directly to her.

"What B'ar Hatfield knows is what I know," she said suddenly.

"Good girl, and promise me you won't ever even pretend there's more to it than that."

"Oh, yes, I'll promise. Dear Silky." She leaned over and kissed him. I fooled him, she thought, it was easy. It always is easy. She was still smiling when Gavin came into the room with a cluster of state troopers and highway-patrol officers behind him. Bogey leapt up and ran round the table to jump up into his arms.

"That's my girl," said Gavin, hugging her.

"Oh, daddy," she said. "Miss Jelke gave me pills and I slept and I missed everything."

"You're a lucky little girl," said one of the troopers.

"I'm pretty lucky, too," Gavin said, across the table to Silky. The painter smiled awkwardly, and looked abashed.

"And that's as true a word as you ever spoke, Mr. Hatfield," said the trooper who had given Silky a hard time, "it certainly was one hell of a lucky break for you that Mr. Sigaux woke up right there just when he did. And it wasn't just that he woke up, Mr. Hatfield, for an amateur, an individual, that is, without any special training, Mr. Sigaux handled that madwoman real well. I tell you, and I think every one of us in the force here would agree on this, that there's nothing I dread more than a deranged person, and when it's a woman into the bargain, I'd rather handle a real mean criminal any day. You picked out a rough spot to get into there, Mr. Sigaux, and for my money you came out pretty well. I'll be candid now, and I won't exaggerate, Mr. Hatfield, but I think it ain't far short of a miracle that Mr. Sigaux got out of it so well as he did. I know one thing for sure though, and I'll tell you what it is, that little girl in your arms is the luckiest girl child in the whole of Congdon county right this minute, and her father, too."

"You know how I feel, Silky," Gavin said, stroking Bogey's head and smiling.

"I think she owes Mr. Sigaux a great big hug, if her daddy can spare him one," one of the highway patrolmen said. "That's what I think."

"We should get back to the Grove, that's what we ought to do, isn't it, young lady, so that we can start to forget all about this," Gavin said.

"Well, if I know my married people, Mr. Hatfield here must be just about dying to get that girl of his back to her mother before she goes out of her mind with anxiety, so we shouldn't detain him here, crowding round him with our chatter and gossip. You're welcome to run along whenever you're inclined, Mr. Sigaux, and I regret any inconvenience the necessary formalities may have caused you. But we have obligations to fulfill and we can't disregard them as we'd sometimes like to do. I'm sure you understand that."

"There is two seventy-eight on these breakfasts," Hannah said quietly. And because Bogey was in Gavin's arms, Silky paid, counting out three dollars from his pocket and adding a dime to make the tip that was too big for Congdon City, and not big enough to celebrate the end of a kidnap attempt. Gavin watched him, thinking, of course, the poor son of a bitch has to think about money all the time. I would have given her a five and told her to keep the change, because I feel happy to have Bogey back. I'll have to find some way to fix that, some way that won't hurt his pride.

283

They drove out into the streets of Congdon City, and past its gaunt Italianate City Hall, a brick, porticoed building which had the air of having gone out of its mind because it had been painted from cellar to attic in brightly gleaming aluminum paint. A faded banner, the relic of some recent drive, flapped under the shelter of the portico, saying something hard to read between the fluted pillars about a finer home town.

"The atmosphere certainly changed when you came on the scene," Silky said. "At one stage I felt I was headed straight for the electric chair."

"Oh, they all know me up here," Gavin said. "A couple of years ago the Governor put me on a special four-man commission to clean up the police department here after the Maramee *Herald* uncovered that bolita scandal. It was a sort of numbers game. The police and the politicians had taken it over from the nigras. We put the fear of God into them all right, and handed the racket back to the coons. I expect they'll be able to keep it for a couple of years before the politicians and the cops get hold of it again."

They drove out of the old city into its newly developed industrial park, through the sprawl of one-story factory buildings dwarfed by massive water tanks standing above them on trestles, and past the recurrent billboards carrying the local administration's slogan "Congdon, sunshine city where work is play and life is fun," along with details of the bribes it would offer businesses to settle there, free factory sites, factory space, and exemption from taxes for ten years. A power line looped from lattice tower to lattice tower across the waste, and along the streets tarred pine poles carried a multitude of shielded cables. On the edge of town a congress of brilliant yellow earth-scraping machines fretted at a vast expanse of raw, freshly exposed gravels. The site already had its label: "The Future Home of Conestin, a Monadnon Subsidiary."

"Is this a real place, Gavin?" Silky asked. "I don't think it's true."

"I don't know. There's a lot of money being made here right this minute. But it could all go to hell in a hat overnight I believe." He looked at Sigaux's drawn face. "Why don't you lie back and try to sleep? You must be all in."

They ran out of Congdon on a secondary road that Gavin took to avoid traffic. It followed an old survey line due south across the sour highland country, an eternity of planted pines waiting in rows for their twenty-year harvesting for the pulp mills. Here and there trees gave way to the desperate farms of Negroes and white trash who couldn't wait twenty years for a crop. Rangy pigs looked for what keep they could find behind their wire fences, tractors that were visible debts on wheels rolled over mean stretches of tilled ground on blowing veils of dust, and here and there men in shapeless sweat-soaked hats held jumping plows into the gravel behind mule teams. One gaunt sun-bleached house with its silvered barns and crazy outhouses succeeded another at the roadside. Each with its surrounding scurf of dead or dying machinery, broken castings, wheel hubs used as dishes for dogs or birds to drink from, holed pots and dishes used as flower pots, and small objects thrown out or just let fall onto the polished, trodden, earth. Gavin barely looked at it all, he knew it. He did not think this is hell, failure, and damnation, he recognized the back country and the manner of life of the wool-hatted crackers who distinguished between what they lived on and what they called cash-money, which could be got by going on up the road to Congdon and signing on at one of the plants up there for a month or two. A man could have his wife at any time, but if he wanted a woman for sport he would need cash-money to buy one in one of the Congdon City or Maramee cat-houses. And it was the same with food, there was what you had, and what you needed cash-money for. As long as a man was content with his own pork and the staples his thin-soiled acres grudgingly yielded he had no need to show up anywhere when a whistle blew to say yes, boss, or no, boss, or to ask anyone a favor. It was only if he wanted soft bread in sealed packages, and fancy stuff, that he had to do that. Gavin knew that the red-necks were ignorant, and prejudiced; and that they, out of a kind of willful contempt for government and interference, as

285

they conceived its function, supported knowingly the kind of corrupt politician whose election amounted to sabotaging the government machinery; but he couldn't dislike the breed as he knew he rationally ought. There was nothing to stop them leaving their world of hardship and hard labor for the cash-money world at any time, they knew the way. But they liked their independence and were ready to pay for it with every one of the comforts and privileges which the money world offered them. They're all right, he thought defiantly, and if they want to live this way that's all right, too.

Bogey leaned against him and slept. Sigaux leaned back into the huge car's softness and slept, too. Gavin thought, with a momentary chill, of Miss Jelke, something broken they were leaving behind them. She would be held under observation for a time, and then certified. After that the state would ship her back to her home state to live out her life in some institution. He wondered if she would have broken up so completely if Silky had not intervened, and what Bogey would have done if she had found herself in Alabama alone with Miss Jelke heading North for wherever it was the nurse had been heading. How long would it have taken her to realize what was going on, and would she have been for it or against it? He could see that it would be fun to be the central star figure in a nation-wide game of cops and robbers, and he decided that at eleven he might have been inclined to give it a try. Later, when they were back at the Grove and the whole story had been told to Ilona, he found that this aspect of the thing had occurred to his daughter. At the end of Silky's recital Bogey turned her face up to Ilona with an expression of something near outrage.

"Isn't it awful, and, mother, do you realize I slept through the whole thing? I missed it all. Every bit of it."

Ilona tousled her hair and bent her head to kiss her.

"So did I. That's awful too, isn't it? There you were being kidnapped and I didn't know. We were all asleep, your father, Mary, Thomas, everybody. Nobody knew but Silky and . . ." Ilona looked up suddenly, and stared across the room and out of the window. "Miss Jelke," she said. "Oh, of course, it was Miss Jelke. I should have known."

"Of course it was Miss Jelke," Gavin said. "That wasn't any sort of mystery."

"No. I don't mean that. I'm thinking of something else, something she did to annoy me, a long time ago. I should have realized that she hated me from that. I should never have trusted her." Her voice changed, and she held Bogey to her. "It's awful to think what might have happened. I was so stupid. But that's the way it always is with servants. The better you treat them the worse it is. They stay with you for years, pretending they like you and doing all sorts of things to show it, and then at the end of it all you find they've been secretly hating you and thinking how they can hurt you most." She stood up, blazing with her sudden anger.

"Silky said it was because she loved me," Bogey said. "That's why she tried to steal me. So she could have me for herself."

"I don't think she hated anybody, Ilona," Silky said with his eyes downcast. Gavin stared at the painter for a moment, and then looked at Ilona. She met his eyes with a curious clouded stare and a sullen expression. He realized why Miss Jelke had wanted to steal the child, not for anything, but simply to get her away; Ilona knew from what, and she knew now that both Gavin and Silky knew, too. Gavin got to his feet and went slowly to Ilona. He put an arm protectively round her shoulders.

"It doesn't matter," he muttered, "she was just a poor old maid going out of her mind. She might just as well have set the house on fire, she could have done anything. You know that."

She shrugged herself free of his arm, furiously. "Bogey," she said, "I shall scream if I see you sitting there in your nightdress and dressing gown for another minute. Go up and put on some proper clothes, there's a dear. You're a big girl now. I'm sure you can manage by yourself." She turned to the two men. "I don't want to even think about this horrible thing any more. Let's all try to forget that it ever happened. I'll always

287

be grateful to you, Silky, you know that, but I don't want to think about what's happened, or what might have happened, ever again. Try to understand how I feel, please try."

"I can understand it very well," Silky said. "But you must excuse me, I think I'm going to go home to sleep for a week, and I've got to go right this minute or I'll drop right where I am." He got up out of his chair and stood for an instant looking at Ilona. "I know how you feel," he said, "I truly do. It's the way I've felt for the greater part of my life about the greater part of my life. I've wished time and time again I could have a complete loss of memory. But then if I did I suppose it would only start me worrying about what I'd forgotten. I just don't know what the answer is, Ilona, but we can try it your way if you want." He went over to her and kissed her on the cheek. "I must go now, or I'll die," he said.

Gavin went out with him to his car, saying nothing until they were out of the shadow of the porch and in the full blaze of the sun. He stood by awkwardly until Silky was in the driver's seat, ready to go. Then he spoke:

"You won't ever try to tell me you're no good again, will you?" he said.

"I wish it was that simple, Gavin, but you know it isn't as well as I do." He started the engine, and sat for a minute with it idling.

"There ought to be something more to say than just thanks," Gavin said. "It doesn't seem quite enough in the circumstances. But you know what I mean."

Silky sat on for a second trying to say what was in his mind, but the words wouldn't arrange themselves in any order that made sense. There wasn't any way to convey to another human being his certainty that what happened in the night had been the wrong thing, the worst for them all that could have happened. He said "So long, Gavin," in a choked voice, and drove off. When he had gone, Gavin went back into his house. Ilona had gone upstairs and all the vast space enclosed in the succession of huge rooms, and in the spreading porches and verandas round them, was empty of life. A sense of anticlimax overwhelmed him, he supposed that even though it was so late he might as well go on down to the office. He had had some thought that Ilona might need him to be there after what had happened, but he had apparently been wrong. He looked in at the drawing-room door and saw Patti Elliot's white handbag in the spot on the mantelpiece where he had put it last night. It looked more like a big white envelope than ever in the daylight, like a piece of mail waiting for someone. It was, he decided, waiting for him, and he went over and picked it up. He put it to his nose. It had a light fresh smell which somehow suggested that life was simple and easy. He slipped the bag into the side pocket of his jacket as he left the room, and a few minutes later he was driving bareheaded down the river road with the light and beauty of the morning all about him.

Chapter Seven

GAVIN stepped out of Cohn and Zimmerman's, the custom tailors on Basin Street, and into the busy street. A fresh wind was coming off the gulf, and everything looked clean and renewed in the spring air. He decided to walk back to the office, and was halfway there when he found himself standing beside Eddie Riemann, waiting for a traffic light to change.

"You've just come from the tailor's," Eddie said.

"How did you know that?"

"You have the startled look on you yet. I must say that when I saw myself in that triple mirror rigged up in knee britches and a tailcoat it startled me too."

"It wasn't the eighteenth-century style that shook me, Eddie, it was the twentieth-century price. Do you realize Cohn is nicking each and every one of us one hundred and eighty dollars for the suit?"

"Ah, that's what you get into when they talk you into being one of Rex's courtiers," Eddie said. "Here's the light, let's go." They stepped forward. "Last year I said to myself that I'd had enough, and that I'd never do it again. I was going to resign. But this year Porgy Armistead came to me and told me his wife had talked him into being Rex, and he begged me to stand by him. So what could I do? And now I'm Grand Chamberlain."

"He put the heat on me, and I'm Grand something or other too."

"His wife is crazy. She's getting a ball dress from Givenchy that's setting her back over eight hundred dollars, and she made him force this thing through about having new costumes for the whole court. It's all her doing. I don't think the committee would have voted the resolution if they'd realized what it was going to mean."

"Those old shiny satin costumes were pretty cheesy, but still, even though I felt like a pig at a ball when I was wearing mine, I'm damned if I see the point of all this. Rex's fifty gentlemen will be shelling out nearly ten thousand dollars between them when you work it out, just for their clothes. If you ask me this whole Pedro Nunez thing is getting out of hand."

"I went into it with Porgy. I believe being Rex through carnival week is going to cost him somewhere around fifteen or eighteen thousand dollars. That's if he's careful. If it goes the way his wife wants it to go it may cost him twenty-four thousand—maybe more than that."

"How do you suppose it got this way?"

"I'll be damned if I know, Gavin. How does anything get to be the way it is? I suppose it began to go badly wrong when the three Allendorfs got to be Rex one after the other. Each one seemed to want to prove he could outspend the others. After that anyone who's really wanted to prove they've got it to burn has tried for Rex."

"Remember how it used to be when I first came down here? When I joined the court the whole thing was just one excuse for a stag dinner the night before the cotillion, and Rex was nothing much."

"Yes, there wasn't anything serious about it in those days. You saw the end of the best of it." Riemann paused. "I'll tell you how it went wrong, now that I think I can see just what did happen. It was the year the ball moved out of the Beverly and into that damned auditorium out in Memorial Park. That was when they started that business of having the grand parade of the debutantes and the presentations to Rex and the queen. I remember standing out against all that, but they voted me down. It went wrong right there."

"I suppose it was a mistake, turning a family affair into a public spectacle."

"That too, but the real trouble was it made it a woman's show, and that sank it."

"You're just a sour old bachelor, Eddie."

"That's not the point, Gavin, the point is there's nothing in the entire universe as serious about being what it is as an eighteen-year-old girl. You're a father, man, you should know that."

"I suppose I should," Gavin laughed.

"Well, it's that utterly serious self-absorption, self-reverence, and I don't know what, which gives them the daemonic power to take over this whole damned city for one week every year, just to arrange a mounting fuss, confusion, tension, and excitement, all centered on them and all released after a hundred and forty hours of social hell when fifty of them walk solemnly round on a boarded-over ice rink before climbing up a flight of steps at the top of which it is publicly and formally announced that they are now physically and mentally ready for copulation, cohabitation, and breeding."

"Eddie, you must have been reading a book," Gavin said.

"Oh, I have a wide variety of interests," Eddie said, and looked thoughtful. "How is Ilona?" he said abruptly.

"Not good, Eddie. Not a bit good."

"I wish there was something I could do to help."

"So do I. I'd ask you to do it, without any hesitation at all."

They walked side by side in silence for a while.

"I heard from Nedda the other day," Riemann said. "They had to leave Palma. Harry went for a man in a night club because he thought he'd been giving Nedda the eye. He got out by paying the man fifteen hundred dollars to cover his medical bills, the poor brute had a broken jaw. Then there was another thousand dollars compensation to make him feel better and to keep him away from lawyers, and a last thousand dollars for the police, to keep them friendly. So that's the end of their six months economizing in Glorious Majorca. The police made Harry clear out in forty-eight hours. They'd been there for just five weeks. The thought of that damned man still acting as if he couldn't trust her not to be unfaithful to him if he turns his back on her for a single second makes me sick. She's been devotedly loyal to him through every squalid mess he's got her into all these years, as it happens, and the whole thing makes me so angry I can't be reasonable about it. I wish he'd die. I'd almost like to kill him myself. I wish I knew why she sticks with him."

"She loves him, Eddie," Gavin said. "That's all."

"I don't believe it. I used to. But I just don't any more. He's just a burden she's picked up for the sake of carrying a burden, or because she's got some ugly craving for ill treatment. You never knew mother, did you? She was before your time. I think Nedda missed her when she was gone. She couldn't live on her own without the woman's utterly unconscious cruelty and injustice bearing down on her. She was like a lost soul from the time mother died until she found Harry. I didn't know what it was all about then. I thought she just didn't know a nice guy when she saw one. But now I know it wasn't that, she didn't want anyone who'd be good to her, she didn't want a nice guy. She was looking for a real heel to get stuck with. Don't tell me that has anything to do with love, it was just a horrible compulsion."

Gavin looked ahead, at the men and women walking towards them and away from them, at the soft face-like fronts of the cars parked diagonally along the curb, at the brazen store fronts hung with their strident signs, and the scraggy sago palms whose fans were rustling briskly in the wind from the gulf. He knew that Eddie had never loved anyone, and he was almost sure that while he had laid a great many women he had never spent a second night with most of them. With the act the point was proved that Eddie could get the woman, and that was it. He would suddenly be overwhelmed, not by desire, but by the necessity of bringing the woman to give herself to him. The woman had to have no specific qualities such as being blond, tall, smart, or even conventionally attractive: she was just suddenly and unpredictably the one who had to be the next with her legs open, her arms round his shoulders, and her hands pressing him closer than flesh to flesh, but bone to bone and darkness to darkness. By which time he was already gone, into remoteness and indifference, watching distantly as a spec-

293

tator for the moment of liquefaction and delight to be signaled by the changes in the woman's breathing and expression which would let him know that he had succeeded once again. Gavin knew that it had once happened to a girl who was a teller in his bank. She had cashed Eddie a check. And because, while counting him out the thirteen tens, two fives, and ten ones, she had quickly passed the tip of her tongue across her upper lip, she had become the next center and focus of his life. She was a Lutheran from Indiana who had come to Maramee when her husband had been assigned to duty at the William Arling Field, and she came with him because she loved him. Eddie's pursuit and his insistence prevailed over everything; upbringing, conscience, long vigils at prayer. He won in the end. She had a long talk with her husband which she opened by saying, "Roger, I have something important to tell you. I am no longer a fit person to be your wife." When the talk which began after she had washed up the dishes at the end of Sunday lunch was over, she left her husband's house with the bags she had already packed and moved to the Whispering Pines Motel where the cottages had a living room, a sleeping alcove, bathroom, and kitchenette. When Eddie met her two blocks from the bank the following evening, expecting to drive her, as had become usual, to a corner two or three corners from her street, she told him. "Don't turn right on Claibourne," she said, "take the Tampa road. I have a cottage at the Whispering Pines." She came to Gavin's office some six weeks later looking calm and still, but with shadows under her eyes. He looked at her and thought she must have been told that she had some serious chronic illness by her doctor. He thought that she had come to him to ask for some kind of help with the cost of the treatment.

"Mr. Hatfield," she said. "I don't like to bother you with a personal matter, but I believe you can help me."

"I'd like to help if I can, Mrs. Meyner."

"I shouldn't do this I know. But I have urgent personal reasons for getting in touch with Mr. Riemann. I don't seem to be able to reach him at his home or at his office. I'm ashamed to ask you this, but I have to, I know you are a friend of his and I think you can tell me where he is. Where can I reach him, Mr. Hatfield?"

"I saw him last a little over a month ago, Mrs. Meyner. He told me he was going up to Aspen, in Colorado, for some skiing. I think he meant to stay for the rest of the season up there." Gavin found it hard to look at her as he spoke. He knew what had happened to her, and he could see from her face that she too had known for some time but was only now admitting it. She sat quietly for a while, stood up as if to leave, and then sat down again.

"I hate to bother you," she said, "but I've nowhere to turn. I didn't realize at the time how little Mr. Riemann wanted of me. I left my husband on his account, and I'm a stranger here. I could handle it on my own if it was just a matter of realizing I'd given him my full cooperation in making a fool of myself, but it doesn't stop there. I've always wanted children, and the one flaw in my marriage was that it had never been blessed. I suppose it was part of my foolishness, but what made me give in to Mr. Riemann and leave Roger was the feeling I had that Mr. Riemann would give me children and be a good father to them. My instinct was sound enough, Mr. Hatfield, and I've started the baby I've always wanted more than anything. I've been to the doctor and it's quite definite. So you can see I'd like to have some word from Mr. Riemann."

"I'll do everything I can, Mrs. Meyner. What do you want me to tell him?"

"I suppose, since he ran away, he doesn't want to have anything more to do with me. I'd like to know if he wants me to have the child, or if he'd rather I had one of those operations. I'm not sure which would be more degrading, to have a child that anyone could call a bastard any time they wanted to, or to have some stranger with rubber gloves on finish what began with love. I feel Mr. Riemann would probably prefer me to have the operation. But let him say. And tell him I'll need money either way."

"I'm sure he'll do whatever's right, Mrs. Meyner," Gavin

said, and instantly wished he hadn't. She looked at him without any expression.

"I don't think you understood when I said I thought Mr. Riemann would prefer me to have the operation. I said I thought he would prefer that because it would be more degrading to me as a woman and a human being. I don't expect anything of him that anyone in their senses would call right. He just does what he has to do, I suppose."

"I can understand your feeling bitterly about this, Mrs. Meyner," Gavin said. "And I'll do my best to make things easy for you."

"I don't feel bitterly, Mr. Hatfield, I feel badly." She stood up and her calm and her face disintegrated. "I wish I did feel bitter. I wish I could hate him. But I can't. He made me love him, and I can't stop. Even though I know now that he just wanted me once to prove he could get me. He could do anything and I'd go on. That's what's so terrible. Roger was good to me all our life together, so good you wouldn't believe it, but I liked him for it. All his goodness only made me feel I owed him a wife's duty, I never wanted to crawl anywhere on my hands and knees on his account. Every bone and nerve in my body says I've got to bring this child into the world, I want it because it's his child, but if Eddie wants me to do this vile, this disgusting . . ." Her voice broke, and she turned her back on Gavin. She stamped her foot with anger at her own weakness, and squared her shoulders. "Then that's what I have to do," she said in an almost inaudible voice.

When the whole dismal and pathetic mess had been cleaned up, so far as it could be, and Mrs. Meyner had vanished from Maramee with enough money for the operation and anything else that might come up within a year or two, Eddie had been grateful to Gavin who had arranged everything which had to be arranged. In his gratitude he had unburdened himself of his story. Eddie knew, if anyone did, what the words hateful compulsion meant, but it was no use talking to him about love, he was a stranger to that country.

Two Negro girls came down the street, daring any white

man to look at them. Their dresses were stretched like skin over their young bodies, and their firm breasts seemed to vibrate as their stiletto-heeled shoes tapped the pavement. There were golden clips like small seashells on the lobes of their ears and their formal mouths were drawn on their lips in a very pale magenta. Gavin looked deeply into the eyes of the girl nearest to him and saw the softness and the sweetness behind the sullenly aggressive face's challenge to him to deny that it was a human face. There was always a person within, and still another within that inner being. There was the outer shell contrived to take the wounds, the inner, wounded creature, and inside, or beyond that, the matrix, the lost twin, unhurt, unspoiled, and uncorrupt. Loving was what? Having the courage to remove the outer shells was part of it, giving oneself defenselessly and without reserve, as oneself, into the hands of another human being in the hope of being rewarded with a return of the same trust and yielding up. But not with that hope as a calculation, loving wasn't for anything, it was a necessity of being—if you were not too enclosed, as Eddie was, in the memory of old wounds and the hideously perfected mechanisms for avoiding further wounds.

"I don't think you'll ever begin to understand Nedda," Gavin said.

"I don't think I'd want to understand what's got hold of her. As for Harry, I'm seriously thinking of going over to break his neck for the pure unadulterated pleasure of it. If I'd known then what I know now I should have let you drown him that time we were all out there at the spring, you had the right idea."

"I never tried to drown Harry that I can—hell yes, I do remember, come to think of it."

"Well here's my corner—let's have lunch on Thursday, at the club."

"It's a date, if there isn't anything in my book. Let's say it's on, and if I can't do it I'll call you when I get back to the office."

While Gavin was covering the hundred yards or so which

297

remained between him and the bank building the spring filled his thoughts. He hadn't been out there for years. The white sand and the brilliant color of the circle of living water ringed by the oaks came vividly to his mind's eye. The place had been so much a part of his life at one time that it was difficult for him to realize how completely it had dropped out of his scheme of things. Marsen had warned him once not to spend too much time there watching the movement of the water under the dome of the sky, and he wondered what the old savage would have said to him if he had ever known that he would come to the stage of even forgetting that the place existed. He hadn't given it a thought for years. And as he gave it thought he recognized with a small shock that he could no longer think about it as the spring, or as Marsen had always called it, the boil. Between him and it there was the last sight he had of Nedda's naked body, drenched in moonlight at the water's edge. It was the place where he had seen what he had lost, without recognizing it. He had just thought then that it was too bad that they had stopped sleeping together, as if Nedda was simply something to be touched, felt, looked at, and enjoyed, that you had or did not have by staking your claim and keeping it staked to the exclusion of other stakes. Nedda had been there for him to discover once. She had offered herself to him, but he had not noticed her making the offer. He had never thought of asking himself what she was, inside the hard shell of her disguise as the party girl who would go the limit for fun. He had been too busy going the limit. Naturally she had dropped him, naturally, naturally. And now her naked body, the sexual apparatus which he had mistaken for her whole self, stood in his memory beside the pool to mark the stupidity of his irrecoverable loss. He thought of the loving, warm, and infinitely generous spirit he had seen for a moment looking out from inside the Negro girl. For a second they had recognized each other, and it was the sort of recognition on which love was based. Loving was living with the discovered inner creature, ignoring the outer shell, and perhaps making so absolute a gift of oneself that an outer shell stopped being a neces-

298

sity at all. In the climate of love the inner creature could throw off its disguise and live as itself, unmasked. Eddie would never know that his sister knew another Harry, who made no squalid scenes, and was honorable, understanding, and kind. She was giving her life to keep that lost and hidden Harry, the real man, who could respect himself and trust himself, alive. There was no way to explain how it could be worth her while. These things didn't explain, didn't tell. They had to be learned. For a long instant, Gavin contemplated the bleak vistas of a life in which they never were learned, and for the first time understood poverty. He came out of his reverie to meet the wide grin on the face of the bank's doorman.

"Good morning, Mr. Hatfield, it surely is one beautiful day, isn't it?"

"It's spring, Charlie."

"Yes sir! The sweetest time in the whole of the year."

Gavin went in through the heavy plate-glass door into his Roman-style temple of divine money. The doorman always gave him a peculiar feeling. He had deceived Gavin and everyone else systematically over the years by cultivating a public personality which was a cross between Uncle Tom and Santa Claus. He stood there opening and shutting the door during banking hours every day making believe he was a happy, good-natured, simple-minded old darkie, delighted to have the honor of dressing up like a Ruritanian brigadier general. He had been given a Sam Browne belt when he was issued a pistol, and at the time Gavin and several other bank officers had thought that this was the high point in his life. But as the years went by and each one of old Charlie's three sons went North in turn to go to good universities on good scholarships it came out that Charlie had never spent a nickel of his wages on any item that was not strictly necessary to keeping himself, his wife and the children alive, clothed, and housed. Every cent he could save he had saved to spend on the text books with which he first educated himself, and had then coached and driven his children up to the highest scholastic levels children who were not prodigies could reach. When Gavin had discovered what he had done, through a paragraph in the Maramee *Herald* announcing that Charlie's third boy had graduated summa cum laude from his college, he went to see him at his home, a four-roomed house in Morgantown which had in it five kitchen chairs, two kitchen tables, one of them for the boys to study at, an iron double bed, bunks made of scrap wood for the three boys, and an old stove that had been rescued from a dump. It had lost one of its metal legs, and needed a brick under one corner to keep it level. There were two chests of drawers, and there was a kitchen cabinet. There were the boys' books and there were as few pieces of china, pots, and pans as there had to be.

"Why didn't you let me help you, Charlie?" Gavin said standing on the porch step, looking into the house's emptiness.

"I never asked any white man for help in my entire life, Mr. Hatfield," Charlie said.

"There's nothing I can do now?"

"No, sir."

Down the street one or two people were standing casually looking into space, devoured by curiosity as to what catastrophe or disaster had brought a white calling on their neighbor; he could be most likely either a debt collector, a process server, or a plain-clothes man. Gavin looked at them, and then back to his employee, standing impassively waiting for him to go away, holding the newspaper he had been reading in one hand and his spectacles in the other.

"If the boys want any help getting jobs just ask me. I'd be proud to give them letters of recommendation."

"I'll remember that, sir."

But Charlie had never asked for any help, and had presented himself at the bank in his role of the dear old darkie just the same as always the next day, and every day thereafter. Gavin had even slipped back into his old way of making the kind of brightly cheerful remark to him that would touch off the broad grin and the characteristic Charlieisms. But always, afterwards, he remembered with a little jolt the dignified and remote off-duty Charlie, who was not even called Charlie at all, but Nelson. And I was going to teach Marsen how to deal with those people, he thought, this time incredulously recalling his greenness as he crossed the marble floor on his way to the elevator. A wall calendar caught his eye, reminding him first how close it was getting to the week of carnival and Pedro Nunez Day, and then how soon after that it was going to be Thomas' birthday. I know, he thought, I'll hand the spring over to him, and the whole piece of property that goes with it. He's got to be the age at which he can do with a little responsibility, it'll be good for him. And the spring, that'll do something for him, if he sees it for what it is. Gavin got into the elevator, pressed the buttons, and slid upwards towards his office.

A few days later Thomas took a classmate of Mary's called Sophy Dawes McCann to see a movie at a drive-in theater on the fringes of Maramee. The film they saw was a poor one, and at the end of it, as they drove out of the place in the convertible which was Thomas' first car and his joy and pride, they both simultaneously said, "Let's go on over and hear the bells," then laughed at the way their thought and their words had chimed together. The bells were over at Sweetwater and were a part, and after the football stadium the most famous part, of Gulf University. When American institutional architecture was in the full flower of academic Gothic, someone, officially described as a benefactor, had hit the university with the gift of a campanile, an enlargement by one-third of a tower at Caen in Normandy, housing twenty-seven real bells, and thirty resonant tubes, all electronically operated from a console in the lower part of the structure. The bells marked the passing of every hour with an elaborate and, to the students, exasperating chime, but the real punch packed by the carillion was unveiled at the Saturday and Sunday-night bell concerts when the resident campanologist would cut loose with unpredictable medleys which would flit from "Good Night, Irene," to "Voi Che Sapete," to "Weel May the Keel Row," to the "Londonderry Air," to the "Tennessee Waltz," to "My Heart's in the Highlands," and to almost anything else that occurred to him as likely to be distinguishable in the vibrating outpouring of his huge machine. The campanologist practiced for these affairs on most nights of the week for half an hour between ten and half past. The tower stood in the university's botanic garden beside a lake which was ringed by a drive, and it had become a part of courtship in that section of the state to go necking at that waterside. The enlaced couples would lie or sprawl in their parked cars in the shadows of the strange-leaved and exotic trees, letting the tingling, clanging, musical goo pour slowly over them, saturating them with its honeyed sweetness. "Let's go on over and hear the bells" could mean more than it seemed to mean, particularly if a girl suggested it to a boy. Thomas was not sure what Sophy intended by the suggestion and did not find out on the drive there. She sat far away from him, leaning back with her face turned up to the sky, and with hands locked under the back of her head. She sang with the singers who were on the platter program which was coming in on the car radio. She seemed utterly uninterested in him, not even bothering to pretend to want to talk. He was glad to be spared the effort, and limited himself to joining her in one or two of the songs he liked. As they passed through the first houses in Aitkens, the jigtown on the Maramee side of Sweetwater, they heard the far off tingle tangle of "Oh, No John, No John, No," ending and dying in the softness of the night air. Nothing followed it.

"Hell, I'm sorry, Sophy," Thomas said. "We've missed it. I thought we had plenty of time, too."

"It doesn't matter," she said peacefully. She rolled her head sideways so that she could look at him.

"Well, I thought you wanted to hear them."

"I did. But really I just wanted to go somewhere with you," she said it without special emphasis, as if it were up to him to make anything he wanted to of the remark. He thought about it, but spoke about something else.

"Did you ever hear anyone tell about the Gulf student who went crazy because of the bells? He hid in the belfry, right up in the top where they're hung. Somebody bet him he couldn't stay there through one of the concerts. He was up there for the whole of one of those Saturday afternoon concerts and . . ."

"I won't even listen to it," Sophy said putting her hands over her ears.

"They have him shut up at that state hospital in Rogerstown still," Thomas said.

They found a parking place under a huge oak at the water's edge, and lit cigarettes as soon as the engine was turned off. A patrol car of the campus police force slid past slowly, and as it went by briefly snapped on a flood lamp. When the driver saw them sitting upright and apart with cigarettes in their hands he cut the blinding glare off again and drove on. When the red glow of his rear lights had gone out of sight they both threw away their cigarettes in curving trains of sparks and, falling into each other's arms, kissed mouth to mouth. This formal opening stage in the proceedings continued for perhaps a minute, until Thomas became aware, by some softening of her body, that he could go on to stage two, in which it would be all right to caress all such parts of her body as he could reach without actually unfastening or unbuttoning anything. When that stage was done with in its turn, he discovered that another level of privilege was being allowed him, she made no movement to resist when his hand went in under her blouse but lay back further to drink more softly and eagerly at his mouth. In a few more seconds he had her blouse and her brassiere unfastened and while he kissed her small breasts and nipples she held his head tightly to her. He returned to her mouth and set his hands traveling gently down the smooth surfaces of her warm back. Suddenly at the exact point, and at the exact instant he expected it, her back arched and she pushed him away from her saying "oh-oh" in a firm tone. He brought his hands quickly up to her shoulders and tried to return to her mouth, but her arched spine was stiff, her hands and arms were no longer soft and clinging, and her head was turned away. He took his hands out from inside her blouse, and instantly found her mouth back again on his, and this time her tongue flickered

303

briefly between his lips. She broke away too soon for him, and briskly asked him to light a cigarette for her, as she buttoned herself back into presentability. He was unlucky here, since he did not know that this was for her the most worldly and sophisticated sexual gesture that a woman could make towards a man. The fact that her father and mother would light cigarettes for each other, according to whichever had the wheel, when they were out driving epitomized for her the fact that the marriage relationship was a sexual one. As she accepted the cigarette which Thomas had had at his mouth and put it to her own lips, she was amazed that she could do anything so mature and carry it off with such poise. A wave of special tenderness for Thomas enveloped her. She lay back softly in the angle of his arm, conveying to him by some subtle language of contact that handling and fondling was, at any rate for the time being, through and that there was to be just nestling and talk in what remained of the evening. He felt it to be so, but although the message came through strongly enough he couldn't resist making certain. He moved a hand slowly upward from her waist to cradle one of her little apple-like breasts. Without moving she uttered the same two syllables "oh-oh" with a bald definiteness that allowed no argument. He let his hand lie there for perhaps half a second to show that he was a man and not to be given orders, and then dropped it obediently to her waist. They drowsed in a warm stupor, conscious of each other, of the starlight filtering through the trees, of their close approach to something glorious and dangerous, and of a narrow escape from it.

"Sophy."

"Mmm?"

"You're a pretty good friend, I mean, really, the best friend Mary's got, aren't you?"

"Yes I am, Thomas, I like her about as much as you can like a person. If I said I loved her it wouldn't be too far off it."

"You talk about pretty much of everything I suppose."

"About everything two people could talk about I'd say. We're friends."

"That's what I thought." Thomas was silent for a while. "I used to be friends with Mary."

"She's still just terribly fond of you, I know that."

"She doesn't act it. She's been impossible—for months now. Nothing she says or does makes sense any more, to me anyway. We used to get along well, too. That's what foxes me. We were close, just like that"—he held up his fingers—"closer. I could sometimes tell what she was thinking, even. Then, whammy, suddenly there's a complete stranger in the place."

"You still *like* her, don't you, Thomas?" Sophy said.

"Sure I *like* her, but we used to be *friends*."

"Well, it's important, because you see, if you didn't like her —and you don't have to just because of being her brother, I mean it's natural but it doesn't always work, my own sister is mean to me all the time, if you want an example, and I almost hate her sometimes. I know just lots of brothers and sisters who don't get on at all. But if you didn't truly like Mary, I wouldn't be able to talk to you about her."

Sophy Dawes McCann then went into an act. She put on the thoughtful, earnest expression which her mother used to adopt when she was going to really get down to the business of nailing another woman to the wall, a process which almost always involved a breach of confidence. The look, and the betrayal, was to Sophy another important part of being adult and mature. It was a kind of stepping outside friendship into the domain of pure scientific psychology. And again it was something her mother did for her father's benefit, and which she did for him because they were man and wife. She was about to give things away to Thomas which Mary had told her under the seal of a dead secrecy on the numerous occasions on which they had spent the night at each other's homes after going to parties or to a movie, and this gave her a thrilling sense of involvement with him. It made her a little closer to being Thomas' mistress. She used the word to herself with a reckless tingling of all her senses. She knew it was dishonorable to give away secrets, but between lovers there just couldn't be any secrets. And she and Thomas were as good as lovers.

"You ought to try to be terribly understanding with Mary just now, Thomas. I mean she has problems. I shouldn't really tell you, but she's in love with this man, she made me promise not to tell anyone, and you've got to promise, too. He's . . ."

"I know. He's Silky Sigaux. The hero who saved Bogey."

"How did you know?" Sophy was bitterly disappointed.

"I don't know. I just knew. I suppose it was my knowing that made her mad at me."

"Well, then there isn't so much to tell. Anyway she's crazy about him, and yet she can't bear it."

"What can't she bear?"

Sophy paused a minute. Now that she was faced with the problem of stating it in words, she was not sure exactly what Mary had precisely told her in an almost incoherent flow of words that meant collectively suffering, and confusion, and uncertainty.

"I don't know," she said vaguely, "the whole thing, I guess."

"I touched her once, there, you know. It was an accident. I don't know just how it happened—sweet Jesus she was mad—she went off like a firecracker. I thought I'd done something terrible. Can't she bear being touched, well, that way?"

"You didn't understand, Thomas. That's well, something pretty special. I mean you wouldn't let a person do it, touch you there, I mean, unless you had thought about a person a whole lot in a particular way which just wouldn't be right if it was a sister thinking about a brother."

"Can she bear to let him touch her?"

"She can't bear the thought of anyone else."

"Well, what on earth's the matter?"

"Oh Thomas, don't be so simple. She can't just go to him and say she wants him. A girl, a woman, can't do that. And then he's a lot older than she is. It's awful for her. She loves him, and he doesn't seem to know she's a proper person who could love him. He thinks she's the little girl who lives in his friend's house. When he takes her out it's awful for her. It's like an uncle taking his niece out. He's kind to her, and she loves him. Don't you see?"

"What do you really think of him? Honestly, I mean."

"I can see what Mary sees in him," she said. "I mean he is sort of beautiful, and it's romantic, his being a painter and having a studio. He isn't just ordinary. But I don't think he's terribly good for her. I don't see how he can be."

"I wouldn't think he was much good for anyone," Thomas said uneasily and sadly. "He's no good for himself."

Sigaux gave Thomas more and more the same feeling, when he thought of it, as a bird with a broken wing, or a dog with an ugly sore festering prominently on its body. The painter gave this impression of being sick, or hurt, not by his appearance but by his actions. And these took some time to understand. Thomas had known him first by Gavin's scoffing titles: "the star boarder" or "your mother's pet highbrow." He had always thought it odd that Sigaux accepted his father's patronizing contempt as if it were what he deserved. But after Miss Jelke's mad attempt to carry Bogey off had made Gavin think him brave, there had been a change. Now that Gavin treated him with respect and as a friend, Sigaux had begun to be ashamed and unhappy in his presence. Something bound him to Ilona, and whatever it was was queerly wrong. He was not sure what made him think so. But he had a sense that there was an edge of pain to every word that his mother drew from the painter. She had him to the house to talk about another world, a world of ballet, plays, pictures, people, and art which was also a world of reputations and success. While he was with Ilona Silky had to pretend to be part of that world and he clearly wasn't. He'd been rejected by it. He lived in Maramee and he drank. Thomas knew something strange was going on when his mother's promptings turned the painter back and back again to the region of his personal failure. He knew that it was something odd too which brought Silky back to have his feelings hurt day after day. It now struck him that it was odder yet for his sister to want to add another element to this entanglement of tormentor and tormented. He did not want to look further into the nightmare landscape which seemed to be opening before him when he thought of what

307

Mary was doing to herself. He turned towards Sophy abruptly. "Turn up your face, look at me," he said in a harsh, almost brutal voice. She lifted her eyes to his in surprise, and when he flung himself on her violently and passionately, bruising her lips, she was terrified to find that she was in the grip of a more powerful force, at once in herself and outside herself, than she had ever before encountered in her life. For a moment she thought, no, I'm not ready, and then she thought simply, Thomas, I'm glad. I've always known it would be Thomas, and, we'll be happy, yes, happy, happy, happy, happy always and forever. His face fell away from hers and he buried his head in the softness of her breasts, a suppliant for reassurance and forgiveness. She stroked his hair gently, feeling infinitely old and wise, protective and proud.

"I'm sorry, Sophy," he said, "I don't know what came over me. Will you forgive me?"

"I love you, Thomas," she said. "There isn't anything to forgive. It wouldn't have happened if I hadn't wanted it."

"I didn't, I hope I didn't hurt you?"

"Not one little bit." She bent down to kiss his ear. "I like the shape of your head," she said. "I suppose that sounds silly, but I mean it. You have the dearest head of anyone I know."

As she spoke she did not consciously think that she wanted a head like that one, made of her flesh and bone and of his, to come thrusting out of her womb into the world but she felt it. Thomas did not think about it either as he listened to her heart beating and enjoyed the warmth of her body, he merely felt safe and at ease just where he was. Sophy spoke again and he listened to her. She was drugged with her delight in him and in his body.

"I'm glad I'm not Mary," she said. "She's been wanting this to happen to her more than anything. She says she'll die if it turns out he doesn't love her. It would be the end to want someone and have them not want you, wouldn't it? You ought to be extra nice to her to make up for it, really you should. She says it's one of the things that's terrible for her, she says you don't understand anything any more. And you used to be so close. She's terribly fond of you, Thomas, I mean she worships you. She honestly does."

"She's told you that?" He felt a warm pleasure at the thought of her telling her best friend that it was so. "It would be pretty awful to be fond of someone you had to be ashamed of, I see she would be upset."

"She isn't ashamed of him, Thomas, she loves him." He sat up and looked at her. "The way I love you," she said.

"You mean you'd love me even if I was awful, sort of sick inside, and messed up? What do you mean?"

"I don't know. Isn't that terrible? I just mean . . ." She sat with parted lips, looking at him. It was something that giving herself to him should have cleared up, something she had always supposed that women, as opposed to girls, knew. It dawned on her that he might take her home and drive off, and that he might never come back. What had happened might mean nothing to him except that he had done it to her. She reached out to touch his bare forearm, and the instant her fingers were on his flesh she knew that she wanted him to have her a great many times, that she would like to have at least four children by him, and that there would be nothing that she could think of that would turn her against him or make her disgusted with him. "I just love you," she said, "no matter what." She turned away from him and turned her face upwards towards the stars. She had read about them in books with an odd feeling that what she read had no meaning, but she now suddenly understood how vast and strange the universe was. Perhaps it all had no meaning. She turned back to Thomas and inspected his brooding, thoughtful face. Perhaps she was just to be his first, the girl with whom he was to find out that he could do it, and what you had to do to get it, the answer to his need of the moment. It was a great happiness to have been that, at any rate, no matter what followed. He felt her eyes on him and looked up. They exchanged a long silence during which she had a moment of panic. If he just takes me again, she thought, it'll be the end, and oh, God, I don't want it to be just that. But he kissed her gently on the cheek, and took her hand.

"You're so nice, Sophy," he said, "you're just so nice. I'm not at all sure I'm nice enough for you, but I'm going to try to be, I really am."

"You don't have to try, Thomas," she said, "you're all right. You really are."

When Thomas had left her off at her home on the Heights, and had seen her vanish through the big nineteen twenty-five Spanish-mission doorway, between the twisted pillars and the two windows with wrought iron grilles over them, he felt serenely happy and thirsty. All the way out to the Grove he thought about being a man to whom a girl had truly and properly given herself, about how wonderful it was that the girl should be someone as miraculously beautiful, kind, gentle and understanding as Sophy Dawes McCann, and about how the minute he got home he would make himself a Boston Cooler. When he got there the first thing he did was to pour a bottle of ginger ale into a large glass and add to it a huge dollop of vanilla ice from a carton in the Deep-Freeze. With his concoction made, he went over and sat himself in Julia Bailey's rocking chair with deep satisfaction. As he spooned into the ice he wondered why the text "many are called but few are chosen" had such an appeal for the fat, placid cook. Julia, who had been around for as long as he could remember, was entrenched in the kitchen, and had adorned it with several of her treasures. The rocking chair of bentwood was hers. She had bought it at auction, when the property of a minister she admired had been sold after his death, along with three identical framed texts which had been in his house. "Many are called . . ." they all said from their different places round the walls. The same cryptic message was embroidered in a variety of colored wools on a plump cushion under his back.

"What do they mean, those words, Julia?" he asked her once.

"It's a beautiful saying of our good Lord, Mr. Thomas,"

Julia said, "and it's the truest thing ever got written on a piece of paper."

Thomas looked at the text on the wall over the stove across the room and saw it in a new light. Not everybody could have the luck to be loved by the person they were in love with, and have that person be Sophy Dawes McCann. He savored the name. Pretty soon she would give it up and become Mrs. Thomas Hatfield, and that would be quite terrific, but meanwhile it was nice thinking of her as S.D.M., my dear sweet, sweet dear mistress, Sophy Dawes McCann. And if there was anything better than a Boston Cooler you had made for yourself, he did not know it. He saw the swing door into the front part of the house opening as his mother came through into the kitchen, carrying a tall glass.

"Hallo there, Tom," she said. She came over and ruffled his hair with her free hand as she drifted by him. She came to rest with her behind propped against the dresser not far from his chair. She yawned widely, looking about her, and Thomas smelled whiskey. Her eye fell on a knitting bag and a stack of dream books which she hadn't seen before.

"Goddamn that Julia," she said, "she's always squirreling away more stuff in here." She wrinkled her nose. "I ought to put my foot down. I ought to throw all this crap of hers out before the whole place begins to stink of nigras."

Thomas looked into his glass and said nothing, and the kitchen clock ticked noisily across his silence. His mother yawned again.

"Sweet Jesus," he prayed, "make her go away and leave me alone."

"I had an idea, just an idea mind you, that I'd find Mary here," she said, "she's out late tonight."

"I expect she's with Sophy," he said, lying with some idea of being helpful to his sister. "I expect she's gone over to spend the night with her, or something like that."

"I don't think so," said Ilona, sipping her Bourbon delicately. The sips were followed by a large hard-drinker's swallow. "No, I don't think so. In fact," she added it in a level tone, as if she didn't really care if he heard her or not, "in fact I know damn well she isn't." She looked for a while at something fathoms deep in her glass. Thomas uneasily gave himself another couple of spoonfuls of ice cream. "Sigaux took her out. She twisted his arm and made him take her to the opera to hear some second-rate touring company moaning their way through *Rigoletto*. That's what happened. And you knew it as well as I did. Didn't you?"

"Well, yes, I sort of knew it, but not for sure."

"And all the same you didn't feel like telling me." A lock of hair fell across her forehead and she brushed it back with too large a gesture, so that she had the air of smearing something across her face. "But then you wouldn't, would you, tell me anything? Not if it was tearing you apart to tell someone, would you? If it was important, that is. If it was any little thing, O.K. you could tell me. But if it was something that mattered, really mattered, I'd be the last, ultimate one to tell in the entire loused-up universe—wouldn't I?"

The clock ticked again, through a period in which Thomas thought that on the whole he would rather she struck him than asked him that kind of hideously unanswerable question.

"I came in here, as it so happens," she said, "knowing damn well it was you and not Mary. I heard that jalopy of yours come in, and there's no mistaking it. I just wanted to pass the time of day, and say how fond of you I am, that's all. Absolutely all. And you won't, you can't, talk to me."

Thomas carefully put his partly finished drink down, hoping as he did so that he would have a chance to pick it up again before the ice cream was altogether melted. He went and put an arm round his mother's shoulders.

"You don't ever have to tell me you're fond of me," he said. "I know that. As for the other thing, you know, about talking, you want us to hash things over with you that—well, it's impossible. You know why—you've done it, growing up I mean. Mary and me, we're doing it. I bet you couldn't talk to anyone, even your own mother, when you were doing it."

Ilona looked at her son with large eyes. She was amused. She had come through to look at him to see if he had made out with his girl that night. She hoped that he had. She wanted all her children to get their sexual gropings and experiments over quickly, without anxiety and regret. She didn't want him to go on wrestling silently with fears and inner confusions for months and years, as she had. She was surprised to find that Thomas knew as much as he did about where he was, and what the score was. There was no invaluable piece of advice she could give him, no talisman which would see him through his years of uncertainty. He was just faced with something difficult which he had to handle for himself.

"I'd forgotten," she said. "Yes, I'd forgotten how secret it all had to be." She rattled the ice against the side of her glass. "It's hell growing up, isn't it? But then it's the same hell being grown up. It never stops. The only thing is not to let any of it scare you."

"I won't, mother." He caressed her with the heavy arm he had thrown over her shoulder, comfortingly and kindly. She looked quickly into his face and saw that he was offering her sympathy and understanding for being much closer to the breaking point than he would ever be. He was pitying her. She recoiled, almost shocked, from his understanding, and with an involuntary movement shook off his protective arm. She had not really looked at him for some time and she was surprised to see that the child she had known had already gone. She could see the beginnings of character, of a man's face, and recognized that he was already stronger than she had ever been. She felt a simultaneous flash of joy and despair. He is my child and I have never known him, she thought, and now I never will know him. This stranger came out of my body. And he's ready, she thought, not just to get himself laid, but for love and a woman. She kissed his cheek, holding her breath as she did so in the hope that he wouldn't smell the whiskey on it. If it's only a real woman he finds, she thought, not just some little local chippie with hot pants. But what chance has he got, what chance? Tearfulness threatened.

313

"I think I'll go to bed, Thomas," she said gently. "Don't bother to wait for Mary. Just leave a few lights for her." She wanted to make some tremendous declaration of love, of apology, but it all dwindled in her mouth into a meaningless compliment. "You're looking very well these days, Thomas, really very well. I'm proud of you. Good night."

"Good night, mother."

He was pleased to find, when she was quite gone, that the ice cream was still not altogether melted. He finished it sitting on the table reading Winchell's column of ten days before. It was on the upper side of one of the sheets of the Maramee *Times-Herald*, which Julia had spread out, as she did every day, to save the immaculate white surface of the oil-cloth beneath. When he had finished the column and the Boston Cooler he sat for a while in the encompassing silence of the sleeping house, staring across the room at the electric clock. He could just hear the faint buzz of its motor. It was three minutes to the end of the most important day in his life so far. He thought of Sophy, and the idea came to him that if he thought about her hard enough she would know about it. The day ended and he stole ten minutes from a new one.

While Thomas was sitting on the kitchen table, Mary was sitting on the big blue sofa in Sigaux's studio listening to a recorded Beethoven quartet. The music filled the loftly white-painted room which had not changed much since he had given up painting. But soon after his aunt's death Silky had turned the space beneath it, where the stalls and loose boxes had once been, into lock-up garages for the use of the people who had apartments in the converted Remington mansion further up the block. He had leased the coach house at the end of the stable and barn to a dealer who used it as a furniture store. Miss Esther would never have allowed any of it, just as she would never have allowed Silky to put up the gilt horse's head, from a French horsemeat shop, crowned with pink and white roses which Silky had hung high on the blank south wall of the studio between the Severini and the Picasso copies he had made when he was a student. But she would have approved his having Mary Hatfield there in the studio alone at midnight. Silky could hear what she would say, just as if she were alive to say it. "That girl has a wonderful background. There may be men with more money in Maramee, but nobody has a better position than Gavin Hatfield. I couldn't pick you a more suitable wife than his daughter."

He looked covertly at her face and wondered what he could do to postpone the moment when she would tell him she loved him. He wondered, too, how he would find words to persuade her that she was infatuated, not with him, but with life. Her face was rapt, she was for the moment intoxicated by the false unity created by the music, and her belief that they were fully together illuminated her with sheer happiness. He saw, against his will, that it was no use pretending that what was flaming through the girl's body was calf love. She was not simply focusing her diffused longings to know more and to feel more on him. Two years back, at the time of Bogey's night adventure, it might have been so. But she was no longer a child with a child's generalized desires to have and to be everything. There was no chance that she would snap out of her dream to discover what she truly wanted in the shape of some boy of her own age. She loved him. He cursed himself for the idiocy with which he had handled the situation at the stage when it was still negotiable. When she had been just an infatuated child he had pitied her. By way of giving her a substitute for the emotion that he couldn't return, he had admitted her fully into his mind, telling her what he felt most deeply about the poetry and music which they both treasured, talking through their meanings with her, and sending away for French and English books she didn't know, which related to the beginnings she had made and which would develop her growing worlds of interest. He felt the more deeply about these things because they were what filled the hollow of evasion at the center of his being. When he talked to her about his intellectual passions and commitments, it was with a real intensity which Mary had always taken as an index of his real feeling for her. So that this fobbing her off with intellectual surrogates

315

for love had boomeranged terribly and made her fall much more deeply in love with him. He was being terribly punished for his hubris in pitying her. He lay back and surrendered to the music, which spoke to him of the vastness of the universe and of man's terrible and unbearably lonely place in it.

The same sounds spoke to her more simply and more urgently, of the power of the emotions in general, and of the strength of her feelings for him in particular. She had no motive for living beyond her longing for him. She wanted to be his, regardless of any consequences there might be. Every minute away from him was a lost one, every hour of delay in his possession of her a waste and betrayal of life. She curled herself up, tucking her legs beneath her, and looked along the sofa at him. He stared away into the immense realms which the music opened to him, through the studio walls out into the deserts of time between the scattering galaxies. She saw the marks of pain and sadness left on his lean face by his knowledge of his own inadequacy. She knew she could remove them. The giant spirit of the music filled her with a sense that she would be able to do anything she wanted with her life. She saw his sensitive hands, with their long fingers, idly clasped on his knee and wanted them to become confident and strong by touching her. She followed the direction of his gaze across the studio and let her eyes travel round its walls. The gilt horse's head crowned with flowers seemed a magical and wonderfully original thing to her, and the big copies each side of it seemed like the splendid banners of a rebel army. If her love were behind him to give him strength to overcome his diffidence and his hesitancy, their life might become the adventure promised by those banners. She knew it would. Her devotion would bring out the greatness in him. The music came to its final moment of discovery and magnificence, and ended.

"Well, there we are," Silky said, getting to his feet. "That was just about the right antidote to that rotten performance of poor old *Rigoletto*." He went deftly through the ritual of sliding the record back into its protective sleeve and glanced at his watch. "Holy cow, it's after midnight—I'd no idea. I must get you home or someone will be after my scalp. Come on, child."

He came over to her and gave her his hand to help her up out of the sofa. She took it but remained where she was.

"I wish you wouldn't call me child."

"Isn't it dignified enough? I'll call you Miss Mary if you want."

"You know that isn't what I want."

"Yes, I do. But even if I call you Mary it won't alter anything. You're very young. Much younger than I am. I owe your youth a certain respect."

He felt foolish, standing over her with his hand trapped in hers.

"I may be young. But I'm not a child any more, and I don't have a child's feelings."

"No, my dear, but you have an awful lot of growing up to do yet."

She dropped his hand and jumping up off the sofa flung her arms round him, burying her head on his chest. Uncontrollable sobs shook her shoulders. Moved by pity he put an arm round her waist protectively, and stroked the back of her head gently with his free hand.

"Come now, it's not as bad as all that, being young . . ." The facetious words struck a wrong note, and he made amends. "You mustn't cry, Mary, please don't cry, please."

"I don't want to. It isn't that I'm sad, or unhappy. It's just that I love you so terribly, terribly much and I can't bear it any longer, the way you keep me at arms' length and treat me like a baby."

"You know I'm very fond of you."

"That isn't enough—fond—you know it isn't enough."

"But, Mary, I'm so much older than you are, and in our situation—I'm a friend of your parents—after all, you must see it has to be enough. It would be dishonorable if I were to take advantage of your inexperience. You must see that."

"That's just something to say. It doesn't mean anything.

317

You know you wouldn't be taking advantage of me. You must know that. You must know how much I love you. Everything's right between us, not wrong. I couldn't be more sure of that."

She turned her tear-stained face up to his uncertainly. He gently kissed her on the forehead, and then feeling the cold sweat running from his armpits broke away from her.

"It's impossible . . ."

She heard his words, and collapsed onto the sofa, burying her head in her arms and sobbing convulsively. He took a desperate turn up to the far end of the room and came back to stare at her from behind the protection of a low marble-topped table in the center of the room. She looked up suddenly.

"You must despise me. You must think I haven't any self-respect at all."

"My poor darling, no . . ."

"Don't dare to pity me!"

She buried her head again, but now lay motionless. He bit his lip to strengthen himself and went round to sit down beside her, managing with an effort to touch her arm gently and comfortingly. She took his hand and laid it beside her wet cheek.

"I'm sorry. I'm being awful."

"No you're not. It's all my fault."

There was a long silence in which he wondered what he could tell her. The truth perhaps? It would be an act of love to tell her the truth, but if he could hardly bear to face the truth about himself, how would it be bearable for someone who loved him to know it?

"I can't marry you, Mary," he said. "And if I can't marry you it wouldn't be right to pretend to love you, would it?"

"I could be your mistress. We could be lovers."

He jerked his hand away with an abruptness which made her look up.

"That's just what we can't be," he said.

"People would say it was wrong," she said. "But it wouldn't be, not if I love you. And besides, nobody but us need know. And you wouldn't be taking advantage of me, you would be making me happier than anybody in the whole world." She reached out and touched him. "If it's just because you don't think you love me, you might come to love me after we'd lived together for a little while. They say that does happen; in books and novels, people get married because it's been arranged, and then they fall in love with each other . . ."

My God, what a little monster, he thought. But his keen pang of physical disgust ceased to stab before he could draw a second breath. It was, after all, Mary who had, in all innocence, been brought to this point. He dropped his hands and swiveled his body to face her.

"I don't know how to say what I have to say to you, Mary. The hardest thing in the world is to tell the truth about yourself to another human being." He faltered and dropped his eyes, failing, and falling into euphemisms. "It's just because we can't be lovers that I can't marry you."

"I don't understand . . ."

He got up and began walking about the room, striking the palm of his left hand with his right fist with every stride.

"That's it, that's it, that's just it, the horror of it, that I've let you into this before you're ready to understand half of what the trouble is. I don't know even that I ought to tell you. I don't know that I shouldn't go on pretending that you're a child and treating you like one. I don't know if you are ready to face the ugliness of some of the things that lie under the surface of life yet. I don't know if I'm man enough to speak the truth to you, even if you were a grown woman with a solid experience of life . . ."

She began to relish the drama of it. He was going to tell her he was secretly married to some women who wouldn't divorce him, or that there was madness in his family—something awful. Whatever it was to be she would take it without flinching, and when he had talked himself free of it she would take him in her arms and comfort him. Whatever it was, her love would be the answer and the cure. He sensed her misunderstanding, and the wave of repulsion returned, bringing with it this time the desire to hurt her.

319

"You are a child," he said. "You wouldn't understand me if I spent a year trying to explain. It's no use, no damned use at all . . ."

"That's an out—isn't it?" She looked at him accusingly. "You nearly got to telling me, and then you chickened out. Can't you at least try to be honest with me?"

"No. I can't. I try, and I can't." There was a silence until while he considered what he could say about himself which would reach her in her innocence. "You can say I'm sick if you want," he said. "Yes, that's the modern jargon for this kind of thing. Say I'm too sick for a woman to live with, almost too sick to live with myself. As for marriage, or an affair, it's impossible. Don't ask me to say more than that."

"Perhaps it isn't for you to judge, not all by yourself. Maybe loving you gives me the right to ask if I can help." She had taken a small square of Irish linen from her handbag and was dabbing at the tear stains each side of her nose with it.

"Don't do that while you're speaking," he said sharply.

"No?" she was surprised.

"It makes you sound as if you had a cold in your nose."

"I've been crying . . ." She put the handkerchief away obediently. "I'm sorry. If it—this trouble—is something in your mind, perhaps living with me would help."

"You don't know what you're talking about." He stopped his pacing. "I've been criminally weak. I don't know how I can have let things drift on to reach this point. I reproach myself for it. But we ought to end it now, before I do you any more damage. We shouldn't ever meet again. I'll go away—take a trip somewhere—and you can forget the whole thing."

"I won't ever forget you. I couldn't forget you. If you were just to drop me now, to go off, I don't know what I'd do. I think I might die. Don't you begin to realize what you are to me?"

"You learned that speech from some book." He managed to smile. "You're too young to know what it means."

"I mean it, every word of it."

He remembered the intensity of feeling of which he had

320

been capable at her age. She heard him mutter, as if to him-self, "God help you, I believe you do." Temptations assailed him. Her father would certainly have settled some money on her in the form of a trust fund for tax-evasion purposes. Her ignorance of life seemed even more profound than he had thought. He could without much effort pull the wool over her eyes for a few years, and perhaps forever. And even if pretenses broke down he could keep things going for a time by undergo-ing treatment at the hands of an analyst or psychiatrist. If she had enough money they could perhaps live in Europe. Even if she hadn't, her father might stump up a large enough allow-ance to keep them in Spain or in Mexico in sunlight and com-fort. He ran his hand through his hair, horrified at the direc-tion his thoughts were taking, and looked at the girl once again. Mary was combing her hair. She powdered her nose and retouched her mouth. She took a last critical look at herself in the small round mirror in her compact when she was done and brushed a few flecks of powder from the front of her dress. The word sublimate crossed his mind: perhaps he could canalize his interest in feminine things into the business of helping her to choose her clothes, teaching her how to wear them, telling her what to do with her hair and make-up, turning her into the fragile, elegant, and desirable thing he would himself have liked to be, and making her an extension of his own real per-sonality, so cruelly buried in a male anatomy. His daydream took on an erotic tinge. When he had made her in his own image he would help her to find a man who would be worthy of her, and of him. She suddenly looked up, trustingly and ap-prehensively, and, meeting his eye, smiled timidly.

"Can you forgive me," she said, "for loving you so much?"

He flushed, and faced with the reality of her innocence was overwhelmed by his own approach to corruption.

"Try to forgive me—I'm not fit for you." He sat beside her again, and took her hand, holding it with a suppliant gesture between both his. "I'm very fond of you, fonder now than ever, and I am your friend. I wish that was enough for you. I had a friend in Paris who was like you. Friendship wasn't

321

enough for her. She was older than you, and much more experienced. So I told her, even though it was difficult, how things are with me." He stopped and swallowed. "I'm sick in a complicated way. I've been to doctors about it, but they can't help. This woman in Paris thought she could help. She thought love was something strong enough to get me out of it. Well, it just wasn't. The whole thing was a terrible mistake." He dropped his face and spoke rapidly to her knees, racing to get his words out before his courage failed him. "We tried and tried, all through one God-awful winter. I would have to get up in the night and go to the bathroom to vomit, and when I came back to bed she would be lying crying in the dark, or lying stiffly trying not to cry—which was worse. She got to hate me and to hate herself, and I came to hate her. And we'd been friends. You may think it would be different for us. You may know it would be. She was just as sure of herself, and of me. I can't let you take on anything like that. I owe it to you not to let you try—because I'm fond of you, because friendship means something. When you're older and more experienced you'll understand me better. You'll know what my trouble is, and you'll thank me. I hope we'll be friends then, and always; but we mustn't ever think of being lovers, or of marriage. I know it's hard for you, but I have to beg you to accept it, and, for your own sake more than mine, to put your feelings for me out of your mind."

She slipped her hand from between his and ran her index finger across the back of his right hand.

"Then you don't love me at all, and you can't try to make me happy."

"You can't try to do that. Either you want to or you don't. Trying would mean misery for us both. I know."

She seemed intent on his hand for a few seconds.

"I'm physically repulsive to you?" Her voice was so quiet that he barely heard it. He felt a wave of relief that she had understood him without further, more precise, explanations, and had no inkling of the simplicity of her thought.

"From a sexual point of view, yes," he said. "That's what makes it impossible, you see . . ."

"I suppose I do. Yes," she said in a flat voice. She looked at her wrist watch and stood up. "It's very late. I should have been home an hour ago. Will you take me home, please?"

They went most of the way to the Grove in silence. At the railroad crossing the scarlet blinker-lights were flashing on and off to give warning of an approaching train. As they sat waiting, they could hear its laboring grumble coming nearer.

"Say you forgive me," he said, uncertainly.

"I'll try to. I don't really know what I'm supposed to forgive. After all, it's not your fault." She sat with a stiff back, looking away from him down the line towards the flare from the headlight on the heavy freight. The humming Diesel roared past at the head of its long string of groaning and shuddering cars, drowning them in waves of noise and hypnotizing them as they sat watching the seemingly endless procession. They sat stunned for half a minute after the caboose had swung past and the train's red tail-light had crawled on northwards.

At the Grove, they said good night without even touching hands, and Silky watched her walk in across the lighted porch, under the whirl of moths and insects round the lamp, as if she were a stranger going into a strange house, someone he had never seen before and never spoken to. He waited to see if she would turn and wave, but the screen door swung to behind her and she vanished without a sign. He sat alone and miserable for a minute, half thankful that it was all over, half sick at the pain he had inflicted, and then he shook himself and drove off.

"He's gone," she muttered incredulously from the place just inside the front door, where she was standing supporting herself by holding onto a table, waiting for him to burst in to tell her that it was all some frightful mistake, some test he had been giving her. She crossed the hall with dragging steps listening to Bailey's dog barking at the retreating car and found Thomas's note left for her on a chair that he had dragged out and placed in front of the bottom step of the stairs. "Sugar-bush you the lastest," it said, "put out the downstairs' lights. Sweet dreams, your loving Bro Tom." She smiled, put the chair back in place, and went round snapping off the switches. In the darkness the thought which she had been keeping at arm's length, as a diffused sense of despair, suddenly crystallized and smashed its way home through her defences as a sequence of unambiguous words. She stood with a hand on the newel post of the staircase looking up towards the faint glow from the night lamp on the upper landing and listened to her own thought as if it was being spoken to her by someone leaning over the balustrade. "Your body is disgusting to the man you love. He can't bear to touch you." She shuddered, as if she had been struck, and ran quickly up the stairs to get into the secrecy and privacy of her room before the tears came.

Gavin was lying, heavy-limbed, spread-eagled naked across a huge double bed in one of the cabanas on the beach out on Rummer's Key. Patti Elliot was beside him. They were both awake, listening to the soft whisper of the small waves hushing themselves onto the sand, and to the dry rattling of the palms round the little house. The sea seemed to be faintly luminous under the starry sky. Patti sat up and ran her hand gently along one of his thighs.

"Gavin, are you awake?"

"Yes."

"If you're going home you'd better think about it now, I mean it's tomorrow, or Sunday that is. It's after one."

"You want me to go, don't you?"

"Why do you say that? You've been in a funny mood all evening, all night. Sort of jumpy and silent."

"You know why. Try a little telepathy. Read my mind. See if you can tell what would make me jumpy if I could read your mind."

"Nobody reads my mind, I don't think ahead enough. I'd have said it before you could read it if I had a thought."

"For once that isn't true, Patti, and that's why I'm sad."

There was a silence. She became quite still, with one hand resting on his thigh, and her eyes on his powerful body.

"Who told you?" she said.

"The manager. He called it a word to the wise. He thought I'd like to know that you have a reservation on that midday plane to New York. He's that sort of man." Gavin looked at the girl's downcast face. "Why are you running out on me, Patti?" He waited for a moment. "Did I do something wrong?"

"No," she said. "Nothing. But I have to go. Even though you are the most attractive man I ever did it with. All things being equal, if you follow me, I could go on forever with you. But they aren't. And you know it. I haven't thought this out. I didn't have to. It's something I know." She cupped one breast in her hand. "It's all right. These things are for kissing, and I got my bangs having them kissed. But they ought to be full of milk one of these days. I want them to be. I want this belly of mine to swell up and get big. I want kids. I'd like it fine if you'd give them to me. But it wouldn't work out. I mean, with you I'm strictly for laughs and the kicks that go with them. You like me, but because I'm not like the rest of your life. You wouldn't want me around all the time, and you can't fool me by pretending you would. With me it's strictly escape, not that you don't know that better than I do, but I have to explain why I can't stay. I mean it's all right for me personally to sit on the beach here waiting till you can get around to slipping away for a couple of hours or for a night, or till you get some trip organized I can go on. But Gavin, baby, it wouldn't be the same with kids would it? I mean absolutely not. I thought I could tell them you were a salesman or something, but you never get away with that sort of thing with kids, either they're bright, or a neighbor's kid tells them, or something blows up and hits them in the face. I thought maybe we could play it straight. I could say to the kids about how your wife wouldn't give you a divorce, on account of being R.C. so we just had to go on without getting married. They'd be nice kids, they'd understand, I'll bet on that, but I don't want my kids

325

to be tolerant where I'm concerned. And I don't want anyone tolerating them either. I mean, it's all right about being a bastard, it isn't the kid's fault, but it's a word that gets tossed around. You know how people say things like, 'He's a *real* bastard.' Well, they mean something by it that isn't nice. So that's out. And, Gavin, that last birthday of mine when you were so sweet and I got to be twenty-four, I was really getting to be twenty-seven. Of course I was lying to you and I felt badly about having done that, and I was crying about that, partly, after you'd done, but what really had me yelling was being that age and letting so long go by without getting down to business, you know, the real business a woman's got when you get down to it. So you see it isn't anything personal at all, I've just got to go. I wanted to run out on you because I didn't want to say good-bye, I just wanted to be gone, because I knew if you lifted a little finger, as the saying goes, or said anything to try to stop me I wouldn't be able to go, and I have to go."

"Yes, you have to go, Patti. I've stolen two years of your life. It would be pretty low after what you've done for me to try to steal some more." He sat up. "I should go home. Yes, it's high time I went off home." He cupped her chin in his hand. "Do you have any regrets, Patti?"

"Not about this, no, none . . ." she said. He dropped his arm.

"Have you really ever regretted anything you've done? I don't believe you have."

"Oh, brother. Are you out on that! The night I graduated from high school there was this ball. You know—we were all in white tulle bouffant skirts and the guys in their first tuxedos, worldly wasn't the word for it, one of the little jerks had a flask and he poured most of it into me between dances. God knows how it happened, but I let him and five men of the football squad get me away into some shed on the school grounds. I must have been unconscious or something. They didn't give me a baby or anything, but they might just as well have. They talked. They gave me a real beauty of a reputation.

326

It was all over town within a week. I was the girl who'd taken on six fellows and was ready for more at the end of it. It's the colorful sort of thing people find easy to remember. If it hadn't been for that, I'd have been married there where I was born when I was eighteen, that year or the year after. The whole thing fouled me up on knowing what I wanted to be, what I wanted to do, for a long time. A thing like that hurts, and there isn't any way you can get it back." She looked into his eyes for a second and then looked away. "I've never known it to fail. I tell a man that and bam! he knows how I got to be the way I am. That fellow I was with when you came along. Tollick, remember? We were soul mates, he said. He could tell me anything he said, and he could pretty well. About how his mother used to get his father to thrash him for every little thing like playing with himself, and how they'd make him kneel down and pray for forgiveness after he'd been beaten, all about how miserable his childhood had been, and then about the girls he had that he couldn't do it with because of remembering praying and being beaten. And then like a horse's ass I told him how my good times had fouled up on me all of a sudden, and after that it was like he was reforming a whore he didn't trust."

She got up and pulled on a light cotton blue and white dressing gown from Japan. She walked out of the room and stood on the porch looking out at the sea. "It's cooler," she said. He went out and stood beside her. "Yes, it's a lot cooler." She grabbed him round the waist and pressed herself closely to him. "I wish to God I spoke your language. I wish I was your kind of person. If I was, perhaps I could explain to the kids how it really was all right about their being bastards, I mean when we had them." She sniffled. "But I'm not, and so this is it." She was silent for a time. "Do you think there's a man anywhere on God's earth who will still love me and trust me after I've told him about what happened after that damned dance? Why did it have to happen to me, Gavin? Why is it I'd have to tell any man about it before I could let him give me a child? Why is it I can't keep my big mouth shut?

327

Will you tell me, Gavin? Will you tell me why?" He held her and smelled her hair as he bent down to murmur comforting nothings into her ear. It was the scent she always used, and which he had first recognized as characteristically hers when he had picked up her handbag in the drawing room at the Grove. It had the light fresh fragrance of an early summer flower and it always conjured up for him the vision of a life which was as simple as it was easy. He knew that all the real comfort he had for her was in the warmth of his body and in the strength of his arms. He had nothing else for her. He could not ask her to stay with him. He did not want her to bear him children, or want her to change as motherhood would change her. He wanted her to stay just as she was, or rather as he had first thought her, simple and easy, everlastingly pretty, and everlastingly young. He did not think she would find a man who would speak her language and be able to take her story of the dance. It contained too much of the truth about what she was.

"There," he said, "there. It'll all come out all right, you'll see." He felt her hold on him relaxing and he stroked her marvelously smooth, marvelously cared-for hair. She looked up into his face with slightly parted lips, and a questioning expression, and he remembered that often after they had made love he would let her know that he was ready to make love again by starting to stroke that shining, smooth mane. He had never known her not to be ready, and she was ready again now. It was good to get back to what was simple and easy, and to what certainties there were. He bore down on her mouth and entered that domain of silence in which they could enjoy happiness and peace of mind for whole seconds, and even minutes.

Gavin got back to the Grove between three and four. He slept till seven and woke with a start, his mind filled with the idea that he should call Patti to tell her to cancel her flight and stay. But when he saw the time he knew it was too early to act. He lay wakeful for a short while and then went back to sleep. It was a few minutes after midday when he woke again. He put through a call to the airport at once, but the flight had gone out on time and Miss Elliot had been on board. Gavin sat up in bed looking about him at the beautiful, light, and somehow entirely meaningless room, wondering why he had come back to it and why he had left Patti. His eye fell on the folded deed to the old Marsen Bunce property lying on the green-leather top of his desk. That was it, of course, he hadn't come home just to spend a pleasant Sunday *en famille*, he'd come back for Thomas' birthday, and for the particular purpose of driving him over to the spring at some stage, to hand him the deed which made him sole owner and proprietor of three thousand acres of the world's surface.

When Gavin came down, his family was scattered all over the north porch in a sea of newsprint. Each of its members was bowed over one section or the other of one of the Sunday papers, the Maramee one, or the *Times*, flown down overnight from New York and theirs for seventy-five cents, forgetting the price of the gas that Fred Bailey had burned up driving in to pick it up at the newstand in the Beverly lobby. There were coffee cups all over the place, but the coffee jug on the table beside Ilona was empty. Bogey ran out to tell Bailey to make fresh coffee.

"Well, this is a nice surprise," Ilona said, ironically. "I didn't think you were going to get away from that convention till this afternoon."

"It broke up early. There was no point in hanging about," Gavin said. "I hope Bailey makes it snappy with that coffee." He looked at Mary and thought she was looking pale and poorly. Not herself at all. The time of the month perhaps.

"This could interest you," Ilona said, handing him part of the Maramee paper. He looked at it.

BANKERS DISCUSS INFLATION THREAT

Bankers and economics experts from financial centers all over the world gathered at Gulf University campus at Sweetwater Friday to take part in a three-day conference devoted to money problems of the U.S.'s rapidly expanding economy. Professor Eberhart, head of Gulf's economics department, stated in an opening address that . . .

329

Gavin yawned. "That was it," he said. "I really need that coffee."

"The last paragraph is the interesting one," Ilona said.

"Oh? Why?" Gavin said. He looked down to the end of the story.

Telegrams regretting their inability to attend were received from J. Barksdale Hornework of Washington D.C., Consultant Economist of the Civilian Space Agency; Wilmott K. Wilmott of the United Kingdom Delegation to the United Nations and St. John's College, Oxford; V. K. Rhanjasidajan of the Bombay Commodities Exchange Bank; and Gavin Hatfield, prominent figure in local financial affairs and member of Gulf's Board of Trustees.

"I see," he said.

"You can still blush," Ilona said. "But, you know, you don't have to. I wouldn't blame anyone for ducking out on three days of chitchat about money. Though it would be nice to know why it has to get worth less and less all the time. You must know about that. I wish you'd explain it to me some time."

"I will, you ask me, sometime when you feel like listening to me saying something serious." They smiled pleasantly at each other. Bogey brought Gavin his coffee and he fell, with relief, into the first section of the *Times* as he drank it. Bogey nuzzled up against his legs and looked at the ads while he read the stories. Thomas got up and left the room, coming back presently with a downcast air. He slumped into a chair and sat scowling into space for a time. Ilona looked at him and wondered how she could have thought he had everything sewn up when she talked to him in the kitchen only a few hours back. Obviously he hadn't. Here he was being the classic troubled adolescent with all the world's problems, unsolved, right on the back of his neck. She touched Gavin's foot with her toe and nodded to him to look at Thomas. As Gavin inspected him, he suddenly catapulted himself out of his chair and came to rest on his knees beside Mary.

"Oh, go away, Thomas, I'm reading the paper," she said, pushing at him.

"No, this is serious," he said, grabbing her arm and pulling her down so that he could whisper in her ear.

"No, I won't," she said. "Because I'm doing something else." He whispered again. "Oh, all right. As it's your birthday, I'll do it."

They got to their feet and went out together.

"I don't like the way Thomas is looking," Ilona said.

"He looks all right to me," Gavin said. "He's obviously got some birthday thing on with Mary, and there's been some hitch. Did he like that casting reel you got for him?"

"He said he did." She paused. "How did you know I was giving him that?"

Gavin looked down at the top of Bogey's head, bowed over a full-page department-store advertisement for girdles and waist pinchers.

"You asked Alfred to get you a really good one, and he told me so. I didn't think somehow you were going to take up bait casting yourself after all these years, so I just guessed."

"I suppose it's natural that Alfred should have told you. It's funny to think of being watched by somebody in every little thing you do. It's rather horrible, too." She stubbed out a cigarette from which she'd taken only a few puffs and lit a new one. "It's boring about that reel, too. Last year it would have been right. I'm not sure that it was exactly a howling success this year. Thomas was polite about it. I had a strange feeling I'd lost track of him when I gave it to him."

"Mother, can I have a waist pincher?" Bogey said, looking up.

"No, you can't. Why on earth do you want one of those things?" said Ilona.

"What does she want?" Gavin said.

"This, daddy. It's only sixteen fifty." She put her hand on his knee. "I really want one terribly badly. Can't I have one?"

"Why, that's ridiculous, Bogey. What on earth do you want with such a thing?"

"Because I want to be grown-up, that's why."

"Oh, my poor baby," Ilona said, "pinching in your waist won't be a bit of help with that."

"You'll just have to wait," Gavin said. "It's only a few years more."

"I don't want to wait. I want to be grown-up now." She stood up. "Even if I'm not, I want to feel grown-up. Why shouldn't I play at being grown-up anyway? I must have one of those things, I must."

"Well, Bogey, I sympathize with your state of mind. I know it's a bore being a child once you get the idea of what fun you're going to have later on. But you've got to grow a bit before you can start acting and dressing like a grownup. Meanwhile you aren't going to have one of those things because it would be a silly waste of money." Gavin hesitated. "I'll tell you what I'll do. I'll put sixteen fifty into your savings account tomorrow. You leave it there till your pretty little girl's figure turns into a woman's figure. When it does you can take it out and get something you need with it. And I'll bet you fifty dollars it won't be a waist pincher. Is that a deal?"

"You're both just so dense and stupid sometimes I could scream," Bogey said. She looked from her mother to her father, burst into tears, and ran out of the room. Ilona and Gavin leaned forward and surveyed the full-page spread on the floor in front of them, with its array of uplifted bosoms, flattened tummies, and encased and confined behinds.

"What a damned queer idea to get into her head, that having one of those things would help any," Gavin said; he shook his head in astonishment. Ilona lit another cigarette with hands which trembled. "Do you think one of us ought to go after her, to be nice to her?" Gavin said.

"No," Ilona said. "She'll be all right. She'll tell B'ar Hatfield how awful we are, and then she'll forget it." She paused. "The frightful thing is, you know, she may have enough in her money box to send away for one of those contraptions. Poor darling. The others will about tease her to death if she does." She stubbed out the freshly lit cigarette and took another one. "I wish to God Silky would get here. I can't think what's keeping him. He's usually here before this."

"That's because you can't start drinking till he gets here, isn't it?" Gavin said. "That's why you've been so nervous this last half hour, or am I wrong?"

"You don't know what you're talking about, so let's not talk about it." She picked a flake of tobacco from the tip of her tongue. "We made an agreement a long time ago that I wouldn't bother you about your necessities if you wouldn't bother me about mine. I don't admire your arrangements with women like that broad—I wish I could use some other word—you keep out on Rummer's Key, but I put up with them. I think we'll both be happier if we just leave each other's weaknesses alone."

"It won't do, Ilona."

"It'll have to do."

"Listen to me. Until that business with Miss Jelke you had yourself under some kind of control. But since then you've been going downhill, and you're going fast now."

"This is really too ridiculous, Gavin. Please let well enough alone."

"I can't. I have to say this. You're forcing me to say it. When Sigaux started coming out here it upset me. I didn't think a lot of him and I couldn't make out why you wanted him around. And then I found out, or I thought I found out. You liked watching him drink himself silly because as long as he was there you could feel that you weren't that bad. But now there's something different going on. I don't know if you know it, but he hardly drinks at all any more, and you're drinking a hell of a lot more than you used to. You hold out till he gets here and then you really start hitting the stuff. I can't make it out. It's as if you wanted to punish him for having saved Bogey from that poor lunatic. God knows how your mind works. I can't begin to follow it any more. All I can do is tell you that you're hurting us pretty badly, but you're hurting yourself even more."

"Have you quite finished?"

333

"All right. I suppose so. I can see it's useless to go on."

"Good. I'm glad you can see that. That helps a lot. You know why Sigaux still sticks around? He pities us. He pities me for being me. He pities me for being married to you. He pities you for being married to me. Oh, he's got a big heart, all right. He pities our children for being our children. He comes here to do what he can for us. You know what? He thinks he made a mistake interfering with Miss Jelke. He should have let Bogey be carried off by that woman because she believed that l-o-v-e spells out love, and the word means something. He comes out here to pity me, because living with you I found out love is four letters, and that m-a-r-r-i-a-g-e is four letters, too. You four letter me and put your four letter in my four letter and that's love until you get bored with my four letter and want better, fresher, four lettering with some other piece of four letter."

"You're going off your head, Ilona."

"That's why he pities me. And he pities you because m-o-n-e-y spells d-i-r-t, and dirt is all you've got for being mister moneybags. Don't touch me. Don't offer me your beastly sympathy. That's what I can't bear from him. His coming here as a duty, to give me pity and sympathy—him! I can't bear it."

They were both standing up, facing each other. The look of horror on her face appalled him.

"Ilona," he said. "Can't you try to see that it isn't like that? Not any of it. He comes here because we like him, because he likes us. He gives Bogey a lot of time because it thrills her to have a real grown-up man listening to her nonsense and treating her as an equal. He's been attentive to Mary because she had a crush on him. He'd have made her miserable if he'd ignored her, and he's done her a lot of good by taking her seriously. He sits with you and talks while you drink because he knows you have some kind of need for him. He's not pitying any one of us." He took her hand and held it in spite of her effort to snatch it from him. "Ilona, try to believe in somebody, in something, just for a minute."

"Let me go, you're hurting my hand." She turned her face away from him. "I've got to have a drink."

"It won't do any good. You know it won't."

"I know it won't. But it'll help, for ten minutes, for half an hour." She kept her face turned from him. "Please let me go."

He let her hand fall. It had become a thin hand. Her arms were getting thin and sinewy, too. Lines were beginning to bite into her face. He saw that her flesh was undergoing the change which had already taken place in his, a subtle deterioration which he had often been forced to recognize when he had seen his own nakedness beside Patti's flawless and unmarked body. Her flesh seemed to have a glowing life of its own, his covered his bones.

"It's Bushmill's you like now, isn't it?" he said.

"It's what I drink, yes."

When he came back with the big glass three-quarters filled with whiskey, ice, and water, she had gone over to the window to stand staring out into the garden. He passed the drink to her silently and she took it with a hand which trembled enough to spill a little out over her fingers.

"Thank you," she said.

"How long do you think you can go on with this without asking for help?"

"That's silly," she swallowed a large mouthful of whiskey, and then put the drink down as she fought with a coughing fit. "I don't need help. I don't need sympathy. I don't need anything."

"I wish," Gavin began, but Bailey came into the room.

"Luncheon is just about ready, Mizz Hatfield, but Mr. Thomas and Miss Mary just went down towards the lake. Do you want for to wait for them, or shall I ring the bell to bring them in?"

"Ring the bell, please, we'll eat right away."

"Don't you want to wait for Silky?" Gavin asked.

"Oh, I was forgetting," Bailey said. "Mr. Sigaux called. He said he wasn't too well this morning, and he didn't think he'd come out till late this afternoon."

335

"Well then, there's no question of waiting for him. Ring the bell and we'll eat as soon as the children come in."

Bailey went out to pull the cord that set the voice of the bell calling down through the ordered lines of oranges, lemons, rough lemons, and grapefruit to the edge of the water where the planting met the strip of cypress wood running along the ground that was too wet and soft to work. Thomas and Mary leaned over the balustrade of the diving dock looking at the swarm of tiny fish sheltering in the shadow beneath them. They lifted their heads as the sound of the bell reached them.

"I suppose we ought to go back?" Thomas said. He lifted his head and looked up towards the house.

"We'd better," Mary said. "Don't look so fierce and sad. I'll think of some way to get to her." They started walking up the slope. "They can't be keeping her shut up in a box."

"They wouldn't let you speak to her," he said, "and they wouldn't speak to me themselves. Three times they said she wasn't up yet, and the fourth they . . ."

"Yes, you've told me a dozen times so far. I have a pretty clear picture."

"What did they say to you, exactly?" He looked so desperately at her that she laughed.

"I've told you a dozen times. Mr. McCann picked up the phone and as soon as I'd said who I was he said, 'I don't think it's at all desirable that either you or your brother should have anything to do with Sophy for quite a while. So please don't call again, Miss Hatfield.'"

"Those were his exact words?"

"Yes, though I can't see what difference it makes. What really happened, Thomas? Did you try and rape her or something?"

"No, for Christ's sake. I love Sophy. I wouldn't try to force anything on her. You know that." He flushed, realizing that Sophy hadn't been asked, and hadn't consented. What had happened had just suddenly been happening. Perhaps it had been a sort of rape.

336

"Well, it happened, anyway," Mary said, reading his sudden coloring, "and now her parents know, and they're mad."

"I've got to speak to her, or get word to her. She's got to know I'm not just letting them get away with it."

"I'll tell you what. After lunch you take me to Ginny Holmes'. She's as close to Sophy as I am, and we'll send her over to spy out the land. That's the only thing I can think of now. But we'll get word to her that you'll be ever faithful and ever true, somehow."

"You're laughing at me."

"No. Love's no laughing matter, I know that much."

"You must think I'm crazy though, to get into such a state, just because I can't get a phone call through to someone I was talking to only twelve hours ago."

"It's all easy enough to understand, you old puddin-head. And I'm sure it'll come out all right."

"It's the hell of a thing to happen to me on my birthday, however you take it. They must have it all wrong. They must think we aren't serious. I suppose they think I'll run out on her, or do something rotten."

"Did you think much about what you were doing?"

"I don't know—I suppose not, and yet we've always liked each other. And then we just seemed to know—don't ask me how—that we're going to get married and, you know, do everything together for the rest of our lives if it all works out."

They came up onto the terrace.

"Make it work out, you've got to," Mary said, as Gavin came smiling out to hurry them in to get the meal started. "Daddy, has Silky come yet?" she said.

"No," Gavin said, putting his hands on their shoulders and pushing them on into the house. "He's got a hangover or something. He won't be out till later. What did you do to him last night?"

"Oh. We sat around talking in his studio. The opera was ghastly. Silky nearly died he was so disappointed, and I was pretty let down, too."

337

"The helpers and bawlers let you down?"

"They hadn't rehearsed properly. And the orchestra was terrible. And the costumes and the scenery were shabby and ugly."

"You can't expect too much of the sort of touring company that gets down here," Gavin said. "You have to make allowances."

"I don't know, it seems beastly always having to put up with cheery things. I wanted it to be terrific, like the records, only more so. Somehow it's awful when the real thing lets you down."

"Well, our poor little opera society can't afford the big stars, and half the orchestra are local amateurs. It's pretty ambitious of them even to try *Rigoletto*."

They were in the dining room, settling into their places.

"Why shouldn't they try something they can do properly?" Thomas said.

"They used to do cute little operas nobody had ever heard of, and nobody went," Ilona said. "I was on the committee in those days. They were sweet little things: *Rodelinda*, the *Man in the Moon, Bastien and Bastienne*, the *Duel*. Harry Bodiner and people like that sang in them. It was all rather cunning. But my goodness what a lot of empty seats there used to be. It was depressing, so they got pros in to help, and then they started to do the big operas. It was quite a lot of fun in the old days."

"Were you in on this, daddy?" Mary said.

"Heavens no. I wouldn't even qualify for a barber-shop quartet," Gavin answered, looking up from carving the leg of lamb in front of him. "I'm afraid I didn't give your mother much help in the days when she was trying to civilize darkest Maramee. I'd just give her a fat check now and again, and that was about all I knew about the opera society."

"I think opera's ridiculous," Bogey said. "People standing screaming at each other a few steps apart, just yelling out stuff they wouldn't even whisper if it was real."

"It's different, it isn't meant to be real that way," Mary

338

said indignantly. "It's not just an imitation of the way things happen. It's more real than just ordinary everyday life."

"If a thing is real it's real," Thomas said. "I don't see how one thing can be more real than another—not if they both exist."

"Art makes things more real than just a string of jumbled-up accidents, it gives real things meaning, everybody knows that," Mary said.

Ilona looked at her daughter with a curious expression, halfway between sympathy and dislike.

"You've got awful high hopes of art, if you ask me," Gavin said. "I'd think twice about leaning on that particular stick, if I were you."

"But art's everything. I mean it makes all the interest, all the importance there is in life. If it wasn't for art man would just be a sort of greedy, destructive animal."

"Some animals aren't too bad," Gavin said.

"Oh you're horrible, daddy, I can't bear people who pretend to be cynical," Mary said.

"He doesn't pretend to be cynical," Ilona said. "I believe he really thinks man is just some sort of animal." She caught sight of a huge mound of food rising up on a fork towards Bogey's wide-open face. "Some people seem to be trying to prove him right, too. Do stop shoveling that food into your mouth and try to behave like a decent human being, Bogey, there's a darling."

"It's horrible the way you pick on me all the time, for every little thing I do." Bogey scowled and arranged a smaller mouthful. "I don't make personal remarks whenever I don't like anything, I don't think it's a bit nice to hurt people's feelings."

"Oh, Bogey, you really are getting impossible," Ilona said. "I almost wish you were grown-up."

"As soon as I am I'll get married," Bogey said. "Then I'll be able to do everything I want, just the way I want, when I want."

"I bet you she will, too," Thomas said. "She'll hook some

poor jerk who'll get her breakfast every morning before he goes to work, you see if she doesn't."

"Let's have a change of subject," Gavin said. "Where did you get that stuff about art being so important? Do they give you that in school, or does Silky feed it to you?"

"That's not what bothers me," Thomas said. "I want to know what she meant by that stuff about the opera or whatever it was being more real than life. I just don't see it."

"You know perfectly well." She was at a loss for an instant and waved her hand helplessly, swinging the fork she was holding in a wide arc. "It's like, it's like, it isn't like anything, it's what happens to you all the time. While things are going on you don't know what's important and what isn't. Afterwards you sort it out in your mind, and then you see. That's what art does, what it is. It's making sense of the confusion of things all round us."

"The way you've been waving that fork about for the last minute isn't art, it's downright bad manners," Ilona said. "Though you're perfectly right to have strong feelings about art, I wish you would occasionally try to behave as if you understood civilization."

"Oh mother, that's cheating."

"I know. But I don't want you making sweeping gestures with the silver." Ilona smiled. "It really doesn't look well. You may not think these things are important, but I promise you they are. You can turn men against you with the strangest little mistakes. One man told me once he'd taken a girl out to dinner meaning to propose to her, he found he just couldn't, because while they were having soup she used her spoon as if she was trying to scrape the bottom out of the plate."

"That's a real Murray story," Gavin said. "Not that it couldn't have been a Hatfield. But your mother is right, Mary, manners are important. If you do ugly, graceless things people get a false idea about you, and it doesn't do you any good."

"I'll try to remember," Mary said.

"I still think you're wrong," Thomas said, looking up from his plate at Mary. "I think you're in semantic trouble on this art thing. I don't think relating things in a pattern can alter their status. You may be giving them false relationships for the sake of comfort or convenience when you do it. But either way, if you're discovering relationships you weren't aware of before, or if you're inventing them, it won't affect the events themselves, not in the way of making them more real."

"What are you talking about, Thomas," Ilona said. "I didn't understand a word of that rigmarole."

"I mean reality is an absolute quality. You can't affect it by the way you talk about it."

"You know when I was your age," Gavin said, "the thing that used to bother me was minus quantities. Zero was nothing, right, I could follow that. But how could you have a finite number that related to nothing, not five, not seven. I didn't see how you could have quantities of nothing. I still don't for that matter. Absolutes scare me."

"Father, for heaven's sake," Thomas said, "that's all pure semantics."

"Somebody's been teaching you how to shove problems under the rug," Gavin said, "that's what I suspect."

"Nobody's shoving anything under any rug," Thomas said indignantly. "It's just if you use language properly a whole lot of problems disappear. That thing about minus numbers is one of them."

"You mean if you fool around with the words it's stated in, a problem that's worried you for the whole of your life can just vanish into thin air, presto, chango, just like that, no more problem."

"That's right. If you work out the grammer of the things you were saying about minus numbers you'll see there isn't a problem there. It's a set of grammatical mistakes. If you correct the mistakes you've got the answer to the problem."

"When I hear you talk like that it stirs dim memories of what a glorious thing it was being eighteen. I envy you, Thomas. But I've got to warn you about something. You've

341

still got an awful lot to learn." Gavin grinned. "And I used to want to kill my father, too, when he said things like that."

The meal came to an end at last, and Thomas and Mary leapt to their feet to escape. But Gavin grabbed Thomas by the arm before he could get away.

"Not so fast, young man. Mary, I want young Thomas for a couple of hours. I hope I'm not busting into any deep-laid plot you two have been working up. But I haven't had a real talk with your handsome brother for a long time, and this seemed a specially good day for it."

"I wish you'd said . . ." Thomas began, but Mary cut into his objections.

"I'll take your car and go to Ginny's. It might even be better if she didn't know you were in on this. I'll just chatter with her a bit and have her put in the call without her knowing why. It might work out better that way."

"That's all right, but I won't know for hours what's going on."

"This all sounds pretty desperate and pretty complicated," Gavin said. "I smell girl-trouble in it. Take it from me though, these things aren't ever as serious as you think." He ruffled Thomas' hair. "Take it easy, it's only a couple of hours, after all. The heavens aren't going to fall in that time."

"Well, leave him off at Ginny Holmes' when you're through with him, daddy," Mary said. "Don't worry, Thomas. It'll be all right. I hope."

"So do I."

"I don't know where you're all going, and I don't much care," Ilona said, "but I am going to remind you, Thomas, that you've invited forty people to a supper and dance here tonight. You're the host and Mary's the hostess. I don't want you back here in dirty blue jeans and looking like death five minutes before the first guests arrive. Come back in good time. And remember it's your party, not mine."

"Oh, mother, for heaven's sake, there goes the surprise party we've all been keeping secret from Thomas for six weeks," Mary said.

"I thought I hadn't asked any forty people to anything," Thomas said. "Whose bright idea was this?"

"I thought it would be fun," Bogey said. "It will be too if you don't spoil it all be being sour and mean. You ought to watch yourself, growing up's making you boring."

"I'm terribly sorry," Ilona said. "How could I be so awful? I just seem to have an instinct for spoiling things. Oh, Bogey, what shall we do?"

"I know, we can pretend he didn't hear, and we'll ask him to pretend to be surprised when the time comes. Then at any rate all the guests we've asked can have the fun they've been working for by saying nothing about it to Thomas all these weeks."

"That's a very reasonable plan, Bogey," Gavin said. "You'll go along with it won't you, Thomas?"

"Oh, sure. Not that I ever felt less like a party in my life."

"Well, it'll all be good practice for your entry into the adult social world."

"Do we have to learn to lie to each other about everything all the time," Mary said, "to be ready for that?"

"Come on now, old lady, it isn't as bad as all that." Gavin smiled at her. "You just have to grease the bearings with a lie or two now and again." He looked at his watch. "Thomas, the hours are sliding away under our feet. Let's get going."

On their way over to the spring Thomas felt an active dislike for his father for the first time. He looked across the width of the open Cadillac at the man and bitterly resented being taken off somewhere where he didn't wish to go to serve some end that wasn't his. He knew his father was kind and well-intentioned, but the fact of his being as nice as he was only seemed to accentuate the defect of sensibility, which left him utterly blind to the hell of anxiety inside his own mind. He simply isn't aware of me as a person at all, Thomas thought, he just plows ahead as if I didn't have any thoughts or feelings of my own. He wondered if it could be that living with that solid, unbreakable indifference for years had been the cause of his mother's drinking. It seemed to him that nothing could be more wounding in the long run than living with someone who was nice, likeable, decent in every way, and even loveable, but bluntly insensitive to everything that went on outside his own head. Perhaps the worst thing about the relationship between his father and mother was not some terrible definable wrong, but just an absence. He wondered how drunk his mother had been at lunch. He hadn't thought she was drunk until the business about the party had come up, and even then he had wondered. It was unusual for her to be plastered so early in the day, but if she was looped already how far gone would she be when the guests began to come into the house in four or five hours' time? He thought, with a sharp flash of intense feeling, like a knife blade among his bewilderments and uncertainties, I don't want any part of such a life, I'm going to make another kind of life altogether with Sophy, however difficult it is to do we've got to do it. He drummed his fingers on the solid, fat top of the car door beside him. It was such a huge, sickening, large machine, when you thought that it existed just to take a couple of people from place to place, or to take one man to his office every day.

Thomas looked westwards in the direction of Maramee and Sophy Dawes McCann, and caught sight, low down on the horizon, of the group of towers clustered together in the city's center. There was a little haze and the tall foolish buildings shone palely in a violet mist. What is that place for, Thomas wondered, why? He had seen his father's picture in the last number of the *Herald*'s annual new-year business review where he was described as one of the makers of modern Maramee. He turned back to his father with the thought of asking him why he had done it, but refrained because there was a smile on the man's face, and he looked happy. Gavin was thinking at that moment, what a tremendous relief it was to have the Patti thing over. There was no bigger mistake than imagining that you could have an affair and keep it on one level. He had taken Patti on straightforwardly to take the shaft when he felt like giving it to her, because she was young and cheerful and good-natured. He had looked forward to his visits to her pretty

344

much as he looked forward to his three weekly games of squash at the racquet club, but she had got in under his guard and made him recognize her as a creature of his own kind with feelings as elaborate and as complex as his own to consider. As soon as that recognition had been established, the liaison had become a burden. He was ashamed that it should be so, but he was glad that the burden had been lifted off his back. He recalled Miss Leigh. He had never been able to think of her as anything else, even in her most ecstatic and abandoned moments. He had indeed passed some kind of milestone with her. Since her day he had come to recognize that his greatest happiness was in absence of pain, absence of regret, absence of feeling. He knew that Patti had attracted him because he could have her for nothing emotionally, and he was glad that it was all over, with nobody hurt. He realized with a start that they had just passed the spot where the Marracombee County Arch had once stood. It had been gone for twenty years, or nearly that long. The car tires hissed on the smooth concrete of the four-lane highway. He had forgotten how much the neighborhood had changed. There were a number of new houses along the roadside, and vast quantities of signs and billboards calling the traveler on beyond Halesville to Tampa and Orlando.

"I can remember this as a two-lane black-top with a rotten surface," Gavin said. "You had to watch it all the time to make sure you didn't meet another car on a culvert—that's a long while ago."

"Before the war, I should think. It's always been like this so far as I can remember."

"Can you remember the war at all, Thomas?"

"Why, yes. Truman firing MacArthur, and the Marines making it out through the snow after they'd been cut off. And then all that stuff about prisoners, and P'anmunjom. But I guess I read about Porkchop Hill afterwards."

"I wasn't talking about that war, not that it matters."

"I remember you coming back from the other one. You had a cane. But I don't remember that war at all."

Gavin began to slow down looking for the Bunces' house

345

and the turn-off for the spring. He expected that there would be a break in the fringe of signs where the boundary of his son's property began. But there wasn't. He remembered that the estate-management section of the bank had been in charge of that side of things. Naturally they had seen to it that the acreage earned what income it could. Gavin saw that they had limited themselves to the more substantial agencies which rented space to national advertisers. The dirt road leading off towards the boil passed between big structures crowned with floodlights which were carrying advertisements for Sunoco and Ford. Gavin looked doubtfully at the track, unsure if it was the right one. He hadn't been down this way, he realized, in years. He looked across the road and recognized the Bunce house by its uncompromising outline and the sheer orneryness of its arbitrary placing, unaligned with anything and unrelated even to the passage of the sun round the earth. It looked across the road at an angle of about fifty-three degrees and was oriented to the east north east. It seemed to stand catty corners to the entire universe. It now had a small neon sign across the upper part of the porch which said it was the Lonesome Inn. Behind it was a row of seven tourist cabins, showing signs of slatternly care. Festoons of washing on lines beside them showed that the place had lost out on tourists and had drifted into the business of housing migrant workers. In the back lot near the cabins two garishly painted-up horse vans stood parked beside a barn knocked up out of scrap wood and corrugated iron. It had a name, Lazy J Rides, carelessly lettered on its doors, and nearby two big-bottomed girls in T.V. Western outfits were slackly currycombing two out of a string of ratty piebald ponies. Gavin took it all in without enthusiasm, but without much surprise, until his eyes fell on the glittering Monel metal diner which had been put down in the field at the far end of the house. This addition to the landscape had a sign reading Bunce's Burgers in letters almost as high as the building all along its roof.

"I don't believe it," Gavin muttered, "I won't believe it.

Even Lorene wouldn't have . . . Just a minute, Thomas, I have to go over there to see what the devil goes on."

He turned the car in onto the parking space beside the diner and got out to walk across to the Lonesome Inn. As he opened the garden gate he caught sight of Edwin bundled up, sitting in a wheel chair on the porch, staring at him. Gavin was amazed to find him still alive, still more astonished by his appearance which was that of a pink and healthy turtle.

"I know you, Gavin Hatfield, but I don't know that young fellow you're with," he said in a dry cackling voice, as Gavin came up the porch steps with Thomas behind him.

"What are you doing in a wheel chair, you old scoundrel," Gavin said, "you can't be a day over a hundred? Those things are for old men."

"Oh, I'm not sick, I'm just loafing. It takes the weight off my legs when I'm moving around. In answer to your question though, I am eighty-six, and I'm just about as surprised to be here as you are to see me here. My heavens, it's a long time since I set eyes on you, Mr. Hatfield. There's been changes, hasn't there."

"I'll say there just about have, I wouldn't have known the place. This is my son Thomas, Edwin. Thomas, this is Edwin Bunce, a real old-timer in these parts."

Thomas took the withered turkey claw offered to him with an effort, it was hard to touch such an old man without feeling endangered, it would be so easy to catch death from him, he had it so badly.

"Well, he's a fine-looking boy, Mr. Hatfield, a credit to you or to some good-looking feller. What do you think of my diner over there, smart isn't she?"

"It looks bright and cheerful enough. But what started you on all this, for heaven's sake?"

"Well Mr. Hatfield, I got bored and Lorene got bored, and the next thing you know she was divorcing me for mental cruelty. I brought countersuit, and I won. I had a bright young Jewish feller acting for me and he proved about the only mental cruelty in it was me being too slow to die to suit her tastes.

347

He was a clever feller, quick as I can't say what, and he tied her up in knots up there in court. I felt ashamed for her the way she was caught out time and time again in front of everybody. Once or twice she made herself so plain foolish there was a snigger run round among everybody there, and some people had to laugh right out. Well, the long and short of it was I had to give her a little bit of money and I was shot of her. Then, of course, there I was with a house on my hands and nobody for company. I found my body cold at night, like King David in the Bible. And my thoughts kept turning in a certain direction. I used to go down to Halesville to watch school come out until the policeman there, Ned Patterson, give me a friendly warning. Well, I could see it was coming to trouble, when by good luck I ran into this Heinzleman couple from a traveling carnival that had gone bust and broken up down south towards Fort Myers. They had these four girls, daughters they'd had one way and another, and all them piebald ponies you see out the back. They asked if they could spend the night here on their way north and turn the ponies out to graze. Well, I could see they were on their uppers, worn tires on the vans, glum looks, and when I'd had a good look at the girls, I knew it was the answer to a prayer. They were all girl-type girls, Mr. Hatfield, and when you get to be my age that type gets a powerful strong appeal. I had this feller Heinzleman in and told him he hadn't no call to hurry on North, he could settle in for the winter. Well, bit by bit I got a hold on him, lending him money for feed for the horses first off, then a little bit more for this, then a little bit more for that, you know how it goes with anyone feeding four girls and eleven horses. I think he had it worked out he was taking me. Well, one day he came in—I judged he was raising one last loan before he cleared out— and started in his usual warm-up routine. I bit him off short. I said no there wasn't a thing more doing in that line. But I said, I tell you what, you can have a partnership in this property, and a reversionary interest to what I've got in the way of cash if I can have something I've set my heart on. Well, he sort of swallowed, and he hummed and hawed, and then he brought

348

himself to ask what I had in mind. So I said I'd like one of your daughters, I ain't particular which one."

Gavin saw Thomas get up quietly and leave the porch.

"You didn't really make him go through with it did you?" he said.

"Of course I did." Edwin gave a screech of senile laughter. "He come to taw, and his wife, and the girl. They all toed the line. Cutest little thing I ever got my hands on. She's got a temper. But she's got everything else as well, so I ride out a storm now and again and I'm pretty well satisfied. Of course, I was running a risk. You know once I was legally married I was in a weak position, or I could of been. They could of stripped me out and cleared off. Well, I thought of that. So I had that young lawyer who handled the divorce fix me a will. It's fixed on sliding scale. Neatest thing you ever saw. The longer I live the more of the property they get, and it's fixed in shares, too, so as to play them off against each other. If my wife should run away they don't none of them get a cent, and her share gets bigger the longer she stays with me. It all works out so they do better every year I stay alive and happy, and they all do a lot worse if I go suddenly as a result of one of them accidents old fellers get to die of when there's eager legatees around. That will's a work of art I tell you. We had a reading of it out here a couple of days after the wedding, you could see the feller was proud of it the way he read it, and he'd put in little explanatory pieces to say what the legal words meant now and again. It was as good as a show. But Maybelle, that's the one I got married to, she's got sugar on her tongue, and she's talked me into things like the diner—that's hers and mine, fifty-fifty —and those cabins her father built out back. I put up money for the materials and I guess that's money lost. But he gets the rents and that keeps him happy." Edwin banged on the floor with a stick. "Maybelle," he called. "Maybelle. You come on out. You might as well see what I've been talking about," he said dropping his voice. "Maybelle," he called again, rapping with the stick.

The door into the house opened and Gavin stood up. He was taken by surprise. He had expected something extravagant, a gum-chewing, sexily dressed young tart. There was a rather quietly dressed high-school girl in the doorway. She had a charm bracelet on one thin wrist and a wedding ring on her child's hand. Her white blouse was fresh and clean and her gray skirt spotless. She was wearing white socks and sneakers. A small crucifix, hung on a thin gold chain, lay in the division between her high and splendid breasts. She looked at Gavin with frank and uncalculating eyes for a second, smiled a small social smile at him and then turned to the man in the wheel chair.

"I didn't know you had company, daddy," she said. "You should of told me. Did you want something?"

"I just wanted Mr. Hatfield to meet you, Maybelle. Isn't she a pippin though?" He beamed. "You wouldn't have a piece of one of your chocolate cakes handy so Mr. Hatfield could taste what a fine little wife I got myself."

"I really couldn't eat a piece of cake, even if you did, thank you, Mrs. Bunce," Gavin said. "You don't have to prove anything, Edwin, I can see you have found a wonderful girl to look after you."

"She's all woman too, Mr. Hatfield. Show him your Marilyn Monroe walk, Maybelle. Go on. It's the best thing you ever saw."

"Go on with you now, daddy. That's private between us and you know it. You'll excuse me, I know, Mr. Hatfield."

"You show him, Maybelle, he's a real old friend."

"Oh, all right then. Though I ought to have heels to do it right. It won't be half good in these sneakers. I'll have to go on tiptoe and pretend I got heels, but you really want a heel to bear down on."

She turned round and walked away from them down the porch.

"Ain't that wonderful," Edwin said, "ain't that the best thing God ever made? Maybelle, you beat all, you truly do."

The girl reached the end of the porch, came down on her flat

350

heels and turned around. She brushed her hair off her face and came back to them.

"It's nothing without heels," she said. "I could feel it wasn't right without. I'll go and get a pair of shoes with spike heels."

"Oh, please, don't bother, Mrs. Bunce. I have to run," Gavin said, terrified by the absoluteness of her innocence or her corruption. "I just dropped in because I was in the neighborhood."

"Well, it's too bad you can't stay," Maybelle said. "When I do a thing, I like to do it right. You know what I mean? I wish you'd drop by whenever you do come this way. Daddy gets lonesome just watching the cars go by."

As Gavin went out through the gate into the diner's parking lot he looked back at the couple on the porch. They both waved and in numb amazement he waved back.

"Who was that God-awful old mummy of a man?" Thomas asked, as his father got into the car beside him.

"His name is Edwin Bunce," Gavin said. "I used to know him a long time ago. I thought he was dead." He drove carefully over onto the dirt road and started in towards the spring. "I'm sorry you had to listen to his story of how he got his wife. It was pretty hard to take I'm afraid."

"What was she like?"

"The funny thing was she was all right. I wish you'd stayed. She might have made you feel better about the story."

"How could she be all right? I mean marrying that old horror. And in that way. Picked out of a lot of four, like a steer. How could she do it? How could her father let her do it?"

"I don't know, Thomas. There's an awful lot I don't know. But in a darned queer way that girl was all right." The car rolled softly through the sand. "The place has gone horrible. I think old Bunce has gone bad. I'll bet Heinzleman and the rest of his brood are pretty odd lots, too. But that girl, I don't know how to put it, she scared me by being so unaware of what you could think about what she was doing. I felt she couldn't do wrong, because she wouldn't know what wrong was. I felt ashamed of myself for having thought badly of her before I'd

351

seen her. From what old Edwin said I'd judged she was going to be vile. But then there she was, a stranger to good, but a stranger to evil, too."

"Isn't that corruption, I mean having everything blurred so you don't know what's good and what's bad any more. Mr. Deacon, he's my English teacher, says 'It's all right if it works' is the most corrupt statement you can make."

"Teachers lead sheltered lives, Thomas, you start learning the important things about life after you get out of their clutches."

Gavin fell silent. He had a gathering sense of disquiet. The road was rutted as if it was used quite frequently, and he kept seeing the shining ends of beer cans winking at him from the borders of the ditch beside it. He had forgotten that the spread of Maramee in the Tampa direction had made the spring much less of a cloistered and remote spot than he had always thought of it. Seminole Acres, the four thousand unit development south of Morgantown which he had helped finance was not more than twelve miles away up Route 189. That was a fifteen to twenty-minute spin, less for a hotrodder. It was only to be expected that kids looking for a place to swim would find it. Gavin pulled up at the edge of the ring of live oaks surrounding the pool. Sunday afternoon, he realized, had been a bad day to pick, dedicated as it was to family life. Ten or eleven cars were parked round the ring, and most of them had brought picnicking families to the spring. Numbers of small boys and girls were snapping at each other with six shooters, plastic machine guns, and death-ray projectors as they dodged in and out through the palmetto scrub. Their parents slept or dozed with handkerchiefs over their faces stretched out on folding chairs placed beside their station wagons and cars. All around the pool, on the virgin whiteness of the clear sand there were the marks of old fires, and the traces of old picnics in the way of torn off handles of bottle carriers, pieces of plastic food wrappings, and cans. The dome of water from the spring still tried to rear itself up on the green surface of the pool, but the true wonder of the sight was hard to see through the lashing arms and legs of the dozen or so teenagers who were making a collective effort to force their way up onto its crown. They shrieked with pleasure and with a delighted fear as the irresistible force of the surging water tore their arms apart and flung them back. Gavin watched the scene, taking in all its details, for several minutes, touching his cheek with his finger tips in his old gesture of uncertainty and self questioning.

"I know this place," Thomas said. "A whole gang of us used to come out here all one summer two years ago—twenty or thirty times. But then a pretty rough crowd from Maramee moved in on us. You know, they'd annoy the girls with wolf whistles and all that stuff, creep up on them while they were changing. We got into a fight once about that. But they were men and we didn't have a chance with them. So we quit. I haven't been here for—oh, I don't know, eighteen months. They say there's some pretty fierce necking here, nights."

"It's funny isn't it. I was thinking it was my secret, and that I was going to give you a great thrill showing it to you. When I first knew it it was miles from anywhere and hardly anybody ever came here. I bought it years ago for you. And I had it in my mind that it was going to be a pretty big thing when I gave you the deed. Here it is. Your unclouded unencumbered and incontestable title to this place and three thousand eight hundred acres of land bounded by Route 189 over there behind us, by the Marracombee River over there, and by a surveyed line that runs out from the road to the river. It's a triangular piece of ground, more or less. This map makes it clear."

"A lot of that land along the riverside is swamp, isn't it?" Thomas asked.

"Yes, just about fourteen hundred acres. But that's this strip beside the river, and the point of the triangle, from about there to there. All this other piece is dry sound land, two thousand four hundred acres."

"It's a huge present," Thomas said. "It takes a little getting used to." He went over and sat himself down on the sand at the foot of one of the huge oaks to begin a grave study of the deed broken by frequent inspections of the map attached to

353

it. Gavin walked out to the edge of the water and stood listening to the screaming and shouting, and to the music of two radios behind him. They were both tuned to the same program so that the break for station identification and the commercials came through with an almost stereophonic effect. "If you have a personal problem with dandruff or itchy scalp you can obtain amazing quick relief with the shampoo that people are talking about all over the United States, Minamar; one application and you look better and feel better. Minamar goes right to the root of the trouble and swiftly ends your discomfort and embarrassment. Minamar . . ." There was no turning away from it, or shutting one's eyes to it, it was inescapable. Gavin looked about and found where the radios were standing on the ground among the folding tables and chairs, the Scotch Coolers, the baskets stuffed with used paper plates and paper cups, and all the other trappings of a Sunday afternoon in the open air. The commercial ended and the announcer stated that it was "your favorite window on the world, Radio Maramee." Gavin stirred the sand with his foot, thinking simultaneously, or nearly so, that he was within a foot or two of the place where he had once seen Nedda standing (Eddie's voice came back to him saying "Starkers! I say, not starkers"); and that he owned forty-one percent of Radio Maramee and its television affiliate. A plump, gray-haired man in a Hawaiian sports shirt, with a peaked straw cap on the back of his head, came across from among the trees, strolling idly, and approached Gavin, smiling.

"My name's Krawitz, Abram Krawitz. I don't remember seeing you here before."

"I haven't been here lately. My name's Hatfield, Gavin Hatfield."

"Well, I'm very pleased I'm sure. It's a great spot, wonderful for kids, not just for playing either."

Thomas drifted up to them, dazed with acreage, lost for words in which to thank his father for a gift which perplexed him.

"This is my son Thomas, Mr. Krawitz."

354

"It's my privilege. A fine-type boy. You could be proud. But as I was saying, that water there has qualities you might not imagine. We originally came here, Bella and myself, with our young hopefuls on a recommendation we had from a neighbor that it was an unusual-type swim—a change from the beach. A break's welcome when you get set in a rut. Well, so we came. And we liked it. The place is nice, and the crowd is nice—one tells another—it's a club atmosphere. Three or four times in a row we came here, and one morning my wife says, 'See the skins the girls have all of a sudden!' One month we are spending a fortune on medications, the next, skins are satin-smooth. Acne, pimples, a thing of the past! Mentioning it around casually I find it's the common experience. Swim at the spring and the skin clears. For girls and boys in a certain stage it's a boon. Miracle Spring Bella calls it on the girls' account. What the magic ingredient is I don't know, but that the spring has this property there's no question. If you've got girls with the problem, in kindness you should be bringing them to the spring so often!"

"That's very interesting, Mr. Krawitz," Gavin said.

"A natural source of skin lotion really would be something," Thomas said.

"All right for you to laugh, young man, but for some the problem is suffering. Don't you forget that! And many have cause to be thankful to Miracle Spring who don't know it!" He turned to Gavin. "Some of us older men who come regularly have an informal Sunday chess club. Each week we have a few games under the trees while the kids amuse themselves. If that sort of thing has any appeal we'd welcome you into our little group."

"Well, that's very kind of you, Mr. Krawitz, very kind indeed, and I'll be very glad to see you if I ever get out this way."

"And you young man you'll find welcome, too. We're always glad to see good-type youngsters round the pool. When we started coming here there was a rough element, with a dog-in-a-manger outlook, but we family men stood our ground and the undesirables melted away."

355

"Well, thank you," Thomas said without irony, and with something akin to embarrassment at having legal title to the place in his pocket. He felt he was deceiving Krawitz. "We have to go now I'm afraid. We're late as it is. I'm sorry."

"That's perfectly all right, my boy, don't apologize. I look forward to your return."

Mr. Krawitz accompanied them to the car in the friendliest way and waved when Thomas looked back. Gavin began to laugh when they were halfway out to Route 189, and had some difficulty stopping. Thomas watched him uncertainly. He had heard of people laughing until they cried and had not believed that the phrase meant anything. But he now heard his father laughing and saw tears rolling down his cheeks.

"Are you all right?" he said.

"Oh, God, no," Gavin said, and quite suddenly was silent.

"You didn't expect it to be like that, all picnicky and folksy?"

"No. I wanted to show you something, I can hardly explain what. That place used to stand for the most tremendous things there are. I used to come out to sit there absolutely alone, in a hushed world. It used to be quieter than silent. There were noises made by the wind, a few bird calls, the noises that make you feel how quiet everything is. I'd sit there while the light went out of the sky. The water in the pool would make a noise almost like a chuckle every now and then, and I'd think that if I could just hold on to myself and feel a little more, be a little more *there*, in it, part of it, I'd suddenly understand the meaning of the universe, and life, and who I was and why I was. It was all there, and while I was there I could almost believe I knew." Gavin paused. "Do you have the faintest idea what I'm talking about?"

"Yes, sir."

"Well, as planned, we were going to sit under the oaks out there, and the magic of the place was going to do its work, and we were going to have a talk in which something really got said. But instead we learned how to get rid of acne, and we met Krawitz. We were even accepted by Krawitz and made welcome to take part in the fuller life of his group." Gavin swung the car out through a break in the traffic and into the north-bound stream on Route 189. "What a flop my big surprise turned out to be."

"You shouldn't say that. It didn't disappoint me. It's a pretty wonderful thing, all that water coming up out of the ground, even if there was a crumby crowd there. I mean Sunday's just about the same anywhere, the way people just come out of the woodwork and swarm over places. If we'd gone there in the week we'd probably have had it to ourselves."

"You could be right. But the place has changed. It'll never be the same again for me. You're too young to know what regrets are. You don't know what it is to find that you've lost something you'll never get back. It's not exactly embittering, but it's saddening. It gives you an odd feeling of powerlessness and futility. Still there's no use crying over spilt milk."

"Perhaps you ought to yell before it's spilt."

"Never yell, just don't spill it," Gavin laughed. "But that's impossible. Was that a good reel your mother got you?"

"Yes, it was. Too good really. I don't fish that much." Thomas rubbed his forehead. "About not spilling milk. I've been a coward. I've been trying to get up my nerve to talk to you for months now. I don't know what I'm scared of but it's something to do with an idea I've got about you. It's sort of impertinent, and hard to explain because of that. I have a feeling you don't get much of what you want, and when I want to stand up against you I feel I'm doing wrong. It makes me helpless. Every time I try to bring this thing up I know it's going to upset you, and I find I can't speak. But it's my birthday, having regrets has got a lot to do with it, I'm eighteen and it's getting late in the day. so I've just got to . . ."

"Take it easy. I'm listening. Go a bit slower and worry a bit less. It'll come out clearer that way."

"I can't go to Gulf, father, it's no damned good."

"That's a pretty big statement."

"I know. I didn't put it the right way. I know it will be a good university some day. But it isn't yet. I don't say they shouldn't have courses on progressive salesmanship and retail economics. I don't say they shouldn't have a course called Twentieth-Century Technics III that used to be called Automotive Arts. I don't say that all the people who graduate out of the School of Electronics turn out to be T.V. repairmen. I wouldn't necessarily agree with anyone who said that Gulf was a diploma mill and nothing more than that, but I do know I don't belong there."

"We're trying to make it a good college. We've de-emphasized football. These things take time."

"I know, and time's what I haven't got."

"Where do you want to go?"

"M.I.T."

"Hell's bells, Thomas. Every kid who ever put his head in a space helmet wants to go to M.I.T. You know better than that. If you want to do physics the science department at Gulf is perfectly all right. We have a cyclotron, and the head of the department got a Nobel prize a few years back."

"I know, Professor Fersen. I went to see him. He said, 'Don't waste your time here.' He gave me a recommendation to M.I.T. My science teacher says I ought to go there. So does the head of studies. They say it's a damned shame I'm going to Gulf. I shouldn't go there."

"If they feel that way why don't they speak up."

"They're scared of you. That's why. Because you're on boards and committees that they have to go to to ask for money. Because you've got power."

"But what'll happen to Gulf if all the good students in the state by-pass it? Do you ever think of that?"

"I don't know. I'm eighteen, just, today. There's an awful lot I don't know. That's one of the things I don't know about. How a Baptist school for training missionaries got blown up to be a huge polytechnic is hard enough to figure out. How it would go on growing and get to be a university I wouldn't know. I don't believe I'd find out by grinding my nose in it. Perhaps I'd find out if I went to a real university. I don't know. But I know I don't want to go into a lot of so-so programs, with a second-rate student body to work with, when I could be up there with the best men of my generation, learning from the teachers who are the real right thing."

"Are you so sure you're that good, Thomas?"

"No. But I want to get in there to find out. I'll never know at Gulf."

"You couldn't be satisfied with . . ."

"No. I've got to go now. If I miss two or three years at this stage I'll always be that far behind. Physics isn't a subject you can play with, there are any number of physicists who aren't quite good enough. It's the most demanding subject there is, that's why it's the most interesting. I can't bear to go into it on the level of the second-rate. You must see that."

"Yes, I can see that." Gavin was silent for a time. "You want to go to pick up Mary at Ginny Holmes' don't you. The Holmes' are out on the Point, or did they move to the Heights?"

"They're on the Heights, on Cristobal, between Wyman and County." Thomas scratched the back of his head nervously. "You understand, don't you? I mean it hasn't been treachery or anything. I haven't wanted to deceive you, but I'm all set to go to Gulf, and I'm all set with M.I.T., too. We've gone through all the procedures, and they've accepted me. I didn't want to make an issue of it, and then have it all for nothing. But now I can see how it looks. As if I had gone behind your back. But I had to do it this way."

"I know. I went through the same sort of thing once, myself. My father had ideas about what I ought to do. And I had other notions."

"Did he make you go into business?"

"No. That was my idea. I had an obsession. I wanted a million dollars. Don't ask me why. It was an ambition that seemed all right at the time."

"What did you want to do with it?"

"That's just it. I didn't know. I just wanted to prove I could get it." Gavin concentrated for a few moments on changing lanes. "It's all right, Thomas. I can see Gulf is one of my ob-

359

sessions, and I suppose physics and M.I.T. have got to be obsessions of yours. Well, if that's the way it is, I suppose Gulf will have to try to get along without you."

"I'm sorry."

"Perhaps when you've jumped your hurdle you'll come back and help to make Gulf's science department what you'd like it to be."

"I don't know that it's a hurdle. I mean what I'm doing isn't like going out for a million dollars. What gets me in science is the way there aren't goals, it's an opening out. Whenever you solve a problem it only takes you further in to see new ones. It's like walking through mountains, every time you get to a good viewpoint you see more good viewpoints ahead." He paused. "I'd like to say, yes, sure I'll come back to Gulf when I've had my licks at what I want to do. But it won't be like that. I mean I'll have to go where the right crowd to be with is, where the work's being done that I'm fitted to do."

"And it won't be Gulf in a million years? Is that it?"

"That's pretty well it. I mean, I don't want to be unpleasant or anything, but that set-up is pretty hopeless. I mean, I can understand the citrus growers wanting a non-toxic dye to make oranges look ripe, but I don't see a university research team doing itself any good taking a fat grant to go out for a thing like that. You look the place over and the talk is fine, but it's actually a research lab for a lot of local industries."

"I see you've been into this thoroughly."

"Yes, I have." Thomas bit his lip. "I don't want to sound stuffy or anything, but I can't afford to be wrong at this stage. Things aren't the way they used to be. You don't get second chances. Not in the important fields."

"I know. I'm sorry. I seem to have underrated your ambitions, or misunderstood them. Perhaps I just ignored them." Gavin looked at him. "You helped by keeping them dark, but then who ever could tell his father that he was planning his own life before he'd done it."

They were close to Maramee, traveling slowly along the six-lane approach to the new bridge, which had been widened to take the increased traffic and renamed for Harry S Truman. The huge road had, for all practical purposes, annihilated Morgantown. The bulldozers had scraped away the foundations of the houses where nine thousand Negro families had lived, and had left untouched only two small parts of the old jigtown, one on each side of the roaring traffic stream. The colored people left in these awkward pockets clung to them for a few weeks and then cleared out in a body to go to the new colored section which had sprung up in Jepson County just north of the Maramee city limits soon after the road widening began. At first the new place had no name. It was located on a gravel ridge, about half a mile from the end of the main runway of the Arling Field, which had been a failure as an orange grove in the early 'thirties. Someone bought the property from Jepson County for the back taxes and parceled it out in fifty-foot square lots, ten dollars down and a dollar a week for a year, and after the first three or four hundred had been sold, everyone was calling it Harlem Heights as if that had always been its name. Not that Morgantown had risen in the world by becoming white. It had become a transients' slum where Northerners from the big cities looking for a fresh start in Florida would spend a few weeks or a few months before finding work and better housing elsewhere, or until they drifted over to Congdon City, or on down the Gulf. Blight spreading outward from the decaying remains of Morgantown was worrying property owners in the surrounding neighborhoods. As a result, a part of the Urban Renewal Program which had been drawn up by the Civic Betterment Committee of which Gavin was chairman called for the transformation of two wide strips on each side of the highway into a belt park.

"It'll really give the town a handsome entrance from the south," Gavin said.

"I read about it in the *Herald*," Thomas said, noncommittally.

"You don't sound too enthusiastic."

"Oh, sure, I think it's a swell idea, having a park."

"But?"

"Oh, I don't know," Thomas said, "just that Harlem

Heights is sort of under the wheels of the bombers as they come in and out of Arling Field. It seems too bad driving the Morgantown people up there, just to make room for a lot of palm trees and banana plants. I suppose parks are a good thing though."

"They are. And when this scheme is through we'll have something better to show people than this run-down slum." Gavin looked ahead, between the tall piers of the widened bridge. "I don't see the bottle."

"There it is," Thomas said, pointing. "Further over."

"It's funny to think how much that damned bottle of Chuck Hallet's used to annoy me. It's hard to find it now."

It was a little thing compared with the huge Husky Tire over the Husky Rubber Company's plant and it was quite overshadowed by the forty-foot sugar packet over the Sweet Southland Cane Corporation's factory nearby. This had a neon routine at night which made Hallet's floodlighting seem positively tasteful. First an italic neon tube flashed on to say 'sweeter'n sweet,' the company slogan, then three banks of neon came on one after another in three shades of red saying 'white, light brown, dark brown,' then floodlights illuminated the whole of the red and yellow carton. In all there were twenty-seven signs of this type, several times larger than the façades of most Maramee houses, facing the river and greeting travelers coming to the city from the south. The bottle was lost in the crowd.

"I'm not very good at talking to you, I'm afraid, Thomas," Gavin said.

"You do all right."

"I was going to try to tell you all sorts of things today," Gavin said as they came out of the business section and started up County Street towards the Heights. "But our friend Krawitz rather took the wind out of my sails. So did old Edwin for that matter. I've been trying to work out what I was going to say, but I see now that I hadn't really thought it out. I was relying on the spring to say it for me, if you see what I mean. I spent half my life nerving myself to meet a test. I felt I'd be called on somewhere or somehow to prove myself as a man, as a human being, and that after it I'd get a pass mark, or I'd know I'd failed. Either way I'd move on from uncertainty to certainty. After that there'd be happiness and tranquility in my life because I'd know, and there wouldn't be anything to be afraid of any more. Well, don't get that idea. It isn't like that. You just do your best. And then you do your best again. But you never reach that haven. It sounds disgusting when I put it into words, it's so trite. But happiness isn't a prize you can get, it's doing your best, and going on doing it. It hasn't even got much to do with having things your own way. In fact if you get things your own way, you may find it's a kind of punishment." He touched the horn and gave two short blasts as they passed over an intersection. "In words these things become worthless, you have to know them. If I tell you the most important thing I know about life you won't even realize I've told you anything. It's no use doing good, you have to be kind."

"Here's Cristobal, father, we turn right."

"Into the heart of Hollywood Spanish America. Tell me which Ginny's house is. She's an attractive girl."

"I guess so. Yes, she's pretty, all right." Thomas pointed. "That's it, where my car is. The sixth house."

The two tons of machinery came to a stop, and by the time Gavin looked round for Thomas he was halfway up the flagstone path leading to the front door.

"Do you want me to take Mary home, or are you going to bring her back? She has to be on hand to organize this surprise you're going to get, and you've got to be there too, remember, if you're planning to fade off into the blue with Ginny."

"Ginny isn't my girl—I'll find out what Mary wants to do."

Thomas vanished into the house without ringing or knocking, Gavin noticed. He recalled that in his day the doors of girls' houses had been formidable obstacles behind which the wrong person was always waiting, the father, the mother, the sister you didn't like, or a hearty brother. Now the young just passed into houses where there were other young people as of

363

right, as casually as flights of birds moving from roost to roost. Mrs. Holmes came out of the doorway and walked casually down to the car. She looked well in the red silk shirt and black matador pants she was wearing. Because she had a snub nose and a pretty smile she had been given the nickname Funnyface when she was twelve, and she was stuck with it, for life now.

"Hi, Gavin," she said, coming up to the car. "Mary's been telling me there's going to be quite a party at the Grove tonight. Think Ilona would like some help? Any excuse to get out of the house on a Sunday night is good enough for me."

"That's sweet of you, Funnyface, but I'm ducking out and taking Ilona off with me. We're just leaving the place to the kids and the caterer's people. Miss Wilbraham will be on hand to keep it all under control."

"And then in two weeks it's going to be Pedro Nunez, and all that stuff will be on us. Are you giving a dance? I should know, but I haven't really studied up on all our invitations yet."

"We're skipping it this year. Ilona hasn't been too well lately. We're just going to look in on one or two of the big things we can't very well get out of. Rex's ball, and the Club Dance."

"Try to come to our party—it's on the Tuesday."

"If Ilona feels up to it we'll be there."

"She's not well again?"

"No, I'm afraid not."

"I know I shouldn't say this, Gavin, but have you tried the A.A. people, they were just wonderful with my sister. I don't mean to be a buttinski, but they really helped her."

"I know they do a fine job for some people, Funnyface, but they can't work with someone who won't work with them."

"It's a shame, Gavin." Mrs. Holmes looked down at her feet, bare in thin-strapped sandals. "They're such wonderful kids, and you're such a wonderful guy. You all deserve something different. I wish there was something we could all do to help." She looked up quickly and met his eyes. "You have an awful lot of friends, Gavin, and they all feel the same way."

"I know, Funnyface. Thanks."

"Well, I'm sure you've got a lot of better things to do than just sit here," she said, and put a friendly hand on his arm. "I'll go and kick those kids out of the house. I think Ginny wants to spend the night at the Grove with Mary. Is that all right with you?"

"Oh, yes, of course. Bogey's off spending the night with some friend, so the house is a girl short. We'd love to have Ginny."

"Goo'bye then, Gavin." She smiled her wide-mouthed, good-natured, smile, squeezed his arm with the lightest of friendly, sisterly, unsexy pressures and took herself off.

In the house Mary had said, "It didn't work, Thomas."

"I'm awfully sorry," Ginny said, "I didn't get to first base."

"What happened?"

"I went over there. There wasn't anybody in the front of the house. I found Mr. McCann sitting out on that terrace by the lily pool round at the back. I said 'Good morning, Mr. McCann,' and he put down the paper he was reading and said 'Good morning, Ginny.' He looked at me so—I don't know— as if I'd done something wrong—anyway I went into a panic. I said 'Can I see Sophy, Mr. McCann?' And he said 'No, Ginny, you can't.' Like a fool I said 'Why not?' Can you imagine, as if I was seven, and he sat there radiating this sort of malevolence, and said, 'Because I say you can't, that's all, Ginny.' And he had me so cowed I just muttered something about being sorry, and I literally crawled out. So I didn't do any good at all."

"I'm sorry, Thomas," Mary said.

They all sat staring into the miniature perfection of the Japanese garden Mr. Holmes had built when he came back after finishing his tour of duty on General MacArthur's staff in Tokyo. The stones, which played a large part in the garden, had been shipped down from Connecticut carefully crated so that they wouldn't be bruised or damaged on the journey.

Word of this had got round in Maramee and Mr. Holmes was now known to a considerable number of people as "the well-known rock collector." Near the two girls and the boy, a thin trickle of water fell from a bamboo spout into a circular basin cut deeply into a large boulder. The sound had a hypnotic effect, and for a few seconds they just listened to it.

"The house felt empty," Ginny said suddenly. "I had a hunch Sophy wasn't there. I don't think Mrs. McCann was there either. And the air in the house was—charged—as if there'd been a terrific row."

Mary and Thomas exchanged a look.

"I'll have to go and see Mr. McCann," Thomas said.

"He's hateful," Ginny said. "I don't know how Sophy can be so nice, with such a stinker for a father." They all got to their feet a little awkwardly, closely united in a friendship that they didn't know quite how to express.

"Ginny and I'll drive out with father," Mary said. "Try not to get too involved with Mr. McCann. You ought to be back before people start to arrive."

"I never felt less like a party in my life," Thomas said.

Mrs. Holmes came through the house calling "Now you kids."

"But don't worry, I'll show up," Thomas said. "We're coming, Mrs. Holmes."

"We're leaving this minute, Mrs. Holmes," Mary said, and took her brother's hand. "Go on and get your dress, Ginny. We can't keep father another second." Her friend went indoors with a cry of "Sorry, mother, it was all my fault, we forgot," and ran upstairs. Mary squeezed Thomas's hand and then let it go. "He'll try to trample on you. You won't let him, will you? He'll try to hurt you. Are you ready for that? Don't go if you aren't."

"I am. I think I am."

"Well, don't weaken, that's all. Don't let her down." She hesitated, and then added a few more words. "And don't let yourself down."

They made their farewells to Mrs. Holmes and passed out

of the house into the bright sunshine on the street. Gavin saw them coming through the doorway and felt a stir of pride. They were fine young people. He could see something of himself in them, something of Ilona, something else altogether different which was entirely their own. He saw Thomas wave to him as he turned aside towards his own car, and he waved back. Well, that was it, the end of the great episode of communication between father and son, he thought, but at least I had a stab at it, which is more than my father ever did. Or did he, he wondered, but at some moment when I wasn't listening, or when my mind was full of my own all-important discoveries about life? He had an impression that Thomas' mind had been elsewhere most of the afternoon.

"What have you two been cooking up?" he said, as Mary got into the car beside him.

"We were cutting up material to make ourselves dresses for Pedro Nunez week. Mrs. Holmes was showing us how to lay out the paper patterns on the cloth. We're going to have terrific dresses out of *Vogue*—really grand—and we're going to show up in a different one every night. It's a sort of an anti-money-swank thing. Some of the girls are getting dresses that cost two or three hundred dollars and we think it's awful. We're going to show them up."

"That isn't what I was asking about, and you know it, you secretive minx. But if you won't talk, you won't talk."

"No, I won't," Mary said. "Where are you taking mother tonight?"

"I thought we'd go on down to Tarpon Springs. Sigaux knows a good Greek place there, or he says he does."

"Oh, that's nice," Mary looked past him. "Here's Ginny at last, thank goodness."

"Yes, and now your poor doting old father won't be able to ask any more awkward questions, will he?" Gavin said smiling.

"Oh, father, that's so unfair. Thomas' trouble is private. I just don't have the right to talk about it, that's all."

"I know. It was stupid of me to ask. It's just that I love you both. I have a lot of experience with one kind of difficulty and another and I can't help feeling I might be able to help with sage advice if I knew a bit more about some of your infant troubles. That's all." Gavin turned himself round to open the door behind him so that Ginny could lay her dress in its plastic cleaner's bag down on the back seat.

"You've brought that glorious blue and green dress after all," Mary said. "I'm so glad. It's my favorite of all your dresses."

Gavin looked at his daughter's face, which was alight with what seemed to be unfeigned pleasure, and thought, It's all so much water off a duck's back, you can't reach them, and you can't help them. He started the engine of the car and drove off as soon as Ginny was in her place beside Mary on the far side of the front seat.

Thomas rang the front doorbell of the McCann's house several times before Mr. McCann came to answer it.

"Well," he said, "well, well! This is indeed an honor. Won't you come in." He led the way across the hall to his study at the far corner of the house. When he reached it, he left Thomas standing in the middle of the room while he filled his pipe from a tobacco jar on his desk. He let the silence stiffen further while he lighted the pipe. Thomas watched him with uneasy fascination. It was, as Ginny had said, hard to believe that anyone could bear such a close physical resemblance to Sophy and yet look wholly disagreeable. Mr. McCann sat himself on the corner of his desk and took a few puffs at his pipe. "Well?" he said coldly.

"I'd like to see Sophy, Mr. McCann," Thomas said.

"I suppose you would. But you're not going to, or not for quite some time."

"I must see her, Mr. McCann."

"Ah, that's a big word, must. It means, well, it means must, and yet there are going to be considerable difficulties about it." He got up and shifted himself to the chair behind his desk.

368

He was a short broad-shouldered man who moved with a blunt forcefulness which made even the act of sitting down seem aggressive. "You see Sophy isn't in Maramee any longer. She left with her mother this morning. They're a long way off now, and you don't know where. We'll say somewhere in the United States. So far as you're concerned it's classified information. I don't think you'll find her very easily for one thing, and for another I don't think you've got time to find her before she goes abroad. Her mother will be taking her to—well, we'll say a foreign country for the time being, shall we?—anyway she'll be in school there for a year. I expect she'll write you from her school, and then it'll be more or less up to you to see what you can do about it when you know where she is, won't it? But meanwhile remarks like 'I must see her, Mr. McCann,' are—well, pitiful, pointless, pathetic, even puerile—wouldn't you agree?" He put his pipe back into his mouth and sucked on it greedily. His eyes gleamed with satisfaction.

"I don't think you understand, Mr. McCann. I love Sophy."

"Well now, that's nice. What do you think I'm having difficulty in understanding?"

"The whole thing."

"Ah, yes. The splendor and beauty of it all. The pledges given and received under the stars, all that crap . . ."

"Sir, you don't have any right . . ."

"I'll tell you who doesn't have any rights in this. You don't. You've lost them. You had them. But you chucked them away when you laid my daughter on her back and went to work on her. You knew what you were doing. Man's work, on a child. And you aren't fit for man's work yet either. You're both children, vicious and dishonorable children. You'll keep your mouth shut and hear what I've got to say. When I say dishonorable, I mean it. You've been a trusted friend in this house for years. You came and went as if it was your own home. I trusted you. My wife trusted you. We didn't hold it against you that you've a drunk for a mother and a skirt-chaser for a father, though we should have if we'd had any sense. We should have known that rotten stock breeds rotten cattle. We

369

were fooled by your good looks and your smooth manners, I suppose. And we trusted our daughter too, with freedom, to go and come in open, friendly, decent houses like our own. We taught her honorable standards of conduct, or so we thought. We thought we'd taught her to know right from wrong. We hoped she'd respect herself."

"She can respect herself, Mr. McCann. We love each other. We mean to get married."

"Oh, you do. It's nice of you to tell me that. You think a quick lay in a parked car is a good foundation for a lifetime of happiness? I don't, strangely enough. I think you took advantage of an inexperienced girl last night. And I think the young swine who would do a thing like that isn't a very good husband for my daughter. I'll tell you something else, too."

"I hope you're not going to say anything more about my mother, Mr. McCann."

"Well, that's good, that's very good, a spark of manliness at last, though it took a lot of getting it out of you, I must say. Well, I'll phrase what I have to say with care so as not to arouse your manly feelings any further. I'll say that you haven't exactly been brought up in an atmosphere of restraint and self-control. At any rate, you don't know much about these things, do you? I mean there was my daughter last night, and you were having a bit of fun working her up, and working youself up, and then you just thought, hell, why not, here we go, who cares about the consequences, let's have fun. That's about the size of it. And then you liked your piece of nooky when you'd had it, so you came around, after sending a girl first, to say 'I must see Sophy, Mr. McCann.' You'd even marry the girl to get another go in there, wouldn't you? 'I love Sophy, Mr. McCann, we mean to get married, maaareeed.'" Mr. McCann drew it out like a lamb's bleat. "Well, again I'm old-fashioned, I don't think you've shown me that you're quite ready for marriage. You've proved to me you can lay my daughter. But you've proved a lot of other things, too. You've proved you haven't the slightest consideration for her honor or her reputation. At least that's what you've proved. You've proved to me, if

370

not to her—she liked it too, she likes you, she'd like to be maaareeed, too—but as I was saying you've shown me you're a greedy, thoughtless brat, without any self-control at all. And I don't think a greedy, thoughtless brat who can't control himself is the husband I want for my girl. You see my point perhaps? And there's another thing, too, that hasn't occurred to you apparently. You're wet behind the ears. You haven't ever done a damned thing except suck stuff out of that great big silver spoon of Gavin Hatfield's. You've never done a lick of work in your life. You've never done anything but play. And you're a schoolboy. You're going to college in the fall. Christ, man, you'll be sitting in classrooms for four more years at least. If you're going to be a scientist worth a damn, you'll be doing graduate work for three or more years after that. Do you have to have a wife to play house with when you get out of classes? Can't you see you're nothing but a kid with seven or eight more years of schooling ahead of you? And don't you know what schooling is? It's education—it's making you, molding you, changing you. You won't be the same in eight years. Sophy doesn't know what she's getting into. You ought to know. You had no right to take her last night, no right at all. So far as I'm concerned you did something unforgivable, wrong, and shameful. That's what I feel emotionally. And I don't think you're being realistic, when I think about it on the practical level. I used to like you. I can even admire the way you've stood up to this tirade. But I don't like you any more, Thomas, and I don't trust you. So I'm putting Sophy out of harm's way for a time. I daresay you'll win back my respect by proving yourself as a man. I hope you will come through, but right now I don't feel at all friendly where you're concerned. So just get out of my house, and, whatever else you do, stay away from my daughter."

Thomas stood looking at him for a full second without moving. He was conscious of the heavy green shadows hanging under the big trees close to the house. The sunlight seemed far away, and the room, lighted only by that diffused green, seemed an underground and lifeless place. Its walls were covered with the icons which Mr. McCann had brought back from Russia after he had done famine-relief work there in the 'twenties. The virgins and saints, the Father and Son, and the archangels, and all the remembered splendor of Byzantium, shone from the painted boards. "What are they, Sophy?" Thomas had said once. "Things father was given by the Russians. They're old." "They look old." "They're spooky though, aren't they, in this dark old room?" "Yes, they are, come on, let's go." That would have been six years ago, perhaps longer.

"I said get out, Thomas," Mr. McCann said. "There's nothing more to be said. Don't just stand there looking fierce. It won't get you anywhere."

"I was thinking of what I ought to say."

"Well, you could apologize, and then you could say good-bye."

"No I don't think I could apologize, Mr. McCann. At least I wouldn't want to. I can see you've had a lot of practice bullying people and hurting people. I can't see much else admirable in you. I may be all the things you say, but if I've done wrong its because I'm young and I've got a lot to learn. But you, well, I hope I'm not like you when I get to be your age, mean, vindictive, foul-mouthed and foul-tempered." He paused and watched Mr. McCann's hands, stiff with controlled fury. He saw the stamp of age on the skin between his knuckles and wrists. He saw a small opening and thrust at it. "I suppose it's pretty disagreeable, if you're a greedy and selfish person that is, to feel that you've had your chances and missed them, and that the future isn't yours any more. It's too bad you have to take it out on your daughter though. Good-bye, Mr. McCann. I don't think you'll succeed in breaking my will or Sophy's. I hope you won't, because if you do it'll mean life's a much more disgusting business than I think it is."

"Well, bravo. Finely said, young man. Now let's see you live up to it." Mr. McCann got to his feet. "I'll see you out." Halfway across the hall he paused. "Oh, Thomas, there's one thing I can tell you. If you want to avoid this sort of thing in future, take a little trouble. The next time you crack some poor kid's maidenhead, stick a towel or something under her ass. Then she won't go home with an ugly blood stain on her dress. It's the sight of blood that maddens us fathers. It's neurotic perhaps, or it could touch some vein of the primitive in us. But there it is."

"Blood?" Thomas faltered. "I didn't know . . ."

"Yes, quite so." Mr. McCann looked at his stricken face with pleasure. "As you are noble enough to admit, you've got a lot to learn. You've learned some of it at my daughter's expense. But not any more, sonny, not if I can help it. Now get out, and get lost."

As the heavy door slammed shut behind him a primeval ignorant horror welled up in Thomas' mind filling it with fear. Mr. McCann had meant it to. Thomas didn't know if he'd done some terrible injury to Sophy, or if he'd hurt her without knowing it. She had said not, but there had been the gasp and shudder that had made him ask. Perhaps she had been very kind, and keeping something back that might have upset him. The only reassurance he had was Mr. McCann's furious voice saying, "She liked it too, she likes you, she wants to be maaareeed." He stood still on the path about ten paces from the house, with the veil of her innocent blood between him and the world. It would be there until he had heard her saying that it was all right, that she still liked him, that the sun would rise tomorrow. And he did not know where she was. He looked up and down the expensive street, seeing nothing but her absence.

"Hi, Thomas, Thomas boy." He looked up and saw Torrey Warner calling to him over the side of his noisy old hotrod from out in the middle of the street. "Are you all right? You look green." Warner hopped out of the car and slammed the door shut, leaving it double-parked. He came up to Thomas and took him by the arm. "You aren't sick or anything? You look as if you'd been clubbed. What goes on? Girl trouble? Father trouble?"

"No, I'm all right. I just didn't feel too good—coming out

373

into the sun suddenly—something like that—it's cool in that McCann house."

"You looked badly, you really did. Say, I've got to run. I've got to go home to get showered and all dressed up for some party—why damn it, it's your party. What are you doing here? You ought to be . . . You still don't look right, man, not to me. Shall I drive you home?"

"No, that's all right, Torrey, don't you worry." He straightened his back and squared his jaw. "It was nothing. I'll see you at the house in about an hour."

"Well you know best, Thos old boy," Torrey said, thumping him on the shoulders. "But take it easy. It's all that brainwork getting you down, if you ask me." He grinned cheerfully. "Take care."

He got into his foxtail-festooned, and star-studded machine, and drove off, a blaze of white, scarlet, and flashing chromium, which was soon lost to sight up the tunnel of date palms lining the street. Thomas followed him a few minutes later, thankful that Torrey had come along just in time to get him to square his shoulders and to lift his chin up off his chest. No, he thought, I won't let myself down, I won't think badly of myself just because that old brute wants me to. But what the hell can I do? He had a paralyzing sense of his own impotence. He concentrated on bringing back before his mind's eye every recollection he had of Sophy. But the images wouldn't come alive, they stayed in the past, he couldn't get round the overwhelmingly negative present, in which he didn't know where she was, what she was doing, or what she was feeling. He ran over his father's words about how he was supposed to live: you did your best, you tried to be kind. Yes, all right—swell, fine—but what did you do when someone like Mr. McCann shot you off into a sort of emotional outer space, where you didn't even know which way was up? How do I do anything at all now? Let alone the right thing?

Gavin drove the car out of the shadow of the towering bamboos into the open space in front of the Grove. He looked affectionately at the tower, the sprawling roofs, the carpenters' fantasies, and the tumbling masses of vines and creepers held up by its porches. Dear house, he thought idly, saying aloud to the girls, "Well, here we are," and felt a moment of pure pleasure at being home. He wished he was going to spend the rest of the evening there, but all things considered, it would be best to have Ilona out of the way before the crowd of youngsters arrived. Ginny, holding her dress up by the wire hook of the cleaner's hanger, turned smiling to him from the foot of the steps. "It's always such a thrill to come out here, Mr. Hatfield. You are the luckiest people in the world to have this wonderful, romantic old house. I mean it's like something in a fairy tale, it really is. It's just beautiful." Gavin grinned at her. "Good girl. It's not everybody who can see that. Why, I've even had people say, 'Why don't you tear this old barrack down and build a modern house that makes sense.'" "Oh, they can't mean it! Why, Mr. Hatfield, that would be a crime. You wouldn't ever dream of it, would you? How could they?" He put his hand on her shoulder and patted it. "No, Ginny, I'll promise you that." "Nothing would ever be the same again if the Grove vanished or even changed, would it, Mary?" Ginny said. Mary looked down from the head of the steps with her hand on the screen door. "Oh, it's all right, it's just a crazy old place, it's not so wonderful when you have to live in it." It was not what she felt, but some instinct told her that Ginny was acting the role of the enthusiastic parted-lips girl for Gavin's benefit. She had a silly look on her face. Ginny was, in fact, thinking at the moment that there was something solid, sure, and strong about older men that young men just didn't have. All her regular dates seemed weedy and uncertain of themselves in comparison with a man like Gavin. Of course, he was Mary's father, and he was married, but still he was terribly attractive. It would be sort of wonderful just to put yourself in the hands of someone who knew what he was about. "Oh, come on," Mary said, moving on into the cool darkness of the hall, "we've got to get dressed." "All right, but we've got hours," Ginny said, hurrying after her, smiling over

375

her shoulder at Gavin with an expression which surprised him. He wondered if she knew what she was doing with her face, and with her body, too. He supposed that it was an instinctive thing with no conscious thought whatever behind it, and followed the children slowly into the house. Miss Wilbraham was coming up the hallway beyond them, holding her finger to her lips. The girls hesitated and stopped, looking back at Gavin silhouetted against the daylight behind them.

"Shh, girls. Hi, Ginny," said Miss Wilbraham softly. "Try not to make a noise. Just go quietly upstairs and start dressing. Everything's all right. Take your friend up, Mary, I just have to speak to your father for a minute. Run along now."

"What's all this Miss Wilbraham?" Gavin said, aloud, not understanding why she was speaking so softly. The housekeeper gasped, and turned her head anxiously towards the open doorway into the living room.

"Who are you shshshushing with out there?" Ilona called. "What are you up to out there, Willy?"

"Go on, do," said Miss Wilbraham to the girls, "now."

"What?" Gavin said coming forward.

"It's Mrs. Hatfield," Miss Wilbraham said. "She . . ."

"She what?" said Ilona holding on to the living-room doorpost. "What about Mrs. Hatfield? Tell me what, Willy?"

"This is no place for you girls," Miss Wilbraham said.

"Now, Ilona," Gavin said.

"Mary, for Christ's sake," Ilona said, "my daughter, my darling daughter, I have a bone to pick with you. I have a personal question I want to ask." She saw Ginny shrinking uncertainly away from her towards Gavin. "Who's that? She's cute. Is she your friend, Mary, or is she daddy's friend? Some cat the dog brought in—"

"It's Ginny Holmes, Mrs. Hatfield," Ginny said wretchedly.

"Well, you watch out, you pretty cute thing, with my great male man around anything can happen." She shook her head. "You wouldn't believe, right here, in this house."

"Madam," Miss Wilbraham said going to her and taking her

arm. "It's all right, girls. She's unwell. Take your friend upstairs, Mary."

"You let me alone, Willy." She shook herself free and took
a few steps forward. "I want to know something. I want to ask
my daughter a question. A simple question."

"Now take it easy, Ilona," Gavin said. "Mary's just come in.
You can have a talk with her later." He made a brushing movement with his arm to get the girls moving. "There's plenty of
time. There's no need to rush anything."

"You sicken me, you gentle good-natured, lecherous slob.
Don't touch me." She saw the girls beginning to slip away, arm
in arm, towards the stairs. "You, Mary. What the hell happened last night? What did you do. Why won't Sigaux come?
I've called him and he won't come." Miss Wilbraham had her
by one arm, and Gavin was holding her by the other. Ilona
rolled her head from side to side, staring now into one controlled, disgusted face, and now into another. "You don't understand. He's the only friend I've got. I need him. And my daughter, my own daughter, she's put herself between us. How could
she do it? What did she do it for? Why did she turn him
against me? That's what I want to know. That's all I want to
know." She looked into Gavin's eyes. "It's what I must know."

"Try to get a grip on yourself," Gavin said. "Go on up to
your room, Mary."

"No," Mary said. She halted with one foot on the bottom
of the staircase before coming slowly back to face her mother.
"I don't know what good it will do if I do tell you," she said
slowly. "What difference do you think it will make if I do?"

"You tell me," Ilona said, "we'll see."

"This won't do any good," Miss Wilbraham said. "Just
leave her be, Miss Mary. It's too late for explanations."

"Don't hurt yourself by getting into this, Mary," Gavin
said. "Run along out of the way."

Mary looked curiously at them both and then into her
mother's smoky eyes, the whites a little yellowish, a little
bloodshot.

"I didn't mean to do any harm, mother, I just fell in love

377

with Silky, with Mr. Sigaux. I hoped something would happen, but it never did. He was very sweet and kind to me. But that wasn't what I wanted. Last night I told him what I did want. And he told me he couldn't take me on any terms, as a wife, a mistress, or anything, because I was physically repulsive to him. He didn't want to hurt me by telling me that, but I made him. So now he's being kind by staying away. He doesn't want to hurt me. He's giving me a few days to get used to the idea that you can love someone who can't bear even to touch you. I don't see why that should upset you, or give you an excuse for making this disgusting scene. I don't know what you have against me, or Thomas, or Bogey, or daddy, or anyone, that makes you act like this. You seem to want to punish us, or to drive us into hurting you. I don't know why you're so cruel to us, and I don't know why you're so cruel to yourself." She ran clean out of words and stood silently looking at her mother, biting her lip unhappily. "What you do to yourself is worst of all, for us," she said abruptly, met her father's eyes for an instant, and then walked quietly away. Ilona's body softened, and Gavin and Miss Wilbraham let go of her arms. She stood watching the two girls going upstairs until they were out of sight at the turn of the flight. When they were gone she shrugged her shoulders and went unsteadily back into the living room to find the drink she had set down. Gavin could see her from the doorway as she drifted from one low table to another, restlessly and listlessly looking for the glass which was in plain view at the end of the mantelpiece.

"She ought to be in a hospital, she's sick," Miss Wilbraham said. "She's going to get worse than this, fast, if you don't do something." She looked at Gavin's face with something like anger. "You've tried kindness. It isn't any good."

"She's shshshushing again behind my back," Ilona said, "tell her to shut up before I go out of my mind. Tell her to stop, Gavin. Go away, Willy, go away."

"Thank you, Willy. I don't think there's anything more you can do right now."

"It's a shame, when everything's been done to make it such a lovely party. She loves ruining things. She just loves it. She's getting mean and wicked. You've got to wake up to what's going on, Mr. Hatfield . . ."

"Stop her talking and send her away, Gavin, please."

"Some other time, Miss Wilbraham, not now."

"It's never now. You won't face it. You've got to face it."

"Miss Wilbraham." Bailey appeared in the dining-room doorway. "Excuse me, Mr. Hatfield. The band has arrived. Will I take them on down to the tent or will you do that?"

"I'll come in a minute, Bailey." The veiled discreet face vanished.

"You'd better do that, Willy," Gavin said. "Did they send the green and white tents we asked for?"

"Yes, Mr. Hatfield. They look lovely down by the water. The dance floor is laid out round that big tree, and the lanterns are all through the grove. The buffet looks very well, and the raft with the fireworks is hidden off, out of sight down by the dam. The kids won't know a thing about them until the first shower of rockets goes up. It was all going to be just about perfect until this started."

"I'm sure you've done your best, Willy, you always do." Gavin saw that Ilona had found her drink at last. "Just leave me to handle this my own way, and it'll be all right yet."

"Oh, Mr. Hatfield, when are you going to catch on? You haven't got a chance. Well, I see it's a waste of time making with my big mouth. I'll go and deal with the band and get on with my job. I'm sorry if I've been talking out of turn."

"That's all right. I understand how you feel." Gavin walked away into the living room, and Miss Wilbraham, slowly shaking her head, walked off into the servants' quarters to meet the bandsmen. Gavin stood with his back to Ilona for a while, fishing a cigarette out of a marble box and lighting it. She watched him, taking an occasional gulp from the glass. His body tapered well from his broad shoulders down into his narrow hips, she could see what the other women went for. He was, in the most daring phrase her mother ever applied to

379

matters dealing with the physical attractions a man might have for a woman, "very nicely made," still. She felt with anger that he was lasting better than she was, in spite of the vile things he could do and did without shame and without remorse. He turned slowly round and looked at her. Because he was tense and upset, the scar sliced across his face by Immortal Maggs gleamed whitely with an unusual sharpness down the side of his face.

"Eugh." It escaped her. "That scar! Sometimes I wonder how any woman can let you . . ."

"That isn't what we have to talk about, Ilona."

"But I suppose some women go for that sort of thing—they can see you've been hurt. There's a kind of thrill in a scar on a man . . ."

"Stop it, Ilona. Did you understand what your daughter told you just now?"

"Of course, she's physically repulsive. We all are. Loathsome animals. What does she think happens to her every month? Something pretty? Something attractive? She had to know sooner or later how repulsive being human is."

"I told you to stop it, Ilona."

"Oh, yes. That's nice. Gavin says life is beautiful. So we just shut up about what it's really like, and tell lies to make him happy."

"Now, look here, Ilona. Didn't you take in a word of what that girl said to you? She's been hurt, I can't tell how badly hurt. She told a man she loved him and he turned her down flat for the cruelest reason I can think of. She's in trouble. What good are you to her at this juncture?"

"Me? What good am I to her? Why, no good at all. What good could I be? What good are you? You go on up there and tell her, 'You disgust the man you love, darling, but don't worry, it's all right, there are lots of other men, you'll find someone to shove it up you before long. You won't miss anything, nothing important, I promise . . .'"

The sound of Gavin's flat hand striking her cheek instantly filled the room with silence. They stood looking at each other,

380

rigid and motionless, as if they were two animals who had come face to face while hunting in the silence of a twilit jungle. Ilona was the first to move, staring intently at him as if she had never seen him before. Her body remained stiff with shock, nothing moved except her right arm which lifted her hand to her face. Her finger tips explored the side of her cheek where she had been hit. Then, as if impelled, her hand traveled across the space between their faces and its finger tips traced the line of the razor's sweep.

"Oh,"—less than a gasp, it was a strengthened exhalation. "He must have hurt you so terribly, I've never realized . . ." Her voice died away.

"Ilona, I . . ." Gavin said, but before he had uttered more than her name she was on her knees holding the hand with which he had hit her and smothering it with kisses. He looked down at the top of her head in amazement, almost as horrified by what she was doing as he had been when he realized that he had for the first time in his life, hit a woman to hurt her. He felt her tears on his hand, and stroked her hair with the other one. She was incoherently begging his forgiveness, he could barely distinguish for what in the roster of offense for which she was condemning herself. She was now holding him round his knees, rubbing her head against his thighs in an ecstasy of self-abasement. He bent down towards her, soothing her, comforting her with caresses, as if she were a hurt child. She rejected his comfort as she clung to him.

"No, no, I'm no good, I've been too awful, too vile, I've hurt you too much. I don't know what to do." It was as much moaning as speaking, and as Gavin tried to distinguish her words he was taken aback to discover that his shock was wearing off and was being replaced by as keen a sense of pleasure as he had ever experienced. She was literally at his feet, and begging, no less literally. He had a sense of his almost godlike power to do anything he liked with her; if he were cruel, he could destroy her self-respect for ever, if he were merciful he could set her on her feet and give her back her life. And she would know, for what remained of it, that she owed

381

everything to him. He could give her or not give her leave to
exist. He realized that he was tasting the heady wine which
Father Prieto preferred to sex, or love, or money, the intoxicating sense of mastery of the whole being of a fellow creature. He knelt beside her and lifted up her chin so that she was
forced to look into his face.

"I can't do anything for you, Ilona, you have to do it for
yourself," he said.

"I've always wanted you to hit me. Once I thought you
were going to, but you never did. You slapped me once when
I was hysterical, at the pool."

"I remember."

"This was different, though. Wasn't it?"

"Yes. This time you're drunk, and I was angry. I wanted to
hurt you. We've come a long way, haven't we?"

"Mm," it was half agreement, half a sob.

"What's it all about, really and truly?"

"I can't bear it, Gavin, being me. I just can't bear . . ."

"Don't do that. You're just sliding away from it. Try to say
it."

"I've been so vile, I . . ."

"No, that's all rubbish. What are you so ashamed of? Why
do you want to degrade yourself with drinking? Why do you
want to be despised for this instead of something else? What
is it? The real thing, the thing that makes you so cruel to yourself."

"I've got to, I've just got to have a drink, Gavin," Ilona
said, trying to get to her feet. "I can't talk any more unless I
have one." Gavin held her by the arms.

"No. You can't dodge it. And I won't hit you again, or
beat you so that you can feel punished and paid up. That's
why you wanted me to hit you, isn't it?"

"No," she looked uneasily about her and then at him, as
if she were not quite sure where she was or with whom. "Yes.
And I didn't want to be responsible."

"Responsible for what?"

"For . . ." She put her hands into her lap again, knotting

and unknotting her long fingers. Her engagement ring glittered as it rubbed against her flesh. "Do you remember giving me this?"

"Yes, at Barnton. I remember it very well. We sat on a dam by a pond. There were fireflies everywhere, and the sky was full of stars. There was some sort of party going on at your uncle's house up the hill and we could just hear the music."

"You remember all that?" She grimaced. "I suppose I do too, when I think of it. But I try not to."

"Has being married to me been so awful?"

"Yes." She put a hand quickly onto his knee. "But I don't mean that the way it sounds. It's because I shouldn't have married you. I did something rotten when I said I would. I just thought it would be worthwhile. I married you for your money, Gavin."

"That's not so terrible, Ilona. An awful lot of women marry men because they want a man to keep them. A lot of men marry housekeepers."

"Do you really think it's any comfort to know that I'm vile in the way that a lot of other people are vile?"

"That was silly of me. All I mean, really, is that it's a long time ago, and I don't mind. I wish you'd try not to mind." He took the hand on his knee and held it. "I don't know what I was thinking about when I married you. I didn't know you very well. I didn't understand you at all. I married my idea of you, I suppose. That was a stupid sort of thing to do, and very unfair. It's been hard on us both."

"Hard on us both. That's so thin—isn't it? Hard's such a little word. You know it began to get hard when I realized I'd cheated myself. I felt like a whore who'd sold herself for forged money. I knew I ought to say, no, when I married you, but I couldn't. I looked up the hill to Uncle Alston's house and I thought, I'll never have it, even a part of all that, if I don't say, yes. And then when we were married I found you didn't want any of the things I wanted. You had your mad dream about this crazy place and this disgusting, ugly town." She shook her head. "You don't know what hell this house is to me. It

383

mocks me. It's an awful parody of the house I wanted and married you to get. I should have left you as soon as I'd found out that you really wanted to live in it forever. But I couldn't." She stopped, staring at him, biting the knuckle of her left thumb. She thought, perhaps if I tell him everything he'll let me have another drink. "I couldn't," she said, letting her hand fall, with the prints of her teeth livid on the white skin. "Because my body wouldn't let me. My body wanted your body that badly. I fought against it but I couldn't hold back. And every time I gave way I despised myself a little more. In the end I hated myself, and then I hated myself more because I still wanted that from you."

"Well, you won that battle in the end, didn't you?"

"I suppose I did." She turned her head and looked at the enormous, enormously expensive, expensively covered sofa beside them; at the antique games table beside it with the inlaid chess board on its top, at the Chinese *famille rose* jar converted into a lamp standing on the table, at the silver wine taster's cup serving as an ashtray lying near it, at the vast glass-fronted bookcase from France against the wall beyond the sofa, and at the early-American and ante-bellum landscapes hanging on the walls. The bookcase was full of eighteenth-century china from English, German and French potteries; anything had been right for Ilona's collection provided it had a bird somewhere on it. Her collector's fever had lasted for just over four years, and had burned out as suddenly as it had taken hold. He had indulged her in so much. "Did you never guess how it shocked me to find you could just take me when you got back from the war? Didn't you have any idea of what I felt then?"

"I thought you were glad to have me back. It was stupid of me, I suppose."

"You were so horribly assured and so powerful. And you'd go on and on, like a great animal, and I wanted you to go on forever. And then I realized that there wasn't anything special about it being us. You'd do it with any woman you could, whenever you could, and it was all one to you, whoever it was as long as she liked it and you liked it. God, how I hated you when I found that out."

"Were you jealous?"

"No, I wasn't jealous. I just felt utterly pointless. What was gone was the thing everything else turned on—when I married you for your money I could at least feel I was letting you have something. That was all I had to keep me from feeling utterly dishonorable. And then at the end of all those dishonorable years there wasn't even that to go on fooling myself with. You took it away, the last little rotten rag of my self-respect. I'd nothing left, Gavin, nothing." The hot maudlin tears began to run down her cheeks and she bowed her head. A clock struck seven in the hall, and a smaller more musical voice repeated the information from the mantelpiece behind them. "The years have gone by, Gavin, and they're lost to me, they're lost to me. I've been false to myself and false to you, and it's all been for nothing. That's what I can't bear, and what I can't live with. I can't bear to admit that I'm worthless. I can't bear to think of what my life has been, and what it's going to be. I'm waiting to die, Gavin. The whole of my life has been nothing else but that." She crouched down, sobbing, and once again he found himself towering over a supplicant. He put a friendly, firm hand on her shoulder and shook her gently.

"Thomas' friends are going to start arriving pretty soon now," he said. "You don't want them to find you here in this state, do you? Come on up to your room and lie down. You'll feel better."

"I need a drink first, Gavin, before we go up." She got to her feet. "Please, Gavin."

"I'll bring you some coffee when we get upstairs."

"A lot of coffee might do." She caught sight of her old empty glass. "I suppose it might."

"This is going to be a turning point, isn't it, Ilona?" Gavin said, still on his knees and looking up into her face. "Now you know what you've been running from, you're going to try not to drink any more, aren't you?"

"Yes, yes, I'll try." Her gaze traveled over his face searching the impenetrable mask for some sign of understanding. The scar was there to show that he had once felt something, but that was his pain, not hers. Now that hers was in words in his head he seemed no nearer to the comprehension she had tried to force on him. Gavin got to his feet in his turn and started her towards the door with an arm round her shoulders.

"You don't understand about Sigaux?" she said. "Even now?"

"I don't think so, no."

"It's pain for him to be alive, too," she said. "He knows how it is with me. He knows what it means to be rotten all through, and pointless."

"Ilona darling," he said. He was piloting her firmly across the hall and up the stairs. "You're going to try to stop thinking like that, aren't you? That's part of the new order of things —you've got to realize that. You're going to try not to drink any more, and you're going to try not to think up excuses for drinking. That's all that stuff is when you take a good look at it. You're going to try both things, aren't you?"

She saw the stairs rising in front of her and went up them step by step as Gavin gently guided her. He moves me as if I were a puppet, she thought, he's even thinking nice, reasonable thoughts for me.

"You don't listen to what I say, Gavin, do you?"

"Not when you start on that Russian stuff about how despicable and vile you are." He smiled. "I know you're not." He steered her into her bedroom, the large airy room, now all pink and white, in which he had not set foot for more than ten years. When he had last seen it it had been blue and white and as neat as it was cool to look at. Now it was pink and warm, and fantastically untidy into the bargain. The closet doors all stood open on the carelessly hung rows of dresses inside them, shoes were scattered at random about the floor where they had been kicked off, and every piece of furniture was covered with a mound of carelessly discarded clothing. A brassiere trailed down one side of the prie dieu, its pendant two thirds emerging from beneath a crumpled silk

386

shirt and a couple of soiled petticoats. Odd stockings were all over the place in cobweb-like skeins. A large cage full of finches was on a table in front of one of the tall windows looking out over the roof of the south porch to the lake, gleaming beyond the tops of the orderly ranks of orange trees in the grove. From where he was standing, Gavin could just see the tops of the big green and white striped tents down by the water's edge, through the cage and the window behind it. The birds cheeped with excitement when they saw Ilona and fluttered with sharp darting movements from perch to perch. She went over to the table and gave them fresh grain from a half-empty paper bag which shared the seat of a chair with a pale blue girdle and an old copy of Vogue. The tiny birds crowded up to Ilona's hands taking grains from her skin with their scarlet bills. She brushed them away and shut the little slide door through which she had passed them their handful of seeds.

"They're pretty little things, aren't they?" she said absentmindedly. "What are we going to do about Mary loving Sigaux. Do you have any thought?"

"No." Gavin was surprised by her tone of detached curiosity, "What did you mean when you said he was rotten all through, just now."

"I don't really know." She took off her bracelets and put them down on the dressing table beside a roughly opened box of Kleenex and a small radio. "It's a feeling he gives me." She took the clips off her ears and put them down with two sharp clicks of the metal on the powder-filmed table top. "So many of those people he talks about, the ones he knew in Europe, are degenerates that I have an impression that he knows a lot more about that sort of thing"—she crossed the room and vanished through the bathroom door—"than he says. But I could be wrong," she said as she vanished. Alone, Gavin walked up to the cage and looked at the birds. "When did you get these—the finches," he called, his voice starting a fluster of panic which sent the small creatures whirling from perch to perch and end to end of the cage, shrilling in alarm.

"They were Bogey's," Ilona said, "it was some craze of hers,

387

and then she got bored with them. They bore me to death too, in a sweet way." She was tying the cord of her silk wrapper from Hong Kong as she came out of the bathroom again. "Are you really putting me to bed, as if I was a naughty little girl?"

"Yes. I wanted to take you down to Tarpon Springs for dinner. But you were too drunk to leave when we should have gone. Now I'm going to have supper with you up here, because I can't trust you not to upset the children by getting drunk again when all their friends are here."

"Miss Ilona is to have supper in her room. Be-cause she has been nau-ghty. Gosh, Gavin. I mean, gosh, that's all." She began dipping into various handbags until she found a packet of cigarettes, and then had another hunt among the book matches in the pockets of the bags for one that had some matches left in it. She lit a cigarette, and blew smoke out of her mouth. "Are you going to undertake my moral redemption? I don't think of you as a Dimitri somehow—not even a Yul Brynner Karamazov. I don't understand that sort of thing though. When you have girls like that Patti Elliot, do you try to make them good, too? Or is it just me you worry about, morally I mean." She walked past him and sat down on one of the window seats, leaning against the window frame. She began combing her hair, but desisted after a few long, slow, strokes. "We'll just be able to hear the band from up here," she said. "That will make it a romantic evening."

"Aren't you going to try?" he said.

"I don't think so. I need it now, Gavin."

"I won't ask you to try for my sake. I'll ask for the children's sakes."

She opened her mouth as if she were about to reply instantly but then shut it again sharply. She put her tongue between her teeth, and looked down at the comb held in the hand lying in her lap. She let go her tongue and he heard her draw in a long breath and then sigh. She stared out of the window slapping the comb against her thigh.

388

"Dirty pool, old boy, dirty pool. You can cut blackmail right out. And I mean that, right out," she said.

"It's something to think about. I think they've all got used to seeing you pretty squiffy, but now Mary's seen you really stinking drunk. I don't know if Thomas has or not. Bogey doesn't miss much."

"Shut up, I tell you, shut up." She threw the comb at him, and then came at him screaming. He held her off.

"I'm not going to hit you again, if that's what you want," he said, holding her by the wrists and making an effort to speak calmly.

"Please try to control yourselves." Mary was in the open doorway. "Ginny is just across the hall, and the others are going to be here any minute." They turned and saw her standing with one hand still on the door knob. Her eyes were ringed with dark pencil, but she had no lipstick on, and her face was powdered with very white powder. The dark-red dress she was wearing was plain and severe.

"That dress is far too old for you, dear," Ilona said.

"Oh, mother, for heaven's sake. I came to tell you you were making a disgusting noise. Anyone can hear you anywhere in the house."

"I'm sorry, dear, your father can be rather exasperating at times. Forgive me. And, of course, that dress is perfectly beautiful really. It's just that it makes you look like a lovely woman, and I've got this silly idea you're still a child. But then I'm a mother, any normal person could see that you look just wonderful. I've been very nervous, and stupid, all day. Try to make allowances for—well, you know what the difficulties of life are."

"Please don't have any more scenes or rows tonight. It'll spoil everything." Mary stood for another instant looking at them and then pulled the door shut on a silence.

"We can't go on like this much longer, can we?" Ilona said.

"You said something just then—you said any normal person could see she looked wonderful."

389

"Yes." Ilona seemed surprised. "Why . . . oh, my God, of course."

"He told her he couldn't lay her or marry her because he was queer. And she thought he was telling her she was physically repulsive. What a damned mess! And how do we straighten it out?"

"Gavin, I can't take any more. I've got to have a drink . . . please."

"One of us has got to think of a way of telling her that she's had the rotten bad luck to fall in love with a homosexual. And we've got to do it first, before she goes out trying to collect convincing evidence that she isn't repulsive to the entire male sex."

"These things cure themselves. You feel terrible for a while —and then you wonder what it was all about. She'll come through it on her own. Everybody does." Ilona went over to the bed and sat down. "Almost everybody does."

Gavin looked at her. Inside his head he heard the sound of engines, and for a split second saw the English coast stretching away northwards in the gleaming razor-sharp light of five o'clock on a summer morning. The Wash was immediately below him. Further up the coast he could see the estuary of the Humber beside which a grounded ship or a crashed aircraft was on fire, throwing up a huge tower of black smoke. Two groups of eighty-one aircraft had made their rendezvous at the right place, time, and altitude, and the whole two-level defensive box was wheeling out into the North Sea on its way to Hamburg. Just beside him *Peggy Ann* emitted a long stream of black smoke from number-three engine exhaust, and a few seconds later feathered a propeller. "He's done it, the yellow son of a bitch," Gavin said, in his inward dream and felt his stomach knotting with envy, hatred, and fear. Harry Travis was taking *Peggy Ann* back to base with engine trouble. The other aircraft dropped back, down, and away from *Plain Jane* and the formation. "Just look at that," said the voice of Enright from the waist gun position over the intercom. "I'll be a monkey's fugging uncle if Travis ain't going home all on his

390

own." "I hope they give him a real nice breakfast," Thurston said. "I wouldn't eat that stuff for breakfast, not what he'll get to eat," Weiss said. "They give it to you in a bucket when you do a thing like that." "That's enough chatter for now," Gavin said. In the bar of the Old Bear Inn at Padgham Market that night, a friendly Royal Air Force Wing Commander leaned across Colonel Littlefield to Gavin and said, "I say, old boy, you know a fellow called Travis, don't you? He was asking me where he could get a bit of trout fishing in these parts the other day and I . . ." "Save it, Wingco," Colonel Littlefield said. "We won't be seeing young Travis any more. He came down with a distressing ailment this morning and he's been whisked away, no man knows whither." "Oh, I say, nothing really unpleasant, I hope," said the R.A.F. man. "Pretty bad, Wingco, old boy, it's a complaint called cowardice," said Colonel Littlefield. "Oh, I'm sorry to hear that. He seemed a very decent sort of chap. I took quite a liking to him," the R.A.F. man said. "Too bad."

Gavin left Ilona sitting on the bed and walked over to Mary's room. Her door was not quite shut and as he came up to it to knock he heard his daughter's voice lifted passionately. ". . . simply can't stand it any more. I've got to get right away." Silence followed his four taps.

"Can I come in?" he said. "It's me."

"Oh, all right."

He went in and found the two girls standing together, united in outrage, by the white marble fireplace on the far wall of the room.

"That's a very pretty dress, Ginny. Do you mind if I have a word with Mary alone for a minute?"

"Oh." Ginny looked doubtfully at her friend. "Yes, sure. I'll wait for you downstairs, Mary."

"Please don't try to apologize or explain, father. I quite understand about mother drinking, and your not getting on."

"I don't think you do, Mary, but I don't want to go over that with you now. There's something else I have to tell you that isn't very pleasant to talk about. I feel I'm butting into

391

your affairs when I do it, which doesn't make things any easier for me. I don't think you quite understand what happened to you last night."

"I think I do. I'd much rather not discuss it, please, father. I propositioned a man and got turned down. It's pretty simple really."

"Well, yes. But I don't think you realize what Sigaux was trying to tell you about himself. You aren't physically repulsive to him because there's anything unattractive to him about you in particular. It's women in general he can't bring himself to have anything to do with. There are men like that. They can't love women, any women at all. They only love other men. You must have heard of fairies, or homosexuals. He's one of them. That's what he told you last night. That's why he can't bear to touch you. There's nothing wrong with you as a woman. It's something wrong with him as a man. I'm sorry to tell you anything as ugly as this about anyone you care for, but I thought you ought to know."

"You aren't just making this up, to try to make me feel better?" Mary said. "Promise me it isn't that."

"I almost wish it was," Gavin said. "I should have warned you. But I didn't realize you'd turned into a woman. I thought you were just a girl with a pash on her mother's romantic friend."

"You aren't telling me all this because you're jealous of him," she said quickly.

"No."

"I can see you aren't." She sighed deeply. "Am I the biggest fool there ever was?"

"No, you aren't. We're all fools at times."

Three cars drove up and there was a stir below as a dozen young men and women came into the house. Ginny was heard to call Mary, and other voices were heard, calling for Thomas.

"I ought to go, father," she squeezed one of his hands and pressed a kiss on his cheek. "I'm sorry I was beastly just now. It upset me to have Ginny hear you and mother quarreling, that's all. I wish I knew where Thomas was."

"I'm here," he said from the doorway. He looked solid, solemn and a little pale, but handsome in his white dinner jacket. "I came in a while back, but I didn't feel very social so I just slipped into my room and had a shower and a bit of a snooze. You look just great, Mary. That pale mouth is really far out."

More cars arrived and the cries for Mary and Thomas were renewed. Thomas took Mary's arm and marched her formally towards the head of the stairs. A burst of clapping and some ironic cheering greeted their appearance. "Wow, Mary," Torrey Warner called, "you look luscious," and girls' voices were heard saluting the dress as gorgeous and terrific. "How was beastly Mr. McCann?" Mary whispered, when they were halfway down the stairs. "Pure hell," said Thomas flashing a smile and waving to the company below, "but he didn't scare me." Somebody began to sing "Happy Birthday" and within a few seconds it was being sung first ironically and then with enthusiasm by some twenty voices. Gavin leaned over the ballasters of the upper landing, watching the mock heroic descent. His eyes traveled from his son's face to his daughter's and back again, within a few years now they would be married people with children of their own. When they were a few steps from the foot of the stairs they both looked up, and as Thomas smiled Mary blew her father a kiss. He lifted a hand from the smooth polished wood of the ballaster rail in acknowledgment of their salute, and smiled too; he knew that they would never suffer from Travis' or Ilona's distressing ailment. He was surprised that it had taken him so long to recognize it for what it was. He was dealing quite simply with cowardice. For a long instant in which Thomas and Mary were absorbed into the cheerful crowd below, Gavin thought he had discovered something tremendous which would change everything, but as he began to walk purposefully towards Ilona's room, his find evaporated into thin air. What difference did it make to him after all, to know that Ilona was a coward. To stop her being one was neither more nor less difficult than stopping her drinking. When he reached the door of her room the handle moved

393

but the door itself stayed shut. She had locked herself in. Gavin shrugged his shoulders and went on down to the kitchen where Julia gave him a plate of cold chicken, a slice of pie, and a can of beer.

"If I'd know you was eating to home, I'd have got you a proper dinner," Julia said. "But Miss Wilbraham she said you was going off out of the children's way."

"I know you would Julia, but this is just fine."

"And about Mizz Hatfield eating. Shouldn't I take her up a little something?"

"She's all right. She'll come and get something later, when she's hungry."

"She ought to eat regular, Mr. Hatfield, she's begun pining away. I had an uncle, Simon Carter, he claimed he was born a slave, and he claimed he was at a big battle at Nashville in the war. He never ate nothing solid at all for fifteen years. He'd just sup on moonshine whiskey and a couple of quarts of milk a day. He withered away till he was like a parchment bag with a few bones inside it. He'd sit there on Aunt Hollis Carter's porch with an old blue navy overcoat on and his hat jammed down over his eyes to keep the light off 'em, and I'd tell him you going to die if you don't stop drinking and start eating, but he wouldn't pay no heed. Aunt Hollis would come and tell me to leave the poor old man alone, she'd say, he got to be a hundred and four or five or whatever playing the fool in his own sweet way and you ain't going to teach him nothing now. She married him out of kindness when she was sixteen and he was seventy-two. He was supposed to be a wore-out old thing then, and she was just nursing him. It's an arrangement a young girl ain't too foolish to make when there's a little bit of property and she ain't got no expectation. She'll do her nursing two or three years or more and then she'll be able to marry after her mind. Uncle Simon sure fooled her though, and she set him out on the porch mornings and took him in again at night for thirty-three years. What he liked best of all, all the time I knowed him, was a young thing like a puppy or a kitten that couldn't hardly mew, he could take it in his hand and be happy by the hour, just stroking it with his finger tips, or he liked to have young hatching chicks or ducks where he could watch them and tease them a little now and again with a piece of straw or grass stem. Some said he wasn't no more than ninety or ninety-five, but Aunt Hollis said others—her mother's family—reckoned he must have been more'n a hundred and ten. He was the oldest-looking thing I ever hope to see, however old he was. You eat another piece of that pie, Mr. Hatfield, it's as good a pie as I ever made."

"It really is a pretty wonderful pie, Julia, I think I will."

It was very pleasant and restful, eating in the kitchen, and listening to Julia running on. Gavin was glad he was not at the Chippendale table in the dining room with the big panels of Chinese papers on the walls around him, eating off the English china. "Didn't Aunt Hollis miss having children, and all that sort of thing?" he asked idly.

"No, sir, she always said a husband that didn't want to mess a woman around all the time was a treasure without price for a woman like her. She'd been broke in, but she didn't ever take to that part of a woman's life, and didn't miss nothing. She said for a woman like her to marry a normal sort of man would be a sin and a shame, misery for 'em both. Here now, I jest made this coffee fresh before you came in."

"Your aunt was a very sensible woman, Julia."

"She was, so. It ain't a bit of good for men and women to go wasting their lives away battling against their natures, that's what she said." Julia handed him a blue and white sugar jar, looking him innocently in the eye.

"Is Bailey down by the lake?" Gavin asked, putting two spoonsful of sugar into his cup.

"Old fool. He says he's got to see the caterer's men do things right, but he ain't no more than getting in the way down there if the truth ever gets to the light of day. But I couldn't begrudge him the pleasure of seeing all them young people dancing around and having fun if he'd come straight out and say it was that he went to see instead of puffing himself up for mister fixit."

395

"You want to sneak down yourself pretty soon if you aren't going to miss the fireworks."

"Oh, I'll stand on the back porch and watch 'em off behind the trees. I'm frightened to get down close to those things, flashing and banging like guns and murder. Didn't you have enough of that in that war you was in?"

"Oh, I had my share. But I think I'll go on down to see the show. I like rockets." He got up. "I ought to have supper with you more often, you make the place seem like home, you really do, Julia."

"A kitchen's the heart of the house they do say," said Julia. "Don't do for a family to get too far from the stove. No it don't."

"Well, good night, Julia, and thanks for the pie."

"Thank you sir, Mr. Hatfield," she said. Adding in a lower tone when he was through the door, "You is sure enough welcome to eat your own food in your own kitchen, any time. Of course, Miss Wilbraham, she wouldn't allow you to eat no piece of pie like that in the front part of the house because that ain't proper and fitting country-gentleman food. And, of course you couldn't tell your housekeeper, nor your own lawful wedded wife what you wants because one learned in school that ain't what you ought to want, and the other she wouldn't give you a thing just because she knowed it was what you wanted. Well, you go on off down to see a lot of your good money turned into little bits of sparks to amuse a parcel of kids old enough to know better, and I wishes you a very good time." She pulled a few scraps off the carcase of the chicken with her fingers and ate them thoughtfully, listening to the faint faraway music from the party. "Many are called and few are chosen, yes sir," she said, "few is right, few is surely right."

Gavin passed down through the empty grove, among the crisscrossed shadows cast by the lanterns hung in the trees. Down by the lake the tents themselves seemed like two big lanterns, filled with soft, warm light. Gavin circled them and came out in the dark belt of trees beside the water, where a number of his field hands and their wives, one or two with children, stood silently watching the dancers and waiting for the fireworks. A waltz came to an end in a scatter of hand clapping and the lights in the tents began to grow dim. A hush fell, followed by a general aaah! of expectation satisfied, as the first fan of rockets rushed up the sky. They burst with a shattering series of reports to become a rain of silver and gold stars floating slowly towards the ground. Flight after flight of rockets filled the air until there was silence and darkness for a long minute. The air was filled with the scent of gunpowder, and fragments of inconsequential remarks. The lights went on again. The bandsmen went back to their places and the music started up once more, drawing first one couple and then another and another onto the circular floor, surrounding the stem of the huge cypress whose branches were hung with paper lanterns. At last it was covered with a swirling mass of dancers, circling and turning, smiling and laughing, in a blaze of youth, health, and color, which seemed to flow round the tree like a stream. Gavin would see Mary with her shoulders rising so whitely from her dark-red dress now as the single hard accent of color in a group of white tulle, now as one of a group of strong colors acting as foils to a single softly voluminous white dress. The young people danced inexhaustibly with an effortless grace, light as feathers, round and round. Gavin watched for ten minutes and then for another ten, and at last managed to tear himself away when the band took a break. When he got back to the house he saw that Ilona's windows were dark. He supposed that she had fallen asleep, and feeling curiously relieved and happy, he went to his room, took a shower, and after reading a few pages of Galbraith, turned out his light. He lay awake for a while listening to the faint music of the band, and then to the noises of the party breaking up, the farewells, and the departures. He thought proudly of Thomas, upright, cheerful, and master of the occasion, and of Mary's courage. They were all right, they were really good people, however you took them. He wished that he had had Ilona on his arm as he walked down through the grove, and that they could have watched the dancing together.

397

She denied herself so much, so many of the small things that added up to happiness even in the middle of crises and dramas, and in the end outweighed them. Looking back over the long day he tried to think what he would remember from its confused tangle of impressions; he knew it would not be any of the big things, it would be the longing to be grown-up written on Bogey's dear face as she begged for her ridiculous garment, the happiness of sitting on the wooden seat of a kitchen chair eating pie while Julia rambled on, the dancers flowing round the tree, or just the gold and silver stars with their trails of ashy smoke drifting slowly down the dark sky towards the inky blackness of the lake.

Chapter Eight

"I'M bored with France," Ilona said, "bored to tears." She leaned forward in her seat and rubbed her half-smoked cigarette into the ashtray among the glasses, knives and forks, plates, butter dishes, and what-not on the restaurant table in front of her. As soon as she had blurred it out she was worrying through her handbag for her lighter and cigarette case, and within seconds she had another going. She blew out a jet of smoke, looked through it at the plate of oysters in front of her, and then turned to Sigaux, who was sitting at right angles to her on the next side of the square table.

"I said I was bored, Silky," she said.

"Bored?" He said it with a rising inflection of interrogation, and then added in a mutter, as if to himself, "Oh, that's natural enough, it is boring here." He looked at her thin, nervous hands restlessly fiddling with her cigarette, and with the fragments of a crumbled roll. It was over a year since she had come bursting into his house in the middle of the night to tell him that she had left Gavin, and he was beginning to get used to the role of companion and courier which she had forced on him. It was, he thought, when she wasn't in one of her jumpy moods, not at all a bad role, and he was even getting the feel of her jumpy moods. He spooned up a mouthful of the orange meat of his *melon au Porto* and ate it with enjoyment. A squall coming off the sea set the branches of the tamarisks in the garden flogging, the red-checked gingham cloths of the tables on the terrace began to flap briskly, a big orange parasol fell over, taking an iron table with it, and a flower vase inside one of the big plate-glass windows fell into a plate of *sole Normande,* washing a mixture of sauce and water into the lap of a woman from Bordeaux. She screamed.

"Oh God, how I loathe the French," Ilona said. "Just look at the drama they're getting out of this." She gestured with her cigarette at the head waiter and his assistant who were mopping at the defiled thighs of the heavily built but still attractive Bordèlaise with lamentations appropriate to a real tragedy. Behind them other waiters, with ballet-like exaggerations of the necessary movements, shut the windows opening onto the sea, while outside a swarm of white-coated bus boys darted about folding up the big sunshades and whipping the cloths off the green-painted tables. Beyond them Ilona saw that the metallic-blue water of the bay was becoming covered with white horses. She could see, out by the headland, agitated figures fighting to get the sails off a wildly pitching yawl.

"The weather is ghastly, and there's nobody here," she said, rounding on Silky. "Why don't we give North Africa a try?"

"I don't think it's for you," he said, "honestly I don't. I loathe Moslems, personally, and I think North Africa's remorselessly squalid in a dismally provincial way. Hell, if we want Asiatic misery we might as well have the splendors with it. That's my feeling, anyway." He ate another mouthful of melon, sizing up her reaction to the word "Asiatic." A gleam of interest appeared in her face, and he pushed on, swallowing quickly. "To tell the truth, I'm bored with these Mediterranean countries altogether. I've had them for the time being. I'd like to go somewhere quite new."

"I don't want to go to Russia," Ilona said flatly.

"What put that horrid idea into your pretty head, my dear?" Silky said. "I can't imagine anything more dreary or obvious. I wish you'd eat those oysters instead of just sprinkling them with cigarette ash. They look awfully good to me, but they'll be a dog's dinner before long."

"Oh, all right." Ilona took off her dark glasses and began to eat. Silky watched her thoughtfully. She had been behaving along the lines of a predictable pattern since she had stopped drinking. Long periods of tranquil contentment would come

400

to an end in a matter of minutes. They would give way to states of mounting nervous tension which would build to an explosive climax at the end of a few days when something pent up in her would be released by a complete change of plans and flight to a new place. Silky recognized the beginning of a new cycle and decided to see what would happen if he forestalled its development and cut through to the end of the jumpy phase.

"Why don't we get out of here and go to India?" he said.

"As long as I don't have to go to see the Taj Mahal," she said. She lifted her head, and Silky saw that a glow of interest had already replaced her sullenly empty expression.

"It would be great. We could go with Betty and Tuggy Amroth. They asked us to join up with them. We could catch up with them in Istanbul. Why don't we do that?"

"Why not? We could do all those countries."

"I think it would be terrific. Nelson Osmington said Siam was really out of this world. Let's do it. And it'll be fun going with Betty and Tuggy, too; they really are darlings."

"I liked Betty," Ilona said, looking at Silky. "I wouldn't be so sure about Tuggy."

"That's just your suppressed lesbian streak, Ilona dear," Silky said. "Still, even if Tuggy isn't nice exactly, you've got to hand it to him that he is always fun."

"Oh, yes." Ilona touched the handle of a knife. "Do you really think Betty's a lesbian?"

"That's too obvious. Betty's a man really, at any rate, psychologically. That's why that first marriage of hers was so grotesque, and it's why she gets along so well with Tuggy."

"I suppose that makes sense." Ilona looked doubtful for the barest part of an instant. "Let's get this started, Silky. Let's drive to Nice tomorrow. We can fly on from there and pick up all the visas we need in Rome. It would be boring going up to Paris. It would be more like getting started if we went to Rome. It's in the right direction."

"All right," Silky said, "we'll make an early start tomorrow."

401

He was elated. There was not going to be any jumpy period this time.

So three days later, the car was in dead storage in Nice, and they were in Rome. It was raining there. Pools of water gathered on the worn stone pavements, and the Roman and Renaissance cornices dripped incessantly. "This is awful, I can't bear this," Ilona said, "Rome's the smallest town in the world in bad weather." They hired a car and drove to Venice to look at Palladio's villas, and moved on after three days when the bad weather caught up with them. Then they were in Athens, hating it because the food was terrible and all the buildings that sounded so wonderful were ruined, and often hard to recognize as buildings. So they moved on sooner than they had intended, and joined forces with Betty and Tuggy at the Hilton hotel in Istanbul. When they went into Betty's suite there were four people there; Betty herself, in blue velvet slacks and a Persian coat; Tuggy looking like an actor playing the part of a country gentleman in the sort of sports clothes that come from a department store; a tall ginger-haired Englishman with a salesman's smile, called Ulick; and a woman who didn't look like anyone's wife, called Fergus, who was married to him.

"I want you to meet the Farquhars," Betty said. "They're terrific and I know you're just going to love each other."

Ilona was disconcerted by Fergus' drawl and by Ulick's military English accent. She had difficulty understanding them, and she was thrown off balance by the way Fergus, who was Irish and had been in English movies, looked her over. Few men had ever examined her with so frank an interest in her physique, and she was surprised to find herself playing up to it.

"Ulick has this marvelous car, like a tank," Betty said.

"It's a perfectly bang-on Land-Rover," Ulick said, "nothing in the least special about it."

"It's divine," Tuggy said, "in a Walter Mitty sort of way."

"Actually it will get us there if anything will," Ulick said, squaring his jaw. "You can count on that."

"Where are you going, Mr. Farquhar?" Ilona asked.

"We're all going, darling," Betty said. "I'm getting a Land-Rover, too. I just fell in love with Ulick's, I had to have one once I'd seen it. And we're all going into the mountains to bag this marvelous kind of wild ram . . ."

"Biggest horns you've ever seen, Mrs. Hatfield," Ulick said, smiling his smile and making a spiral motion with his hands in the neighborhood of his ears. "Terrific chaps."

"You will come, Ilona, won't you?" Fergus said leaning forward with a sudden passionate intensity. "It'll be fun, I promise you."

"Of course, they're coming," Betty cried. "It's on our way, darlings, we'll go on through the mountains into Persia, and then to India. It'll be much more exciting than just flying there, like everyone else."

"Do come," Fergus said, "I want you to come. I mean it."

So they all spent three weeks together night-clubbing in Istanbul while the second Land-Rover came from Italy and was cleared through the customs. Every morning Ilona spent a long time staring out of her window, across the Bosporus, with its coming and going of ships and boats, to the further shore and the hills beyond. Asia began over there, and she wondered what would happen to her when she went into it. She wondered if something quite different would begin. She was eager for something new. During the day she went sightseeing with Silky and the others, and the sense of the town's age, which had at first been exciting, slowly become oppressive and terrible. She had sometimes envied countries with long histories, but here she felt history as a burden. The past seemed to sit on the chests of the living in Istanbul, mocking them with the knowledge that whatever they did would crumble away and become pointless in the end. When the second car came at last, she was more than ready to get away and to leave the dead emperors and dead sultans behind her. She was, too, half-excited and half-frightened by the ambiguous relationship which was slowly developing between her and Fergus. She felt that the other woman was playing with her, and establishing a kind of domination over her that she couldn't quite understand. She didn't know what Fergus intended and she wanted to find out. She learned, when the party reached the uplands over on the Russian frontier where the rams were supposed to live. They spent five weeks searching for them in bad weather in a countryside more desolate and sad than any place which Ilona had ever imagined as existing. The mountain villages were miserably poor, and the landscape seemed to have been abandoned in a raw, unfinished state, so that the hills looked more like dumps waiting treatment and disposal than like the work of nature. At times there seemed to be nothing in the world but misery, the roar of mountain torrents, and the endless bluster of the wind. When Ilona had been seduced by Fergus, she discovered that Fergus was having an affair with Betty. She then found that there was an understanding that women who had affairs with Fergus always had to comfort Ulick. He was always miserable until he had caught up with his wife in this way.

"Do let the poor lamb have his kicks, Ilona darling," Fergus said. "After all, who cares what a man does to you?"

"Did you do this just to corrupt me?" Ilona said.

"Steady on, darling," Fergus said. "You've got some terrible ideas, if you ask me. I'm not asking you to be cruel or dishonest or anything. I'm just asking you to keep a poor drip of a man cheerful. I wouldn't dream of asking you to do it if he didn't like you, after all, there are limits."

"Do I have to?"

"Well, not tonight, if you don't want to, darling. But it would help."

Silky and Tuggy were having an affair, too, and it made them very giggly and silly. They invented new practical jokes designed to make Ulick look foolish every day, and they had a competition between them to see which would have the most success with the boys from the villages. Their behavior had been annoying Ulick for some days, and at supper, the night after Ilona had refused to sleep with him, a lightly meant remark of Tuggy's made him burst into tears and leave the tent.

"Oh, my God, when men turn on the water works what can you do?" Betty said.

"Go and be nice to the poor slob," Fergus said.

Ilona got to her feet slowly, and after looking at the four faces round the table went out to find Ulick. After they had made love, he cried and told Ilona how awful it was being married to Fergus because her behavior made it impossible for people to respect him. When he had gone, Fergus came in through the tent flaps.

"No, Fergie, please," Ilona said. "I don't think I can stand it."

Fergus chuckled; there was not much chance of stopping her when she wanted something. She was a strong-minded girl. All the lovemaking took place on canvas cots under the billowing and straining pitched roofs of the tents. Inside, under the wind-proofed canvas it was always stuffy no matter how strongly the wind outside was blowing, and the enclosed air smelt of chemically treated light alpine clothing, damp wool, and rain-soaked earth.

In the mornings Ilona would try to get Silky off by himself to say: "I'm going out of my mind. I can't face another night with Fergus and Ulick; we've got to leave." But he was not sympathetic and answered her impatiently.

"Oh, be grown up, darling Ilona, it's all in fun."

The mornings were often lovely, with thin sunlight breaking through rags of scudding clouds to light up the awesome nakedness of the huge bone-bare mountains all around them, and the swift streams boiling among the rocks in the valleys below. Ilona finally killed two rams with the first two shots, and the only two shots, fired by the party. An endless gentle slope of stone scree ran up into the clouds which drove along in cottony masses just below the edge of the snow line. Ilona and one guide, separated from the main party, were just about to turn back to camp when a break in the cloud pack suddenly gave them a glimpse of two thousand feet of snow-field, golden in the afternoon sun, a skyline, and a patch of dazzlingly blue sky above it. Ilona, soaked through and through, looked at the sunlit patch thankfully and patted the wet neck of her pony. Some day, she thought, I'm going to be dry and warm and comfortable again. The guide excitedly edged his mount up alongside hers and pointed. Less than three hundred yards away they could see two rams floundering like rocking horses across a four- or five-acre patch of rotten snow below the main field. They urged the ponies upwards over the sliding shale, and where the snow began Ilona dismounted to pull her heavy rifle out of the bucket holster beside her saddle. The rams were yellow against the white background. Their wool was almost exactly the color of an old man's tobacco-stained moustache, and their seesawing as they fought their way through the soft, rain-sodden snow was pitifully slow. Ilona fired twice, feeling that she heard the thump of the heavy bullets going home each time, even through the doom-laden resonance of the shots echoing from mountain to mountain all around them. The clouds closed in again a minute later, and they brought the two dead animals back to camp in driving sleet. Their huge spiraled horns and their grave faces with heavy-lidded eyes gave them the look of two wise, dignified, dirty priests. Every time she caught sight of them, Ilona felt sorry she had fired. But it was too late then. They were slung across the backs of the ponies and their heads were nodding as they were jolted about. The sleet clung to their wool, and the heat of their cooling bodies was not quite enough to melt it. The return seemed interminable.

In the evening Ulick made a terrible scene. It appeared that Ilona had done altogether the wrong thing in shooting the rams. It was just like her, as an American woman, to shoot out of turn. As leader of the expedition, he should have had first shot; she had no right to shoot until he had done so. In the circumstances he felt there was no use in going on, he was going to break up the camp in the morning and call the whole thing off. It was a bitter disappointment, but there it was. Oddly, Fergus backed him up. She came to Ilona's tent that night saying that she couldn't leave without one last bash, but she complained bitterly afterwards that she did think it was too awful of her to have spoiled poor Ulick's party. "You really should have known better, gorgeous, but I suppose you Americans don't have etiquette about that kind of thing. But I do think you might have thought."

So they split up in the morning. Fergus and Ulick went back to Istanbul, and after a little discussion Ilona, Silky, and the Amroths went on into Iran. To the bewilderment of the Turks, the two rams were abandoned. Nobody wanted to be bothered with either the hides or the heads.

Silky and Tuggy quarreled in Teheran and the Amroths flew on to India. The day they left, Ilona met the American Ambassador in Iran who turned out to be Jock Lambton, the second husband of Stewart Murray's oldest daughter, Harriet. "So I'm as good as your cousin, Mrs. Hatfield," he said, smiling with a beautiful show of even teeth in his wonderfully youthful pink face. "You must come along and have dinner with us. I know Harriet will be delighted, just delighted, to have a chance to talk about Barnton and the old days. Now do promise me you will."

Jock's nephew, Steven deWitt Lambton, III, was at the Embassy when Ilona and Silky went there a few nights later. He seemed to take to Silky right away, and by a coincidence he happened to be looking for someone to go with him to Kabul by way of Meshed and Herat.

"Oh, all right, if we don't have to shoot anything, but I am, honestly, sick to death of mountains," Ilona said.

But she was actually rather excited by the idea of going to Afghanistan. Silky had taught her not to be boringly enthusiastic about things, and to suppress what he called "the all-American girl" in her makeup.

"Do you really want to go with them?" Harriet said, when they had a moment alone together in the Embassy library. "I mean Steven is sweet in a retarded sort of way, but he's awfully like a lost dog when you get right down to it."

"What does he do?"

"He's in the Foreign Service, but he's not doing very well. It's things like this. He ought to fly to Kabul to get back to his

407

job there, but he's dreamed up this Meshed-to-Herat idea and now nothing will stop him until he's done it. Every now and then someone gets fed up and sends him home, but so far Jock has had enough influence with the Secretary to get him sent somewhere else before long. I've told him he's heading for Rangoon or Addis, but he won't listen—and actually I don't think he cares. But I just thought I'd warn you that he's not very responsible."

"Well, I'm not very keen on responsible people just now. Gavin was terribly responsible."

"I'm sorry that didn't work out."

"So am I. But I was just making everyone, including myself, miserable by staying on, and I believe they're all much happier now. I know I am."

"Still it must have been hard to just pick up and go."

"It would have been much harder to stay."

"I suppose so. Is there going to be a divorce?"

"I don't think so. Unless Gavin wants to marry again. He doesn't seem to want one now."

"You don't feel rather defenseless—the idea of being just on the loose with nothing settled would rather frighten me."

"I don't know what there is to be frightened of. I suddenly woke up—the night I ran away from Gavin—it's a silly story —there was a party for the children, Thomas' birthday, it was, and I'd dropped off to sleep. And then the fireworks woke me —they were letting off rockets down by the lake—and the room was dark—all I could see was these silver and gold stars floating down the sky and winking out one by one as they fell. I suddenly knew I had to go. That the worst thing couldn't be worse than what I was doing. So I cleared out. You frighten yourself—there isn't anything to be frightened of, not really."

"I wish I had your philosophy. You always were a gutty little thing, though, when you were a child."

"You can't mean that."

"Goodness, yes. I remember how you used to take the most enormous show jumps on that huge horse of yours. It would have scared me to death even to get up on its back."

"It's funny, isn't it. I turned out to be the world's worst coward."

"You can say it, but I'll never believe it."

So they crossed Iran. The irrigated fields were dazzling with the first flush of green shoots, and the yellow-twigged poplars, lightly brushed over with new leaves, lined the water courses like torches, the orchards were smoky with drifts of white and pink blossom. In the north they came upon a region of shallow lakes surrounded by drifts of wild irises covering hundreds of acres. When Ilona cried out in delight and said that she wanted to stay there forever, Steven, who had taken to wearing a huge round Kurdish hat of black sheepskin, said that in a few months the lakes would burn up in the summer heat and that these flowering steppes would turn into dusty wastes of cracked mud and blowing dust. They went on into the mountains, into the air that was like frozen wine after dark, and which vibrated night and day to the humming roar of boulders being rolled down the beds of the rivers by the tumbling rush of snowmelt. Ilona would lie awake for a few minutes before she dropped off to sleep listening to the sound, feeling that what she heard and felt was time itself grinding the universe away. A few days beyond Herat, Steven was silent and unresponsive all through supper, hunched deeply into his thick sheepskin coat. His big Kurdish hat was tipped forward so that his face could hardly be seen. He ate scarcely anything. Ilona thought he had quarreled with Silky, and Silky was afraid that he had somehow offended him. "Did I do something wrong, Steven?" he asked. "I'm not a bit well," Steven said. In the morning Steven's bedding was sodden with sweat, and his greenish-white face was filmed over with the approach of death. He drank tea incessantly all day but couldn't eat anything solid without immediately throwing up with exhausting convulsions. Silky, Ilona, and the interpreter talked endlessly about what they ought to do and agreed that Steven was too sick to stand a night-and-day push to get him over the high pass ahead of them on the road to Kabul. The interpreter thought that they might get to Kabul in three or four days if they drove continuously, but he didn't think they could keep Mistah Lambton alive while they did it. On the third day, Steven took Ilona's hand as she knelt beside him to wipe the sweat off his face, and held it.

"I'm going to die," he said. "I'm going as soon as the sun goes behind that hill and the valley fills with shadow. The cold that comes with the shadow is going to kill me."

"Don't give it up like that, Steven."

"If it was a matter of giving up I would have gone last night. I just wanted one more day. But I can't hold on through another night. Will you write letters to mother and my sister saying nice things about my not having any pain, and thinking about them to the end, and all that?"

"Yes, I will."

"The addresses are all in the little blue leather book." His teeth chattered for a moment. "I'm so cold. My guts have turned into a great big black cold stone, a wet stone." She put her hand into his sleeping bag and felt the still-intense heat of the bottles filled with hot water they had packed in beside him. "I shall float off into the coldness when the shadow comes pouring down the mountain side." He smiled, a mere tightening of his white lips. "Do me a favor and gather me a little bunch of flowers, any you can find that aren't yellow. I hate yellow flowers."

When she brought him his bunch of small alpines, like a doll's posy—pinks, blues, violets, and whites—the sun was sliding down towards the castle-like rock face to the west of their camp. Steven looked quickly up at it, and then back to the bouquet. "Ass that I am, I've dazzled myself, and now I can't see them." He covered his eyes with one white hand and Ilona saw a few tears run down his cheeks. After five minutes had gone by he tried again. "Hold them up one by one," he said. She did so, and he muttered their names as he identified them, hesitating once or twice, and calling back one small blue flower for a revision. A herd of belled sheep was being driven along the track on the far side of the river with much bleating, shouting, barking of dogs, and off-key clanging of beaten copper. One minute the jostling mass of animals was in full sunlight and the next in shadow. Ilona quickly turned her head and saw that the sun was going. The bar of shadow under the steep crag was rolling irresistibly out across the softer grazed space of the alpine meadow on which they had made camp.

"Give me your hand, Ilona."

"Don't be afraid, Steven."

"I'm not afraid."

Some instinct brought Silky to the far side of Steven's sleeping bag to take his other hand. The shadow rushed over them, and in a few seconds the air turned bitter cold. The dying man's grip on their hands tightened, and then relaxed as he fought for breath with a long growl-like groan. The heartrending sound of struggle ended. After a long moment of incredulity, Ilona hesitantly closed the dead man's eyes. She knelt for a while looking at his crew-cut scalp, at the greenish-white marble of the face which had seemed so invincibly healthy a few weeks before in Teheran. They both stood up.

"I'd never seen—that—before," Ilona said in a musing tone.

"Poor Ilona," Silky said, without irony.

"Poor Steven," she said. He watched her face as she stood looking across the shadow-filled valley to the peaks on its far side which towered up through the thin, clear air into the sunlight. It was still broad day up there, and warm. Ilona had the expression of an emigrant who turns on the deck of the ship which is bearing him away for one last backward look at the shoreline of his native country.

"To know so much, and to feel so much, just to come to that," she said. "It doesn't seem fair."

"Do you want more?"

"No, it's funny, but I don't think I do."

The interpreter came towards them, an odd figure in Afghan tribal costume but for neat clocked socks and smart tan oxfords, a knitted pullover pulled on on top of his other clothes and a threadbare British army overcoat.

"If our poor friend Mistah Lambton has shuffled off this moral coil as I suppose, I think we should inter him without further delay."

"You mean mortal coil, Ayub Kahn," Silky said.

"Mortal?" he frowned. "Mortal, mortal. Is that correct?"

"Yes, that's quite correct," Silky said. "It seems so hurried, just to put him away at once."

"The villagers whom I hired to prepare the grave could then fill it in and prepare a cairn before returning to their homes. They would then require a more modest sum than if they were to return to complete these sad offices tomorrow."

"Did you have a grave dug before he was dead?" Ilona said, shocked.

"Madam, Mistah Lambton made a request that I should do so early this morning. It appears that he had a peculiar horror of being pecked at by the fowls of the air, ravens were his particular aversion. He told me that it would be a comfort to him if he were aware that the necessary preparations were in hand."

So when the moon came out that night, Steven was already stretched out under a pyramid of stones not far from the tent in which Ilona sat writing a long letter to Thomas, about the final meaning of life. When she had finished it she read it over to herself, tore it into very small pieces and threw it away. She then sat for a long time looking at the flame in the lantern hanging on the tent pole, occasionally running her fingers through her still-lustrous and beautiful hair. She wondered how long she would have to wait, and if she would be afraid. Towards dawn she lay down on her cot and fell almost instantly asleep.

Mary was surprised to get a letter from her mother posted from Bombay. She sat on her bed and opened it in a rather gingerly fashion as if she expected it to contain something

412

unpleasant, a magic hair that would turn into a serpent and bite her perhaps. The rounded immaturity of her mother's boarding school handwriting upset her, as did the running inconsequence of her style.

Dear pet, such a long time since we left France and feel foolish about not writing at so many places. Was madly disappointed in Athens after Rome and went on to Turkey where the weather was too awful and we were involved with some really rather terrible people who had seemed nice. We went near Mount Ararat and the ark would have come in handy it rained so, but Persia was lovely, flowers and flowers like tapestry, and Jock Lambton at the Embassy was sweet when he found I was his Harriet's cousin. She is a dumpy jolly matronly woman and couldn't have been more motherly and protective which I couldn't get used to because I remember her as a rather dashing fifteen-year-old when I was ten. I dimly remembered her being married to her first husband who was killed in World War I in Sicicly—that's not right—Sicily I mean and very blushing and jeune fille in billowing white veils so as Jock's wife she was a surprise. We had a rather terrible journey through the mountains to Kabul in Afghanistan which was somehow a fierce and killing place, but while we were there we met a delightful Parsee, a director of Tata's whatever that is, who has introduced us to all sorts of people here, and we are off to look for tigers next week with two most beautiful Indian women and a real maharajah who is great fun. It is very hot here but beautiful, and such lovely saris. We think of Christmas in Hong Kong where a lot of our friends seem to be heading. I hear it is V. beautiful. Oh dear I had so much to say which I don't seem to have said but here is Indira to take me off somewhere so I shall just say I am missing you and send you hugs and love, your mother.

Mary put the letter away in the drawer where she kept important documents. After she had closed the drawer she looked at herself in her mirror for a few seconds, reopened the drawer, took the letter out and tore it up. She then de-

413

cided she would go for a long walk, right round the lake, to make herself feel better. She walked down the bamboo-lined drive and turned right where it joined the dirt road that led to the north end of the lake. A short stretch along the road she found an Air Force colonel sitting in a small foreign car. He was looking about him with a puzzled air and as she tried to hurry by he spoke to her.

"I wonder if you could help me, ma'am."

"I don't know. What do you want?"

"Well, I'm looking for a house. I thought it was on this road. I don't really remember it at all, but my mother has told me about it so often I sometimes think I do." He climbed out of the car and produced a photograph from his wallet. "This is the house I'm looking for."

"I've never seen it. It's rather like our house, though."

"That's the big house back there. My mother told me about that. You passed it, and then went down the hill about a quarter of a mile, and then you came to the second house, that was our house."

"Oh!"

"Oh?" The colonel took off his cap and Mary was startled by his good looks. "That sounds bad."

"Well, I've just remembered. There was a big house which burned down, just along here. I'll show you the cellar hole. My brother and I used to hunt snakes there."

"I wish you would do that."

They walked side by side down the soft, sandy road.

"It's nice of you to do this. You see, I was stationed in Spain a year or two ago and while I was there I went off and found the place where my mother's family originated. It was just four farms clustered together round a little bit of a chapel up there in that Basque country. It was rugged but it was pretty good in an off-beat way, and the people there were as nice as they could be. Particularly when I got through to them that we were blood relations. I had a lot of fun up there. I even learned to milk a goat, if you can imagine. Well, when I got back it gave me the idea of looking up the place my father's family came from. I'd heard so much about it from my mother, I didn't think I'd have much trouble finding it." He paused. "You may have heard older people speak of the family, Lascomb was the name. I'm Herbert Wingfield Lascomb."

"I'm Mary Hatfield. I've heard the name, but that's about all." She searched her brains. "Somebody called Lascomb sold us the Grove, and died soon after. Then the family moved out of their house and went North, and a year or so later the house was burned down. I don't know what happened. I've heard people say that children broke in and set it alight by mistake, playing house or something." She turned off the road on a barely perceptible track. "You can see there was a garden here by all these flowering shrubs and creepers." She looked about. "It's all changed so much since we were little, I don't believe I really know where it was any more."

"That magnolia's huge. Almost as big as the ones they have on the campus of the University of Virginia. Did you ever see them?"

"No, I've never been there."

"It's one of the most beautiful places there is. What sort of tree is that?"

"That's an avocado."

"It's a fine tree." Suddenly they both pointed.

"There it is."

"Yes, that's it. That's all there is left, that hollow in the ground and a few baulks of charred timber under the vines. It's a great place for snakes. I suppose it's a sort of sun trap. Thomas and I, he's my brother, used to come here to shoot them with his .22 in the first spring days when they were sort of slow and sleepy. Then all of a sudden it seemed a cruel and pointless thing to do and we stopped. I haven't been here for more years than I like to think about."

"I can't even visualize it as a house." He pulled the photograph out of his wallet again. "But that's how it was, right here." He handed it to her. "That's my father on the porch, standing beside his father's chair."

415

"What a dear little boy he was."

"I would have killed my mother if she'd ever dressed me up like that."

"I think those sailor suits are just darling. It's terribly sad about the house though, it looks so settled and solid and permanent in the photograph. It's hard to think of it just roaring away in flames in a few hours."

"Oh, in my line you get used to that idea. I saw an awful lot burn up in Korea, and we spend a lot of time learning new and sophisticated techniques for burning things up. It seems quite natural to me to find that part of my past has burned." He smiled. "That's quite a thought, isn't it?" He turned his back on the cellar hole and looked about him. "Is that the lake glinting down there among the trees? Mother said I'd be able to see the lake from the porch and all the upper rooms."

"Was she very fond of the house?"

"No, she detested it. She was upset when I said I wanted to come. She said it was an unlucky house and that I'd be a fool to look for it. All I gleaned from her about it I picked up while she was giving me good reasons for not coming. It may have been an unlucky house, but I don't feel it's an unlucky place. Do you?"

"No, I don't."

A silence prevailed between them. She looked at the photograph again.

"Your grandmother was lovely."

"I didn't say she was my grandmother." He took the photograph back from her and looked at it. "I didn't say anything about her."

"The little boy's very like her. And so are you." She smiled. "She must have been your grandmother." He lifted his eyes from the picture and looked curiously at her.

"Don't you see . . . ?" he began on an interrogative note, and then bit off his question. "It doesn't matter, does it?"

"Do you show that photograph to everybody you meet, right away like this?" she asked.

"You're an odd girl to run into by chance on a country

road," he said. "You ask the damnedest questions, Miss Hatfield."

"Well do you? If I knew that I might be able to tell you whether it mattered or not."

"I do as a matter of fact. I can't help it. It's the only photograph of my father I ever saw. My mother may have had some, but if she did she got rid of them. This is a copy of a photograph I found slipped into a book for a bookmark. My father, or perhaps his mother, slipped it in there. It was dry, on brittle paper, so I sent it to one of those places that advertise . . . I keep telling myself I'll junk all the copies, stop carrying a copy, or stop showing it to people, but I don't do that. It's a compulsion I suppose."

"Then it does matter, doesn't it?" Mary pulled a leaf from a vine. "I was starting out for a walk when you spoke to me," she said. "I was going round the lake. Do you have time to do that?"

"Why, yes, I do, as a matter of fact, Miss Hatfield." They both turned towards the road. "May I call you Mary?"

"Oh, all right. But I can't call you Herbert, I loathe that name, and Wingfield's pretty stiff, too. What do people call you?" she said. "People who like you?"

"I don't know that an awful lot of people do," he said.

"That's because you have this chip on your shoulder," she said. "Did it ever occur to you that it might not matter much to anybody but you?"

"When I feel good I can believe that for days and weeks together. But when I feel low it gets me down. All this month I've been feeling like hell about it. The commanding general put me on a committee making a study of the morale problems of an integrated unit in a segregated area. It's a three-man committee. There's me on it, an Italian called Agrigenti, and a wasp called Lynch."

"What's a wasp?" Mary said.

"White Anglo-Saxon Protestant. And his name is Lynch. It doesn't seem credible anybody could do that by accident. And then I wonder what I'm doing on the committee. I wonder if

General Klaempfer has guessed, or been tipped off by some-one. I wonder if I'm supposed to be the colored man on the committee. It's the sort of thing they do to get at you."

"Who are they? The people who gave the medals in Korea and promoted you up to colonel?"

"No." He was silent. Two boys in blue jeans and white shirts with cheap cowboy hats on their heads came down the road in front of them on horseback. The horses were trotting and their footfalls kicked up spurts of soft dust, leaving a haze behind them on the road. The horses were beautifully cared for and the black tack on them was studded with silver stars and moons.

"Hi, Miss Mary," they said as they passed.

"Those are *they*," Lascomb said, when they'd gone. "They'll say, 'We saw Mary walking along the road with a Air Force colonel' now. If they knew what my grandmother was, they'd say, 'We saw Mary with a dinge back there.'"

They turned out of the long tunnel of oaks and their hang-ing gray tails of Spanish moss, onto the white sand road that ran along the water's edge at the north end of the lake.

"You don't want anyone to miss it, do you?"

"How can anyone miss it?"

"I don't think anybody could possibly know, unless you told them. But I didn't mean that. I was thinking that it was funny that you should be so anxious to let people know how much you mind. Was it so awful for you when you first found out?"

"Why do you ask that?"

"I don't know. I suppose people who've been hurt too badly become very self-centered. I suppose they want to inflict their pain on everybody. When I see somebody pushing their agony around, I always wonder what hit them." She paused, and they walked quietly along for some time without speaking. "What else did your mother say when she tried to persuade you not to come looking for this place?"

"Oh, all sorts of things."

"Such as?"

418

"She said my father failed in life because he had no proper pride. She said she hoped I wasn't going to go the same way."

"But you came, looking for a house that wasn't here, just to make yourself miserable, didn't you?"

"You're a funny girl."

"Oh, I'm a very ordinary sort of girl," she said.

"I don't think you are," he said. "No, I don't think so," and he laughed. "I think you're the special girl I've been looking for for a long time."

"Well, don't you rush me," she said, "I'm not in any mood to be rushed. You wait till you've spent some time finding out what's on my mind and then we'll see if you've been looking for me or not."

One day a few months later, when Gavin and Mary were having a late swim, there was a noise of ripping silk and three jet fighters came skimming over the roofs of the sprawling house. They climbed a little over the lake and banked and turned a mile or so beyond it. They came back to swing round the lake in a close turn and then rocketed up and away in an almost vertical climb which took them out of sight into the immensity of the afternoon sky.

"Well I see you have a new young man," Gavin said, as three contrails began to appear. "Tell him not to do too much of that sort of thing. My nerves won't stand it. Is he nice?"

"Oh he's quite nice," she said lazily looking upwards under the shadow of a hand. "He's complicated but he's awfully nice when you get to know him."

"Am I going to get to know him soon?"

"I think you might bring out the worst in him. You'll have to wait until I've built him up a bit."

"I'd like to see him before you actually marry him."

"We'll see." She stood up. "I may just vanish for a week or two and come back married. Then you won't have to worry about a big snazzy stupid wedding."

"Don't do anything like that, please."

419

"Do you want me to have bridesmaids and ushers in tails, the whole works?"

"In an odd way, I do."

"I don't know that I'll be able to stand it. I honestly don't. How would it be if we got a little married first and then had a pretend wedding later? Just to make you happy."

Gavin sat up and considered her. "Are you breaking it to me, by any chance, Miss, that you've been to some sniffling old justice of the peace and had five dollar's worth of law before sneaking off to a motel for a couple of hours of honeymoon? I'll put you over my knee if you have."

"Would you really be very angry?"

"I don't know. If he had two heads or if he was colored I might be upset for an hour or two." He stopped short. She had turned very white. "Am I going to be very upset?"

"I think so. He's a colonel stationed at Arling. He, his name's Herbert Wingfield Lascomb."

"Lascomb? That name rings a bell." He climbed to his feet slowly. When he was up he stood in front of her speechless for a space which was a little too long for comfort. He took her chin in his hand and lifted it so that she had to meet his eyes. "This isn't some character test for aging fathers you and Ginny have worked out between you, is it?" She shook her head. "You've really gone and done it?" She nodded. "Well I'll be damned." He held her chin up for a second longer. "Mrs. Lascomb, well, well." He walked off down to the end of the dock, stared for a moment at the far shore, and then came back. "I can't pretend to be absolutely delighted, my dear, because I don't know your husband from Adam. I knew his father, Manuel Lascomb. He always called his mother Donna Anna, or spoke of her as such. The story was she was Spanish —Cuban, at any rate. I don't really think she was. Do you know what I'm driving at? What does he say he is?"

"He knows about his grandmother."

"Oh, he does. And when did you find out? Before or afterwards? It's got a lot to do with whether I'm going to like him or not."

"Before."

"Really and truly?"

"Yes."

"Mary." He took her hand. "Why couldn't you trust me?" She looked at him and he dropped his eyes.

"No I don't suppose you could have. I'd have sent you abroad like poor Thomas' Sophy. I'd have done all I could to break it up. I think. Unless he's awful nice. He's really it, is he?"

"Yes, he is. I—I love him very much."

"I see you do." He put his arm round her shoulder. "So you're all fixed up, an old married woman with a husband."

"I'm sorry," she sniffed.

"Now don't start crying. You haven't anything to cry about. Not yet, anyway." He patted her back. "Well, this'll be news for Thomas, or is it a secret for the time being?"

"No, now you know, it's all right. Anyone can know."

"You realize what you've done?"

"Yes, I do."

"I wonder if you do," he said. "I wonder."

"It's going to be all right," she said. "I promise you, father. I'm going to make it be all right."

"You do that, you keep that promise," he said and he managed to smile. He inspected her. "Don't rush into having babies. Give yourself time to settle down, in a couple of years you'll know the fellow better. It's hard to get to know a man when you've got children on your hands. And besides, they complicate matters if things don't work out. I know it's hard for you to realize it at this stage, but things don't always go as you'd like. On that score, I'll only say quit if you find you've made a mistake. Don't let false pride stand in your way if you do find you've bitten off more than you can chew." He smiled in embarrassment. "That's not what I want to say. I want to wish you well. It sounds as if I want things to go wrong. But I truly don't."

"I know you don't." She put her hand beseechingly on his

421

shoulder. "I know you'll like him. You really will. He's nice. I love him."

"I'll like him for that reason. It's good enough." He swallowed. It ought to be, he thought, but it as sure as hell isn't. Her first love had been a fairy, and now she had taken on a colored man. The words of an old song drifted up from the depths of his memory. "Go home and tell your mother, she certainly made a wonderful job of you." That's not fair either, he thought, patting her hand and looking into his child's eyes with love, and sympathy, and horror—we did it to her together.

"Come on," he said, "come on up to the house, Mrs. Lascomb, and we'll see what Julia has for our lunch."

Chapter Nine

FOR Thomas there was a pure delight and excitement in being at M.I.T., a constant renewal of the pleasure he had experienced on the long journey up to Boston. He arrived in the sticky fag end of summer, when its heat and lassitude were spilling over to make a stagnant autumn. And then abruptly there was a bite in the air at night, the air became limpid and winelike, and the sullen summer-worn trees began to flame with clear vivid colors, brilliant singing yellows, and reds of a breath-taking purity. There was an exhilaration in the prospect of cold, hard weather ahead which he had never felt before, and which he could feel building up, for all that the weather continued mild, all through November and December. After Christmas the cold came. And when the first heavy snow fell, Thomas took a long drive lasting all one weekend for the pleasure of looking at the movement of the snow-covered rock-strewn hillsides visible through their veil of covering woodland. All the trees were bare and a townsman would have said lifeless, but in them the sap was beginning to stir and the young twigs at the branch ends were showing color; red, dark green, and yellow. The snowy slopes appeared through a smoke-like mist of soft color made by the crisscrossed twigs. It was all new and wonderful to him, and he had difficulty in deciding what about it most delighted him. In the end, he settled for an embracing everything, from the demure white houses with their elegant clapboard planking, through the underlying rock and the endless web of stone walls, to the sharp night air which transformed every light and gave it a jewel-like brilliance. Towards the end of his long swing round Boston, following roads more or less at random, he found himself lost in the southern end of the Berkshires, looking up at a sign saying Wychbury, pointing in the direction which was the right one to take him back to Boston. A short while later he was driving slowly up the hill into the center of the town with its short row of cozy old-fashioned-looking shops on his right hand and the Civil War monument silhouetted against the darkening sky in front of him. The shops looked as if they had always been there, and he imagined his father as a small boy swinging a bicycle across the street in a wide circle to fetch up in front of the drugstore where they still had the sign up for the ice cream that had the screaming eagle as a trademark for the sake of the execrable pun, if it could be called that, "I scream for ice cream." A pick-up truck passed him with a threshing of chains and turned off to the left at the monument where the rifleman stood with snow on his shoulders and on the visor of his cap. Thomas followed it on an impulse and found himself traveling slowly up a splendid avenue-like street which opened up at a right angle to the main road. Huge trees lined it, and their snowladen branches gave the effect of a magnificent Gothic vault. Behind the trees, across stretches of wide lawn, were rows of widely spaced houses with a stern, sensible, eighteenth-century beauty to them, a beauty which had an inevitableness about it, as if there really was no other way of building a house or any other style. Thomas turned at the fork at the top of the street and drove slowly back down again, liking it more and more. A particular house caught his attention on this second inspection, because all its ground-floor rooms were filled with light and the glow from them lit up its snow-covered lawn. Thomas slowed to see if he could make out what sort of people there were inside, and as he slowed saw the mailbox with its lettering, M. Hatfield. An impulse seized him and he pulled in to the curb, beside the high frozen wall flung up by the snow plow. He hesitated briefly and then climbed out of the car into the keen cold of the fading evening, at worst they could snub him, so why not? And a minute or two later he was on the step, speaking through the open door to a pleasant-faced woman with graying hair pulled back into a bun.

"My name's Thomas Hatfield," he said. "I believe you are some sort of cousin of mine. My father, Gavin Hatfield, we live in Florida, came from here. I happened to be passing by on my way up to Boston, and I thought I'd look in and say hello."

"Who is it?" said a voice from the hallway behind the woman, who began to smile.

"Do come in," she said, and then, turning, added, "Oh, Mark, this is exciting. Here's one of the lost tribes."

"A missing Hatfield!" Thomas found himself being looked over by a tall thin-faced man whom he took to be the woman's husband. "You certainly are a Hatfield. One look is enough to settle that. My goodness. How exciting. A brand new Hatfield!"

"Thomas, dear, lost Gavin's son." They both beamed at him. "Well take that great sheepskin coat off. I'm Alice, and this is my husband Mark."

"I knew Gavin very well when he was a boy, Thomas," Mark said. "Our fathers were first cousins. But for our purposes all Hatfields have cousin's rights. It's a sort of tradition. Well, it is good to see you. Now come in and meet my young people, Christina, Lawrence, Dunce. Christina's a young woman. She's just going to be married, we're in the middle of making the preparations for the great event. Lawrence graduates from Harvard in July, and Dunce is in her freshman year at Radcliffe."

"I'm at M.I.T."

"Oh, well then, you'll be seeing a lot of each other in Cambridge." Mark put his hand on Thomas' shoulder and propelled him across the hall towards the living room, and the years of family life and friendliness Thomas had missed.

Christina was too absorbed in her own immediate future to pay Thomas much attention, but Lawrence and Dunce were interested and curious. The meeting took, and they began to see each other frequently in Cambridge, and at weekends in Wychbury or skiing in Vermont. They introduced him, too, to the various Hatfield cousins in and around Boston, the Louisburg Square Hatfields, the old Hatfields out at Concord,

425

and the Linnaen Street Hatfields who had a Pollock and a Brancusi. Thomas wrote amusing letters about them all to Sophy, and she wrote back, cheerfully at first and then with a gathering unease. Spring came and turned into summer, and the unease in her letters began to infect Thomas. "I don't know what's the matter," she said, "but I'm tired all the time. It's all I can do to get through the day. I used to get low in the winter sometimes, but I'd always pick up in the spring. But now it's all beautiful and warm, but I'm limp as a rag and it's all I can do to stay on my feet after lunch. I just fold." Thomas agitatedly told her to go to a doctor, and got his answer soon enough. "Of course I've been to not a doctor but doctors, stupid. Squads of them. But they don't seem to be much use. They just don't know what gives." So that Thomas was left with a faint nagging worry. Sophy was not only far away, but mysteriously afflicted also, with something intangible and un-fightable. His days were filled with life and interest, but some-thing vital to him was out of his control, and going wrong. His worry began to show in his face and in his manner. One after-noon in early June, when he was on Ipswich beach with Dunce soaking in the sun after a quick plunge into the cold sea, she spoke to him about it. She lay on her stomach on a towel be-side him with her head turned so that she could watch him. His head was cradled in his arms, but his body was tense. He looked as if he was trying to stare down through the sand into some storehouse for the answers to riddles hidden deep in the earth.

"What is it?" she said. "What's the matter, Thomas?"

So he told her the whole story and for the moment experi-enced a certain relief. Since he had been parted from Sophy he had not showed the inside of his heart to anybody, and Dunce's silent attentiveness had given him a happy sense for the moment of not being alone. It didn't matter that when he had told her there was still nothing they could between them do to improve matters, it was enough that she knew, and that she wished to help. He did not realize that she was beginning to be in love with him, or that he was beginning to be in love

426

with her. Before that had to be faced the crisis in Sophy's life came. She wrote Thomas on a Monday, and on Friday he was reading it.

Thank goodness, they've found out what the trouble is at last. I sort of hate it, it sounds so dreary and depressing, but it's good to know. It turns out I have had some sort of infection in, eugh! my gall bladder, whatever that is. Apparently it's been poisoning me right along. It means an operation, but not a very big one. Probably by the time you read this it will be all over and I'll be starting to get well. Oh, Thomas, it's all been so long and I've been so miserable thinking I was going to be feeble and dreary when we did get to see each other again. Now I am going to be well again and I feel so much happier. It's as if I knew a day when I was going to see you and touch dear you again, at any rate it makes me believe in us again. It's been so terrible being afraid I wasn't going to be good enough to be part of us when all this . . .

He read the long letter again and again on the Friday, on the Saturday, and on the Sunday, and then no more because he knew it all by heart. On Tuesday he had the second letter in an envelope written by a stranger, a little piece of white paper from a memo pad, covered with a few lines in a scrawl which was hard to read.

Dearest,
I had my operation but something went wrong and I have been bleeding a lot. I am scared stiff and I feel terrible! But the doctor says I am O.K. and they are going to take me in to put everything all right soon; soon, dear Thomas, so don't worry. I know I'm all right. Love,

Sophy

Thomas called the Grove and the bank and everywhere else he could think of where Gavin might be, but for hours he couldn't trace his father. When he ran him down he was at a

427

hotel in New Orleans, dressing for a dinner with some oil-men. His father turned him down. He wouldn't help him to get to Switzerland. "You don't know anything about it, when you get down to it, Thomas. All you have is two notes from a scared girl. She may be just frightened. You always feel terrible after an operation, much worse than you are."

"It's because she's frightened and scared I have to go to her, father."

"I know how you must be feeling, Thomas. But I'm sorry."

"Please, father."

"Now, Thomas. Don't be hysterical. I can't send you to Europe just because Sophy is sick and upset. Be a little realistic. I'll call Mr. McCann in the morning and when I've got some definite news we'll make a decision. But I can tell you right now that Sophy will have to be very, very sick indeed to justify your going out there."

"Please call Mr. McCann tonight."

"Now, Thomas, get a hold of yourself. Be a man."

"Father." Thomas put the phone down realizing that his father had hung up. For the next thirty-six hours, time leaked away minute by minute as Thomas stayed as near as he could get to the phone on which Gavin would call him. But Gavin had forgotten to call Mr. McCann the next morning. He had flown from New Orleans to Houston in Texas, and, when he had done a full day's business, from there back to Maramee before he remembered. By then Sophy was dead. Gavin wired Thomas saying when he would reach Boston, but the boy didn't come to meet him at the airport. When Gavin came into his room in the dormitory building looking over the flat expanse of the Charles River, Thomas didn't get up, and didn't look at his father. He looked at the ceiling.

"You didn't have to come," he said. "I knew as soon as I had your wire."

"I'm sorry, Thomas."

"There's nothing to be sorry about."

"All I can say is I wish things hadn't turned out this way."

"So do I."

428

There was a silence in the room, through which a radio in another room could be heard faintly as it reproduced a piano sonata superbly but dispassionately played.

"Why did you come?" Thomas said.

"I just thought . . ." Gavin hesitated, looked at Thomas, and then looked out of the window at the thrumming traffic outside, at the river, and at the sprawl of Boston across the water. "I thought it would be easier if you heard it from me. She died under the anesthetic. She had no pain, no fears. She didn't know anything about it."

"Swell. Just great."

"I said I was sorry."

"I told you what I think about that."

"Well, I guess you don't want me around in your present mood. I'm going over to see if they have a room for me at the Ritz. I expect they have. I'll be there if you want to give me a call or to come over and talk, for a couple of days anyway." He paused. "Take my advice. Get up off that bed just as soon as you can and get back to work. You're not doing yourself any good lying there. And being bitter won't do a bit of good. This is something you've got to put behind you."

"Thanks."

"What?"

"I said, thanks. That's all. Thank you."

Sophy's last letter reached Thomas the next morning. He held the envelope in his hand for a long time before he found the courage to open it. It seemed all wrong to be getting a communication from someone who was lost and gone. She would never write, or speak, or smile, or breathe again. He had resigned himself to her silence, and here, breaking it, was one more word. He tore the cover open and read it once, taking in the words, and then a second time understanding its meaning. Behind the words he read the message, that time was not on his side, that there was something inimical at the heart of things, a darkness hostile to all love and warmth, and to all the fragile brightness of human joys and delights. It had killed Sophy, and it would presently kill him. He looked at the weakly traced

429

words a third time, seeing no words but feeling through them Sophy's pain at what she had learned and what he was to learn.

Dearest, dearest Thomas—
I love you so and I don't think it's any use. I wish you weren't so far away. I would like to see your dear face more than anything. Everything is going wrong. I've had two operations and they're going to try again. They are scared but I'm too feeble and tired for that. I've had so many transfusions and things I've lost count. I'm still bleeding and I know it's our life draining away. I wish we had been allowed to be happy together. I hope you will soon find someone to make you happy. They say I am tiring myself and must stop. I love you so much Thomas, good-bye, darling, and be happy for me, promise to be happy for me.
                                                                Sophy

Thomas folded the letter carefully and put it away in a box with all her other letters. When he had done that, he looked about his room for a few seconds as if he had never seen it before. The photographs of Ilona and Gavin on a shelf over his bed caught his eye, and his gaze lingered on his father's face. "I'd better go and see the poor son of a bitch," he muttered abruptly, "though God knows what there is for us to say to each other." On the way over to the hotel he thought of a solution to the problem of concealing himself from his father's sympathy without adding to his sense of guilt. He drove him down to Cape Cod and they spent the rest of the day walking along the south beach. The sea was calm, and a lazy surf, pushed by a rising tide, murmured to them as they walked through an opalescent haze. When they had gone, the flouncing waves lapped up across the bare sands and washed away their footprints.

"We had a good day, didn't we?" Gavin said, as Thomas dropped him at the hotel. The boy nodded and smiled without opening his mouth. Fatherly, comforting, and remote beyond measuring, Gavin patted him on the shoulder.

"Get to bed early," he said. "Have a good night's sleep. Sleep's more help than anything at a time like this."

"I know. Good night, father."

Thomas went to bed early, but he did not sleep. He lay awake in a rage of anger at his own condition of helpless dependence and powerlessness. They had just taken Sophy from him and he had been able to do nothing about it. He racked his brains for a clue to some quick route to freedom and invulnerability and at last fell asleep towards the morning with his fists clenched.

The next weekend Thomas went down to Wychbury with Dunce and Lawrence. They were concerned about him and wanted to cheer him up; Lawrence because he thought his distant cousin was a good fellow, and Dunce because she couldn't bear to see him enclosed in sadness so completely that he seemed almost unaware of her. The sight of him so deeply hurt had finished the process of falling in love for her, she now loved him and was beginning to be aware of it. They sat three abreast on the front seat of Thomas' car on the way down, and she found herself consciously enjoying the mere fact of their being physically that close together. A few curves pressed her close to him and she tended to remain snugly with him for longer than was necessary, to her own surprise. On the last stages of the journey she fell into a reverie trying to imagine what Sophy had been like. She conjured up a picture of someone small, snub-nosed, and cute and felt sure that she would never have been good enough for Thomas. And yet she must have been all right or Thomas would not have loved her. The thought crossed her mind that it was a good thing that Sophy was dead. She instantly recoiled from it. Oh! I don't mean that! That's awful! But then she wondered what exactly she did mean if it was not that. In perplexity, she separated herself from Thomas and pulling her compact out of her bag examined her face in its mirror. How awful was she, she wondered? And was she in love with Thomas? She snapped the compact shut and turned to consider Thomas' set face, watch-

431

ing the road ahead. Perhaps she did. She couldn't be sure. She would have to go to bed with him to find out.

At Wychbury Alice told Thomas to put his things in the guest room on the street side of the house across the wide corridor from Dunce's room. He was beginning to think of it as his own. He always slept in it when he stayed with his cousins, and assumed that he would go to it. The room was all white but for the dark, almost black, wooden furniture, and the corn-flower blue of the curtains and the hangings on the fourposter. There was very little furniture beside the bed, two chairs, a tall-boy, and a sturdy table. But the sparseness and the plainness of the room delighted him. It was so bare, and still there was the sense of enough and more than enough about it. When he had unpacked his bag he hid it in the closet and stared about him happily, sniffing the faint odor of lavender which seemed to have become through the years an integral part of the room. Dunce called to him from the open door of her room, where she was standing looking out in her dressing gown.

"Oh, Thomas, can I ask you a favor?" she said. "I was go-ing to have a bath before dinner. I'm all undressed, and I find I've left my hand lotion behind. Could you be an angel and pick up a bottle for me at the drugstore?"

"Oh, yes, I'd be glad to." He smiled at her as he said it, and happiness instantly lit her face. He took it that she was grate-ful for his willingness to do her the small service, and the thought entered his mind that Dunce was really very nice, even nicer than she seemed to be, which was saying a lot. The mellowness of the moment went with him as he walked down to the end of the street in the cool shadow under the arching trees, and stayed with him as he stepped into the drugstore through the swinging green-painted screen door. He had to wait his turn to be served while the druggist made up a pre-scription for a spotty youth who leaned on the counter hum-ming "Que sera, sera," under his breath. The druggist came to the counter with the little packet he had made up and held it up disparagingly to the blue-eyed and red-faced young man.

"Alfred, are you sure you know what you're doing? It's not

too late for you to change your mind," he said. "This darned stuff is going to cost you four dollars and eighty-seven cents. You could have the big bottle of Dr. Martin's pills for one twenty-five, and they're every bit as good. You take my word for it."

"Aw, Mr. Higgs, Dr. Martin's is old-fashioned stuff, everyone knows that. You'll be trying to get me onto snake oil next thing you know."

"Old-fashioned or not, the pills are cheap and they work. I can tell you that much."

"But I been to the doctor, Mr. Higgs," the youth said in an unhappy whine. "What's the good of that if I don't do what he says?"

"Doctors don't know everything. You'd do better to listen to me when it comes to some things. But there, you're determined to be robbed, and if somebody's going to get your money I'd just as soon it was me. That's four dollars and eighty-seven cents, National Druggists' Association price for a dollar's worth of humbug. When you find it hasn't done you a bit of good, scrape up five quarters and come back for a bottle of the sulphur tablets. They'll do the trick for you."

"Did you say sulphur?" Thomas said.

The druggist and the gangling young man eyed him suspiciously.

"I did, as it happens, though I wasn't talking to you," said the druggist, taking the money. The hobbledehoy, who not only looked as if he came from a farm, but even smelt a little that way, flushed and went out with a muttered, "Good night, Mr. Higgs." The druggist looked after him as the screen door flapped shut with a twang of its rusty coil spring.

"Worried about his spots, poor kid. Spent seventeen dollars on one thing and another this year alone. I've told him a dozen times there's nothing the matter with him that a little sulphur and a bit of time won't cure."

"You said sulphur, again," Thomas said. "Is that all Dr. Martin's pills are?"

"That's all. Yellow sulphur. Can't beat it. My mother used

to dose us with it every spring in these identical Dr. Martin's tablets. She said it stopped our blood heating or thickening or some such thing. Whatever the rights of it are, there's nothing to beat it for clearing the skin."

"Well, thanks," Thomas said, beginning to leave the store. "Good night, Mr. Higgs."

"Say, aren't you forgetting what you came here to pick up?" Mr. Higgs said.

"Oh, yes. A bottle of that hand lotion Dunce uses, and you might give me a small bottle of Dr. Martin's, just for luck."

"What's so interesting about sulphur pills to a fellow like you?" Mr. Higgs asked.

"Nothing really," Thomas said. "They just remind me of a man called Krawitz, that's all." He smiled and added, "Goodnight."

So Thomas canceled his summer plans to go out to Oregon to work for a lumber company, and headed south to Maramee after he'd seen Lawrence graduate and had attended the subsequent rally of Hatfields at Wychbury which honored the occasion. He didn't stay at the Grove, but lived in a tent near the spring, working with the drilling crew which he had hired to take test cores all over his property. As the work went on and the numbered samples from the parallel lines of drilling spots accumulated, an elaborate picture of the soil beneath the surface of Thomas' property began to appear. The largest element in it was a deep bed of almost pure sulphur lying close to the surface under more than four-fifths of the ground. Thomas' expert, a graduate student from the Wisconsin School of Mines, made a detailed map for him when the drilling was finished and calculated the tonnage lying in the deposit.When he had finished work on his report, they went over and had a celebration supper at Bunce's Burgers, chicken-in-a-basket and beer.

"How did you come to get hold of this piece of ground, Thomas?" said the engineer.

"My father gave it to me, Harry. I've never figured out just why."

"Do you think he knows what he parted with?"

"No, I don't think he does."

"You lucky son of a bitch."

"Am I so lucky?"

"Don't you know how lucky you are?" Harry put down his knife and fork. "Haven't you taken in what you've got there? Didn't you understand what I put in that report?"

"Well, yeah, there's a hell of a lot of sulphur there."

"Sulphur, man, it's money in the bank. Don't tell me you don't know—" His voice broke off into a groan. "What do you think it's worth?" He leaned across the table, staring at Thomas. "How much would you say at a guess?"

"I haven't really figured it out. Four or five million dollars, something like that, isn't it?"

"Holy Gee, as my aunt used to say." The engineer looked down at his plate and pushed it aside. "You take my appetite away. I have a lifetime of honest goddamned toil ahead of me working for people like you and I begin to see what it's going to be like. This silver spoon your father gave you . . ."

"Don't talk like that to me."

"What?"

"Say anything you like, but leave silver spoons out of it."

"All right . . ." The engineer suddenly looked subdued. He went on in a flattened, tired voice. "Well anyway, what you have out there over the road is worth between forty and sixty million dollars."

"It is?" Thomas looked out of the window, across the parking lot, through the screen of billboards, to the wide stretch of grazing land with the dark mass of woodland hiding the spring beyond it. "That's good. I like that." He laughed. "Nobody's ever going to push me around ever again."

"I don't think they are," the engineer said, looking at him curiously. "Say, I could do with another beer."

"You're the fellas was drilling for oil all summer acrost the road," said the waitress. "Too bad you didn't find nothing. You can't be lucky all the time though."

"Oh, we can't complain," said Thomas. "Make it two more

435

beers, will you. There's nothing like experience after all, is there?"

"That's the attitude you have to take," the girl said, "it's the way to get along in this world." She went off smiling.

"I envy the way you can get people to eat out of your hand," the engineer said. He nibbled at a drumstick and put it down. "That spring's the only problem. Have you thought about it?"

"We'll cap it. They're crazy for water in Maramee and down in Halesville, too."

"It's sort of wonderful the way it is. It's too bad to spoil it. It really gets you if you sit by it on a still night. It sort of chuckles as if it knew something you didn't."

"I know, but it's a detail. It can't stand in the way of the big thing."

"What's the big thing, in this case?"

"I don't know. Progress. Something like that. I feel it instinctively. What I'm going to do over there has to be done. It's the next stage—that's all—there's no alternative in my mind."

"You scare me." The engineer hesitated. "At the beginning of this job I thought you were just a kid playing with some dough his father or someone had let him have. I felt way ahead of you. But now, I don't know. There's something in you I'm not sure I understand." He paused and added in a lower tone, "I'm not sure that I want to."

Gavin had a chance to measure that something a year later when Thomas had sold the deposit to Gulf Sulphur for a huge sum in cash, a block of stock, and royalties on every ton of sulphur taken off the property. Huge machines moved in onto the grazing land and began to peel the topsoil off the soft yellow bed beneath it. Wind drifted the dust from the workings onto the trees round the pool until a logging crew came to cut them down, burning the soiled foliage and the toppings in huge stacks which burned for days at a time. As the snarling power saws bit in closer and closer to the pool, Mr. Krawitz became almost crazed with anxiety and distress. He formed a Save the Pool Committee of citizens of southern Maramee and tried to raise a fund to buy a few acres round it.

Contributions came in with an illusory suggestion of massive support, thirty or forty a day. But when the total was added up, thirteen hundred donors had put together only eleven-hundred-odd dollars. Too many children had sent dimes and quarters, only a few adults had gone to five dollars. Mr. Krawitz, with despair in his heart, went to see Gavin to beg him to plead with Thomas for the spring.

"It's not for myself I'm asking, Mr. Hatfield, it's for the children, for the future, this beautiful thing should be preserved. I implore you that you should stop this outrage, Mr. Hatfield. Your kid's a kid. He don't know what he's doing. A word in season from a father might work a miracle . . ."

"I'll do what I can, Mr. Krawitz."

Thomas' voice on the telephone only made Gavin realize how far Boston was from Maramee and how great the distance between them had become. "Yes I'll think it over, father," Thomas said. "Yes, I know what I'm doing. . . . It's not my decision any more, father. The property belongs to the corporation now. . . . Yes, I am an officer of the corporation. . . . It's a matter of efficiency, father. I can't tell engineers how to go about their business. . . . I'll write to Krawitz and explain the position." Gavin was chilled when he put the telephone down, and even more disheartened when Mr. Krawitz silently put a letter from Thomas on the desk in front of him a few days later. Gavin looked up from the stone-cold parody of the sort of inhuman business communication he had himself written a thousand times a year, in any given year, and encountered the warm human faces of Mr. Krawitz and the members of his delegation.

"Well, gentlemen, I'm sorry. You have his decision. There's nothing I can do."

"His father," Mr. Krawitz said. "From his father's mouth we have it—there's nothing I can do."

"I'm sorry."

"You should be sorry. Sorry is what you will one day be!" cried Mr. Krawitz.

"Now, Krawitz, please . . ." A member of the delegation

437

grabbed his arm. "To Mr. Krawitz, you understand, the spring has connotations," he said apologetically. "We all feel deeply about the pool as a facility, you understand, a community asset is the expression I would favor, but for Krawitz here there's a mystical significance like it was the pool of Siloam or some kind of holy place, if you follow me. It's obsessive with him."

"I know what he feels," Gavin said. "I want you to understand that this is even more of a blow to me, Mr. Krawitz, than it is to you. It's my son who has done this." Krawitz looked at him for a moment with indignation and dislike. He shrugged his wide shoulders.

"So we have a sympathizer already," he said sourly to the rest of the Save the Pool Committee. "Something stinks around here. I feel nauseous. If it's all one to you, Mr. Hatfield, we'll be leaving."

"I wish you would try to realize how much I regret the whole business," Gavin said.

"In your regrets our kids should go swimming? You make me tired." Mr. Krawitz paused. "You bore me."

"Come on, Krawitz, you already said too much," the apologetic committeeman said. "Like I said, Mr. Hatfield, we understand the position. But with Krawitz here it's emotional."

When they had gone, Gavin sat empty-minded at his desk for a long time and then on an impulse called Hoskins of Gulf Sulphur. The call was routed through the Gulf Sulphur office by a short-wave link to his plane which was somewhere beyond Mobile heading for Texas. They exchanged civilities.

"Say, what are you and Thomas up to between you?"

"Oh, that boy of yours. He's terrific. You should be proud of him, Gavin. He just moved in on us. I've never seen a youngster do better. He knew what he had. He knew what he wanted. He knew how to get it from us, and, by God, he got it. I was impressed, Gavin. You've got a real comer there. I don't know where he's headed, but I'm darned if there's anything that'll stop him till he gets there. I wouldn't like to try to stand in his way, I'll tell you that much. I wish I could say as much of my own boy. I envy you, Gavin. You don't know what it is to worry about what half-arsed thing your own son is going to pull on you next. I don't mean there's anything bad about Nick, but he just hasn't got your kid's sense. It would have done your heart good if you'd been a fly on the wall when that young sprout of yours was putting us over the barrel. Let's have dinner Friday when I'm back on Steamboat Key. When I tell you what he took us for, you'll have to laugh. But seriously, the boy's just fine and I'm very happy to have him in with us."

Hoskins had nothing but good to say of Thomas, but it was strangely not what Gavin wanted to hear. He had wanted to learn something that would make him feel that his son might still have some need of him for advice or protection. He had not wanted to discover that his son was already powerful, determined, and far advanced on a path of his own that might never bring him back. The boy was lost, and the man who had replaced him was someone he did not know at all, and would probably never know. He fiddled with the things on his desk top, picked up a pen and set it down, opened one folder and then another, and then slumped back into his chair. He turned his mind to Mary and Wing and wondered how that marriage was going. He had pulled every string he could reach and had got his son-in-law posted to the Embassy in Madrid as air attaché. They had both seemed to be grateful and excited at the time, but he was beginning to suspect that something was wrong there. Mary was writing back odd, almost anti-American letters that he found hard to understand, filled with hints that she knew that he was ashamed of her, and as good as saying that he had got Wing the posting simply to get them out of the way. She didn't seem to come within a mile of realizing that he had done his best for her, or what value there would be in the future to every scrap of authentication she could raise for that thin Spanish-grandmother story. But she, like Thomas, was to all appearances determined to build a wall between them. He had only Bogey left, and because she could twist him round her little finger he had for her own good sent her up

439

North to boarding school. The thought of the child who had from the first been more his than either Mary or Thomas cheered him up, and he quickly wrote her a letter full of their old private joking references. He read it over, chuckled with amusement, and fully restored, settled down to his work again.

When Thomas had gone back North at the end of his summer's drilling, Dunce had been delighted to have him back. The nature of her pleasure was unmistakable, and Thomas, realizing that he could take her, had taken her. He did not ask himself if he loved her or not, the thing was that she wanted him and he liked her. They settled easily into the pattern of a university affair, making love in the afternoons when they could and getting away for as many weekends as possible. When they were at Wychbury, Dunce would tiptoe across the wide corridor as soon as the house was still, and would slip away again soon after dawn. Alice knew immediately, by instinct, what was happening and closed her mind to it. Mark knew when he looked out of a window one summer morning and saw Thomas standing close behind Dunce in the wisteria arbor saying something quietly to her. She had turned her head to look over her shoulder at him and when she nodded in reply to whatever it was he had said he bent a little forward and kissed her on her neck below her ear. Mark saw the slow smile spread over his daughter's face as the two of them stood entangled in the sensual enjoyment of the moment, in the dapple of light and shade under the vine. "Of course," he said, and understood the flowering of Dunce's beauty which had until then just seemed to be another part of her growing up. But it was Dunce's affair, according to his rules, and if she didn't want to say anything about it, then it was no business of his. But he felt a pang of concern nonetheless. Thomas seemed very nice, unusually nice, but there was something ruthless in his makeup, underneath the good manners and the charm. Mark hoped that Dunce was aware of it. And because he didn't want to think of Dunce being hurt he turned away from the window and consigned his new knowledge to the remotest corner of his mind. So nothing was said by anybody for a year, until Dunce appeared for a March weekend sun-burned to a golden brown.

"Good heavens, how did you get that tan?" Alice said. "Where have you been?"

"Oh, Thomas had to go down to Maramee for a few days, so I cut classes and went with him."

"You've been to Florida?"

"Yes. It was wonderful. They sent a plane up just for us, and they brought us back too. You've no idea how plushy it is being a tycoon."

"Does Thomas really have his own plane? I'm beginning to think anything is possible."

"Oh, no. It belongs to Gulf Sulphur. But he sends for it when he wants it."

"Who did you go with?"

"Oh, nobody, just us."

"Dunce dearest. I don't want to scold. But if you go off on a trip like that again you must take another girl with you. You can't do that sort of thing—not too blatantly anyway."

"It's all right, mother, really; we're engaged."

"It really isn't all right—please don't be brazen." She sighed. "Do you really mean engaged? Do we have to start making plans for a wedding?"

"Oh, we're not all that engaged. Not yet."

"Now that's not good enough. Try to understand that breathing the word 'engaged' into the air doesn't make it all right for you to act like a little trollop whenever you feel like it. I don't want to tell you how to behave, but I'm going to insist on your being discreet."

"I'm sorry, mother. I didn't mean to upset you."

"You don't have to worry about me, but I do think you ought to consider your father's feelings. He doesn't mind what you do, but he doesn't want to have to think about it. So try not to be obvious."

"I will. And don't worry, mother. I do know what I'm doing."

"I hope you do, dear."

441

The conversation repeated itself in masculine terms the following day, when Mark found himself alone with Thomas among the plants in the glassed-in winter garden on the west side of the house.

"I find you a puzzle, Cousin Thomas," Mark said. "You seem to know so much about some things and so little about others."

"I'm sorry. I hope this doesn't mean I've offended you in some way."

"No, not a bit. I've just been thinking things over." Mark sucked on an empty pipe and then began filling it with his slender fingers. "You and Dunce have been thinking of marriage, haven't you?"

"Yes, we have."

"I wonder if you should."

"We've thought a lot about it. We didn't want to say anything until we were quite sure. The cousin business seemed against it, but the relationship isn't that close."

"It's not that I'm thinking about. I wonder if you've thought what you'll be doing. Your father made such an effort to get away. Do you think you'll be wise to come back?"

"I like the life here, Cousin Mark, and I know I love Dunce."

"I think you may love Dunce. But I don't know how well you know our lives. My father taught me to despise businessmen because they were greedy, politicians because they were vulgar or dishonest, artists because they were sloppy, ministers because they were hypocrites, and the poor because they were mercenary. The worst thing father could think of to say about anyone was that they were pushing. I remember when he decided to give up his chair—he was professor of Ancient History of the Middle East, at Harvard. 'I find,' he said, 'that some of the younger men,' sniff, 'are doing something they like to call research. It's no subject for a gentleman any more. They'll be asking me to take archeology seriously next.' He was very nervous when I began to be interested in the law. 'I hope it isn't in your mind to become an attorney,' he said. 'A life given up to courtroom trickery would be a shoddy thing to have to

442

look back on at the end of one's days.' He was greatly relieved when I settled into my lectureship in Pre-Renaissance International Law. 'I was very much afraid that you intended to practice,' he said. I don't think I can tell you how dreadful he made that word sound."

Thomas remembered how the word 'married' had been made to sound by Mr. McCann, and imagined it very well.

"You make a strong case against all that, Cousin Mark," Thomas said. "But there's something about life up here that I like. You all seem to know what you're doing and why. It's enviable."

"We did know. But now we're just hanging on to a fading vision. If you look at this part of the world more carefully, I don't think you'll find a fine thing finely done that's not at least fifty years old. This place was given its character a full century and a half ago. It was added to for fifty years—and then it turned sterile. For a hundred years, houses, lives, everything that counts has been getting meaner, poorer, and uglier."

"But Wychbury is still a marvelous place."

"You're in love with our past, young man. And it's all over. Don't be beguiled. Our setting may look all very well, but we don't even believe in ourselves any more."

"I don't quite know what you mean by that."

"We thought that if we were decent, moderate, temperate and, within limits, honest, everything would turn out well because of the power of our shining example. We thought we could drive from the back seat with our hands folded in our laps. And while we were being modest and good they took our America away from us."

"They've left you an awful lot."

"The outward show, nothing more."

"Even if that's true, I still love Dunce."

"If you have children . . ."

"We will, and they'll be fine children. I know it."

". . . they'll be Hatfields on both sides. If you knew us better you might not be so sure. The Hatfield blood is running

443

thin, Thomas, thin and poor. We all envied Gavin the get-up-and-go that took him away. But we stayed. It's been the same in every generation. Some Hatfields cleared out, and some stayed. We're the stayers. We've been sitting here in our beautiful houses being ironic and detached while life has been passing us by. We pride ourselves on being above all the vulgar thrust-ins, we tell ourselves and anyone else who'll listen that we're less coarse, more civilized, better in every way than the rest of America. But it isn't refinement as I understand it, it's debility, the grace of weakness and decline. We're an exhausted, worn-out stock. It's that aspect of the thing that worries me about you and my girl. You may be in love with her, but I'm not sure that it isn't Wychbury—the ready-made family, the settled life, the tranquility, that you're after. Perhaps it is Dunce herself you want, but it could be that you see in her a talisman that's going to protect you from the rawness and the brutality of the life you know. And I don't know about her. I believe she sees you as someone from outside, someone who will carry her off into the activity and bustle of a fuller life." Mark sighed. "Has it occurred to you that you may be dreaming the wrong dreams, fatal dreams, about each other?"

"We've talked the thing through, we know what we're doing," Thomas said. "I promise you that."

"I hope you do, Thomas, I truly do." Mark Hatfield got to his feet, shaking his head. "God knows I don't want the life in this house to end. But don't look here for your salvation. You'll be climbing onto a sinking ship if you do."

"But if this place isn't home, where do I belong?" said Thomas, rising. "Where should I go from here?"

"Ah! That's it!" Mark said. "That's it! That's what bothers us all." He put his arm around Thomas' shoulders as if to comfort him. "We're all in the same boat when it comes to answering that question. You're a free man, absolutely free, horribly free—we all are—free to live where you want, and to do what you like with yourself and your life. You may feel it's being lost, but it's called freedom, and we're all supposed to believe in it, passionately. I'm not sure that I do, in fact I know that

I don't. But there it is, Thomas, you belong where you choose to belong, and wherever you do settle down, there will be an infinity of alternatives left open. You'll be able to pull out at any time to go somewhere else. And everything you think you want will be waiting for you wherever else it is you decide to go to. So there isn't any answer to those questions of yours. It's the condition of our lives that there can't be."

They both looked round as the door into the house opened. It was Dunce bursting in upon them.

"I'm all packed up, it's time we were heading back to Cambridge, Thomas." She paused, catching his stricken look. "Goodness, you look depressed. What have you been doing to him, father?"

"I've been telling him all the things I don't believe in any more, Dunce. What do you believe in? Perhaps you can cheer him up by telling him that?"

She stood facing them with a sudden gravity. "I believe in Thomas," she said slowly, and then with a gathering rush of confidence, "I don't have to believe in anything else, it's all in that."

She looked at the man she had chosen and he looked back at her, and neither of them heard the older man's long, drawn-out sigh, which could have been of relief, or admiration, or of pity, or even a compound of all three.

445

WHEN Pedro Nunez week came round that year Gavin moved out of the Grove and into a suite in the Beverly. Bogey was at first dissatisfied with this arrangement because she had wanted her coming-out to be marked by a ball with fireworks at the Grove which would eclipse all that she had heard of Thomas' eighteenth birthday party. While they argued the point Gavin wondered just how much of Bogey's fixation on Thomas' long-forgotten party had to do with her return home to find that her mother had vanished while it was going on. He felt anxious about her. Her body was fully mature and she was in a raging flower of sensual awareness of herself and of men. But although she was nearly eighteen, or two months and some odd days from that age, she was still in many ways unpredictably childish. As she expressed her dislike of the idea of having her coming-out party away from home she pouted and her face grew sullen. She lay back in her chair in a way which made him think of her refusing to go to bed in advance of Mary and Thomas when she was about ten. She looked like a child, and disturbingly like Ilona, too.

"I just can't face driving in and out of town four, six or eight times a day, Bogey," he said, "so you'll just have to humor me on this."

"I hate hotel parties."

"Even if you had it at the Grove the Beverly would do the catering. It won't make that much difference being in the starlight room and not at the Grove."

"It'll be a horrible party and I'll hate it."

She finally settled for a guest list of four hundred, a name band from New York, and a chartered plane to bring the Eastern friends she had made at St. Timothy's down from New York. When he had stacked up his bribes to a sufficient height she gave in, but not gracefully.

"It could be sort of fun, being right in the middle of everything all through the week," she said.

So on the Sunday afternoon before the week began officially they moved into one of the four modernized penthouse suites on the Beverly Roof. It had two bathrooms, two bedrooms, a kitchenette, an enormous living room, and a private terrace garden. It was furnished in a magazine version of Mexican style and it was called the Hispaniola suite. The management had filled it with white flowers in honor of Miss Hatfield's coming-out, and further evidence of good will arrived in the hands of a bellboy before they had been in the place more than a couple of minutes. This was a huge basket of improbably large fruits ornamented with an outsize bow of green satin and protected from harm by a cover of unpleasantly medical-looking clear plastic. A card that came with it was printed in simulated handwriting. *Hi there!* (it said) *it's an old Florida custom, hospitality without stint. We, the management of the Beverly, speaking for all the Beverly family, bid you welcome and hope you'll have a pleasant stay in the warmhearted city of Maramee.* There was another message on the other side of the card which was just as friendly and sincere. *These choice fruits were personally chosen for you by Harry Kisch, of the Beverly concourse's famous fruit and flower salon. Call me on the house phone should you have any further requirement for top quality fruits or flowers. A boy will bring your order to the door within minutes. And should you wish to be remembered to friends in the area we'd be happy to be of service.* When Gavin had read these communications he wandered round the room, disliking it, and then drifted through to Bogey's room to see how she was getting on. She was talking on the telephone at first, but as soon as she saw him coming through the doorway she cut the conversation off short. "I can't talk any more now," she said, and hung up.

"Who was that?"

447

"Just a person—someone you don't know. A girl as a matter of fact."

"Oh." He was amused by her transparency, but troubled by her desire to deceive him. "You're getting very secretive."

"It's so boring having to explain every little thing. It's just one of the girls I was at school with here before you sent me up North."

She became active with her clothes, taking them out of her cases and spreading them about the room before she started hanging them in the closets. Gavin went over to the window and looked out at the wind-bruised terrace garden.

"Did I make a great mistake sending you up North to boarding school, Bogey?" he asked. "I didn't know what else to do at that time. I felt I didn't know how to handle you. You were wild for a time after Ilona took off."

"It was all right," she said. He waited for her to say something more, but after she had pulled a great deal of tissue paper from the inside of a dress she vanished into a closet. Gavin turned and stood waiting for her to reappear, looking at the variety of dresses for morning, afternoon, and evening which were lying here, there and everywhere, spread out across the bed, over the writing desk, and draped over the backs of chairs where she had first set them down. The room grew curiously still. A panel of the triple mirror on the dressing table on the far side of the room caught his eye. It gave him a view into the closet. Bogey was standing there motionless. Her arms hanging straight down, were pressed into her sides and her fists were clenched. A corner of her lower lip was clamped between her teeth. Her eyes were tight shut. He could feel the intensity which she was putting into the wish that he would go away and leave her alone. "Bogey!" he said, startled. But before he could add anything to the exclamation, the telephone purred beside the head of the bed.

"I'll get it," she said, leaping out of her hiding place.

At first she stood with her back to him while something urgent and forcible crackled into the room through the instrument. Then she slowly turned round to eye her father with a peculiar expression of helplessness and distress. It hurt him because it so closely resembled the look he had seen on Mary's face when she had discovered that her mother had not run away alone, but had gone with Silky. He wondered what he would have to try to explain this time, and, while he did so, saw Bogey's face flush with sudden anger. She stamped her foot.

"No, I will not. I told you I couldn't talk. My father is here. I told you I'd never speak to you again if you called me here once more. I told you I'd call you." She hung up. Father and daughter faced each other in a silence which became marked.

"Are you in any kind of trouble, Bogey?"

"Oh, I . . . ." She trembled on the edge of a confidence and decided against it. She controlled her voice with an effort. "I'm just tense at the thought of all these parties. I want to go to them but they scare me. I don't know why. My own party is going to be pretty awful, but the thought of being presented on Thursday seems even worse. I dread being looked over by all those people. I don't know why I thought I wanted to do it so much. Now I want to crawl away and hide." She dissolved suddenly into tears and ran to him to sob onto his shoulder.

"That's only a part of it—isn't it?"

"Yes." She cried for a moment, clinging to him and then sniffed. "Everything's so awful. I had one of those ghastly letters from mother yesterday."

"They're bad, the way they don't say anything, aren't they?"

"They make me want to die."

"And now out with the rest of it. Who bothers you and bullies you on the telephone? What's it all about? I'd like to help if I can. But I can't do a thing if you won't tell me."

"It's a boy—a man."

"And it's serious trouble?" Gavin said, digesting the possible information about his daughter contained in the distinction.

"Not really. We had a stupid quarrel. I made him angry and then he said things which made me mad. Now he wants to make it up, and I don't want to."

"Did he say such terrible things?"

449

"Oh." She bit her lip. "He said I was a spoiled brat without a brain in my head. He said I was utterly corrupt and that I didn't care about anything except sex and money. He said I didn't begin to understand love. He said I didn't have a spark of decent human feeling in my body. He said I was contemptible and disgusting."

"Gosh! He's really keen to make you like him, isn't he?"

"It's not a joke, father." Her attention was caught by a dress which might crush if she left it where it was on the bed. She wiped away her tears with the back of her hand, slipped a hanger into the dress and hung it in the closet. "It might be a joke if he wasn't perfectly right."

"What do you mean?"

"I brought it all on myself. I told him why I wouldn't dream of marrying him. He knows . . ." She blushed and looked down at her hands, "well, he knows I'm attracted by him physically. He can't see why that isn't enough. He hasn't any money, he despises money. He's a poet but he doesn't write. He says writing is through. He says poetry is speech and rhythm and sound. He won't put anything on paper. He talks into a tape-recorder. He works for Mother Gooses' Juices when he gets broke. As soon as he's got enough money to take a month off he quits and starts making tapes again until he runs out of cash. He has a loft in Spanishtown—it's weird, really weird, just a huge white room with nothing in it. Just a few boxes and crates for furniture and a mattress on the floor." She blushed again. "I told him I'd die if I tried to live like that. With nothing. I told him what I had to have. He called me a greedy, gutless bitch and he threw me out."

"He sounds like a real charmer. Why don't you say good riddance to bad rubbish? There are an awful lot of other men in the world, and quite a few of them are hard-working and kind. What are you worrying about?"

"I told you father. I said he . . ." She swallowed. "He attracts me physically."

"I see."

"And it's not just that. I believe in him. The sounds he gets out of his tape-recorder are really terrific. They make my blood pound with excitement. And there's something about the way he just doesn't care what people think or say that's wonderful. When I'm with him its like skiing on frozen snow. I know if I keep on I'll get hurt. But I don't want to stop."

"But he threw you out. Doesn't that make it a good time to break it off?"

"He's thrown me out before."

"But you went back?" Gavin was startled.

"I go back every time. We don't speak for four days, for five days, for a whole week. Then he calls me and I go. I say I won't, but I go." She hung up another dress. "He says I've got to go to him tonight. I've told him I can't, but he says I've got to. He says I've got to walk out on you, on the whole business of being a debutante and rich-bitch, tonight, once and for all. He says its the end if I don't. He'll wash his hands of me if I'm presented at the ball. He says I've got to leave all these clothes behind. I'm not to take anything with me . . ."

"Not even money?" Gavin said, smiling, thinking he would score a point.

"Not even money. He says money is stolen if you haven't worked for it. He despises me for needing it."

"Does he now?" Gavin suddenly felt a thrust of uneasiness. The unknown young man might be more formidable than he had imagined. "And how do you feel about that?"

"I believe him when I'm with him. When I get away, I feel I've been sick. I feel having nice things and not being squalid must be right. But when I'm with him I feel he's right. I feel it's mean-spirited to be the way I am. But I don't know what I'd do if I had to have babies in his place. I can't trust life the way he says I've got to. And each time I go back to him I'm a little more scared that this time there won't be any argument. He won't throw me out. I'll just stay."

"Do you mean it, Bogey?"

"Yes, father. If I go once again I may be a goner. In fact, I know I will. I'm scared of him, I want him so much. I don't know what to do."

451

"Are you asking me for advice?" Gavin studied her for a few seconds as she fidgeted nervously, brushing a hair off her cheek, turning her head restlessly from side to side, and keeping her fingers in constant motion. "It's late," he said. "You should have told me what was happening to you before this— it's never so easy to straighten things out when you've reached the end of your tether."

"Please don't lecture. I don't think I can stand it. Don't you realize what the danger is? I'm holding myself back from going out through that door, now, this minute, to start something that would be miserable and violent and awful for years and years."

"But there must be something likeable about him, or you wouldn't want to go to him as much as you do." Gavin hesitated. "You won't ever find a man who hasn't got defects to set off against his virtues."

"Oh, daddy, can't you see I can't bear him? He frightens me. It's just what he does to me. I hate myself for going back, just for that."

"Ah, I begin to see it." Comprehension dawned on Gavin's mind. "I've been thinking of you as my little girl. Habits are hard to break. I suppose I just didn't want to face that as a possibility with you. I suppose it was bound to come."

The telephone rang and Bogey put her hand up to her mouth with a quick intake of breath.

"Take it easy," Gavin said. "It could even be for me." He picked up the instrument. "This is Hatfield speaking," he said. "Who's there?" He listened to the sound of breathing for a few seconds and hung up when he heard the click of the caller at the other end of the line putting down the receiver. He turned and found Bogey standing looking at him with parted lips and a half-sickened, half-excited expression on her face.

"What am I going to do?" she said.

"Go away. Get out of his reach. Give yourself time to think. You could go and stay with Mary and Wing in Madrid for a while. I should think the pretty sister of the air attaché's wife would have quite a good time there. You'd better do that. If you find you can't live without your demon lover you can always come back to him. But I'd go now just to get a breathing space. It's hard to be objective when what seems to be the most important thing in the world is just round the corner waiting for you."

"I'll have to start at once," she said. "I won't be able to hold out through the night here. I know I won't."

"Is it so bad?"

"Yes." They faced each other until she took a few steps which brought her to his side. She took his hand and locked her fingers with his. "Am I too awful?"

"No worse than anyone else." He considered her cheekbone and her generously sensual mouth. "But I think the sooner we get you started for Madrid the better. I think I ought to call down and see what the travel agent can do for us right away." He moved away from her and sat on the bed beside the telephone. "You've got a valid passport still from that trip we took to Caracas at Christmas time—and you had the vaccination certificate then, too. If you know where they are we might get you off to Europe tomorrow."

"They're out at the Grove. I know just where they are."

"Well, we'll get your tickets and then we'll pick the passport and the other things up on the way out to the airport."

He picked up the telephone and she came and sat beside him, leaning her head on his shoulder. He put his free arm around her as if she was still a little girl. She looked down at her brown legs and her small, perfectly made feet, but she didn't see them. She saw the thin mattress lying on the boards in the huge white room, and saw the thin, muscular man walking up and down barefooted and naked but for the blue jeans belted round his narrow waist. He had taught her to look at, and to touch, every part of his body as shamelessly as he would look at and touch every part of hers. "It's all me," she could hear him saying, "you like me. Its no damned good trying to pretend you only like the bits of me that are shown in public. You can't just shut your eyes on what you don't like. Open them. Look at it. Open your mouth and say what you want me

453

to do to you. Go on say it, say it." Those words stuck in her throat. She did want him to do that to her, but that was only part of what she wanted. She wanted the gentleness and consideration which was embodied for her in the phrase, "I want you to love me and cherish me all the days of my life." "You want the rod, you silly bitch, you fouled-up boarding-house bitch," he said, "that's what you want. You don't make a deal for it, you just take it. I'm not bidding for you in any goddamn auction. I'm not promising anything." And then there would be the row which would end either in ecstasy on the mattress or with her being bundled naked out onto the landing at the head of the stairs leading down to the street door to dress herself and turn herself back into Miss Alice Hatfield, the banker's daughter, as best she could. This time she was not going to crawl back. She was going to escape for good. She was never again going to leave the world of decency, kindness, and goodness. She was going to prove that she didn't have to submit herself to anything degrading to reach happiness. "I know I'm doing the right thing," she told herself, but her brimming eyes overflowed and first one scalding tear and then another ran down her cheeks. She heard his voice crying, with an accent of despair, "How can you be so gutless? You haven't got the nerve to love, to let go, to live. You're too mean-spirited to trust anyone. You're nothing but a greedy little parasite."

Beside her Gavin shifted himself uneasily. He was sitting on something which made him uncomfortable. He passed one hand under his buttocks and drew out the slightly flattened body of B'ar Hatfield. Bogey took it from him and held it in her lap. The stuff the toy bear was made of was almost worn out and was getting a greasy look. One of its button eyes was gone and the darned patches at the various salient parts of its anatomy where the pile fabric of its original covering had given way had begun to have the ugly look of scars that had not properly healed. Bogey stood up and dropped the toy into the wastepaper basket beside the dressing table. "All right then," she heard her father say, "make it B.O.A.C. to Madrid via London."

When Gavin came back from the airport between midnight and one in the morning he found that the suite had been tidied in his absence. Its anonymity had been restored by practiced hands. Gavin was reminded by its impersonality of all the tedious explaining that he would have to do when the news of Bogey's precipitate departure on the eve of her coming-out party began to spread. There would be no end to the gossip and to the inventions. He turned out of the emptiness of the living room and walked into Bogey's room in search of some trace of her presence that would be comforting. All the tissue paper that had been strewn about in the havoc of her last minute repacking had gone. Her jettisoned clothes were neatly put away in drawers or hanging in the closets. The only trace of her passage was B'ar Hatfield, who had been rescued by an unknown hand. The toy was sitting plumped out on the dressing table with the back of his head, two profiles, and many of his patched wounds reflected in its glass. Gavin examined it without touching it. He remembered buying it for Thomas at F.A.O. Schwartz when he was up in New York on a business trip soon after the boy's third birthday. He could recall walking over to the toy shop from the Plaza, stopping in at Bergdorf's for a present for Ilona, and then looking up at a sky full of the promise of snow as he crossed Fifth Avenue. He looked away from the bear and out of the window at the night sky, pink with reflected neon glare. He suffered once more the pang which had torn at his heart when he had learned that Thomas had gone down to Maramee with some girl and had gone back up North without coming to see him. He wondered emptily how long Sophy McCann would stand between them. "God damn it," he said aloud, "it wasn't my fault." But Thomas was not there to listen or to understand. There was nothing for him to do but to go to bed, where he lay wakefully, thinking of explanations that he could give for Bogey's sudden disappearance and absence from her own coming-out party. When the telephone rang, towards seven o'clock in the morning, he gathered himself slowly feeling sure that he had only just dropped off. He had some difficulty at first in understanding who it was who was talking to him from Madrid. There was a lot of static on the line.

"Who? Who did you say?"

"Me, Wing. Lascomb. Say, are you Gavin Hatfield?"

"Yes, I am. Oh, Wing. I'm only half-awake. Did you get my cable?"

"About Bogey. Yeah. It suits us fine."

"Good. She'll be with you tomorrow sometime. I have the time and flight number here if you'll wait a second."

"You gave them in the cable. Don't bother again." The faint tinny voice paused. "Look, Gavin. I didn't call you about that; I'm afraid I've got sad news for you."

"What's that, bad news?"

"Not good, but sad rather than bad. The baby Mary started. She lost it. She's not in bad shape but she's pretty much upset. You can imagine. That's why its a good idea Bogey's coming out."

"I'm sorry, Wing."

"So am I."

"I'm terribly sorry. Anything I can do?"

"Nothing, nothing I can think of right now. But thanks all the same."

"Keep me posted on how Mary is, Wing. And don't hesitate to ask if there is anything I can do."

"I'll do that. Is Bogey in any kind of trouble?"

"No. Nothing really. She just needs a change."

"It'll be the best thing for Mary, having her around. She's pretty blue right now."

"I can't tell you how badly I feel about the baby, Wing."

"These things can't be helped. The great thing is that Mary's in no danger. I wanted you to know she's all right."

"Give her my love will you? Tell her to get well and not to worry."

"I'll do that. And I'll meet Bogey. So don't you worry."

"I won't. And believe me, Wing, I wish anything but this had happened."

"So do I. It's a great blow to us both."

"It's a great blow to me. I mean it."

When Wing hung up, Gavin lay back and realized with shame that his feeling was one of relief. He was off the hook. He had the perfect explanation for Bogey's flight. He sank into a deep and serene sleep in that assurance. It wasn't going to be so hard to get through the week after all, there was not, in fact, going to be any difficulty at all.

Gavin slept late on Thursday, the day after what was to have been Bogey's party, and the big day of the carnival week. As soon as he was out of bed he went out onto the terrace to see if the ship bringing Pedro Nunez and his party to Maramee was in sight. But there was still no sign of it. For a moment or two he was conscious of the smell of rubber which a soft southwest wind was bringing up to the penthouse, from the Husky Tire plant, but at the end of a minute he was inured to it. He leaned on the parapet and took in the wide expanse of the sprawling town, enlivened for the day by the bright flutter of strings of signal flags flown by all the freighters lying at the commercial wharves and by the hundreds of yachts and power boats lying in the shallower basin between the City and the Point. Across the river, City Park was beginning to look as if it had always been there, and as if Morgantown had never existed. The line of the south-bound highway slicing diagonally through the Park towards Maramee drew his eye. He followed it into the haze which hung over the open country out beyond the new developments, down towards the Marracombee line where the old county arch had been and where the Bunces had lived. He stared for a while into the obscurity, seeing with his inner eye the peculiarly ugly concrete structure which now crowned the spring, and from which emerged the conduit pipes which took its water away to the showers and tubs, the toilets and quick car-washes, the plants and workshops, of Halesville and Maramee. The big live oaks were all felled, and Gulf Sulphur's dredges, roaring and clattering, worked night and day in a haze of soft yellow dust as they cut long trenches through the deposit. He was glad that he could not see this new raw wound in the earth which caused him pain every time he had

to take the southern road out of town. He could not help
thinking of the whole operation as Thomas' revenge on life
for Sophy's death. He remembered the sequel to the visit
Krawitz had paid him at the bank as the spokesman of the
Save the Pool delegation. Gavin had sent their petition to
Thomas as he had promised, but the boy had not acknowl-
edged receipt of it to his father. He had replied direct to
Krawitz, who had shown it to Gavin in shocked astonishment.
It would take him a long time to forget it.

> Dear Mr Krawitz,
> Maramee and Halesville both need water.
> The United States economy requires abundant sulphur
> at competitive prices.
> More than adequate bathing and recreational facilities
> are available at a variety of resort areas in the Maramee
> area.
> The work in progress by the Marracombee River, under-
> taken by this company, must therefore proceed as planned.
>> I am, yours very sincerely,
>> *Thomas Hatfield.*

It amazed Gavin that his son should have found that steel
in him. He straightened up and cast another look out to the
empty green surface of the gulf; there was still no sign of the
ship that was to bring Pedro Nunez in from the sea. The va-
cancy and the salt breeze off the water combined to bring it
home to him that he had missed breakfast. He went indoors to
call for eggs and coffee, to take a shower, and to get himself
dressed.

When he came out again three quarters of an hour later he
had binoculars with him and he soon found the ship he was
looking for. It was a big white-hulled topsail schooner. Its dress
startled Gavin. In the old days no bones had been made about
who and what Pedro Nunez was, a pirate who had stolen a
Spanish pinnace in Cuba and who had got into the gulf by
mistake. He had intended to make his way up the Atlantic
coast of Florida, but a storm had set him a long way off in his

458

reckoning. He had made a bewildered landfall at Maramee, where he had surprised and burned a small Seminole village. He and his nine followers had butchered fifteen Indian men and had taken their women captive. They had lived on a sandspit on the site of the present post-office building for about seven months and had then sailed south in an aimless fashion, looking for some new adventure. A Spanish warship had caught them near Key West two or three months later, and they were taken back to Cuba and hanged just one year and ten days after the beginning of their adventure. For all that Pedro Nunez had been the first European to set foot in Maramee, he was still a pirate and a bad lot, and the ship which brought his representative to the carnival had always in the past admitted to the facts by flying the traditional flag of the buccaneers. But now Gavin's glasses showed him scarlet Maltese crosses on the schooner's square sails and a variety of vaguely ecclesiastical banners and streamers at the mastheads and elsewhere. Curious to know more about the meaning of this change, Gavin left the hotel and made his way downtown to the municipal dock in the half-acre Theodore Roosevelt Park beside the yacht basin where the Pedro Nunez landing always took place. His prominence in local affairs and his membership on several of the Pedro Nunez Day committees saw him through all the police lines between him and his destination, and at last got him a good place among the semi-official notables on the steps of the Rough Rider Memorial. Gavin stood close to the boots of bronze Teddy, who waved his bronze hat and kept his bronze teeth bared in a wide-mouthed yell as he urged his invisible army to follow him in a wild charge out into the yacht basin. Gavin looked up and saw that a rude word had been written six times round the flat brim of the warrior's hat in white chalk, and looking down found Eddie Riemann close beside him. They exchanged greetings and Gavin gestured at the memorial.

"Did he ever have anything to do with Maramee? I thought his lot trained out on Long Island, somewhere near Montauk.

459

I always had it in mind that they went straight to Cuba from New York."

"I don't know about that. I know no Rough Riders ever got within miles of Maramee though. A National Guard unit from Ohio was here for a few weeks, and they may have shipped out from one of the commercial wharves. Look, boy, here come the women."

Eddie leered as a platoon of teen-age girls from St. Teresa's Parochial School in South Maramee, dressed in the uniform of George Washington's Continental Army, marched into the park from the Shoreline Drive. The American Legion band played them in, and out of gratitude they put on a brief display of close-order drill before falling in on the dock where they were to take post as Pedro Nunez' honor guard.

"All those firm young thighs pumping up and down in those tight white breeches really give you ideas, don't they?" Eddie said.

"I wish they wouldn't use lipstick if they're going to dress up as soldiers," Gavin said. He looked over his shoulder and saw some Shriners swaying by on an elephant. When they had gone past in their scarlet blazers and tassled fezes Pete Heinrich, the Mayor, and three of his public relations staff drove up to the entrance of the park in a long black city-owned Cadillac. Two of the P.R.O.'s in the Mayor's party were wearing fringed Indian outfits and Indian war bonnets, the third was dressed as Uncle Sam. He was carrying a huge gold key tucked under one arm, and he had a spare Indian headdress draped over his free hand.

"Come on, be a sport, Mr. Mayor," he said plaintively, as Heinrich strode purposefully towards the dock.

"Leave that damn thing in the car. I won't wear it," the Mayor snapped. The public relations man looked helplessly round him from under his silver-spangled top hat. He caught sight of Gavin, and recognized him as a man who had influence with the Mayor. He beckoned him down off the memorial steps and out of the crowd.

"Be a pal, Gavin," he said, "get Pete to put on his bonnet.

Tell Mr. Heinrich everybody knows Pedro Nunez met Indians when he landed here."

"No Seminole ever wore a goddamned Pawnee war bonnet," the Mayor snarled. "And you're not going to make a monkey out of me." His face was scarlet. "I'll not lend myself to degrading the office."

"This is a parade to make the kids happy, Mr. Mayor," one of the Indians said. "It's only one day in the year."

"It's all in fun Heinrich," Gavin said.

"I wasn't clowning when I took office," the Mayor said, "I don't propose to start now."

"I'll wear it," Gavin said, sensing some hidden desperation behind Heinrich's reluctance to wear the feathers, "If there have to be Indians."

"That's great, Gavin," said Uncle Sam. "I'll be damned if I know what's biting Pete, though," he added, as he helped Gavin to put the bonnet on. "He's been sour as hell all morning, and jumpy too."

When Gavin straightened up some of the crowd greeted him with war whoops and he whooped back as another group of bystanders led by a wolfishly grinning Eddie Reimann sang "For he's a jolly good fellow" in ivy-league glee-club style. They were drowned out as the Husky Rubber band marched by to take its place in the parade. As the oompah oompah of its brasses and drums and the squeal of its fifes faded away along the Shoreline Drive there was a sudden hoarse cry of "here she comes." Most people looked out towards the harbor mouth, where the schooner had swum gracefully into view, but Gavin, Eddie, and a number of others turned their heads in the opposite direction to watch the arrival of Miss Maramee with her maids of honor, Miss Jepson County, Miss Citrus Fruits, Miss Your Neighborhood Store, Miss Local Industry, and Miss Harlem Heights, who had all driven up together in a station wagon. Miss Maramee had a rhinestone crown on her head, a scepter in her hand, and a regal cloak of red velvet and ermine hanging from her shoulders. Beneath it, like the other girls in her entourage, she wore a tighter than skin-tight white bath-

461

ing suit made of so powerful an elasticized material that it pressed and molded her body into a standardized bathing beauty shape, as formalized and sexless as that of Mrs. Noah's in the old-fashioned toy Noah's arks. The girls, tottering on their white opera pumps with high spike heels, clustered uncertainly at the entrance to the park wondering where to go and what to do until a gathering storm of wolf whistles and throaty murmurs of "Yeah man! Local industry!" caught the attention of Uncle Sam. He darted back from the dock to take them in hand and presently returned like the father of the bride with Miss Maramee on his arm. The other girls followed on behind, holding out the beauty queen's train in a wide circle. The Mayor took one look behind him at the approaching mass of pearly smiles, bare legs, and swaying hips, and then stared fixedly out to sea with a scowl of nervous irritation on his face.

"What's biting you today, Pete?" Gavin said, edging up to him. "You know everything goes, and nothing counts either way on Pedro Nunez Day."

"Oh, my ulcer's giving me hell, Gavin, and that's only the half of it. The comptroller came to me last night. For ten days now we've been trying to run down this twenty-eight-thousand-dollar deficiency in Public Welfare. Well, we know where the money went now. My damn fool brother-in-law swiped it. So I'm in no mood for making with funny hats."

"I'll be glad to let you have the money if it isn't too late to cover up, Pete. My one condition is that you fire Jennings. He may be your wife's kid brother but he's no darned good and he never was."

"I know it, Gavin. He never had me fooled. I appreciate your offer, but I've already fired the little jerk and put the money back in the treasury on my own account. But I'm not covering anything up. The Grand Jury gets it Monday. I came in on a clean-government ticket and I'm sticking to it. Friend Willy Jennings has had one last chance too many. It's the last time he gets caught and gets away with it. He'll go to jail for this if I have anything to say in the matter." He mopped his

462

face with a large white handkerchief. "There. I feel better already for blowing off a little steam. But you keep it quiet till I give it to the papers on Monday." The Mayor suddenly grinned and stepped forward to slap Uncle Sam on the back. "Sorry I've been mad at you, boy. I must of got out of my bed on the wrong side this morning. To prove I've no hard feelings and to make it up to you I'll even kiss the hand of that piece of ass standing beside you if you've got a cameraman around who wants a silly picture."

"You will?" Uncle Sam's face brightened. "Ed, hey, Ed," he called to one of the Pawnee braves. "Get Wilson and the Maramee *Herald*'s man for pix."

"They're right in front of you."

Uncle Sam managed to catch the attention of the two photographers, and soon they were photographing the Mayor as he bowed low, twice, to kiss Miss Maramee's hand, and afterwards, as he made a tremendous pursed up mouth as if he was about to kiss her on the cheek. While they were posing in the second of these positions the queen smiled sweetly and said quietly: "Call me a piece of ass again, Mr. Mayor, and I'll knock your teeth right down your throat." She said it as if she was saying something very pleasant indeed.

The Mayor smiled just as pleasantly. "It's a compliment if you take it right, my dear, you shouldn't have such easy-to-wound feelings."

"I don't have any feelings in particular, mister, but you've no right at all to call me names just because I work in show business."

"That's my favorite show, my favorite business," the Mayor said.

Their exchange was broken off by the blaring of ships' sirens and yacht klaxons all over the port area. The schooner with Pedro Nunez aboard was alongside and tying up. A couple of dozen men and women in Spanish costumes followed a splendidly dressed conquistador ashore. Gavin noticed that Pedro Nunez was getting pious as well as making social advances. There was a friar right behind him, and behind the friar a boy carrying a cross. Pedro Nunez was William Kendrick, the regional manager of Brighter Budget Super Stores, and the friar was Matty Callahan of Matty's Sporting Goods Store. Gavin knew almost everyone in the ex-pirate's train. Marks of Hi-Test Produce Stores; Jimmy Hall of Hall's for Fat, Short'n'Tall; Stebbing of Maramee Appliance, and Harry Weil of U. R. Furnishings. They were formed in a half-circle, simpering, and the Mayor read a proclamation from a sheet of typescript fastened with Scotch tape to somebody's old parchment law-school diploma. When the Mayor had said his piece, welcoming Nunez and presenting him with the freedom of the city for a day, Uncle Sam stepped forward to present the key and Miss Maramee to the visitor, and the girls of the Continental Army presented arms. A soprano in a satin evening dress came forward and sang "My Country 'Tis of Thee" while the Legion Band played softly. Many men took their hats off and some stood at attention. Gavin noticed that the form for Indians on such an occasion was to adopt the folded-arms posture, at least that was what the P.R.O.'s did until the soprano was through. After a moment's hesitation Gavin decided against doing the same thing, but compromised by coming to attention. When the song was over, the official group moved on to the steps of the Rough Rider Memorial for the re-enactment of the original founding of the city. Kendrick climbed on to the top step of its plinth and produced a large roll of parchment with a heavy wax seal attached to it. He unrolled it and began to read, in a voice throbbing with a genuine emotion.

"Future and yet unborn citizens of Maramee to be," he began, "know by these presents that by God's grace I, Pedro Nunez . . ."

"Hey, hey there, hold it—," cried Uncle Sam, "this mike is out. Nobody out there can hear"— His words were suddenly taken up by clusters of loudspeakers on poles and lamp standards all along the Shoreline Drive—"a goddamn thing. Oh, Christ." There was a roar of laughter, broken by some cries of "shame," and "cut out the cussing, you fellers," and the disturbance was renewed when Kendrick's whispered question,

464

"You want for me to begin all over again?" came hissing out through the whole public address system even more loudly. Giggling fits swept the Continental Army, and Miss Your Neighborhood Store had to bury her face in the fur border of Miss Maramee's train. Kendrick, badly rattled, plunged ahead, and when he was audible again had gone beyond his first stopping point.

". . . here found a city which shall be for the glory of God and the happiness of man. I dedicate this city, and those who shall hereinafter be its citizens, to the higher service of higher things, to truth, to freedom of speech and worship, to family life, to good government, and true democracy."

"That's one hell of a far-sighted speech for a sixteenth-century Spaniard to get off his chest, isn't it?" Eddie muttered in Gavin's ear.

"In memory of our dedication of this noble city of our dreams to the preservation of and fulfillment of these ideals, I do ordain and command that from this day forth, forevermore, so long as dreams and ideals shall endure, the citizens who live here shall lift up their hearts and set toil aside to remember me in merriment and gaiety on each future anniversary of my landing here with my right good and true companions. Given under my hand, and sealed with my seal, Pedro Nunez, on this day, the fourth of May, in the year of our Lord fifteen hundred and twenty-five."

When the proclamation had been read, the Mayor made his way to his car and disappeared, and the rest of the company were removed one by one as the parade got under way. Pedro Nunez and his companions went off on the first float, which was made to look like a galleon. Miss Maramee left on the second, with Miss Jepson County and Miss Harlem Heights on each side of her. Miss Your Neighborhood Store was carried off in front of a little pageant of ethical retailing, while Miss Local Industry presided over a tableau showing harmony between capital, management and labor. Miss Citrus Fruits climbed onto the seat of a huge swing, hung between two metal masts, on the biggest of all the floats donated by the

465

Citrus Growers Association. As she went off up Shoreline Drive, her mane of vivid red hair fell free. The crowd gasped with pleasure as she swung up and down, to and fro, and the band beneath her played slow waltzes. There were thirty more floats carrying displays by commercial firms, all-girl choirs from the city's churches, the Maramee All-Star pro basketball team, the National Guard's newest anti-aircraft rocket, a recruiting tableau of Marines, a better-health display, the Gulf University football squad, and much else besides. Between each float there were contingents of marchers and groups of drum majorettes from high schools, students from colleges, and members of national societies, the Maramee Irish, the Maramee Spanish, the Italians, the Sicilians, the Scots, the Germans; the Knights of Columbus, the Shriners and their elephant, the Elks, the Teamsters, the Longshoremen, the city departments, and at the end of it all the huge Air Force band and the security battalion from the Arling Field in their blinding polished helmets. When the parade had moved off on its long circuit of the town, Eddie and Gavin left the little park. They joined the tide of strolling people moving up towards City Hall where Pedro Nunez would hand Rex the gold key to the city, which Uncle Sam had given him on the dock. When Nunez gave the key to the king of the carnival, the fun really began. As Miss Maramee took her place on the empty throne beside Rex's at the top of the City Hall steps the bands changed their tempo from marches to dance tunes. They would play on all over the city until long after midnight. During the afternoon, people slipped off home to change out of their day clothes and into fancy dress. By dusk there was nobody on the street who was not masked and transformed, and either dancing, or hurrying to one dance from another. Every street was roofed with banners and strings of colored lights, and the pavements were littered with real and paper flowers, balloons and streamers. Sometimes all the dancers in a club room or a ballroom would, with a common impulse, suddenly form a snake and move off down a street and across a block to another place, leaving their own band to rest beside

466

a deserted floor. At other times a marching band would turn the corner of a street, empty but for a few strollers and couples sitting talking on the curbs, and, breaking into a lively tune, would within a minute fill the roadway with dancers who would come bursting out of almost every house along its length.

Gavin did what everyone else did all through the afternoon. His Pawnee war bonnet was seen everywhere, exciting much applause and admiration, and very little derision. He danced when he felt like it, and when he felt hungry ate the snacks provided at the buffets of all the solvent clubs in the city. Everybody was a friend and every door was open on Pedro Nunez Day. Towards eight o'clock he went back to his suite in the Beverly to take a shower and to rest for a while before putting on the eighteenth-century Venetian suit with the beaked mask, which he had to wear as one of Rex's gentlemen at the grand ball. When he had ordered his supper from room service, he stepped out onto the terrace in his dressing gown. Seen from that height, the town appeared to be incandescent, and it hummed and throbbed with music. Every now and then a flaw in the soft evening wind would bring the sound of a single instrument up to the level of the terrace, a bar of melting sugar from a tenor saxophone, or a long wild riff on a horn, or the pulsing of some deeper-toned drum than the others. The waiter who had brought his meal called him in, and he sat down to it with a pleasure which was more intense because he was alone. The telephone rang as he was finishing his coffee.

"I hate to bother you, Mr. Hatfield, this is Ned Stanton of the *Herald*. I've a crisis on my hands. Nothing bad, but still a nuisance. We've got an awful thin paper tomorrow anyway, but on top of that the lawyers made us take out the whole of the "Point of View" on the center page because they say it's libel. I'm trying to fill the space with a sort of off-the-cuff anthology of optimistic statements about Maramee's future by all you big shots. Can you give me something, Gavin, I'd be really grateful if you could."

"Why, yes, I'd be glad to, but just what do you want, Ned? Read me something somebody else has given you, to give me the idea."

"Ah—just a minute—here we are: this is from Dean Bodmer of the Episcopalian Church on Laurel and Gold. 'I have been impressed all through this decade by the deepening spiritual awareness of the American people and their discovery that there is a greater meaning to life than mere living. Maramee has taken part in this quickening of America's religious life, and I think that in the decade to come, our city may hold up the beacon of leadership to the entire state and perhaps to the nation. The true glory lies ever further on.' I don't know just what he means, but he filled a nice little piece of a column. Here's another, perhaps more in your line, from Hansen Laforgue, the Solid Fuels man. 'There may be dark days ahead on the international scene, but existing contracts give Solid Fuels a certain future which present tensions can only serve to maintain. The two thousand Maramee folk who are part of our family now can make plans for the next ten years with real certainty, and I think that before long we'll be offering careers to another fifteen hundred of the elder boys and girls at present in the city's schools.' Get the idea?"

"Yes, Ned, I think so. 'Since 1525 the trend here in Maramee has been up. I think it has a long way to go. Fortune has been kind to us, and I think we've so far only scratched the surface of what we can do here. Home owners and property owners can look forward to a steady rise in values over the coming years. Industry is going right ahead, faster than the national average, and new job opportunities are opening up all the time. The trend is up, and Maramee is going up with it.'"

"That's fine Gavin, but I'm not sure about that last sentence. It has an ambiguous ring to me. How about, say, 'and Maramee is going to be one of the leaders of the trend.'"

"Yes, that's much better. Put it that way."

"Well, thanks. That's great, just what I wanted. Good night, have a good time at the ball."

"Will you be over later on?"

"When I've put the paper to bed, I might. Anyway, I'll see you next week on that Urban Renewal Committee."

"Yes, that's right. If we don't meet any sooner it'll be good to see you then."

Gavin dressed in his courtier's costume, with its buckled shoes, lace at the sleeves and throat, and jewelled buttons. Last of all he put on the Venetian Carnival mask of leather, with its almond eyes, rounded apple-like cheeks, and beaklike Roman nose. When he gave himself a final inspection in the mirror on the inside of his closet door before going out, he felt that the mask gave him the evil look of one who was ready to meet everyone and everything with a dry mock. He realized that all day he had been pursued by his knowledge that Bogey's lover was somewhere in the city hating him and despising Maramee and all its works. It was odd how strongly the unknown man's passions had come to him through Bogey, so much so that he felt that he knew him quite well, even though he had only just heard his breathing for those few seconds before the telephone had gone dead. He would see me as an evil and destructive man, Gavin thought, if he saw me now, but what harm can there be in dressing up to go to a ball, in an evening's innocent fun at the end of a silly day? He clapped on his big tricorn hat and went out into the whirling confusion of the carnival.

In the ballroom, under the two huge chandeliers, Rex's enthronement and everything else went off as it should; the debutantes were presented, the queen was enthroned, and the aspiring ladies who had passed muster were led out of the non-dancers enclosures round the dance floor to waltz with Rex's gentlemen in the *valse noble*. Ginny Holmes found Gavin after the main ball had broken up, towards two in the morning, when he was eating scrambled eggs with twenty or thirty people who had drifted over to Eddie Riemann's. His mask was lying on the ground beside him. Ginny picked it up as she sat down and held it in her lap. They were side by side

469

on the edge of Eddie's glowing blue swimming pool, floodlit from under the water.

"Hallo, Gavin," she said. "I looked for you at the ball, but I couldn't find you. These masks really make it impossible to tell one person from another."

"I didn't see you." He yawned. "God knows who I was dancing with most of the evening, women I didn't know existed."

She had taken off her shoes and was dabbling her toes in the cool water.

"You like me don't you, Gavin?"

"Why, yes, of course I do, Ginny, everybody likes you."

"Yes, everybody likes me, but nobody loves me. That's funny isn't it?"

"Oh." Gavin yawned. "You've a long way to go yet. You'll find someone soon, never you fear."

"I do fear though, Gavin. Do you remember the year I fell in love with you?"

"Yes. That was years ago. You were still a child. It was a crush."

"But you knew I really wanted you, didn't you?"

"I was shocked."

"With me—or with yourself?"

"Both. It upset me, if you want to know the truth."

"I was terribly disappointed when nothing happened." She paused. "Why didn't anything happen, Gavin?"

"It was impossible." He considered her. He was surprised to see how much the gap between them had widened in four years. Ginny was no longer an adolescent filled with a direct urgency for simple experience of the kind that it would have been easy for him to give. She had become a nervous, tense, and complicated young woman. "There was too much time between us then," he said.

"Is it too late now, Gavin?" she said, looking downwards into the water with an expression of inexplicable sadness.

"Good grief, Ginny! What's got into you? Aren't there any young men in Maramee?"

"There are." She dipped the fingers of one hand into the pool and then shook a sprinkling of a dozen droplets of water out across its surface. She watched the rings made by their fall spreading and interlocking. "But they seem either loutish or lost and scared. I don't like the hearties, and the others don't seem to like me—some because they don't like girls in general, and some because I'm supposed to be difficult. I scare them, Gavin. I begin to despair. I'm beginning to wonder if there really is something wrong with me. I know there isn't. But still, time goes by. I begin to feel very old."

"You don't know what being old is, Ginny. It comes when you've used up your future bit by bit, and you've nothing left. You don't know how it is when your heart burns out. Even death stops being a frightening idea. You've got a future. Mine's all used up. I couldn't have taken you when you wanted me so badly for that reason. You wanted to make me happy, but it wasn't possible. You couldn't have done it by giving yourself to me. The only way you can give me happiness is by being happy. There's no way you can give me back the dreams I've had, and which I won't have again."

"Wouldn't it have been worth giving it a try? I felt so sure. And when Ilona ran away, it seemed as if fate was clearing the way for it."

"It was too late, Ginny. I'm all through with risks and gambles. If you want to know the bitter truth, Ginny, I don't believe in myself any more. Not enough to launch out into any new ventures."

"I can't stand it, Gavin. They've all been so horrible to you, walking out on you, going away and leaving you hurt and disappointed. I don't want you to be like this. I want you to be happy again."

"I'm not so unhappy, Ginny. In a funny quiet sort of way I'm all right. Things don't bother me as much as they used to."

"Did love and loving bother you?" She tipped the mask up so that it faced her, and saw through its empty eye sockets

471

into the blue water of the pool. "That's a horrible word to use."

"Life can be horrible. And love can be a horrible part of it." He looked at her, sitting with her lap full of her drawn up skirt. "Love can tie you to an alcoholic who hates life and hates himself, or to someone who likes pain more than pleasure, or to someone like me who doesn't believe in anything any more. I believed in money once, but I don't now. I learned a lot in losing my faith. If you were my age and you knew what I knew, we could live together very well. We could share silences. Sometimes you would look at me and you'd know what I was thinking, and I'd look back and know what was in your mind. But you still believe in happiness and in saying things. You believe in your own will and its power to get you what you want. That's what's really between us. I haven't the courage left to watch another person's heart die in her. Not from close to, anyway."

"How can you admit it and bear to go on living?"

"Ah, that's the funny thing, Ginny. I couldn't go on living if I couldn't bear to admit it. Now that I've learned my lesson, I don't torture myself any more." He smiled. "Ginny, find out what you're running from. Don't waste any more time pretending that our little feeling for each other was a tragic disappointment. Have a good look at life and see if it's as bad as you think. It may not be. If you want me to be happy, be brave and happy on your own account. Don't come shrinking to me to get warmth from my cold bones."

"You talk to me as if I was a child. You must think me very silly and stupid." She got to her feet and stood slipping her feet into her shoes, looking down at him and about her at the other people talking, sleeping, drinking and embracing, in couples and groups all over the garden. A fight between two men started inside the house. A woman screamed, a chair fell with a clatter, and as something made of glass broke, an indignant voice said "Why, Jesus, you clumsy son of a bitch." As half the party stood up in alarm, or froze in postures of atten-

472

tion, a sudden silence fell. Gavin found himself on his feet with Ginny clutching at his arm.

"Will it always be like this, Gavin," she asked, "with something going on I don't understand, and with me wanting it to be different, and wanting it to make sense?"

"It's the way things are, Ginny. There's no doing anything about it."

"No." She stared at him with wide eyes. "I won't believe it. I can't believe it. I won't have it so."

For a moment they held hands. Then she left him and walked slowly to the garden gate. She hesitated for a moment in the opening, looking back, and then stepped out into the darkness with her head held high.

Gavin did not go back to the hotel that night. Near dawn, when he had slept for an hour or two on a chaise longue beside Eddie's pool, he drove straight out to the Grove, still in his Venetian clothes. The day was clear and the air still. The house seemed to lie under an enchantment as he drove up to it. Nothing stirred and silence hung about the place. Cocks crowed far away, standing challenging each other from the tops of their coops behind the cabins lining the old river road. As Gavin swung his legs out of his car he heard their faint clamor filtering through the heavy motionless mass of leaves and foliage on the towering trees. He stepped onto the porch and approached the front door. It had been closed in his absence, and as he crossed the wide expanse of boarding between it and the head of the steps he seemed to see a dark figure inside the house rapidly and silently coming down the darkened hallway to meet him. Gavin reached the door and recognized the figure as his own reflection when it copied his movement towards the doorknob. He pushed, and the big slab of mahogany and etched glass swung aside. The interloper swung with it and vanished. There was no one in the hall, and the stillness in the house was so complete that Gavin hesitated for a long time before crossing the threshold. He waited for some sound or some movement which would dispel

473

his suspicion that nobody had ever lived there, and that the whole of his life, since he had first set eyes on the Grove, had been some curious entanglement in a dream that was not even his own. His own dreams were of happiness and warmth of a house full of laughter, and the frank contentment of hard-working people, who knew what they wanted and saw to it that they got it. He had done his level best to make his dreams come true, but here he was, and the house, so full of things bought and paid for, was still as empty as it had been on the day when he had first found it, and had come up onto the porch to peer in through this same door into these same accumulated shadows, darknesses, and silences. "Tell me, tell me, what I did wrong!" he said, speaking as if he expected an answer. But there was no one in the house to reply to his words, which were absorbed without echo by the shuttered void.